PENGUIN F

Orphan X

Gregg Hurwitz is the *Sunday Times* bestselling author of *You're Next*, *The Survivor*, *Tell No Lies* and *Don't Look Back*. A graduate of Harvard and Oxford Universities, he lives with his family in LA, where he also writes for the screen, TV and comics, including Wolverine and Batman

gregghurwitz.net
facebook.com/gregghurwitzreaders
@GreggHurwitz

Orphan X

GREGG HURWITZ

PENGUIN BOOKS

PENGUIN BOOKS

UK | USA | Canada | Ireland | Australia
India | New Zealand | South Africa

Penguin Books is part of the Penguin Random House group of companies
whose addresses can be found at global.penguinrandomhouse.com.

First published in the United States of America by St Martin's Press 2016
First published in Great Britain by Michael Joseph 2016
Published in Penguin Books 2016

004

Set in 12.5/14.75 pt Garamond MT Std
Typeset by Jouve (UK), Milton Keynes
Printed in Great Britain by Clays Ltd, St Ives plc

A CIP catalogue record for this book is available from the British Library

B FORMAT PAPERBACK ISBN: 978–1–405–91070–5
A FORMAT PAPERBACK ISBN: 978–1–405–92889–2

www.greenpenguin.co.uk

Penguin Random House is committed to a
sustainable future for our business, our readers
and our planet. This book is made from Forest
Stewardship Council® certified paper.

To all the bad boys and girls, rulebreakers and vigilantes –

Philip Marlowe and Sam Spade, Bruce Wayne and Jason Bourne, Bond and Bullitt, Joe Pike and Jack Reacher, Hawk and Travis McGee, the Seven Samurai and the Magnificent Seven, Mack Bolan and Frank Castle, the three Johns (W. Creasey, Rambo and McClane), Captain Ahab and Guy Montag, Mike Hammer and Paul Kersey, the Lone Ranger and the Shadow, Robin Hood and Van Helsing, Beowulf and Gilgamesh, Ellen Ripley and Sarah Connor, Perseus and Coriolanus, Hanna and Hannibal, the Man with No Name and the Professional, Parker and Lucy, Arya Stark and George Stark, Pike Bishop and Harmonica, Lancelot and Achilles, Shane and Snake Plissken, Ethan Edwards and Bill Munny, Jack Bauer and Repairman Jack, the Killer and the Killer, Zorro and the Green Hornet, Dexter and Mad Max, the Dirty Dozen and Dirty Harry, the Terminator and Lady Vengeance, Cool Hand Luke and Lucas Davenport, Logan 5 and James 'Logan' Howlett, V and Vic Mackey, Hartigan and Marv, Sherlock and Luther, Veronica Mars and Selina Kyle

– for being so wicked that they're good.

Ripley: What you're doing is wrong.
Luther: Yeah, I know.
Ripley: Why do it then?
Luther: 'Cause it's *right*.

– from *Luther*, created by Neil Cross

Prologue: Trial By Fire

Evan's twelve-year-old body is stiff in the cushy passenger seat of the black sedan as he is driven in silence. His cheek is split and his temple bruised. Blood slides warmly down his neck, mixing with panic sweat. Raw skin rings his wrists where the handcuffs were. His heartbeat thunders in his chest, his head.

He uses all his will to give nothing away.

He has been in the car only five minutes. The leather smells expensive.

The driver has given his name, Jack Johns. But nothing else.

An old guy, at least fifty-something, with a wide, handsome face. He's built square like a catcher and has a baseball squint to match.

Jack tugs a handkerchief from his rear pant pocket, fluffs it out, and offers it across the console. 'For your cheek.'

Evan looks at the fine linen. 'The blood'll stain it.'

Jack's face registers amusement. 'It's okay.'

Evan wipes his face.

He was the smallest of the kids, the last one picked for sports. It was only through a savage set of challenges that he found his way into this seat, that he'd managed to get himself chosen.

None of them had known what to make of the Mystery Man when he first materialized at the edge of the cracked basketball courts, eyeing the boys as they'd played and fought. Hidden behind Ray-Bans, dragging his fingers along the chain-link, smoking cigarette after cigarette. He walked slowly, never in a rush, and yet every time he seemed to vanish as quickly as he'd appeared. Theories abounded. He was Chester the Molester. A rich businessman looking to adopt. A dealer in human organs on the black market. A recruiter for the Greek mob.

Evan had been willing to take the leap.

He has been taken out of circulation as surely as if he'd been zapped off the streets by a flying saucer. Trial by fire, yes – a recruitment of some sort, but for what, Evan still has no idea.

All he knows is wherever he is heading now has to be better than what's behind him in East Baltimore.

His stomach gives off a rumble that embarrasses him even here, even now. He glances at himself in the side mirror. He looks malnourished. Maybe where he's going, food will be abundant.

Or maybe he'll be the food.

He works up his nerve. Clears his throat. 'What do you want me for?' he asks.

'I can't tell you that yet.' Jack drives in silence for a time, then seems to realize that his answer isn't satisfactory for a kid in Evan's position. 'I may not tell you everything right away,' he adds in a tone that stops shy of apologetic, 'but I will never lie to you.'

Evan studies him. Decides to take him at his word. 'Am I gonna get hurt?'

Jack drives on, looking dead ahead.

'Sometimes,' he says.

1. The Morning-Beverage Measure

After picking up a set of pistol suppressors from a nine-fingered armorer in Las Vegas, Evan Smoak headed for home in his Ford pickup, doing his best not to let the knife wound distract him.

The slice on his forearm had occurred during an altercation at a truck stop. He usually didn't like to get involved with anything or anyone outside his missions, but there had been a fifteen-year-old girl in dire need of help. So here he was, trying not to bleed on to the console until he could get home and deal with it properly. For now he'd tied off the cut with one of his socks, using his teeth to cinch the knot.

Home would be good. He hadn't slept in a day and a half. He thought about the bottle of triple-distilled vodka in the freezer of his Sub-Zero. He thought about a hot shower and the soft sheets of his bed. He thought about the RoamZone phone in his glove box and how it was due to ring any day now.

Forging west through gridlocked Beverly Hills, he entered the embrace of the Wilshire Corridor, a stretch of residential towers that in Los Angeles qualified as high-rises. His building, the flamboyantly named Castle Heights, was the easternmost in the run, which gave the higher floors a clean line of sight to Downtown.

Unrenovated since the nineties, it had an upscale dated vibe, with gleaming brass fixtures and salmon-tinged marble. Neither posh nor trendy in a city that revolved around both, Castle Heights suited Evan's needs precisely. It drew the old-fashioned well-to-do – surgeons, senior partners, silver-haired retirees with long-standing memberships at country clubs. A few years back, a middling point guard for the Lakers had moved in, bringing with him fifteen minutes of troublesome press, but he'd soon been traded away, allowing the residents to settle back into their cushion of quiet, low-key comfort.

Evan pulled through the porte cochère, gesturing to the valet that he'd park himself, then turned down the ramp leading beneath the building. His pickup slotted neatly into his space between two concrete pillars, shielded from much of the floor and the glow of the overhead fluorescents.

In the privacy of his truck, he untied the sock tourniquet from his forearm and eyed the cut. The edges were nice and clean, but it was a sight. Blood had caked in the faint hairs, and the cut itself hadn't fully clotted off. The damage was superficial. Six sutures, maybe seven.

He retrieved his cell from the glove box. The Roam-Zone was constructed of hardened black rubber, fiberglass casing and Gorilla Glass. He kept it within earshot.

Always.

After checking the rearview to make sure the garage was empty, he got out and changed into one of the black sweatshirts he kept stashed behind the seat. The pistol suppressors were shoved into a paper grocery bag. He tossed the bloody shirt and sock on top of them.

After checking the RoamZone battery (two bars), he slid it into his front pocket and took the stairs up one level.

Outside the lobby door, he allowed himself a deep breath, readying for the transition from one world to another.

Thirty-two steps from door to elevator, a quick ride up, and he was clear.

He stepped into the lobby, the cool air scented of fresh-cut flowers. His shoes chirped against the tiles as he threaded through the bustle, smiling blandly at the residents moving to and fro with their shopping bags and cell-phone conversations. He was in his mid-thirties and quite fit, though not so muscular that he stood out. Just an average guy, not too handsome.

Castle Heights prided itself on its security measures, not least of which was that the elevator was controlled by the security desk. Evan gestured at the guard reclining before a bank of screens behind the high counter.

'Twenty-one, please, Joaquin,' Evan said.

A voice came from behind him. 'Just say "penthouse", why don't you? It *is* the penthouse level.' A clawlike hand closed over his injured forearm, squeezing, and Evan felt a surge of burning beneath his sweatshirt.

He turned to the stubby, wizened woman at his

side – Ida Rosenbaum of 6G – and produced a smile. 'I suppose that's right, ma'am.'

'And besides,' she continued, 'we have our Home-owner Association meeting in the conference room on *ten*. Starting right now. You've missed the last three, by my count.' To compensate for hearing loss, her volume was prodigious, acquainting the entire lobby with Evan's attendance record.

The car arrived with a ding.

Mrs Rosenbaum's grip intensified. She fixed her imperious stare on Joaquin. 'He'll go to the HOA meeting.'

'Wait! Hold the elevator!' The woman from 12B – Mia Hall – hip-checked her way through the glass front door, heavy purse swinging in one direction, her son in the other, iPhone pinched between her cheek and shoulder.

Evan released a weary breath and gently twisted his arm free of Mrs Rosenbaum's grasp as they stepped into the elevator. He felt the blood running again, causing the sweatshirt fabric to cling.

As Mia hustled toward them, dragging her eight-year-old by his arm, she finished singing into the phone in double time: 'Happy late birthday to you, happy sorry-my-car-broke-down-and-I-went-to-the-mechanic-who-told-me-I-needed-new-brake-disks-for-an-arm-and-a-leg-and-so-I-missed-picking-Peter-up-from-school-and-he-had-to-go-to-a-friend's-which-is-why-I-forgot-to-leave-you-a-message-earlier biiirrrtthday, happy birthday to you.'

She lifted her cheek, letting the phone drop into her

capacious purse. 'Sorry! Sorry. Thanks.' Rushing into the elevator, she called across, 'Hi, Joaquin. Don't we have an HOA meeting right now?'

'Indeed we do,' Mrs Rosenbaum said pointedly.

Joaquin raised his eyebrows at Evan – *Sorry, brother* – and then the doors were closing behind them. Ida Rosenbaum's perfume, in close quarters, was blinding.

It did not take her long to break the relative silence of the car. 'Everyone with their phones plugged into their faces all the time,' she said to Mia. 'You know who predicted this? My Herb, may he rest in peace. He said, "One day it'll be so that people talk to screens all day and won't even require other humans".'

As Mia took up the conversation, Evan glanced down at Peter, who was staring up at him with charcoal eyes. His thin blond hair lay lank, aside from one lock that swirled up in the back, defying gravity. A colorful Band-Aid had been applied to his pronounced forehead. His head tilted as he peered down at Evan's foot. Slowly, Evan became aware of cool air on his bare ankle. The missing sock. He took a half step, sliding the offending ankle out of the boy's line of sight.

Mia's voice floated over him.

Clearly she had asked him a question. He looked up at her. A scattering of light freckles, not visible under weaker light, covered the bridge of her nose, and her glossy chestnut hair was a lush, piled mess. He'd grown accustomed to seeing her in frantic single-parent mode – runs in her stockings, slightly out of breath, juggling Batman lunch box and satchel briefcase – but the glow from behind the panels cast her now in a different light.

'I'm sorry?' he said.

'Don't you think?' she repeated, mussing Peter's hair affectionately. 'Life would be boring if we didn't have other people around complicating everything?'

Evan felt the fabric of the sleeve wet against his forearm. 'Sure,' he said.

'Mom? Mom. *Mom*. My Band-Aid, it's coming off.'

'Case in point,' Mia said to Mrs Rosenbaum, who did not return her smile. Mia fussed in her purse. 'I have some more in here somewhere.'

'The Muppet ones,' Peter said. He had a raspy voice, older than suited an eight-year-old. 'I want Animal.'

'You *have* Animal. On your noggin.'

'Then Kermit.'

'Kermit was this morning. Miss Piggy?'

'No way. Gonzo.'

'We have Gonzo!'

As she smoothed the new Band-Aid into place with her thumbs, kissing Peter's head at the same time, Evan risked a quick glance down at his sleeve. He was bleeding through, the black fabric even darker over his forearm. He shifted, and the pistol suppressors clanked together in the paper grocery bag dangling at his side. A wet splotch had appeared on the bag – the bloody sock leaking through. Gritting his teeth, he spun the bag around and set it on the floor with the stain facing the wall.

'It's *Evan*, right?' Mia had directed her attention at him again. 'What do you do again?'

'Importer.'

'Oh? What kind of stuff?'

He glanced at the floor indicators. The elevator seemed to be moving glacially. 'Industrial cleaning supplies. We sell to hotels and restaurants, mostly.'

Mia shouldered against the wall. Due to a missing button, her knockoff blazer gaped wide at the lapels, providing a generous view of her dress shirt. 'Well? Aren't you gonna ask me what *I* do?' Her tone was amused yet stopped shy of flirtatious. 'That *is* how conversations work.'

District attorney, Grade III, Torrance Courthouse. Widowed five years and change. Bought her small unit on the twelfth floor a few months ago with what remained of the life-insurance money.

Evan produced a pleasant smile. 'What do you do?'

'I am,' she said, with mock grandiosity, 'a district attorney. So you better watch your step.'

He hoped the noise he made sounded appropriately impressed. She gave a satisfied nod and produced a poppy-seed muffin from her purse. From the corner of his eye, Evan noticed Peter again staring at his bare ankle with curiosity.

The elevator stopped on the ninth floor. Fresh from the social room, a coterie of residents crowded in, led by Hugh Walters, HOA president and monologist of the highest order. 'Excellent, excellent,' he said. 'A good showing at tonight's meeting is essential. We'll be voting on which morning beverages to offer in the lobby.'

Evan said, 'Actually, I –'

'Decaf or regular.'

'Who drinks decaf anyways?' asked Lorilee Smithson, 3F, a third wife with a face turned vaguely feline by decades of plastic surgery.

'People with A-fib,' Mrs Rosenbaum weighed in.

'Knock it off, Ida,' Lorilee said. 'You just talk down to me because I'm beautiful.'

'No. I talk down to you because you're *stupid*.'

'I say we offer kombucha,' Johnny Middleton, 8E, chimed in. A hair-plugged forty-something, he'd moved in with his widowed father, a retired CFO, some years back. As always, Johnny wore a warm-up suit with the decal of the mixed-martial-arts program he'd been attending – or at least talking about incessantly – for the past two years. 'It's got probiotics *and* antibodies. *Way* healthier than decaf.'

A few more residents piled in, crowding Evan against the rear wall. His skin prickled; his blood hummed with impatience. Theaters of war and high-threat zones focused his composure, but Castle Heights small talk left him utterly devoid of bearings. Mia glanced up from the muffin she was picking at and gave him an eye roll.

'We haven't heard much from *you* lately, Mr Smoak,' Hugh said with a practiced air of superciliousness. Probing eyes stared out from behind black-framed glasses so old-fashioned they were trendy again. 'Would you like to weigh in on the morning-beverage measure?'

Evan cleared his throat. 'I don't have a strong need for kombucha.'

'Maybe if you worked out once in a while instead of

playing with spreadsheets all day,' Johnny stage-whispered, the dig bringing a titter from Lorilee and glares of condemnation from others.

Fighting for patience, Evan glanced down, watching the stain on his sleeve slowly spread. Casually, he crossed his arms, covering the blood.

'Your sweatshirt,' Mia whispered. She leaned toward him, bringing with her the pleasing scent of lemon-grass lotion. 'It's wet.'

'I spilled something on it in the car,' Evan said. Her eyes remained on the sleeve, so he added, 'Grape juice.'

'*Grape* juice?'

The elevator lurched abruptly to a stop.

'Whoa,' Lorilee said. 'What happened?'

Mrs Rosenbaum said, 'Maybe your augmented lips hit the emergency stop button.'

The residents stirred and milled about, livestock crammed in a pen. A blur at Evan's side drew his attention – Peter crouching, his little fingers closing on Evan's pant cuff, lifting it to reveal the curiously bare ankle. Evan pulled his foot away, accidentally knocking over the grocery bag. One of the pistol suppressors rolled free, the metal tube rattling on the floor.

Peter's eyes flared wide, and then he snatched up the suppressor and shoved it back into Evan's bag.

'Peter,' Mia said. 'Get up. We don't *crawl* on the *floor.* What are you thinking?'

He rose shyly, twisting one hand in the other.

'I dropped something,' Evan said. 'He was just getting it for me.'

11

'The hell *was* that thing?' Johnny asked.

Evan elected to let the question pass as rhetorical.

Johnny finally unstuck the red lever, and the elevator continued up. When they reached the tenth floor, Hugh held the doors open. He looked from Peter to Mia. 'I take it you didn't arrange child care?'

The eight or so women in proximity bristled.

'I'm a single mom,' Mia said.

'HOA guidelines expressly specify that no children are allowed during committee meetings.'

'Fair enough, Hugh.' Mia flashed a radiant smile. 'You're the one who's gonna lose the swing vote on the hanging begonias in the pool area.'

Hugh frowned and moved on with the others into the hall. Evan tried to stay behind with Mia and Peter, but Mrs Rosenbaum reached back and fastened her hand over his forearm again, cracking the developing scabs beneath the sweatshirt. 'Come on, now,' she said. 'If you live in this building, you'll do your part like everyone else.'

'I'm sorry,' Evan said. 'I have to get back to those spreadsheets.'

He loosened Mrs Rosenbaum's hand. Her pruned finger pads were smeared with his blood. He gave her hand a formal little pat, using the gesture as cover to wipe her fingers clean with his other palm as he withdrew his arm into the elevator.

The doors closed. Mia folded the remains of her poppy-seed muffin in the paper wrapper, jammed it into her purse, and shot a sigh at the ceiling. They rode the elevator up in silence, Evan holding the paper bag, the top crumpled down to cover the stain. He kept his sockless foot and bloody sleeve facing the wall on the far side of Mia and Peter.

Peter held his gaze dead ahead. They reached the twelfth floor, and Mia said goodbye and stepped out, Peter trailing her. The doors started to close behind them, but then a tiny hand snaked through the bumpers and they jerked and retracted.

Peter's face appeared, his solemn expression undermined by Gonzo staring out from the Band-Aid on his forehead. 'Thanks for covering for me,' he said.

Before Evan could respond, the doors had slid shut once again.

2. Fortress of Solitude

The façade of 21A's front door matched the others in the building precisely, adhering to HOA regs and passing unnoticed before the eagle eye of Hugh Walters on his monthly floor inspections. What Hugh *didn't* know was that the thin wood laminate concealed a steel door fire-rated at six hours, immune to battering rams, and effective in repelling hinge-area breaching charges.

Arriving at his place at last, Evan slid his key into the ordinary-looking dead bolt. When he turned the key, a concealed network of security bars inside the door released with a sturdier-than-normal clank.

He stepped inside, locked the door behind him, deactivated the alarm, dropped the bloody grocery bag on a glass accent table, and exhaled.

Home.

Or at least his version of it.

Copious windows and balconies maximized the corner penthouse panorama. Twelve miles to the east, the downtown skyline glittered jaggedly, and Century City rose to the south.

The condo's layout was largely open, gunmetal gray concrete floors split by a freestanding central fireplace, numerous pillars, and a steel staircase that spiraled up to a rarely used loft Evan had converted to a reading room. The kitchen featured poured-concrete counters, stainless-steel appliances, brushed-nickel fixtures and a backsplash of mirrored subway tiles. The broad island overlooked a spacious, sparse plain broken by training mats, various workout stations and the occasional sitting area.

The windows and sliding glass doors were made of Lexan, a bullet-resistant polycarbonate thermoplastic resin, and the retractable sunscreens added a second layer of discreet armoring. Built of tiny interlocking rings like chain mail, the woven metal was composed of a rare titanium variation. The screens could stop most sniper rounds that might penetrate the bullet-resistant panes. They added an additional protective shield from explosive devices while obscuring the sight line of would-be trackers or assassins.

And they provided excellent shade from the sun.

Even the walls themselves had been reinforced. Evan had undertaken these upgrades slowly over the years, using different suppliers each time, shipping the equipment piecemeal to various addresses, assembling much of the gear off-site. When he needed to hire installers, he ensured that they never knew precisely what they were installing. With meticulous planning and patience, he had built a fortress of solitude without anyone's taking notice.

He had great affection for the world he'd created behind the door to 21A. And yet he was prepared to abandon it at a moment's notice.

He crossed now to the kitchen, his shoes tapping on

the polished concrete. The one flare of whimsy and color came in the form of the so-called living wall installed beside the stove. A vertical garden fed by a drip system, it grew everything from mint and chamomile for fresh tea to cilantro, parsley, sage, basil, and peppers for omelets. Though it was December, the chamomile was flourishing within the carefully controlled environment of the penthouse.

On occasion it gave Evan pause that the only living thing with which he shared his life was a wall.

But he had the Commandments, and the Commandments were everything.

Reaching the Sub-Zero, he pulled from the freezer drawer a frost-clouded bottle of U'Luvka, a Polish vodka named for a style of crystal glass. He poured several ounces into a shaker over distilled ice, rattled it until his palms adhered to the frozen metal, then tilted the contents into a chilled martini glass. He drank, letting the cool burn move past his lips, closing his eyes into the pleasure of it.

He drifted through the scent of the vertical wall and stepped out through one of the south-facing sliding doors. The floor of the balcony was layered with quartz stones that crunched loudly underfoot, which was precisely the point. Shatter-detection software embedded in the windows and doorframes picked up the precise audio signature of the crunched rock, alerting to the compression sounds of any object over fifty pounds. The sensors also were triggered if anything of size neared the glass.

A square planter toward the balcony's edge held an assortment of squat succulents and a base-jumping parachute, tucked behind an inset panel in the event that Evan had to make a rapid exit.

Setting his elbows on the railing, he sipped again, feeling the vodka warm his cheeks. In the distance the crescent of Marina del Rey sparkled at the continent's edge, riding the lip of the night-black Pacific.

Movement in the neighboring building drew his focus. Evan faced apartment 19H across the street. Joey Delarosa flickered into sight behind his vertical blinds, eating out of a pot with a wooden spoon, a football game shimmering in the background. A low-level accountant at one of the big firms, he spent most of his off-hours eating and watching TV. About once a month, he'd go on a drinking jag, stumble home from the Westwood bars and call his ex-wife, crying. These calls were met with a stony reception; Joey hadn't honored the telephonic restraining order or paid child support in three years. His last domestic interlude had put his then-wife in a two-day coma and left his son with a permanent limp, growth plates being what they are in six-year-olds. The service door in Joey's kitchen, which let out near the trash chute, sported a Schlage wafer lock that Evan could get through in five to seven seconds with a forked tension wrench.

Evan made it his business to be intimately acquainted with his setting. His head held a catalog of directories and blueprints for anything within eyeshot – every resident, every stairwell, every electrical closet and yapping dog.

The Third Commandment, beaten into his head from the age of twelve: *Master your surroundings.*

For a time he sipped the crisp vodka and breathed the crisp air.

Habit beckoned him to check the black RoamZone phone again. Despite the high-power-density lithium-ion battery, it was down to one bar. He went inside at once, plugged it into its charger on the kitchen counter, and synced the ringer to the built-in speaker system so he could hear it anywhere in the seven-thousand-square feet of the condo. The number was easy enough to remember.

1-855-2-NOWHERE.

It featured one digit more than was necessary, but given the condition that callers were in when they dialed, they required something simple and memorable.

The black phone hadn't rung in ten weeks. Which meant it might ring soon or it might ring months from now. He never knew. No matter how long it took, he would wait.

Feeling impatient, he repeated the Seventh Commandment in his head like a mantra: *One mission at a time. One mission at a time.*

He stripped down to his boxer briefs, then started a fire with birch logs and burned his clothes, the stained grocery bag and the bloody sock. Carrying the twin pistol suppressors, he padded back to the master bathroom and set them on the counter. The centerpiece of the room was a Maglev bed that literally floated two feet in the air, a slab repelled from the floor by preposterously strong neodymium rare-earth magnets. Cables tethered the slab in place, preventing the slightest wobble. The Finnish design company claimed that the magnetism had a healing effect, but medical evidence was scant. Evan just liked how it looked. No legs, no headboard, no footboard – minimalism in extreme.

Heading for the bathroom, he nudged the frosted-glass shower door, which rolled aside silently on its tracks. He turned on the shower, as hot as he could stand. The water scoured away the grime and sweat and gave him a clearer look at the wound on his forearm. Not bad at all. It was a fairly neat cut and should heal well. Stepping out of the shower, he toweled off, then attended to the wound. Deciding against sutures or butterfly stitches, he pinched the skin together and superglued it closed. As the skin healed, it would push the dried glue out.

He moved back into the bedroom. His bureau held twenty or so gray V-necked T-shirts, a dozen pairs of matching dark jeans and the same number of sweatshirts. After he dressed, he hesitated and stared at the bottom drawer.

He exhaled. Slid it open. Shoved the folded squares of boxer briefs to one side. A fingernail-size divot at the edge of the wood was the only indication of the false bottom.

He reached for it. But his hand stopped a few inches above the wood.

He contemplated the item hidden beneath, then rearranged the boxers and closed the drawer. It had been a long day, and there was no need to open up that false bottom and everything that came with it.

After a quick detour to the kitchen to grab an ice cube, he returned to the bathroom and scooped up the pistol suppressors from the counter. Stepping into the still-wet shower, he gripped the lever handle that controlled the hot water and turned it the wrong way. The lever was electronic, keyed to his palm print. As he pushed it through the point of resistance, a door concealed seamlessly within the tile pattern swung inward, revealing a hidden room.

He mentally referred to the irregular four hundred square feet beyond as the Vault. During an ostensible remodel, he'd 'walled off' the awkward storage space in the back of his condo. Crammed beneath the public stairs to the roof, the room had exposed beams, rough concrete walls and the underbellies of steps descending from the ceiling to crowd the head. No other condo had such a space; no one would know to look for it, let alone miss it.

Accessible only through this hidden door, his armory and workbench lined the wall beneath the inverted stairs. A central L-shaped desk constructed of sheet metal held a confusion of computer towers, antennae and servers. A bank of monitors along one wall showed the innards of Castle Heights, various angles of halls and stairwells. The video feeds were easily pirated from the cheap but sturdy Taiwanese-make security cameras installed about the property.

One computer unconnected to the Internet held his

banking information. His main account was stashed in Luxembourg under the name Z$Q9R#)3 and had a forty-word password in the form of a nonsensical sentence. The account could be accessed only over the phone and his money transferred solely via voice commands. There was no electronic access, no virtual transactions, no debit cards. He'd sprinkled secondary accounts through other areas of nonreporting – Bermuda, Cyprus, the Caymans – and any paperwork was directed through a series of trusts and shell corporations based in Road Town, Tortola.

As Jack used to say, *Ball bearings within ball bearings.*

Evan had come a long way from the projects of East Baltimore.

Beside the mouse pad on the central table, a glass salad bowl held a fist-size aloe vera plant nestled in cobalt glass pebbles. Evan dropped the ice cube into the clutch of serrated spikes, a simple watering that Vera required every week.

He put the suppressors away in one of the weapon lockers and then emerged, sealing the Vault behind him.

In the big room, he sat at last. Cross-legged on the area rug, his back straight, hands resting gently on his knees. Meditating. He observed the shape of his body from the inside. The pressure of his bones against the floor. The weight of his palms. The breathing channel, nose to throat to chest. The aroma of the burning birch logs tinged the back of his throat. He noticed the whorls in the sandalwood cabinet, individual threads of the Turkish rug, the way the blinds diffused the city lights into a gauzy orange glow. The aim was to see everything as if for the first time. That was the aim everywhere. All the time.

His breath was his anchor.

He veiled his eyes, neither open nor closed, turning the space around him dreamlike and vague, and there was no past and no future. He released the day – the four-hour drive from Las Vegas, the slashing knife, the drone of Hugh Walters's voice in the elevator. Air-conditioning tickled the back of his neck. His forearm wound radiated a throbbing heat that was not entirely unpleasant.

His left shoulder, he realized, felt out of whack, and he relaxed it from its slight hunch, lowering it a few millimeters and feeling the muscle stretch. He aligned himself, flesh and thought, until he became the breath and only the breath, until the world was the breath and there was nothing else.

For some time he sat like this, lost to blissful stillness.

And then Evan was yanked out of his trancelike state on the Turkish rug. He blinked a few times, acclimating his eyes and reorienting himself. He realized what had jarred him from his meditation.

The black phone was ringing.

3. Broken Like Me

The ringing of the RoamZone phone seemed straight-forward enough.

However.

The direct-inward-dial number itself, 1-855-2-NOWHERE, originally acquired through a Bulgarian Voice over IP service, was set up so that calls were digitized and sent over the Internet through an encrypted virtual private network tunnel. The tunnel was routed through fifteen software virtual telephone switch destinations around the world to the Wi-Fi access point and VoIP adapter belonging to Joey Delarosa in apartment 19H across the street. From there it was popped back into the Internet via Verizon's LTE network. If, by some miracle beyond miracles, the secret-handshake men ever traced the data stream to that point and stormed Joey's place, Evan could watch the whole debacle from behind his lowered sunscreen.

After every significant contact, Evan rotated the phone service where he parked the number. Right now it was housed by a company in the Jiangsu province of China, a jurisdictional and logistical nightmare for any inquiring mind. The phone hooked seamlessly into the GSM network, functioned in 135 countries, and utilized prepaid vending-machine SIM cards that Evan crushed and replaced on a regular basis.

He rose, his bare feet tapping the polished concrete as he crossed to the kitchen counter.

He answered the phone as he always did. 'Do you need my help?'

The voice came in on the faintest delay. 'Are you . . . I mean, is this a joke?'

'No.'

'Wait. Just . . . *wait*.' A young woman, late teens. Hispanic accent, maybe Salvadoran. 'You're real? I thought you was like . . . like some urban legend. A myth.'

'I am.'

He waited. Heard breathing, faster than usual. This was common.

'Look, I'm in trouble. I don't have no time to screw around if . . . if . . .' A choked-down sob. 'I don't know what to do.'

'What's your name?'

'Morena Aguilar.'

'Where did you get this number?'

'A black guy give it to me.'

'Describe him.'

The First Commandment: *Assume nothing.*

'He had a beard, all scruffly like, with some gray. And his arm was broke. In a sling.'

Clarence John-Baptiste. A meth gang took over his house in Chatsworth last fall, held him and his daughter captive. Clarence and his girl had not been treated gently.

24

'Where do you live?'

She gave an address in Boyle Heights, East L.A., in the flats below the Los Angeles River. Lil East Side territory.

'When should we meet?' Evan asked.

'I can't . . . I don't know.'

Again he waited.

'Tomorrow,' she said. 'Tomorrow in the middle of the day?'

'Where can you meet?'

'I ain't got no car.'

'Is it safe to meet at your residence?' he asked.

'Midday, yeah, it is.'

'Noon, then.'

Noon was good. He would require three hours to sweep the surrounding blocks, to case the house, to check for digital transmitters and trace signatures of explosive materials. If this was a trap and he had to engage, he'd engage on his own terms.

The Ninth Commandment: *Always play offense.*

Later, in the Vault, Evan drank fresh chamomile tea as he ran Morena Aguilar through the databases.

Aside from hard-core terrorist intel, law-enforcement databases are by and large connected to the Internet. The vast majority of criminal and civil records can be accessed by any local police department's patrol car with a mobile data terminal. This includes any Panasonic Toughbook laptop hooked to the dashboard of a basic LAPD cruiser. Each of those laptops talks directly to CLERS, CLETS, NCIC, CODIS and literally hundreds of other state and federal databases.

Once you crack a dashboard computer on a single cruiser, you can get your hands on Big Brother's control board.

Evan wasn't a master hacker by any stretch of the imagination, but he'd made his way unattended into various cruisers and uploaded a piece of reverse SSH code into their laptops, leaving a virtual back door open for himself.

Now, tucked in the hidden room, Evan cruised the information superhighway to his heart's content, gathering particulars for tomorrow's mission and sipping the last of his fragrant tea.

For the past forty-five minutes, Morena Aguilar had been sitting on the overturned recycle bin on the front porch of the dilapidated tract house, her hands wedged beneath her legs so her thin arms bowed outward. Her bare feet bounced nervously on the splintering wood, her knees jerking. Her dark hair was cinched back so hard that it conformed precisely to her skull before tumbling curly and wild from a rubber band. Darting eyes, ducked head, a hint of sweat sparkling at her temples.

Scared.

Parked past the intersection behind a rusting heap of an abandoned car, Evan scanned the street again through a detached rifle scope. On a patch of dead grass in the front yard across from Morena's house, a teenage mom, also Latina, emerged with a diapered infant under her arm. She set him down to play in an aluminum-foil turkey pan filled with sand. The child looked to be mixed race, bright-green eyes offset against caramel skin. As he started digging in his makeshift sandbox, she lit up a Marlboro Red and blew a stream of smoke at the sky, scratching at a strawberry birthmark on the underside of her arm. She couldn't have been older than eighteen, but her face was grim. A cell phone bulged her back pocket. Another teenage mom shoved a baby stroller up on to the dead lawn next to her. The first one flicked a cigarette up from the pack in offering. They didn't speak. They just stood side by side, smoked, and watched the street. Two young women with nothing else to do.

Once Evan was convinced they were harmless, he lowered the scope, picked up a black metal briefcase, and got out of the truck.

As he approached, Morena saw him coming and rose, clutching one arm at the biceps. He stepped up on to the porch. The years were heavy on her face, stress lines and a hardness behind her pretty brown eyes. The smell of hair spray was strong.

'I'm hawking reverse mortgages door-to-door,' he said. 'You're not interested. Shake your head.'

She did.

'I'm going to go around the block, loop through the backyard. Your rear door is unlocked. Please keep it that way. Now look annoyed and head inside.'

She banged through the screen door, and he stepped off the porch and kept on up the street.

Ten minutes later they were seated across from each other in torn lawn chairs in the tiny living room of the house. Evan faced the grease-stained front window. On the coffee table before him sat his locked black briefcase. If the combination was input incorrectly, it threw off eight hundred volts of electricity. It contained a voice-activated microphone, a pinhole lens and a wideband high-power jammer that squelched any surveillance devices.

And it held papers.

The stifling air stank of birds. A ragged parrot rustled in a cage in the square adjoining bedroom. The open door looked in on two mattresses on the floor, a dresser and cracked mirror and a battered trumpet case leaning against a long-disused fish tank.

'Carrot, please!' the parrot said. 'Please! Please don't!'

Over Morena's shoulder Evan could see the street clearly, the two young mothers still smoking silently in the yard across from them. The baby's wails grew audible, but neither mother made a move to comfort him.

Evan shifted on the chair, and at his movement Morena's back went arrow straight. Perspiration spotted her shirt, a stiff button-up with a BENNY'S BURGERS decal and a peeling name tag. She made fists in the fabric of her polyester pants.

'You're nervous,' he said. 'That I'm here.'

She nodded quickly, and at once she looked like a kid again.

'Do you know how to handle a gun?'

The pause drew out long enough that he wasn't sure if she was going to respond.

'I've shot some,' she finally said, and he could tell she was lying. She blotted sweat from her hairline. Her plucked brows arched high, and an empty pierce hole dimpled her nose.

He removed his pistol from his hip holster, spun it around and offered it to her. She stared at it there on his palm.

The Wilson Combat 1911 high-end variant had been custom-built to Evan's specs. Semiauto, eight rounds in a stainless-steel mag with number nine slotted in the chamber. Extended barrel, tuned with ramp-throat work for flawless feeding and threaded to receive a suppressor. The straight-eight sights were high-profile so that the suppressor, when screwed in, wouldn't block them. Ambidextrous thumb safety, since he was a lefty. Grip safety on the back to ensure it couldn't fire if not in hand. Aggressive front-frame checkering, eighteen lines per inch, and Specialized Simonich gunner grips so the gun grabbed him back when he fired. High-ride beavertail grip safety to prevent hammer bite on the thumb webbing. Matte black so it disappeared in shadow, giving no glint.

He gestured again for her to take the pistol. 'Just while we talk. So you don't have to be nervous.'

She lifted it gingerly from his hand, set it on the cushion beside her. When she exhaled, her shoulders lowered a bit.

'I don't . . . I don't care about me no more. It's her.

Mi hermanita – my li'l sis, Carmen. Me, I been a screwup from the beginning. But that kid? She never done a wrong thing in her life. She's in school right now. And she's *good* at it. She's just eleven.'

Evan glanced over at that battered trumpet case in the bedroom, then back at Morena. 'How old are you?'

'Seventeen.' She took a gulp of air. Another lengthy pause. She seemed unaware of how long she let her silences go. She wasn't sullen, but withdrawn.

'My dad left when we was young. *Mi mamá* found out he died a few years ago. She . . . um, she passed away last year. She had the ovarian cancer. And then *he* came in. He took over the rent for our house. He keep us here in it.'

Across the street the baby cried and cried. One of the mothers reached out and grabbed the stroller, pushed it back and forth soothingly. 'Carrot, please!' the parrot squawked from the bedroom behind him. 'Please! Please don't!'

Evan focused on Morena. He did not want to ask any questions. He wanted her to have space to tell her story her way.

She tugged a cell phone from her snug pant pocket. 'He gave me this. So he can text me whenever he want. I'm on call, right? But it's okay. He only use *me*. Until now, I mean. My sister, she's getting older. She's almost out of time. He said she's "coming mature".' At this, Morena's upper lip wrinkled. 'He wanted to already, with her, the other night. I . . . distracted him. Like I know how. But he said next time . . . next time . . .' She

30

bit her lip to stop it from trembling. 'You don't understand.'

'Help me understand.'

She just shook her head. Outside, tinny rap music announced a car's approach. A guy sat in the rear of a flipped-open hatchback, holding a big-screen TV in place as his buddy drove. The car vanished, but it was a time longer before the sound faded.

'Do you have anywhere to go?' Evan asked.

'My aunt. She in Vegas. But it don't matter.'

'Why doesn't it matter?'

Morena leaned forward, suddenly fierce. 'You don't *get it*. He say if I take her anywhere, he'll hunt us down. They have them databases now. He can find anyone. Anywhere.' And just like that, the anger departed. She made a fist, pressed it to her trembling lips. 'Calling you, it was stupid. Just don't say nothing to no one. I'll figure out something. I always do. Look, I gotta go to work.'

He knew that her shift didn't start for two more hours and that the burger stand she worked at was only a seven-minute walk away. He remained sitting, and she made no move to exit.

She swayed a little. 'I just don't want . . .' She blinked, and tears spilled down her smooth cheeks. 'I just don't want her to be all broken like me.'

She lifted a hand to wipe her cheeks, and he saw on her inner forearm what looked like an angry inoculation mark. But it couldn't be, not given her age.

It was a brand.

Evan's eyes shifted to the young mothers across the

street. The first raised her cigarette to her mouth, and it struck him now that the strawberry birthmark wasn't a birthmark at all. His gaze dropped to the arm of the other woman, pushing the stroller back and forth. Sure enough, a similar maroon splotch marred her skin in the same place.

Morena noticed his attention pull back to her, and she lowered her arm quickly, hiding the brand. But not before he'd registered the burned circle. About the size of a .40-caliber gun barrel.

Like, say, that of the Glock 22 that was standard issue for the LAPD.

He replayed Morena's words: *He can find anyone. Anywhere.* The ultimate abuse of power. Human slavery right here in the open. Those girls across the street had on-call cell phones, too. And babies. He understood now the grimness of their faces, the hollowed-out resignation.

Morena rose to leave. She smoothed the front of her work shirt, then tilted her face back so no tears would spill. 'Thanks for coming and all,' she said, 'but you don't get it.'

'I do now,' Evan said.

She looked at him.

'The whole street?' he asked.

She sank back into her chair. 'The whole *block*.' Again her voice faltered. 'I just don't want him to get my little sister.'

Evan said, 'You don't have to worry about that anymore.'

4. I'll Be Waiting

On his way home, Evan ran the circuit of his safe houses, checking up on them. He owned numerous properties spread throughout the area – a town house on the Westside, a cottage in the Valley, a ranch-style home in the crappy neighborhood beneath the LAX flight paths. He made sure the lawns were watered, junk mail cleared off the porches, lighting-control systems varied. The banal façades hid alternate vehicles, mission-essential equipment, weapon caches. Jack had always stressed the importance of maintaining multiple 'loadouts,' gear prepped for a grab-and-go.

After all, Evan never knew when he'd have to vanish. He held a place of honor on numerous most-wanted lists, but none that could be advertised. He had to be careful at airports, borders and embassies, though he'd been to an embassy only once in the past five years, and that was to neutralize a clerk who'd been a key player in a human-trafficking ring.

By the time Evan reached Castle Heights, the setting sun bathed the building's side in an orange glow. He parked and headed through the lobby, passing a half dozen kombucha bottles floating in a tub of melted ice on the refreshment stand. Apparently the beverage initiative had not been the rousing success the HOA had hoped for.

In the seating area across from the door, the *L.A. Times* sports section rustled and dipped, Johnny Middleton's face appearing above the top of the page. He was staking out the kombucha.

Evan sped up. The swish of nylon sweatpants accented Johnny's slide off the cushioned chair. 'Evan. *Evan!*'

Evan had no choice but to halt.

Johnny caught up. Clearly peeved, he glanced over at the forlorn beverage tub. When he looked back, a smug expression filled his round face. 'You should really come by for a workout.' He tapped the martial-arts logo on his sweat jacket, which showed two fists colliding. Innovative. 'I can get you a free pass.'

Before Evan could respond, Johnny feinted at him with a jab.

The fist came in lazy and offline. Evan saw the angles with perfect clarity – a double-hand deflection, gooseneck the wrist, shatter the bone and rake the elbow tendons, then a chicken-wing arm control for the takedown, his knee crushing Johnny's floating rib upon impact with the floor.

Instead he flinched slightly. 'Not really my thing,' he said.

'Okay, chief,' Johnny said, backing away, arms spread in a show of magnanimity. 'Consider it an open offer.'

Evan walked over to the elevator and stepped inside when a tumult by the door to the garage drew his focus.

Mia and Peter stumbled into view, their arms laden with grocery bags. Evan held the elevator for them while they shuffled inside, crowding him. As they ascended, he could barely make out Peter beneath the oversize shopping bags.

'Need a hand?' Evan asked.

'We're good, thanks,' Mia said.

An iPhone rang somewhere on her person, the theme from *Jaws*. Kneeing apart the various items she was carrying, she fumbled for her purse. A plastic drug-store bag slid off her hand, and Evan caught it before it hit the floor. The phone stopped ringing, and Mia sighed with resignation, then began hoisting various bags back into position.

Evan became aware of Peter's stare on the side of his face. Peter lowered his head, scrutinizing Evan's ankle. Evan subtly tugged up his pant leg, a *ta-da* move to show off the sock. *Move along. Nothing to see here.*

The intense stare returned to Evan's face.

'Evan *what*?' the boy asked.

'Excuse me?'

'What's your last name?'

'Smoak.'

'Like from fire?'

'But spelled different.'

'What's your middle name?'

'Danger.'

'Really?'

'No.'

Nothing. And then the boy gave the faintest grin.

35

Mia looked away to hide her own smile.

The elevator dinged its arrival at the twelfth floor. 'If you're done giving Mr Danger the third degree . . .' Mia said, mussing Peter's hair and tugging him out after her.

Too late, Evan looked down, noticing Mia's drugstore bag still twisting in his fingers. He reached for the doors as they bumped shut, and then he was riding up to the penthouse level with her belongings. Returning them would have to wait.

Tonight he had work to do.

He tossed Mia's plastic bag on the kitchen counter and consulted the vodkas neatly arranged in the freezer, settling on the flask-shaped bottle of Jean-Marc XO. Made using four varieties of French wheat, the vodka was distilled nine times, then micro-oxygenated and charcoal-filtered. As he poured two fingers over ice, he noticed that a box of Band-Aids had partially slid out from Mia's drugstore bag on to the counter. Muppet-themed, of course. The gaudy colors, so out of place against the gray slab and stainless steels, leapt out at Evan. He found something unsettling about the Day-Glo oranges and vibrant greens, though he could not put a name to the feeling.

He slid the box into the bag again and sipped his drink on his way back to the Vault. The vodka felt silky going down his throat, the texture of purity.

Morena Aguilar had armed him with two things: her on-call cell phone, now resting on the sheet-metal desk next to his trusty aloe vera plant, and a name.

Bill Chambers.

There was no scarcity of information on William S. Chambers of the LAPD. As a result of several big, well-timed busts, he'd worked his way up from patrolman to detective II, finally landing a spot in the coveted Gang and Narcotics Division four years ago. That explained how he'd managed to carve out his own little despotship in the middle of Lil East Side-controlled Boyle Heights. He was in an ideal position to do favors for the gangbangers if they helped him in turn. And so they left him to his concubinary of coerced girls, maybe even threw influence to protect him and guard the block he'd turned into his personal labor camp. Evan uncovered multiple Internal Affairs investigations, all of them hindered by misplaced evidence or about-faces by key witnesses. Next he searched the money. Chambers's bank accounts showed multiple cash withdrawals and deposits just below the ten-thousand-dollar threshold for mandated bank reporting. Questionable activity. But not ironclad proof.

And the First Commandment demanded ironclad proof.

Evan picked up Morena's on-call cell, a crappy plastic unit with a smudged screen, as light as a toy phone. It was a disposable model out of Mexico. When he thumbed up the text message history, he felt a sudden drop in the temperature of the Vault, a coolness at the back of his neck. A number of explicit texts from a recurring phone number contained sexual directives and instructions for Morena, some including photo references of clearly underage Latina girls in particular poses. He stared at the face of a child who couldn't yet have been fourteen. Her features were leached of affect, the dead, red-rimmed eyes wholly detached from her body and what it was doing.

He traded the phone for his drink but found he'd lost his taste for vodka. Or anything else. Indignation burned, and he had to evoke the Fourth Commandment: *Never make it personal.*

In the years he'd been doing this, he'd never broken a Commandment, and he wasn't willing to do so now.

Back to the databases with renewed energy. The phone number of the sender Evan sourced to a batch of prepaid phones bulk-sold to Costco last year. A simple bit of reverse-proxy code let him slip behind Costco's firewall, and he checked data files at the store locations nearest Chambers's home address. Nothing. Next he looked at several Costcos between Chambers's house and various locations including Boyle Heights, finally ringing the cherries on a store en route to LAPD Headquarters. An account in the name of Sandy Chambers. The membership photo showed Bill's wrecked shell of a wife, wan-faced and slight beneath the industrial lights, her shoulders hunched as if she were trying to fold in on herself and disappear. She'd managed a smile, but it looked separate from her face, something pasted on.

Starting several quarters back to coincide with the date that the batch of prepaid phones had shipped, Evan scanned Chambers's purchase records. Cases of

Heineken, Trojan condoms, deck furniture, jumbo food purchases, a digital camera. And there, seven disposable phones, bought 13 February along with a set of oven mitts and a pack of soft-bristle toothbrushes.

There was no denying that taken as a whole the facts had a certain heft to them, but the evidence could be configured a variety of ways, telling a variety of stories. When Evan got involved, there was a single outcome, and that outcome demanded certainty before the fact. He lifted his melted drink and wiped the condensation ring with his sleeve, leaving the desk surface spotless.

Morena's cell phone rattled on the desk, indicating an incoming text.

TMRW NITE. IO. HAVE HER READY.

Evan stared at the words, waiting for his disgust to abate, for his anger to settle into something calm and unbroken. Then he texted back.

I'LL BE WAITING.

5. Other Things

Evan returned his highball glass to the kitchen, washed and dried it, and put it away. The refrigerator contained an array of items, neatly spaced on the clear shelves. He drank a bottle of water as he coated an ahi steak with coriander, paprika and cayenne pepper and seared it in a pan. When it was ready, he garnished it with a sprig of parsley from the living wall and set the plate down on the island counter, centering it between knife and fork. The fish flaked perfectly beneath the blade. He paused with the bite halfway to his mouth.

The Band-Aid box, visible through the thin plastic of the drugstore bag, glared back at him. Kermit's big green head, that watermelon-wedge smile.

Evan exhaled. Put down his laden fork.

Picking up the bag, he headed out.

He could hear the ruckus the moment he stepped from the elevator. Blaring TV, a boy's high-pitched voice, Mia's admonishments muffled through the door of 12B. The Honorable Pat Johnson stuck his turtle head out of condo 12F, swinging a lazy gaze to Evan as he passed. 'I suppose she has her hands full,' the judge said charitably, and withdrew.

Evan's first two knocks went unheard. He knocked louder, and then the door was flung open.

Mia, hair aswirl, kitchen towel stuffed quarterback style down her sweatpants, stood holding a steaming pot. Behind her, Peter ran laps around the coffee table, up over the couch, and around the kitchen, stirring up a wake of Lego, action figures and comic books. A manic Daffy Duck cartoon provided an inadvertent score. Stray crayon marks marred the walls from waist level down. Pursuing an imaginary adversary, Peter waved a lightsaber, which emitted a futuristic wail piercing enough to vibrate one's teeth. He had a coaster over one eye, pirate fashion, secured with what appeared to be duct tape. A bowl of mac and cheese was inexplicably overturned on the counter.

Evan held up the bag for Mia to see.

Hands full, she gestured with her elbows. 'Can you just . . . uh – come in. For one sec. Please. I'm just –' Her head snapped around as her son zoomed past. 'Tell me that's not duct tape.'

Peter halted in his tracks. 'If I set a place, can Evan Smoak stay for dinner?'

Evan sat before a bowl of spaghetti with red sauce and a fruit-punch juice box with a bendy straw.

'I'm so sorry,' Mia said. 'I forgot to pick up anything else at the grocery store –'

'This is fine,' Evan said. 'Really.'

Across from him Peter beamed. His hair was

41

missing a few patches at the sides where Mia had cut the duct tape free. 'Wanna see my room?'

'Maybe after dinner,' Mia said.

'It's that one, there.'

From the Batman stickers, Kobe Bryant poster and pirate-themed KEEP OUT! sign, Evan had gleaned as much.

'My bedroom is on the same corner,' Evan said. 'I'm straight up nine floors.'

'I thought you were in 21*A*, not 21*B*.'

Evan hesitated.

Mia produced a quick smile. 'He's got a bigger place, honey.'

'Oh,' Peter said. 'You're richer than us.' Mia took in a gulp of air. Before she or Evan could respond, Peter tilted his arm up, examined a fresh scrape on his elbow. 'I need one of the new Band-Aids for this.'

'*Another* cut?' Mia said. 'How'd that happen?'

'Dodgeball.'

'I thought dodgeballs were soft.'

'Yeah, but the ground isn't.' Peter shot a look over at Evan. 'I'm adopted,' he said. 'Which sucks, 'cuz I'll never really know where I came from. My mom couldn't have babies, because she has poor-quality eggs. My dad died.' His head swiveled back to Mia, who was wearing a frozen simulation of a smile. 'Can we get a Christmas tree?'

Evan was still acclimatizing to the collection of non sequiturs that constituted the conversational patter of an eight-year-old.

Mia tilted her forehead into her hand, clenched her bangs in a fist. 'We talked about this, Peter. It's too early.'

'It's December fourth!'

'It'll be dead by the time Christmas gets here.'

'Then we can get another.'

'We're not *rotating* trees, Peter.'

And so it continued, Evan taking it in silently. He reached back into his memory to find a reference point for this domestic scene but found nothing.

They finished the meal, and Mia asked Peter to put his laundry away.

As Peter disappeared into his room, Evan rose to help Mia clear. She neither asked for the help nor thanked him for it.

They washed and dried, side by side.

'You're probably wondering how I afford living here on a DA's salary,' she said. 'My husband's life-insurance money.'

'Oh,' Evan said.

'It's nice and safe here.' Mia handed Evan a plate with a few suds still on the back, so he handed it back, and she passed it again through the water. 'As a DA I sometimes get threats.'

'Direct threats?'

'Usually it's shit we pick up online. The idiots these days, they brag about everything on Facebook. What they've done, what they're gonna do. Their *accomplishments*.'

'That doesn't seem so clever.'

'If they were smart, they wouldn't be thugs.' She shrugged. 'We live in a celebrity culture now. Or a wannabe-celebrity culture. The name of the game is *visibility*. If you aren't tweeted, liked, YouTubed, or Instagrammed, you don't exist.' She scrubbed hard at a stubborn bit of dried sauce, her hands pinking up beneath the steaming tap. 'Fine with me, though. Makes it easier to keep tabs on guys I've put away.'

'That ever get scary?'

'Sometimes.'

'Let me know if you ever need me to keep an eye out.'

She smiled, gave him a little bump with her elbow. 'You're sweet. But these guys are killers. Not importers.'

'Good point.'

'How about you?' she asked.

'I'm not a killer.'

'Very funny. You know what I mean.' She circled her hand in the air. 'Where are you from? You have family in the area? All that.'

'I don't have family anymore.'

'Oh. I'm sorry.'

She handed Evan the last plate, and he dried it and set it in the cabinet. A photo magnet of Peter with a soccer ball pinned a sheet of paper to the refrigerator. It was a handwritten note: '*Act so that you can tell the truth about how you act. – Jordan Peterson.*'

'What's that from?' Evan asked.

'A book I read,' Mia said. 'I try to post rules from it around the house, change them out every coupla days.'

'That's a lot to keep track of.'

'It's a lot of work,' she said, 'raising a human.'

Evan flashed on a memory: *Jack standing beside him at the firing range, hand on his boy-thin shoulder, assessing his shot grouping.*

'Yes,' he said. 'It is.'

The dishes were done. As Evan thanked Mia for dinner, Peter emerged and gave him a little fist bump on his way out. It left his knuckles sticky with fruit punch.

Back upstairs, Evan stared at his dinner plate where he'd left it on the gunmetal gray counter. The ahi steak, uneaten, centered on the white plate. The subway tiles of the backsplash gleamed darkly, throwing off a multitude of reflections, his tiny form bathed in the soothing blue light of the cityscape.

Scraping the fish into the garbage disposal, he noticed the knuckles of his right hand, tinged a faint red from the fruit punch.

He circled the island and washed his hands.

6. Please Don't

Killing a cop was no small business.

Evan sat in the dark of the cramped bedroom that Morena Aguilar shared with her eleven-year-old sister. The chair, dragged in from the kitchen, barely fit between the twin mattresses. In his loose fist, he held one end of a common household string that arced across the room to where it was tied to the lever handle of the closed door. Perfectly still, he waited.

The drawn curtains glowed faintly from the street-lights beyond, and he heard distant voices from various yards. Even here in the locked room over the stench of the birdcage, he caught the faintest whiff of barbecue.

The Victorinox watch fob clipped to his belt loop showed 9.37. He'd been in position for over an hour, and still twenty-three minutes remained until Detective William S. Chambers's scheduled rape of Carmen Aguilar.

'Please don't!' the parrot squawked. 'Carrot, please!'

On Evan's right knee rested Morena's on-call cell phone, on his left his Wilson Combat 1911 with the suppressor twisted on. He'd painted a tiny arrow on to the steel of the suppressor so he could index it to the identical position every time. In addition to the magazine in the pistol, he carried three more in his cargo pockets. They were go-to-war ready, validated in the desert on a makeshift range. As Jack used to say, *The loudest sound you'll ever hear in action is a click.*

Generally Evan preferred Speer Gold Dot hollow points, but tonight he was loaded with 230-grain hardball. The heavier round traveled at 850 feet a second, just below the speed at which it would break the sound barrier. The suppressor would take care of the sound signal of the gun's firing, but given the bustling neighborhood, Evan needed to ensure the bullet didn't make noise on its own.

The parrot shifted from claw to claw in the darkness, the cage clanking. The faded yellow sheets mussed on one of the mattresses were patterned with watermelon slices. The dinged-up trumpet case leaned in the corner by the door. A single red Converse shoe lay on its side in the closet, the toe worn through. Elmo looked out from a peeling sticker on the stained, empty fish tank, reminding Evan of Peter and his lively Band-Aids. Then Evan thought of the grown man en route to this room.

'Please don't!' the parrot squawked cheerily. 'Please don't!'

Evan breathed. *Never make it personal. Assume nothing. Never make it personal. Assume nothing.*

He felt the weight of the pistol resting on his thigh. The weapon, it was always there for him, tried and true, a constant. Steel and lead, they responded predictably. They were finite, unchanging, able to be mastered. He could count on them. People failed. He couldn't rely on flesh and blood, sinew and bone.

Too often it ended badly.

There is still dark at the windows of the dormer room when the alarm screeches, but Evan is already awake. Most of this first night in Jack's house he has spent staring at the ceiling. He rises and regards the room. The rolling chair is perfectly centered at a desk, and the shelf above holds a row of books ordered by height and a cup filled with unsharpened pencils. Shutters are folded back from a bay window, letting in the first glow of dawn. There is no trace of dust, of disorder. Every item squared up, aligned, stacked with precision.

Evan's new home is a two-story farmhouse set behind an apron of cleared land in Arlington, Virginia. His window looks out on a green blanket of oak trees. It is like nothing he has seen outside of television.

He finds Jack downstairs in a study lined with dark wooden bookshelves. He is reading a volume on something called the Peloponnesian Wars. Classical music issues from an old-fashioned record player. On a side table rests a picture of a woman in a tarnished silver frame. She has long dark-brown hair down to her waist and a slight chin, and her eyes are smiling behind large glasses.

At Jack's feet Strider lifts his Scooby-Doo head and notes Evan's presence. The dog is at least a hundred pounds with a reddish tan coat and a wicked-looking strip of reverse fur running down his spine.

Evan waits for Jack to look up, but he does not. He sits as motionless as a carving, focused on his book. Everything about him seems different from the Mystery Man with his slender face and sallow skin, always lurking in shadows, peering through the chain-link, flicking up a flame to catch the tip of a new cigarette.

Finally Evan asks, 'Why'd you pick me?'

Still Jack holds his gaze on the page. 'You know what it's like to be powerless.'

The intonation is that of a statement, but Evan realizes it is in fact a question. More precisely, something he is being asked to answer.

Evan's face burns. His lips firm, but he forces the answer. 'Yes.'

'For what we are about to embark on,' Jack says, the book at last lowered to his knee, 'I need someone who knows that. In his bones. *Don't ever forget that feeling.*'

Evan would do anything to forget it but knows better than to say so.

'No one can ever know your real name,' Jack says.

'Okay.'

'*What* is your last name?'

Evan tells him.

'You like it?' Jack asks.

'No.'

'Want to pick a new one?'

'Like what?'

A long silence ensues. Then Jack says, 'My wife's maiden name was Smoak. With an a in the middle and no e on the end. Want that one?'

Evan notes the past tense and recognizes that this is a gift. As he weighs the cost of accepting it, he does his best to keep his eyes from the framed picture on the side table. Then he says, 'Sure.'

'You will use that name in your personal life only,' Jack says. 'The people you work with will never know that name.'

'What will they know me as?'

'Many things.' Jack rises, keys in hand, his face severe. 'It's time,' he says.

Leaving Strider with a full bowl, they take a truck instead of the sedan, which makes sense since most of their journey proves to be off-road. After a half hour, they turn sharply uphill and bounce violently along a trail, branches screeching against the windows. They emerge at the back of a barn.

Evan follows Jack into the barn. It smells of hay and manure. Jack shoves the heavy door closed behind them. There is only a dangling lamp swaying slightly over the stables, throwing insufficient light.

Evan feels his heart rate tick up, and he looks at Jack, but Jack does not look back.

There comes a crunching of boots across hay. A big man steps from the shadows, a dense beard crowding his ruddy face. He holds a hooked knife. He doesn't smile so much as bare his teeth.

'Hello, son,' he says. 'I'm here to teach you about pain.'

A full-body buzz of fear rolls through Evan. That wicked blade sways in the man's bulky fist, catching the light seeping around the cracks of the door.

Jack's square face points down at Evan, and he says, gruffly, 'The First Commandment: Assume nothing.'

The bearded man spins the blade expertly and offers it, handle out, to Evan. He says something, but Evan cannot make out the words over the thudding of his heartbeat.

The voice comes again. 'Take the knife, son.'

Evan does, his fingers trembling. Then he looks at Jack. What now?

The bearded man says, 'Stab yourself in the palm.'

Evan looks from the man to the hooked blade and back to the man.

'Oh, for Christ's sake,' the man says, seizing the blade from Evan. His thick fist encircles Evan's wrist, and then the steel tip pokes down, popping the tender skin of Evan's palm.

Evan gives a little cry.

'That hurt?' the man asks.

'Yeah, it —'

The man slaps Evan across the face, hard. Evan reels back, the nerves of his cheek on fire.

'Doesn't hurt now, does it? Your hand.'

Evan stares at him dumbly, his ears ringing.

'Does your hand hurt?' Each word drops deliberately, one stone after another.

'No. My face hurts.'

The man shows his teeth again, that slash of a grin. 'Pain is relative. Subjective. A hangnail hurts until someone kicks ya in the nuts. I'm gonna teach you the difference between physiological pain and felt pain.'

He grabs Evan's other wrist and raises the knife, and Evan flinches, ducks his head, the sting in his lowered palm flaring to life again. The knife does not descend. The bearded man's eyes stay locked on Evan's.

'Anticipation of pain leads to fear, and fear amplifies pain,' he says. 'Expectation of relief from pain increases the opioids in the brain, makes the hurting stop. How your mind reacts to pain determines how much pain you actually feel.'

Jack's voice floats over from somewhere beside Evan. '"Pain is inevitable",' he says. ' "Suffering is optional".'

Evan yanks his hand free. Blood drips from his other fist. He senses Jack at his side, doing nothing, and a feeling of betrayal spreads fire-hot beneath his skin.

But Jack is not doing nothing. Jack is watching. And Evan realizes that this is a test like the ones that have come before. He understands that how he reacts now will determine everything, that this is in fact the biggest test so far.

Before Evan can say anything, the bearded man says, 'You need to learn to rein in the brain centers that fire when your body detects pain. Control your insular cortex, get distance from the sensation by focusing on your breathing. I'm gonna teach you to attend to pain, put it in a box, put the box on a shelf, and go about your fucking day.'

Evan's throat clicks as he swallows. 'How are you gonna do that?'

The man's beard bristles again around his grin. 'Practice makes perfect.'

Evan looks up at Jack directly now for the first time and thinks he sees Jack give him a flicker of a wink, a tiny vote of confidence. Or maybe Evan has imagined it altogether.

The stink of damp hay thickens the air. Evan holds a breath in his lungs until it burns. Then he exhales. Turning back to the bearded man, he extends his arm, opens his other hand, exposing the pristine palm.

'Then what are you waiting for?' he says.

Morena's on-call cell phone chimed in the darkness, interrupting Evan from his thoughts, and he lifted it from his thigh.

A text message: IM OUT FRONT. U HAVE HER WAITING?

Breathing the reek of the birdcage, Evan thumbed an answer: BEDROOM.

A moment later Detective Chambers's reply came in: GOOD. U CLEAR OUT NOW. I WANT HER ALONE.

Beyond the lavender curtains, a car approached, a heavy American model by the sound of it. It idled a moment, the engine deep-throated and growly, then went silent. The neighborhood sounds drifted back in – someone laughing in a backyard, a rapid-fire Spanish commercial on a blaring radio, a jet arcing overhead. And then the crunch of footsteps approaching the house.

Evan wondered how often Morena heard those footsteps as she waited here in this room.

The parrot grew restless. 'Please don't! Please, please don't!'

The footsteps led to the metal-on-metal purr of a key entering the front door, and then the hinges squealed. The floorboards creaked. Closer, closer.

The bedroom door handle jiggled up and down. Locked.

A gruff voice came through the thin door. 'I'm sure you're scared, Carmen, but I'll be gentle.' The rasp of a palm against wood. 'Your first time doesn't have to hurt. I know how to do this right.' The handle rattled again. 'I know how to take care of you.'

Evan set Morena's on-call phone down and lifted the pistol from his other thigh.

Out of the memory mist sailed another Jack-ism: *Big problem, big bullet, big hole.*

'Come on, now. I brought you flowers. Open up and let me show you.'

The door handle rattled a bit more roughly this time. The parrot squawked and squawked some more. Evan's hand tightened around the string.

'I'm getting tired of playing games, little girl. Open the door. You open this fucking door right –'

Gently, Evan tugged the string. It tightened, causing the door handle to dip, the lock releasing with a pop.

Chambers's voice, once again calm: 'There you go. Good girl.'

The door creaked inward, propelled by a strong slab of a hand. A muscular forearm came into view, bulging beneath a cuffed-back sleeve. Chambers's face resolved in the darkness as he squinted into the dark room. Blotchy clean-shaven skin, cropped hair, hard eyes.

Chambers stepped forward, his shoes rustling over plastic sheeting. His face changed. 'Who the hell are *you*?'

He looked down, only now noticing the drop tarp unfurled beneath his feet. When he looked back up, his eyes were different.

'Oh,' he said. 'Oh, no.'

7. Who's Who in the Zoo

'Wanna hear the testicle smasher of the year?' Tommy Stojack asked, ambling around his workbench and sucking the last bit of burn from a Camel Wide. 'Pretty soon I'll be able to just *print* your ass a gun. Type some shit into a program and it spits out a mold. Love to see the baby-kissers in D. C. regulate *that*.' He plucked the cigarette from beneath his biker mustache and ran the butt under a sink tap before depositing it among a dozen others floating in a red keg cup filled with water. One stray ember could turn the workshop into a meteor crater. 'But hey, let's not panic the sheeple, right?'

Evan followed him across the dim space, which, given the slumbering machines, sharp-edged blades, and weapon crates, felt more like a medieval lair. The Las Vegas sun had baked straight through the walls, and the air smelled of spent powder and gun grease. The heat made the knife cut on Evan's forearm itch, the skin tingling as it healed, shedding dried bits of superglue.

Tommy customized weapons. He specialized in procurement and R&D for various government-sanctioned black-ops groups, though he'd never stated as much directly. From his slang and demeanor, Evan guessed he'd learned the trade in Naval Special Warfare. About seven years ago, they'd met through a labyrinthine tangle of connections, and he and the nine-fingered armorer had slowly built rapport. It was difficult to develop trust without any personal information being exchanged, and yet, after circling each other like wary sharks over the course of several covert meets, they had landed on a version of it. Somehow, through coded talk and pointed references, they'd gotten the bearings of each other's moral compasses and found them aligned.

'There are drawbacks, of course,' Tommy continued. 'To printed guns. Quality-control issues. But hey, what do you care? You're a trigger-puller. As long as it goes *boom*, you're happy, right?' He winked, gestured at the sticky coffeepot on the counter behind Evan. 'What say you pour me a hot cup of shut-the-fuck-up and we get to what we're getting to.'

Tommy built many of Evan's weapons. Because he had access to virgin-stock pistol frames without serial numbers, he could provide him with sterilized guns, guns that did not technically exist.

But today, the morning after he'd killed a dirty cop, Evan required a different service.

He reached for his Kydex high-guard hip holster, molded in the shape of the gun. The Wilson 1911 came free with a click, and he rotated the pistol sideways and offered it to Tommy.

'I need you to puddle the barrel and firing pin,' Evan said.

'You been throwing lead.'

'I have.'

'It catch any bad guys?'

'One.'

'And the Lord said, "Keep justice, and do righteousness".'

Tommy's nine fingers moved at blackjack-dealer speed, disassembling the Wilson across his bench. He put on a set of welder's goggles, fired up the cutting torch, and reduced the barrel, slide, firing pin and extractor to slag. Then he popped a new slide assembly on to Evan's pistol frame and handed the weapon back.

'Wa-la,' he said. 'It's a ghost again. Just like you.'

Evan clicked in a fresh mag, let the slide run forward, and started to holster the pistol, but Tommy said, 'Whoa, cowboy.' He pointed to a test-firing tube in the shadows. The four-foot-long steel pipe, filled with sand, was slanted downward at a forty-five-degree angle. Donning protective eyes-and-ears gear, Evan aimed at the mouth of the tube. He ran through a full mag test-firing the gun, the deadened smacks of metal into sand reverberating around the lair.

He gave a nod and turned back to Tommy, who downed the last of his coffee and popped open a tin of Skoal, tucking a meaty wedge into his bottom lip. Evan had come across a lot of men with a lot of habits but had yet to see someone hop from stimulant to stimulant with Tommy's ease and enthusiasm.

'I know you prefer burning powder, but in case you get stuck fighting at bad-breath distance . . .' Tommy grabbed a stout folding knife off his bench and flipped it at Evan. 'Just got these in. Figure you could use an update.'

Evan thumbed up the black-oxide blade. Heat-treated, S30V steel, titanium and G10 handle, tanto tip to punch through body armor. A Naval Special Warfare model, Strider make. Evan was a passable eskrima knife fighter, though not superb; an adversary who had truly mastered the Filipino form would carve him to pieces. Because of this he always made a point of bringing a gun to a knife fight. 'Thanks,' he said.

'I know you like you a Strider,' Tommy said.

'I had a dog once with that name,' Evan said.

'I don't picture you having had a childhood.'

'White picket fence, apple pie, Wiffle ball.'

Smirking, Tommy fell back into a chair, letting it roll across the slick concrete and come to rest near what looked like an old infantry mortar. He hoisted up a round from a wooden crate, the drab green thin projectile thicker than his forearm. 'What say we take a drive to the desert, play big-boy lawn darts?'

'Tempting,' Evan said. 'But I gotta get back.'

'All right. Let's get some bucks in my jeans, you can be on your way.'

Evan handed off a folded wad of hundred-dollar bills, and Tommy tossed it on the bench without counting it. Evan started for the sturdy metal door. As he neared, compulsion overtook him and he crouched to make sure the mounted security camera by the frame was in fact unplugged, as per their arrangement.

It was.

He shot an apologetic look back at Tommy.

Tommy glanced up, caught in the act of counting the bills.

Both men grinned sheepishly.

'It doesn't hurt to be safe, now, does it, brother?' Tommy spat a stream of tobacco through the gap in his front teeth, tapping the wad of cash into his shirt pocket. 'Never know who's who in the zoo.'

8. Unmarred

The scent of the grill intermingled with car exhaust, thickening the air around the splintering picnic tables artlessly arrayed outside Benny's Burgers. Inside, customers sat scattered among the booths and two-tops, but the dead L.A. heat had dissuaded anyone from eating out here on the square of crumbling concrete that passed for a patio.

Evan dropped on to one of the picnic-table benches facing the restaurant. Through the windows he observed a young girl sitting alone in a corner booth, coloring with crayons, her tongue poking out one cheek in a show of concentration.

He considered just how young an eleven-year-old was.

A few moments later, Morena backed out through the kitchen's swinging doors, plates expertly stacked up along her forearms. She delivered the meals, checked on her younger sister, then set about busing tables. After a while she breezed outside, squinting into the sun, and dropped a ketchup-sticky laminated menu in front of him.

'Take your order?' She finally looked over her at-the-ready pad, registered his face, and jerked in a breath.

He said, 'Exhale. Smile. Nod your head at me as if I just asked you something.'

She did all three unconvincingly.

'It is safe now?' she asked.

'Yes.'

He hadn't noticed how clenched-up she was until her shoulders unlocked, settling a solid inch. She lowered pad and pen, and he saw the shiny wine-red scar on her inner forearm where she'd been branded by the heated muzzle of Detective Chambers's gun.

'Can we go back there?' she asked. 'Pack up our stuff?'

He'd told her to take Carmen and stay at a friend's house until he contacted her again. It had been only one night, but he could see in her face that for her it had felt like an eternity.

'Yes,' he said.

'Can you take care of Pokey? He was *mamá*'s.'

It took a moment. The bird. 'I'll figure something out,' he said.

'What happened to *him*?'

Evan shrugged. A small gesture, but she understood.

'What if they think it's me who did it?'

'He had a lot of enemies,' Evan said. Still, she looked unconvinced. 'When he turns up,' he added, 'it'll be clear that no seventeen-year-old girl could have done that.'

His peripheral vision caught Carmen's face moving from profile to full circle in the window across from them. He clicked his eyes over, and sure enough, she'd paused from her coloring to watch him. She must have sensed his stare as he'd sensed hers, because she quickly took up her crayons again.

Evan raised the menu, pretended to peruse it.

'I have to go now,' he told Morena. 'I have one thing to ask of you. Only one thing. So please listen carefully.'

'Okay. Anything.' Morena was holding her breath again.

'Find someone who needs me. Give them my number: 1-855-2-NOWHERE.'

'I remember it. Of course I remember it.'

'It doesn't matter how long it takes you. It matters that you find someone in as bad a situation as you and your sister were. Someone trapped and desperate. You tell them about me. Tell them I'll be there on the other end of the phone.'

Morena took a beat. 'That's *it*?'

'That's it.'

'That's the only charge?'

'Yes.'

She looked incredulous. They always did. And he knew she would buckle down and honor the commitment, as had every client before her. Evan had never come into contact with a single one of them after a mission was over, and yet the next call had always come.

'Okay. I mean, I'm *happy* to, believe me, but . . .' She looked down at the fat, untied shoelaces of her knock-off sneakers.

'What?'

'Why don't you just find them people yourself?'

'If I looked, I would find the same sorts of people in the same sorts of situations. Do you understand?'

Morena's face remained blank, her plucked eyebrows arched and still.

He tried again. 'When *others* look, they find people needing my help who I might not find myself.'

''Cuz we go different places? With different folks?'

'Yes. And you've experienced things I haven't. Which means you can *see* things I can't.' He set down the menu. 'So I need your help like you needed mine.'

What he *didn't* add was that the act of helping was itself empowering, even healing. He wanted Morena to have something to do, the focus of an important task. She'd have to search and assess and then finally step in to give a second chance to another person who had been battered into helplessness. And when she completed her job, when she handed off that untraceable number, she'd be on the other side of the equation – a leader, not a victim.

Closure was a myth, but the undertaking might help her get her foot on the next rung of the ladder.

'I'll find someone, then,' she said. 'I'll do it quick. I wanna get all this behind us as fast as I can. No offense.'

'None taken. Do it quick, but do it right.'

'I will.'

'Give my number to only one person. Understand? Only one. Then forget that number forever. This is a onetime service, not a help line.'

She bit her lower lip. 'So we're done?'

'Not yet. Your biological father. You were right. He died a few years ago. He had some assets, still unclaimed. A checking account with $37,950 in it. You're a cosigner on the account.'

'No, I'm not.'

'Now you are.'

She slid the pen behind her ear, dropped the pad into her apron, coughed out a note of disbelief. 'How?'

He smiled. 'The bank'll be mailing an ATM card in your name to your aunt's address. Your dad had a union job, came with a small life-insurance policy. A lump sum of fifty grand, never claimed. You're now the beneficiary. That'll get you started. You're eighteen in two months. You can get emancipated or remain under your aunt's care until then. You have your life back.' He stood and stepped away from the picnic table. 'Now we're done.'

He noticed movement in the window across the patio again and glanced over to find Carmen looking out at them.

'You've taken good care of your sister,' he said. 'You should be proud of yourself.'

Morena's eyes moistened. She blinked a few times quickly and gave her sister a little flare of the hand.

Carmen raised her hand to wave back, revealing the unmarred skin of her inner forearm.

When he walked away, Morena was standing with her knuckles touching her lips, regaining her composure. She didn't thank him.

She didn't have to.

The next afternoon, between checking on his safe houses, Evan swung by Boyle Heights and took a pass around Morena's block. The young mothers were there in the front yard across the street, shoving their strollers and smoking. He parked one street over and cut through the backyard into Morena's place.

The lawn chairs had been left behind, as well as the mattresses in the bedroom, but the bedding was gone and the closet was empty. The stained fish tank remained with its Elmo sticker. Evan checked behind the door and saw that the girls had taken the trumpet, and this gave him an unexpected flicker of happiness.

'Carrot?' the parrot squawked. 'Please, please? Please don't! Carrot?'

Standing in the empty room, he placed an anonymous call to the Humane Society and asked them to send someone to this address.

He walked out into the main room toward the tiny kitchen nook. The surfaces had been wiped down, everything left tidy. On the counter a half-filled bag of birdseed pinned down a handwritten note, which read, *'I don't have this month's rent. I don't know when I will. I'm sorry. I hope you don't come after me.'*

Evan looked at the note for a time, then crumpled it up and laid down six hundred-dollar bills.

He fed the bird on his way out.

9. A Damn Saint

The ice cube singed Evan's fingertips as he twisted the palm-coded hot water lever in the shower and stepped through the hidden door into the Vault. He crossed to the sheet-metal desk and nestled the cube gently into the spikes of the tiny aloe vera plant. Vera seemed not unappreciative.

He slid the black RoamZone into his pocket, though it wouldn't be ringing anytime soon. It had been only five days since he'd put three bullets into Detective William Chambers. It would take a while for Morena Aguilar to find the next client. The shortest time between the end of a mission and the next caller had been two months. Now was Evan's brief window to settle back and relax.

He thought about taking a drive to Wally's Wine & Spirits on Westwood Boulevard and picking up a bottle of Kauffman Luxury Vintage vodka. Distilled fourteen times and filtered twice, once through birch coal, once through quartz sand, it was produced from the wheat of a single year's harvest, making it one of the only vodkas released with a specific vintage, like wine or champagne. Excessive, perhaps, as was the price tag, but it was as pure and clean as any liquid he'd tasted.

He threw on a sweatshirt, grabbed his keys, and

headed down in the elevator. Inevitably, it stopped on the sixth floor, and he smelled the flowery perfume even before the doors parted to admit Mrs Rosenbaum.

Evan braced himself for more tales of her beloved Herb, may he rest in peace, but instead Ida cast a caustic glance over the top of her rose-colored spectacles and announced, 'I hear that you've been sneaking out of Mia Hall's place at all hours.'

The Honorable Pat Johnson of 12F, acting less than honorable, must have spread the word.

Evan pictured the sleek teardrop bottle of Kauffman vodka, his reward if he could make it through this elevator ride and afternoon rush hour. 'No, ma'am.'

She sniffed. 'We have enough problems around here, what with the dry rot. Can you believe it? Here in Castle Heights! The whole frame around my front door, falling to pieces. Ten complaints over two months, and do you think the good-for-nothing manager's done a thing about it?'

'No, ma'am.'

'Well, my son, he's coming in for the holidays, bringing his wife and my two beautiful grandchildren. And he said if my door's not fixed by then, he'll do it himself. Can you imagine? A name partner in a major New Brunswick accountancy firm, and he'd do carpenter work for me?'

Mercifully, they reached the lobby, and when Ida paused at her mail slot, Evan made a getaway down the stairs to the garage. He'd just stepped around the pillar, bringing his pickup into sight, when a voice called from behind him.

67

'Wait! Evan!'

He turned to see Mia run-walking toward him in her midheel shoes, still dressed from work.

She paused, looked down at her shoes. 'Screw it,' she muttered, yanking them off and continuing toward him in stockinged feet. 'Look, sorry, I know this is weird, but can I borrow your truck?'

Evan was speechless.

'That woman from 3B blocked me in with her stupid Range Rover. Beth someone.'

'Pamela Yates?'

'Sure. Whatever. Beths and Pamelas are the same *type* of woman. Everyone knows that.' She reached him, her foot skidding in an oil stain. 'I have to run over to my brother's in Tarzana and pick up Peter. It's a schlep, I know, but he doesn't get a lot of time with . . . well, male role models. Wow, *that's* a dated phrase. But you know what I mean. I just came home to drop off some files, ran up, and now – look.' She flailed an arm at the SUV boxing in her Acura. 'I can't find Beth-Pamela anywhere.' She only now seemed to register the keys in Evan's hand. 'Oh. You're *going*, not coming? Where?'

He blinked once, twice. 'To get vodka.'

'That qualifies as an outing? What a life. Look, can I *please* just take your truck to get my kid? I'll grab you vodka on my way back. What do you like? Absolut? Smirnoff?'

He just looked at her.

Her phone gave a personalized ring, the theme song from *Peanuts*. She snapped it up. 'I'm *coming*, Walter. On my way.' Hung up. 'Come on,' she pleaded. 'I promise I won't crash. And if I do, I'll prosecute me.'

'I don't loan my truck out.'

'Why? Cocaine stashed in the wheel wells?'

He looked at the door to the lobby, hoping that Pamela Yates would miraculously appear, but it remained stubbornly closed.

'Come on,' she said. 'It's a semi-emergency.'

He forced a tight grin. 'I'll drive you.'

'Oh *shit*,' Mia said.

Her foot had smeared oil on the spotless passenger-side floor mat of Evan's truck. Evan tried to assess the damage without being too obvious. 'It's fine,' he said.

However, she was looking not at her feet but her phone. 'Missed a work call.' She speed-dialed while gesturing for Evan to get on to the 405, which was as jammed as a parking lot.

Driving in traffic. To Tarzana. To pick up a kid.

It kept getting better.

Next to him Mia spoke sternly into the phone. 'This is District Attorney Mia Hall. I need that update ASAP.' She hung up, leaned back, and sighed. 'Thank you. Seriously. You saved my ass on this one.'

She clicked the button to lower the window a few times, and nothing happened.

'Why won't the window go down?' she asked.

Because there was no room for it to retract after Evan had hung Kevlar armor inside the door panel. The windows themselves were made of laminated armor glass. The Ford F-150 came with a beefed-up suspension to handle the added weight, and as the best-selling vehicle in America for decades, it had the added advantage of blending in virtually anywhere. He'd taken other steps to prepare the truck as well, disarming the safety systems, removing the airbags, and disabling the inertia-sensing switches in the bumpers that render power to the fuel pump inoperable in a collision. To protect the vulnerable radiator and intercooler, he'd added a built-to-spec push-bumper assembly up front. If shot or punctured, the run-flat tires self-sealed with a special adhesive compound distributed internally with each rotation, and a support ring 'second tire' hidden at the core served as a contingency to that contingency. In the back, flat rectangular truck vaults neatly overlaid the bed, providing secure storage while remaining inconspicuously lower than the tailgate. Like him, the vehicle was prepared for varied and extreme contingencies while never drawing a second glance.

Mia clicked the window button again. 'Well?'

'It's broken,' he said.

'Oh.' Her stare dropped to the sleeve of his sweatshirt. 'Where's the stain? From last week?'

It took him a moment to realize she was talking about the blood that had sopped through the sweatshirt when they'd been crammed into the elevator together. What was he gonna say? That he kept a dozen black sweatshirts mission-handy?

'It came out,' he said.

'Grape juice. Came out.' She eyed him skeptically, then settled into her seat, at last noticing the traffic. 'Oy,' she said. 'Why didn't you take Sepulveda?'

Evan waited at the curb outside the little clapboard house, engine running. At last Mia emerged from her brother's front door with Peter in tow, his hair still spotty on the sides from the duct-tape incident. His backpack, nearly as big as he was, bounced on his shoulders, threatening to topple him. As she helped him into the compressed backseat of the truck, her iPhone rang with the *Jaws* theme. She frowned down at the screen, then wiggled it at Evan. 'Sorry. This is that call. Confidential.'

'I really need to –'

'I know. Buy vodka. Gimme a sec?'

Before he could reply, she'd stepped away.

Silence from the backseat. Evan looked across at Mia pacing on the browning front lawn, phone at her cheek, gesticulating intensely. The call didn't seem to be wrapping up anytime soon.

Evan had to tilt the rearview mirror to bring Peter into sight. Evan cleared his throat. 'Your mom's pretty busy with work, huh?'

'Yeah. She puts away killers and stuff. This one guy? He shot someone. How do you shoot someone anyway?'

'Twice in the chest, once in the head in case they're wearing ballistic armor.'

Peter swallowed. 'I meant, how could someone just *kill* someone?'

Oh.

'Practice. A lot of practice, I'd imagine.'

'I don't get people who hurt other people.' Peter cradled his arm gingerly, and his shirtsleeve slid up, exposing a bruise on his biceps.

Evan thought about the boy's injuries the past few times he'd seen him – the scraped forehead, the skinned elbow – and put it together. He turned around in the driver's seat, tilted his chin at the bruise. 'That's not from dodgeball, is it?'

Those big charcoal eyes took his measure. Then Peter shook his head. 'Josh Harlow,' he said, in his raspy voice. 'A *fifth*-grader. What am I supposed to do?'

'Take out a knee.'

'Really?'

'If he's bigger, yes. But I'm joking. About you doing it, I mean.'

'Oh. Then what *should* I do?'

'I don't know. Ask your mom.'

'Yeah, right.'

Mia was across the front yard now, back turned, jabbing a finger at the air, the work call veering into some sort of conflict. Evan drummed his hands on the steering wheel impatiently. He wondered where Morena and Carmen were at this precise moment. Heading to their aunt's or perhaps already there. Safe. He thought about the way that Chambers's arm had jerked up when he dropped on to the plastic tarp, his expression illuminated by the strobe of the three suppressed muzzle flashes – shock, then fear, then terrible recognition.

Peter had said something.

Evan lifted his eyes to the rearview. 'What?'

'Every time he comes after me, I think I'm gonna *do something*,' Peter said. 'Stand up for myself. But I never do.'

Evan felt an itch beneath his skin, the urge to leave this conversation, this house, Tarzana, to get home to his pristine kitchen and shake a martini so thoroughly that the pour left a sheet of ice crystals across the surface. Peter jounced his heels lethargically into his seat, a disheartened thumping. Evan looked at the kid and felt something tug at his chest.

He inhaled deeply. 'You know the two best words in the English language?'

Peter turned his eyes up at him.

'"*Next time*",' Evan said. 'Everything can change. And not just for good, right? You could win the lottery or get run over by an APC.'

'What's an APC?'

'Armored personnel carrier.'

'Oh.'

'But that's the thing. "Next time" means the world is wide open to you. "Next time" is possibility. "Next time" is freedom.'

Mia tugged open the passenger-side door, hopped in, and gave the dashboard an impatient little tap. 'You ready to go yet?'

Peter lolled in Mia's arms, asleep. She struggled to carry him out of the elevator to her condo. When they reached the door, she swung her hip toward Evan and

73

said in a loud whisper, 'Keys are in my purse. Hurry. Hurry.'

A woman's purse, filled with intimate items. He hesitated a moment before plunging his hand into alien territory.

'No, the side pocket. *Other* side pocket. No, those are work keys. Yeah, those. Great. You're a doll.'

The minute the lock clicked, she pivoted inside, bumping the door and leaving the keys dangling from the knob. Evan pulled them free and followed her in to set them down.

'Sorry,' she whispered hoarsely over her shoulder. 'Come in for a sec. Oh – but don't use that bathroom.' She jerked her chin toward the powder room. 'Turns out Play-Doh doesn't flush.'

She vanished into Peter's bedroom, leaving Evan standing in the living room. He set down the keys and turned to leave silently but then noticed another Post-it stuck by the wall-mount phone. It was one of Mia's handwritten notes from that book: *'Pursue what is meaningful, not what is expedient.'*

How different these rules were from the Commandments he lived by. Penned in a feminine hand, slapped on walls and refrigerators. What had Mia said? *It's a lot of work raising a human.* He considered these alternate lives lived under a different code, this road not taken and never illuminated. He read the Post-it again and decided what the hell.

Rather than taking a quiet leave, he sat on the couch, waiting in the hush of the condo.

A few minutes later, Mia emerged from Peter's room, stretching her lower back. '*Man*. I gotta stop that kid from growing any more.'

She detoured through the kitchen and came to the couch with two glasses of wine, one of which she placed in Evan's hand.

She plunked down on the cushion next to him. 'He's a good kid. Thank God.' She took a sip, pursed her lips.

Evan sensed she had more to say, so he remained silent.

'My husband and I couldn't have kids, so we adopted a year after we got married.' She shifted forward to set down her glass, and her skirt slid a few inches up from her knees. 'Had just bought a house when . . .' She took up her curls in the back, slipping a hair tie from around her wrist to make a ponytail. 'Pancreatic cancer. That's just not how that story's supposed to end, you know?' She slapped her knees gently with her palms. 'But that's how it ended.'

A night-light plugged low in the opposite wall back-lit her and suffused her thick chestnut hair, tinting the edges. He noticed the delicate curve at the base of her neck, the birthmark on her temple, the way her full lips met. He had noticed a lot about her before. But never these things.

'Do you regret it?'

'The marriage? Not for a minute.' She pouted her lips thoughtfully. 'I will tell you what I *do* regret. Not the fights, because everyone needs to fight. But the *stupid* fights. I mean, did he take a condescending tone to me at dinner? Did I tell him to put that thing on the calendar? The dumb-ass escalations. A day of thawing out. So much wasted time.' She shook her head, and the glow played tricks in her hair. 'Don't get me wrong. It was a real marriage with real problems, sure, but we loved each other. Oh, did I love him. A guy can love a million women. But a *man*, a man loves one woman a million ways.' She reached again for her wine. 'God, listen to me. It would've been so much easier if he'd just left me. Ran off with some secretary.'

'Do people do that anymore?'

'I don't suppose.' Another sip. 'But *dying*?' She shook her head. 'It's torture, because he never dies really, now. He's martyred. A damn saint. He's perfect in my mind.'

'He's lucky,' Evan said.

She looked him full in the face for the first time since she'd sat down. The air conditioner blew cool on their necks, and a light hummed in the kitchen, and far away he could hear the elevator stir into motion.

'God,' she said. 'I'm just talking and talking. I guess that's what people do around you. Fill the space.'

His gaze had dipped slightly to her lips, and he sensed that she was looking at his.

A buzzing emanated from his pocket, so out of place that he didn't at first register what it was.

The black phone.

Ringing. Now.

Five days from completing his last mission. Morena had said she wanted to move fast, but this was too fast. It could only mean one thing.

Something was wrong.

The phone had never rung when he was in someone else's presence. He was infrequently around others, and the calls were rare.

It struck him that he had tensed on the couch beside Mia. He fished the RoamZone from his pocket and rose.

'I'm sorry,' he said. 'I have to go.'

He'd already turned for the door when he registered, after the fact, the flicker of hurt in her eyes.

Stepping into the hall, he answered the phone. 'Do you need my help?'

'God, yes, please.' A feminine voice, one he didn't recognize. 'They're going to kill me.'

10. Cloak and Dagger

Evan felt a surge of distrust. He realized he was pressing the phone tightly to his cheek and forced his hand to relax. 'Where did you get this number?'

'A girl. A Hispanic girl.' The woman on the other end of the phone was breathing hard, sending bursts of static across the connection. 'Are you the Nowhere Man? Really?'

To hold the signal, he took the northeast stairwell up, jogging but landing lightly to preserve the steadiness of his voice. 'Did the girl give you a name?'

'I can't remember. Wait, Miranda something. No – *Morena*. She wouldn't say what her last name was.'

'What did she look like?'

'Pulled-back hair. Skinny. Tweezed eyebrows.'

'Any marks on her arms?'

'She had a scar – inoculation mark, maybe.'

Evan felt microscopically reassured. He recalled Morena's words: *I'll do it quick. I wanna get all this behind us as fast as I can.* But still.

'What's your name?' he asked.

'I don't want to give you my name. These guys after me, they're *serious*. How do I know you're not with them? Or that girl you sent? This could all be a ploy.' Her speech was pressured, the sentences tumbling out one after the other.

'So what would you like to do?'

'I don't know. I don't know. God, how the hell did I get here?'

He moved up several more flights, holding the phone to his ear, leaving her the silence to draw her out. Given his suspicion, he wanted more data – a change in tone, background noise, a trip in her cadence that suggested that her words were rehearsed. Were it not for her sharp breaths, he would have thought she'd hung up.

He reached the penthouse floor and moved swiftly down the hall toward his place.

'Meet me somewhere public, then, I guess,' she said. 'Where you can't hurt me.'

'Public.'

'Yes. Like a crowded restaurant. Hello? Are you still there?'

He slid into his condo, put his back to the closed door. 'I'm listening.'

'Bottega Louie. Downtown. Tomorrow at noon. I'll wear amber-tinted sunglasses, even inside.'

She hung up before he could respond.

Evan liked nothing about it.

He didn't like not knowing the client's name. He didn't like her setting the meeting place. He didn't like the cloak-and-dagger setup, contrived enough to make it feel like a trap. But would any party dangerous enough to try to take him down actually attempt such a hackneyed approach? The maneuver, torn from countless Hollywood movies, pointed to inexperience. Or, to

79

play the figurative double negative, was it intended to *appear* bumbling and therefore catch him with his guard down?

He had elevated even his usual level of caution, switching out his pickup for a white Chrysler he kept stashed at the safe house near LAX. He sat behind the wheel of the forgettable sedan now, facing off the fourth floor of the open-air parking structure. Through tactical binoculars, he looked across West Seventh at the designated meeting spot of Bottega Louie below.

The caller had wanted a crowded public place, and the upscale patisserie definitely qualified. Work-casual patrons crammed the ten thousand square feet of marble that stretched from Baroque bar to brick oven. More diners waited at the take-out counters near the front, clamoring over sumptuous tiers of macarons.

A woman wearing the promised amber-tinted sunglasses sipped water at a table flush with one of the showcase windows. Evan had tried three parking levels to find the right angle, and here it was, sniper-perfect.

She was either tactically unsophisticated or dangling herself out as bait.

She looked to be in her late thirties and was strikingly attractive, though it was hard to get a good look at her face given the oversize sunglasses. Her shiny black hair, dyed, was collected in the back just below her crown like a gathered drape, ending in a blunt line at the nape. Blood-red lipstick struck a contrast with her porcelain skin. A three-inch band of bracelets ringed her right wrist – thin leather straps, beads and colorful herringbone weaves. Her fingernails, a rich shade of eggplant, tapped nervously on the table. High, choppy bangs capped off the hipster vibe.

Evan upped the magnification, zeroing in on a tattoo behind her ear. The inkwork proved to be a mini-constellation, three stars in an oddly pleasing asymmetrical pattern. He searched his mental database but produced no military or gang affiliation that matched the markings. Another personal touch, then, nothing more.

Her body language stayed tight and closed, her arms crossed, her shoulders angled away from the hubbub. Beneath the table her knee jacked up and down.

She was either nervous or a damn fine actress.

He checked his fob watch, then dialed his phone.

The hostess picked up on the second ring. 'Bottega *Lou*ie.'

'May I please speak to Fernando Juarez?'

'Fernando Juarez? Who is that?'

'One of the barbacks who works there. It's an important matter regarding his tax returns.'

'Oh. Okay. Sorry. Hang on.'

Through the mil-dot reticle of his binoculars, Evan watched the waitress thread through the tables and speak to the bartender. Her attention shifted to a man stocking bottles. The same man had taken a smoke break in the alley before opening shift, giving Evan opportunity to approach with a folded note and a crisp hundred-dollar bill.

The waitress handed Fernando Juarez the cordless

phone. Pinning him in the crosshairs, Evan saw the man's mouth move even before the voice came across the line.

'Hello?'

'Repeat after me: "Yes, okay. I will handle this when I get home".'

'Yes, okay. I will handle this when I get home.'

'You remember our arrangement?'

'I do.'

'She is sitting at table twenty-one. Now is the time.'

'Thank you, sir.'

Fernando hung up. He finished with the bottles, wiped the bar, then walked over to the woman in the sunglasses and handed her the note. Evan watched her unfold it.

It told her to exit the restaurant and go to the news-stand across the street.

As she read the directive, her back curled in a para-noid hunch. Her sleek hair whipped her cheeks as she turned her head this way and that, looking around the restaurant, eyeing various diners. He watched her face. She was scared. She took a sip of water to settle herself, then gathered her things and hurried out.

Grand Avenue, one of Downtown's main thorough-fares, hummed with traffic, and she had to wait for a break before darting across. Evan followed her with the binocs. As she neared the newsstand, he dialed another number. The worker there, sitting on a barstool reading a thrice-folded edition of *La Opinión*, picked up a cracked phone receiver held together with electrical tape.

'*Hola*. L.A. News 'n' Views.'

'There is a woman approaching wearing dark glasses. Over your left shoulder. There. May I please speak to her briefly?'

The man glanced over, gave a disinterested shrug, and offered her the receiver. 'Iss for you,' he said, returning to his magazine.

The woman stepped away, stretching the telephone cord. 'What *is* this?'

'I'm not sure I can trust you either. I will meet you at a crowded restaurant, but it won't be one you choose. Do you see that bus up the hill? In a minute and a half, it will stop at the bus shelter a block south of you. It will take you to Chinatown. Get off at Broadway and College. Lotus Dim Sum is in the Central Plaza. I will meet you there. Go now.'

Her head snapped up to watch the bus's wheezing advance. 'And if I don't?'

'Then I can't help you.'

This time he hung up first.

Evan had taken numerous precautions, but now was the vulnerable moment, where nothing was left except the approach. The woman sat at the edge of the bustling restaurant, her back to the window. Lobsters and catfish stirred lethargically in tanks, and shiny metal dim sum carts flew to and fro, trailing steam and tantalizing scents.

Evan's Woolrich shirt featured fake buttons for show, but the front was really held together with magnets that would give way easily in the event he needed quick access to his hip holster. His cargo pants were tactical-discreet, with streamlined inner pockets that hid extra magazines and his Strider knife while giving no bulge on the silhouette. He wore Original S.W.A.T. boots, lighter than running shoes, which looked like nothing special with his pant legs pulled over the tops.

He was as ready as he was going to be.

As he made his way through the obstacle course of waiters and carts, the woman's head jerked up and she paused from chewing her thumbnail. He saw himself approach in the lenses of her amber sunglasses, an average guy of average size, the kind of man you'd easily forget.

'Switch seats with me,' he said.

She jerked in a quick breath, then obeyed.

The window left his back vulnerable, but he preferred to face the restaurant and, more important, he preferred to sit where she – and whoever she might have in her orbit – hadn't planned for him to sit. As the Ninth Commandment decreed: *Always play offense.* He had never broken a Commandment and was not about to start now.

They settled into the curved metal chairs, regarding each other warily.

Her pale skin was almost luminous. She rolled those red, red lips over her teeth, then pursed them anxiously. She would have been distractingly attractive were he in a mood to be distracted.

'Tell me your name,' he said.

She looked down at her hands.

'Listen,' he said. 'If I am with whoever's trying to hurt you, then I'd already know your name, wouldn't I?'

She kept her eyes lowered. 'Katrin White,' she said.

'And I would also know why they – or we – are trying to harm you.'

A cart paused at their elbows. Without looking over he pointed and a few items landed on the starched tablecloth before them.

'I owe the wrong people money. A lot of money.'

'How much?'

'Two-point-one.' She scratched at her neck, keeping her gaze on the untouched food. 'It's a Vegas situation.'

'You're a gambler.'

'It doesn't mean I deserve to die.'

'No one is making that argument.'

'Well,' she said, '*someone* is.'

A guy in a baggy shirt entered the lobby, and Evan stared across the restaurant at him. Their eyes caught for a moment, and then an older man in a tailored business suit shouldered in front of the guy to the maître d' stand. When the view cleared again, the man in the baggy shirt was greeting a woman he'd presumably come to dine with.

Evan returned his focus to Katrin. 'Which casino?'

'It's a backroom deal. Private. It moves around. No names, no addresses, nothing. You give them your number, they call you, tell you where to be. You buy in.'

'Minimum?'

'Quarter mil. Then they stake you.'

'Can get out of hand in a hurry.'

'You're telling me.' Her knee bounced beneath the table as it had at Bottega Louie, and he wondered how long she'd been this jittery. He could see the strain in the lines of her tensed face. 'These guys are big on making examples. They unzipped a Japanese business-man from his skin. Peeled him while he was still alive. At least he was for most of it. And now . . .' Her voice cracked. 'They have my dad.'

She ran a finger beneath the oversize sunglasses, first one side, then the other.

After a moment she said, 'All I have is a phone num-ber. They told me . . . they told me I have two weeks to deliver.'

'How long ago was that?'

'Ten days.'

Her delicate shoulders trembled. 'It's my fault. It's my fault he's involved. I don't have the money, and they're gonna kill him.'

'I have never lost anyone I've helped,' Evan told her.

'Not ever?'

'Not ever.'

Her glasses settled back on the bridge of her nose, and in them Evan caught a glint of reflected light through the window behind him. Instinct tugged at him, straightening his vertebrae. A dim sum cart was rattling past, and he slid his foot out and caught it, stopping it dead in its tracks, plates and steamer baskets clanking. The server barked her displeasure at him, but he wasn't listening.

In the stainless-steel side of the cart, he saw a distorted reflection of the three-story apartment building behind him.

In a window on the third floor, a perfect disk of light caught the sun.

A sniper scope.

He grabbed Katrin's thin wrist. As he yanked her sideways, a round snapped past his ear and punched a hole through the solid chrome back of her empty chair, penetrating the spot where her heart had been an instant before.

Sprawled on the hot metal of the overturned cart, it occurred to him that he was, for the first time in his professional life, playing defense.

11. What Now?

The first rule when drawing fire: *Get off the X.*

Evan rolled off the upended dim sum cart, jerking Katrin away from the window as two more rounds splintered the table. They came in not with the *pop-pop-pop* of a smaller rifle but the sharp crack of a major caliber, .30 or up. Echoes of the muzzle blast bounced around the room, a hall-of-mirrors effect as disorienting as it was unnerving. Evan half dragged Katrin toward the heart of the restaurant, trying to get clear of the sniper's vantage.

The other customers exploded into a confused stampede toward all exits. Evan kept Katrin's arm as he led her through the tumult, hip-checking another cart and sending forth a volley of pork bao. His hand drove straight through his shirt, popping the magnets, and ripped his pistol free from the holster.

A chunk of floor gave way at their heels, bits of tile biting at their calves, and then they were clear of the kill zone. An older woman fell to one knee, nearly getting trampled, but a surge of bodies flung her back on to her feet, and the human tide whisked her out of a side door. A baby's high-pitched mewling rose above the screams.

'They followed you!' Katrin was shouting. 'Did you do this?'

Evan ignored her. Only the exit route mattered. Over the wall of receding shoulders, a single face pointed back toward the restaurant interior, a man standing eerily still in the middle of the rush.

Not the guy with the baggy shirt. The older man in the tailored business suit.

His head and upper torso were visible, the rest of his body a murky shadow behind the fish tanks that split the lobby from the restaurant proper. His fist rose, clenched around a pistol. The barrel flashed, and a woman in front of them screamed and spun in a one-eighty, a crimson spray erupting from the shoulder of her blouse.

Though Evan and Katrin had hit the brakes, the surging crowd drove them toward the man in the suit. No backing up. Too many civilians to return fire. A shooter unconcerned with collateral damage.

Evan straight-armed Katrin to the floor and dove forward over one shoulder. He finished his somersault rotation and hammered both feet into the lobster tank's base. It was sturdier than he'd hoped, sending shock waves through his legs, but the glass above gave off a sonorous warble that sounded promising. A splash of salty water slapped Evan's face. He blinked hard, saw the shooter looming above, aiming down.

Then the tank toppled.

The man's arms swung up, the gun discharging once into the ceiling, and then gallons of green water wiped him from view. Lobsters twitched and flopped on the slippery tile, claws secured with blue bands. Washed halfway across the lobby, the shooter scrambled after his pistol on all fours. As the last of the customers dashed out, he reached between their fleeing legs and scooped up his gun. He'd just turned to rise when Evan hit him from above with a modified roundhouse, the points of his first two knuckles crushing the skull at the temple. The squama of the temporal bone was usefully thin there, and it caved pleasingly beneath the well-placed blow.

The man fell, his cheek and chest slapping the floor. His hands and feet curled inward, twitching, the last impulses shuddering from his brain.

Evan turned to find Katrin standing behind him, breathless, her pale skin ashen with shock.

'He's dead?'

'Follow me. Close.'

He kept the pistol pointed at the ground as he shoved them through the double front doors into the bright light of the plaza. Red and yellow plastic pennants rode the wind, fluttering overhead on strings, and the smell of incense tinged the air. Terrified passersby swept through his field of vision, running haphazardly in all directions, but he focused on a rental minivan parked dead ahead, blocking an alley, hazard lights flashing. The back doors were swung open, a few boxes of produce stacked on the ground as props.

The restaurant now blocked the sniper's angle, but Evan didn't want to give him time to reposition. Taking Katrin's arm, he dashed through the crowd, heading for the wall of shops and the blocked alley. A panicked flush had overtaken her cheeks, a strand of glossy dark hair caught in the corner of her mouth.

'Wait,' Katrin said. 'Where are we going? There's nowhere to –'

Evan hit a remote-controlled key fob in his pocket, and the minivan's facing door slid open. He shoved Katrin in, diving after her. He'd left the backseats flattened for precisely this contingency. His thumb keyed the autofeature again, and the sliding door rolled shut behind them, absorbing a bullet from the big rifle. The sniper had picked them up. Another round hammered the door, punching a hole the size of a dinner plate over their ducked heads. Inside the box of the minivan, the clang of metal on metal was deafening. The sniper was working the bolt fast, and if they didn't want to ingest lead or shrapnel, they had to get clear of the van.

Evan yanked at the opposite sliding door and spilled out the far side into the cramped alley, tugging Katrin so she landed on top of him. Behind them the minivan rocked some more, the windows blowing out.

Katrin's hands hovered by her ears, her eyes brimming.

'Save it for later,' he said.

Their shoulders scraped either side of the narrow alley, leaving flakes of dried paint in their wake. A kitchen's back window exhaled hot air and the stench of fish. They reached a T at the alley's end and peeled right. Six paces down, his Chrysler sedan waited, pointed at the main line of Hill Street. They jumped in and he tore out, blending into a current of traffic.

His eyes darted from the road to the rearview to the road. Katrin jerked in one breath after another.

'Who did you tell you were meeting me?' he said.

'No one.'

'Which phone did you call me from?'

Her hand dug in her jeans, came up with a Black-Berry. 'This one, but –'

He snatched her phone, flung it out his window, watched in his side mirror as the pieces bounced.

'What are you doing? That's the only way they could reach me about my dad –'

'We don't want them to reach you right now.'

'They followed you.'

'No,' he said. 'They didn't.'

'How do you know?'

He screeched into a liquor-store parking lot, eased behind the building. 'Out.'

He met her around back and pulled from the trunk a black wand with a circular head. Starting at her face, he waved it over her, scanning her torso, arms, legs and shoes for electronic devices. The nonlinear junction detector showed nothing. She made no noise, but tears spilled down her cheeks and she was shaking. He spun her, scanned down her back. Clear.

'Get in the car.'

She obeyed.

He veered out from behind the liquor store, shot across the street, and merged on to the 110.

Her hand was at her mouth, muffling the words. 'What now?'

For once he did not have a ready answer.

12. A Woman's Job

'You're expensive,' Dan Reynolds said, a flirtatious skip in his step keeping him beside the woman leading him down the corridor of the inn.

Candy McClure didn't break stride. 'I'm worth it,' she said.

Assemblyman Reynolds, the vice chair of the Health Committee, had managed to amass a big re-election war chest while remaining dog-to-bone for patient advocacy. This combination made him atypical. His bedroom proclivities were equally atypical.

Which had something to do with the black leather duffel bag swinging from Candy's shoulder. Her cropped white-blond hair had been sprayed into a call-girl shellac, and her muscular calves flexed beneath navy blue fishnets, but her dress was decidedly upscale, a strapless tweed knee-to-bust number fitted to show off her firm hourglass figure. She'd chosen it for the zipper back, easy to step out of.

Floral-patterned runners padded their footsteps. Candy had of course selected the most private room, the end unit on the outlying wing of the property. The quaint bed-and-breakfast, a few miles from Lake Arrowhead, had low occupancy for December. Fresh snow had been scarce, and the real holiday break was still a few weeks off. Low occupancy was good. They'd be making some noise.

Reynolds sped up, trying to get a glimpse of her elusive face. After checking in, she'd let him in a back entrance as they'd agreed. As a semiprominent politician, he couldn't be seen. Not here, not with her.

A big brass key swung from her finger. Her nails, cut short and unmanicured, were the only aspect of her image not polished to a high feminine gloss. Her work required ready use of her hands.

Reynolds gestured at the weighty duffel bag. 'Give you a hand with that?'

'Do I look like I'm struggling?'

At her tone the excited flush crept further up his neck. 'Can't wait to see what you've got in there.'

'You don't have a choice. But to wait.'

The color spread to his cheeks, and his breathing quickened. She shoved through the door into the room, which had a nausea-inducing Laura Ashley country-chic vibe, all potpourri and frilly pillows and watercolors of geese. A four-poster bed dominated the space. The sliding door to the bathroom had been rolled back to reveal a copper soaking tub.

The copper tub was why she had selected the place.

The duffel clanked on the floorboards when she slid it off her shoulder. She unzipped it and removed a rubber fitted sheet. He tried to peek over her shoulder to see what else was in the bag, but she closed it and slapped him. His fingertips touched the mark on his cheek, and he made a strangled little sound of pleasure.

She clicked the wooden blinds shut, then yanked off the bedding and laid the rubber sheet over the bare mattress. At last she turned to him. 'Strip.'

He complied. He had the build of a former athlete, soft around the middle. His pants snagged on his heel, and he almost tripped in his eagerness. 'We need to specify a safe word. Mine is "artichoke".'

'Inventive.'

'Abrasion, fire play and breath control are off-limits. Pretty much anything else is cool with me.'

'I'll bear that in mind. Sit.'

He lowered himself on to the bed. She secured his wrists and ankles to the four posts.

'I'm usually down with warm-up —'

'That's nice,' she said, and popped a ball gag into his mouth.

His face seemed to bulge around the red ball, but she noted the gleeful anticipation beneath his straining. She had few skills, but those she did have she'd mastered. One of them was reading men.

Candy had grown up in Charlotte, North Carolina, under a different name, and her childhood had been a parade of useless males, from the proverbial absent father to the usual handsy dads of friends. She'd pretty much raised herself. At sixteen she'd gotten her driver's license, and a few weeks later, after a strategic tryst with a zit-faced DMV worker, she'd secured a bus license as well. The money was good, but the training sucked. Mr Richardson with his stale coffee breath and walrus mustache. Any little mistake she made, he'd announce,

'You just killed a kid.' The tires touching the dotted yellow line – 'Just killed a kid, sugar britches. Steady on the wheel.' Braking too hard – 'Killed another kid, sweet sauce. Easy on the pedal.'

Men. The pleasure they took in the commands they gave.

Well, now *she* gave the commands.

The oak cheval mirror in the corner threw back her image, her goddesslike stance at the foot of the bed. She reached behind her and slid the zipper down from between her shoulder blades to the base of her back. The dress bowed forward, and she let it fall. On the bed Reynolds responded, mind and body. Who could blame him?

She squatted to dig through the leather duffel bag, giving him an unabashed view of her backside. A fitness junkie, she knew precisely what she looked like from every angle.

She came up with a swim cap.

Around the rubber ball screwed into his pie hole, Reynolds looked puzzled but game.

She tugged on the cap, then blue surgical gloves. Next she removed an industrial blender and set it on the floor. Given his constraints, Reynolds was tough to read, but he wasn't standing at attention as he had been earlier.

From inside the bag, her cell phone erupted with the chorus of 'Venus', the distinctive ringtone she reserved for one thing.

The sound of the next job zeroing in on her.

Of course, she preferred Bananarama's cover: *I'm yer Venus . . . I'm yer fire . . . At your desire.*

She held up a blue-latex-sheathed finger to Reynolds.

When the big man called, everything went on hold – no matter how awkward the situation at hand.

She answered. 'Yes?'

'Is the package neutralized?' Danny Slatcher had the voice of a middle manager, throaty and bland. Aside from his size, bigger than your average bear, he *looked* boring, too. Button-up shirts, weave belts, dust-colored hair in that white-guy side part, even the start of a spare tire around the midsection – she was never clear if the getup was costume or genuine. The only appealing thing about him was his lethality. When the shit went down, he was transformed, all precision and timing, latent rage, hidden muscles sending bodies and furniture spinning like tops. She'd let him fuck her once, in the adrenalized aftermath of a double hit, and once was enough. They'd been on the rooftop of a resort in Tamarindo, thunder vibrating the adobe tiles, the smell of gunpowder and fresh blood drifting up from the balcony below. But in men's brains, 'once' was an open invitation. She'd given Slatcher a taste, and he'd carried the memory for years, aging it like a wine, fantasizing about popping that cork just one more time.

Candy began unloading her supplies from the duffel and setting them beside the industrial blender. Hacksaw. Safety goggles. Hand ax.

Over on the bed, Reynolds made muffled sounds.

'Just about,' she answered.

'Good,' Slatcher said. 'A bigger job just went sideways.'

'Clearly you brought in the wrong team, then.' She took out a long roll of black construction sheeting, placed it delicately on the floor, and gave it a nudge with her instep. It rolled smoothly across the floorboards, leaving a wide band of protective cover.

Slatcher cleared his throat. 'I was overseeing them personally.'

'*They're* not *me*.'

Carefully, she extracted from the duffel two jugs of concentrated hydrofluoric acid, effective at dissolving bones. It had to be stored in plastic, since it ate through everything from concrete to porcelain – what the majority of American bathtubs are made of. The copper soaking tub would react with the acid, sure, but it would just come out shinier, all the oxide stains eaten away. At the end of the day, Candy McClure would be just another considerate guest leaving a room cleaner than she'd found it.

The sounds of panicked thrashing carried over from the bed.

'I have a man down,' Slatcher said.

'That's what you get for sending a man to do a woman's job.'

A thick vein stood out on Reynolds's forehead. He was trying to say something through the ball gag, but she'd secured the straps good and tight.

Candy set down the jugs, then carefully tucked her stray hair beneath the swim cap. She would leave no DNA on the scene. His or hers.

99

'Get here,' Slatcher said.

At his tone her playfulness evaporated. She calculated the naked man's girth, the size of the tub, traffic conditions down the mountain. Four hours and change. She picked up the hand ax and started for the bed.

'On my way,' she said.

13. Professionals

Evan chose a mid-level motel in a less-nice part of Santa Monica several miles from the beach. With Katrin clinging to his arm in the role of browbeaten spouse, he checked in using a fake driver's license and paid with a credit card tied to a cul-de-sac of a bank account. He booked three rooms on the ground floor with connecting doors for their extended family, due any minute now. Then he led Katrin into the middle room and waited patiently in a rickety wooden chair while she cleaned up in the bathroom. The sink water ran for a long time. When she came out, the red rims of her eyes looked pronounced against her alabaster skin.

She sat on the bed, pressed her hands between her knees. 'God,' she said. She glanced over to the little desk, on which Evan had set out a stack of cash and a burner phone, and made a noise deep in her throat.

'Don't leave this room. Order in only, have them set the food outside, slide the money under the door. Don't use the phone unless it's to call me. Understand?'

'This isn't real. This can't be real. We have to call them. We have to find out about my dad, and now they can't call me since you took my phone and –'

'Where did Morena approach you?'

Katrin jogged her head back and forth slightly, as if

to clear her thoughts. 'I was playing roulette. Shitty odds, I know, but I was down to my last thousand . . . It was a Hail Mary. I thought if God or karma or whatever you want to call it was on my side, I could hit ten on the wheel. And then again. And again. Until I had two-point-one million. Until I could save my dad.' She misted up and had to pause. 'I didn't know what to do. I don't have anything. I don't have money like that. Look, I really think we need to contact these guys —'

'How did she pick you out?'

'How do you think? I must've seemed like a fucking mess — because I *was* a fucking mess. And then this kid comes up. Looked barely old enough to be there. And she said, "Are you in trouble?" Like she was *searching* for me.'

Morena's aunt lived in Vegas, and she'd made it clear that she and Carmen were heading there. What better place than a casino to search out someone in desperate shape?

Katrin continued, 'And you know how sometimes someone asks you the wrong question at the wrong time? I just started crying. And then we sat down, and she told me her story. And I told her mine. Well, part of it. But enough. And she gave me your number. I didn't know what to think, whether I should trust her. I drove back to L.A., mulling it over. Then I gave in and called.'

'You told her your story? Even though you'd just met her?'

'A version of it, like I said.' Katrin's neck firmed, and he saw a trace of steel beneath the green eyes. 'Wait a minute. Is this some sort of test? After what you just saw? Like I *made up* almost getting shot? You seriously don't trust me?'

'If I didn't trust you, you wouldn't be here.'

Her throat clicked as she swallowed.

'There's no question they're trying to kill you,' Evan said. 'I just need to understand precisely what happened.'

She stood up, and he followed suit. 'What about my dad?'

'We'll get to that.'

'They said. They said I couldn't tell *anyone*. Me calling you? That could've killed my father.' She twisted a hand hard in the hem of her shirt, as if working out a violent impulse. 'We have to call. We have to –'

He took her arms gently and moved her back a step. 'The first thing we do is nothing. If we do nothing, nothing can happen. Adrenaline is up right now, everyone will be amped, excitable, prone to making mistakes. Let them calm down. We want nerves to settle. We'll call tomorrow, negotiate your father's release.'

'There's no negotiating with them. There's no moving them.' She scanned the room, as if noticing for the first time the print bedspread, the shitty pastel art. 'This was all a mistake,' she said. 'I have to go. I have to get my car and . . . and –'

'You're not getting your car. It's not safe to leave. The sniper is still out there. He was working with at least one other person. There might be others.'

'The guy. The one you killed. Did you see him? One

eye was still open . . .' Her blood-red lips pressed together to keep from trembling. 'And you think there might be others?'

'Maybe.'

'Because a *sniper* isn't enough?'

'I won't let them lay a finger on you.'

'I'm not worried about a *finger*.' Then she did something completely unexpected. She laughed. A real laugh, too, that beautiful mouth even wider, half hidden behind a raised hand. A few strands of jet-black hair had fallen across her eyes, and she left them there. As quickly as her dark amusement had bubbled to the surface, it departed.

She sat again on the bed, and he settled back into the wooden chair.

'It broke my dad's heart when I married that asshole,' she said. 'He warned me that nothing good would come of it. Though I can't say he expected *this*.'

'Your husband's involved in this somehow?'

'My ex. And no.' She took a breath, held it a moment. 'We were married five months. If it wasn't so typical, I'd have the sense to be embarrassed. Adam Hamuel, a real-estate tycoon. Planned communities in Boca Raton, that kind of stuff. It kept him busy. The land deals, the building permits, the other women.' She ran her hand along the chintz bedspread. 'So when he'd travel, I'd gamble. My dad taught me to play poker.' She wet her lips. 'My mom died young, so dad taught me pretty much everything. How to throw a baseball. Drive stick. But cards, Dad was great at cards.'

'What's his name?' Evan asked. 'Your father.'

'Sam. Sam White.' She blinked back emotion. 'Right before I got married, Dad moved to Vegas, so I'd visit him and I'd play and play. And for a brief time – five months – I had money. A different level of money, I mean. Adam always told me not to worry, that I couldn't *spend* enough to make a dent in what he earned. And so I didn't worry. I played in those backroom games, and I drank the free booze and pushed the markers. Stupid, right?'

'Not given what you knew at the time.'

She breathed for a bit. 'One day at home, I found a leopard-print thong between the couch cushions, and then I couldn't pretend I didn't know anymore. I called him on it, and he left and filed the next day. I'd signed a big prenup, and he just turned off the tap. Everything's tied up in family trusts, offshore accounts, all that kind of stuff. People can hide money where you'd never find it.'

Evan gave a little nod.

'So I have a big house in Brentwood that I can't pay the heating bill on, let alone the mortgage, a shiny leased Jag that they're gonna repossess any day, and a marker for two-point-one million I owe to some guy on the other end of a phone number or he'll kill my dad.'

'What's the phone number?' Evan asked.

She recited a direct-inward-dial number, like his, which he committed to memory.

'I don't have anything,' she said. 'I told them, but they don't believe me. Look at my zip code. I wouldn't believe me either.' She sank to the bed, blew the hair from her eyes. 'It's my fault. I made a stupid fucking mistake, and my dad's paying for it. Maybe right now. Do you have any idea how that feels?'

The red glow of an elevator sign. Jack's callused hand against Evan's cheek. The sweet smell of sawdust cut with something else.

'Yes,' he said.

'I wish you *hadn't* yanked me out of the way at the restaurant. I wish they'd just shot me and let my dad go.'

'Who's to say they wouldn't have shot you and *then* your dad?'

'Oh, just let me be a martyr for a second.'

'Tell me when you're done.'

The faintest hint of amusement firmed those lips. 'I'm done.'

'What can you tell me about this gambling circuit?'

'Like I said, not much. Texas Hold'em in basements of restaurants, rented suites, like that. There was security and dealers, but I never saw the face of anyone behind it all. Even the players, we used fake names. It was impossible to tell who was the house. They were smart enough not to leave a trail.'

'How'd they find you?'

'People find you in Vegas. I was at a table. They approached.'

'Just like that.'

'I make an impression when I play.'

He asked her to walk him through whatever specifics about locations she could remember. Then he asked,

'How did you find out about the Japanese businessman they killed?'

'They sent a picture to my phone. It autodeleted a few seconds after I saw it.' She smoothed an invisible wrinkle from the bedspread next to her. 'A few seconds was enough.'

'You said they skinned him. But we're dealing with a sniper, maybe a team. Why the change in approach?'

'I have no idea,' she said. 'It's not exactly my field.'

Rising to go, he realized that he knew the answer to his question already. Given the size of Katrin's loan and her failure to deliver the money promptly, they'd gone to the next level.

They'd brought in professionals.

14. Dream Come True

In a form-fitting dress, Candy McClure waited at the bus stop on Ventura Boulevard, duffel bag resting near the pointed toes of her thigh-high vinyl boots. Passing cars brought wolf calls, which she basked in along with the morning sun. A bus hissed to the curb, and a group of would-be gangstas unpacked from it. They shuffled past, all lowered trousers and top-buttoned flannel shirts. The leader, not unreasonably taking her for a hooker, pivoted to shake his hips in her direction. 'Hey, Catwoman, wanna play with this?'

'Love to.' She reached out, grabbing his crotch through a baggy expanse of denim and squeezing. He made a noise like a whinny as she steered him around, depositing him on the bench next to her. She played him like an instrument, crushing at will, bringing forth various sounds as his friends circled in a sort of animal panic. When she released him, he rolled on to the side-walk. She'd managed to squeeze out a few real tears to go with the inked ones tattooed at the corner of his eye.

Boys.

He struggled to his knees and then to a hunched approximation of standing.

'Thanks,' Candy said, checking that her press-on nails remained intact. 'Good session.'

His friends conveyed him up the street.

A few minutes later, a rented Scion sedan pulled up, the window lowering. Crammed into the driver's seat, Danny Slatcher hid behind mirrored aviators and a mustache imported from 1980. A larger vehicle would have suited him.

''Bout time,' she said.

With a long arm, he reached across and flung open the passenger door. 'Get in. And change. You look like a whore.'

And *he* looked like an insurance salesman. Which she supposed was the point.

'Wow,' she said, climbing in. 'A crappy purple Scion. Like in the song.'

'What song?'

'Train,' she said. '"50 Ways to Say Goodbye".' A brown grocery bag in the footwell contained her cover outfit. As he drove, she pulled on the new clothes. 'It's about a guy making up outlandish ways his girlfriend died so he doesn't have to –'

'You handled the esteemed assemblyman?' he asked.

'Excessively,' Candy said.

Ten blocks later, when Slatcher parked at one of the seedy tourist motels off the 101 near Universal Studios, she emerged from the car a new woman. She wore clunky espadrilles, a shapeless skirt pulled too high at the waist, and a loose blouse with fussy ruffles to hide her va-va-voom figure.

Slatcher unfolded himself from the car. He was quite tall at six-three, but that didn't account for his size – it was more his *breadth*. He wasn't athlete-stacked but rather pear-shaped, bulky like the outermost Russian nesting doll. His capacious midsection always surprised Candy, and yet there was no flab, just firm mass and muscle, a rock-hard gut billowing beneath a checkered taupe golf shirt. His true-blue jeans, pleated, served as another nod to out-of-towner aesthetics, as did the Oakley wraparounds worn backward on his head to rest at the bulge in his neck.

He hoisted three ballistic nylon Victorinox suitcases from the auto-opening trunk and set them down. Brusquely, he handed her a floppy sunhat, which she set gently atop her Farrah Fawcett wig. The brim wobbled expansively around her head, every tourist's bad beach-fashion statement.

Telescoping one Victorinox handle up, she tilted the case on to its embedded wheels, feeling the weight of the contents as they clanked. Side by side, like mismatched flight attendants, she and Slatcher headed for the tiny reception office.

Their entrance was heralded when the opening door knocked a bell – actually cheery jingle *bells* – affixed above the frame. A wattle-necked woman looked up from a paperback. 'Welcome to Starry Dreams Motel,' she said.

'Heavens to Betsy,' Candy said, arming sweat off the band of brow exposed somewhere between her big shades, the feathery Farrah hair and the straw brim that shielded much of her face. 'Such a *dry* heat.'

'Where you folks in from?'

'Charleston,' she said. 'Checking in under Miller.'

'Ah, yes,' the woman said. 'I have you in Room Eight.'

'Will you please put hypoallergenic pillows in our room?' Slatcher asked.

'I'm afraid we don't have hypoallergenic pillows here.'

Candy rested an elbow on the counter. 'You know what they say. They just don't make men like they used to.'

Slatcher gave an annoyed marital grunt.

The woman processed two key cards and handed them across.

'What time does breakfast open?' Slatcher asked. 'We're heading early to Universal Studios.'

'There'll be coffee and Danish out from six a.m.'

'Bless my stars,' Candy said. 'We'd *better* not be waking up that early.'

'It's three hours later for us,' Slatcher said. 'That's nine.'

'Look at that,' Candy said, grabbing her suitcase and heading for the door. 'He can add, too.'

The minute they entered their room, Candy yanked the sunhat off, Frisbeed it on to one of the queen beds, and tugged her head free of the wig. She scratched at her hair. 'Fuck me,' she said. 'That shit is hot.'

They unzipped the suitcases, laying out pistols, magazines and boxes of ammo on the floral bedspread. Candy inspected the barrel chamber and bore of a Walther P22. 'So this broad. Katrin White. What's our leverage?'

They'd spoken briefly on the phone on her way down the mountain.

'Our leverage is Sam.'

'Who we have a bead on.'

'Sam,' Slatcher said, 'is under control.'

'Then why'd Ms White drop off the radar?'

'Because he took control of the situation.'

'The Man with No Name?'

'That is correct. He killed one of my freelancers.'

'Kane?'

'Ostrowski.'

'Huh,' she said. She'd never liked Ostrowski.

'I've brought in a field team for us,' Slatcher said. 'Former Blackwater.'

'Hoo-*rah*.'

'This guy's very dangerous.'

'I assumed as much.'

'He does not want to be found.'

Candy unzipped her duffel bag. 'Well,' she said, hoisting out a jug of hydrofluoric acid, 'then let's make his dream come true.'

15. Tick, Tick, Tick

It all checked out.

Katrin White, the divorce from Adam Hamuel, the dead mom, the father in Vegas, even the byzantine contortion of family trusts into which her ex-husband's money had vanished.

What *didn't* check out was the direct-dial number Katrin had for the kidnappers. Camped out in the Vault, chewing a tart Granny Smith apple, Evan traced the eleven digits through various electronic switchboards as they ping-ponged around the globe and then vanished into the Internet ether in a manner he found frustratingly familiar.

They wouldn't be backtraced any more than he would.

Time was key. There was no point in chasing his tail around Las Vegas searching for an itinerant backroom poker game. Evan had to be in touch with the sniper and his people soon. He didn't want their vexation to simmer, turn to rage, then desperation.

He ran his hands over his face, gave Vera a look. She looked back from her nest of cobalt-blue pebbles, offering nothing. At the base of his brain, he felt the *tick, tick, tick* of paranoia. His gaze moved from the little plant to the RoamZone phone beside it. He removed the SIM card, crushed it under his heel, and replaced it with a new one. Then he jumped online and moved the phone service from the outfit in Jiangsu to one in Bangalore.

Earlier he'd lifted Katrin's fingerprints from the passenger-side door handle of the Chrysler sedan, which he'd wiped clean before approaching her in Chinatown. From the databases he knew that she was who she said she was, her story literally battle-tested. Nonetheless, in honor of the First Commandment he went back through everything again, plumbing her Social Security records and bank accounts, looking for the slightest hiccup or red flag.

Nothing.

Though she'd been stoic when he'd left her in the hotel room, he could read the fear in her eyes. He'd returned to bring her food, some toiletries and new clothes of various sizes, which she seemed to find vaguely amusing. Then he'd driven back to Chinatown.

At least ten police units had been on-site, lights flashing, as well as multiple unmarked sedans. The shattered windows of Lotus Dim Sum gaped, a row of jagged mouths, and shards still littered the sidewalk. Across the street from Central Plaza, cops swarmed the apartment building. Slowing as he drove along Broadway, Evan picked out a solemn congregation of detectives on the balcony of the third-floor apartment, centered almost precisely on the spot he'd picked up the glint of the scope. Getting a look at the crime scene would have to wait. Evan had coasted by, then switched out cars at the safe house and driven home.

In the Vault now, he took one more bite of apple and tossed the core toward the trash bin in the corner. He bricked the shot, the remains bouncing wetly on to the concrete. He stared at the disobedient apple core, his jaw tense. Then he rose, picked it up, and wiped the floor clean.

As he dropped back into his chair, his eye caught on a rugged gray-haired man peeking out from the clutter of open windows on his computer desktop. With a click of the mouse, he brought the DMV photo to the forefront.

Sam White. Katrin's father.

Held hostage this very minute by men unafraid to fire into a crowded restaurant in broad daylight.

Sam wore a half smile that crinkled his eyes, his skin toughened from sun exposure. He'd worked as a construction manager and looked the part. A guy you'd want to share a beer with, watch a game. Someone to teach you to play poker.

Evan had put Katrin through the paces – changing the location, a bus ride, leaving her car behind, switching her chair at the table. A pattern of movement designed to keep her off balance and himself safe. But one that clearly had aroused the interest of the sniper or the men behind him.

Any meeting that carefully orchestrated obviously went against their wishes and directives.

Katrin's words returned with a sting: *Me calling you? That could've killed my father.*

A pulse beat in Evan's temple. The walls of the Vault

retained a bit of dampness, enough that he could feel moisture in his lungs on the inhale. Through the vent he could smell tar from the roof. For a time he sat there, that picture of Katrin's father staring back at him. He thought of the false-bottomed drawer in his bureau and what it contained.

Never make it personal.

Just make it right.

Tomorrow he'd call Sam's captors. He'd give everyone a night's sleep to settle down, then engage under the light of a new day. In one fashion or another, he would engage.

Exiting through the shower and walking back to the big room, he sat to meditate, setting his pistol on the area rug beside him. Crossing his legs, he relaxed into his flesh, felt the tug of his bones, the weight of himself against the floor. His eyelids half closed, and beyond the blinds the city lights streaked into comets of yellow and orange.

He inventoried the minor aches from the day, starting with his feet and moving up his body. A slice on his calf carved by a shard from the blown-out window. A bruise on his left hip. Some joint tenderness around the shoulder.

The pain flickered in these spots, warm, pulsing. He focused on the hot points, breathed into them, smoothing them out with each exhalation as if beneath a rolling pin. And then they were gone, everything gone but the rise and fall of his chest, the coolness at his nostrils.

The breath was his anchor.

There was nothing else but his body and the chill air moving through it, feeding the blood in his veins, centering him here in this instant, his life measured one breath at a time. For a while he drifted across a blank slate, mindful and aware and yet without thought.

And then, as if stumbling, he lost the thread of the present, spinning back twenty-five years.

16. The Two Wolves

On the drive home from the dark Virginia barn, Jack lays out some facts, serving them to Evan like a well-earned meal. 'You are part of what is called the Orphan Program. You are exceptionally well adjusted and even-tempered in the face of the unknown, selected for the program precisely for these qualities. There are others like you. You will never meet them.' His blocky hands command the steering wheel, the vehicle, the road. 'You will be trained impeccably for your profession.'

'What's my profession?'

'Weapon,' Jack says.

The truck thrums across some railroad tracks. The vinyl seat has grown hot beneath Evan's legs. His head goes swimmy, like he's in a dream. But it's not a bad dream.

Finally Evan asks, 'A weapon for what?'

'For solo, offline covert operations.'

Jack seems to forget that Evan is a kid. Or perhaps he speaks to him that way, the vocabulary just out of reach, making Evan stretch, stretch. Evan thinks for a time, piecing together what that might mean.

'Like a spy?'

Jack's chin dips, his version of a nod. 'Like a spy. But you'll be different from other assaulters.'

Assaulters. *Evan likes the word.*

'You'll be a cutout man,' Jack continues. 'Fully expendable.

You'll know only your silo. Nothing damaging. If you're caught, you're on your own. They will torture you to pieces, and you can give up all the information you have, because none of it is useful. You will go places you are not allowed to go and do things you are not allowed to do. Everyone at every level will deny any knowledge of you, and this will not be entirely false. Your very existence is illegal.'

'An Orphan,' Evan says.

'That's right. This is your last chance to pull the ripcord, so consider carefully. If you die, you will die alone and no one will know of your sacrifice. No one but me. There will be no greater glory, no parades, no name on a monument wall. That is the choice before you.'

Evan thinks about where he came from – secondhand shoes, food out of cans, low ceilings and cramped walls. Jack Johns seems like a portal to a vast, wide-open world, a world Evan had always imagined existed somewhere beyond reach. Now maybe there could be a place out there even for someone like him.

Evan pokes at the cut in his palm bestowed by the hooked blade. 'Sounds good,' he says.

Jack looks over at him. Back at the road. 'There is only me. I'm your handler. I am the only person who will ever know who you are. I will protect you. No matter what.' The trees scroll by behind that rough-hewn profile. 'You and I are all we have. Do you understand?'

Evan watches the foliage whip by. 'I think so.'

'Equivocal answers aren't answers, Evan.'

'Yes. I understand.' Evan looks down at his arms, dotted with puncture marks. 'So I'm gonna do more training? With that guy?'

'Him and others. Under no circumstance are you to reveal to them your name. They will know you only as "Orphan X".'

'X as in the letter or the number ten?'

Jack appears pleased with this question. 'Alphabet.'

'So there were twenty-three Orphans before me?'

'Yes.'

'What happens when you run out of letters?'

Jack laughs. It is the first time Evan has heard him do so. It's a rich laugh, aged in his chest. 'Then I suppose they'll go to numbers.' He veers around a wood-paneled station wagon, a family out for a Sunday drive. 'I will only interject one instructor at a time into your life. At the beginning of your training, you will never be alone with an instructor. I will always be there. Like today.'

'Yeah, but I'll never be as good at handling pain as that guy.'

Jack pulls a thoughtful frown. Then he says, 'You don't have to. You just have to do better than you did last time.' Jack looks across at him. 'You know the two best words in the English language?' he asks.

Evan is at a loss.

' "Next time",' Jack says.

Evan feels unconvinced.

Jack says, 'You've read the Odyssey, right?'

'No.'

'We'll change that soon enough.' Jack takes a moment to look displeased. Then: 'Odysseus is not as skilled a fighter as Achilles. Not as great an archer as Apollo. Not as fast as Hermes. In fact, he's not the best at anything. And yet overall? He is unrivaled. "Man of many wiles".' Jack's eyes move from the rearview to one side mirror, then the other. 'Your job is to learn a little bit *about everything from people who know everything about something.'*

Evan's next years are spent doing precisely that.

He is taught hand-to-hand from a Japanese master who is maddeningly calm, even as he delivers devastating attacks. There are no belts, no dojos, no special white pajamas; it is junk martial arts, the most effective destructions, a little of the best from each form. In Jack's sweaty garage, Evan spans the globe in a single fight, finding himself on the receiving end of an around-the-world offensive. A muay thai teep-kick *interception of his right cross leads to a Wing Chun* bil jee *finger jab to the eye that sends him reeling. Before he can restore his equilibrium, an Indonesian pencak silat open-hand slap to the ear leaves his nervous system ringing. Half blinded by static, he swings, but the master delivers an upward elbow Filipino Kali* gunting *combined with a hand trap, smashing Evan's fist against the tip of the ulna. Evan sits on the floor, hard, the collective wisdom of four cultures distilled into a single ass-kicking.*

He doesn't know which part of himself to check first.

The master bows to him respectfully.

Evan swipes blood from his lips. 'This guy ever lose his temper?'

In a beach chair to the side, from behind a tattered copy of Vidal's Lincoln, *Jack says, 'He doesn't have to.'*

Evan dips his head, drools blood into the cup of his palm.

'Next time,' Jack says, and gets up to go into the house.

Evenings they spend in the study with its towering bookshelves and mallard green walls, where Jack conducts what he calls 'Area and Cultural Studies.' Evan learns rules, etiquette, history, sensitivities. How to respond if he accidentally steps on someone's foot

121

in the Moscow subway. What Armenians think of Turks. The proper way to proffer your business card in China. How to sink the French r in his throat. There are elocution lessons as well, eradicating every last trace of East Baltimore until Evan's accent is as nonspecific as that of a midwestern newscaster. Soon enough, when he speaks, he offers no information beyond what he chooses to divulge with his words.

As the seasons pass, he grows accustomed to the forty-five-minute drive to Fort Meade. Jack always enters through a back gate, the guard station left conspicuously empty for their approach. Most of the activities take place in and around a clandestine set of hangars at the foresty rear of the base. A half-crazy battalion captain with an angry snarl of scar tissue for a chin runs Evan ragged, teaching him how to move under live fire. He uses concealment to head toward cover, zigzagging through tree trunks as rounds bite chunks of bark overhead. The captain's gleeful bellowing stalks him ghostlike through the boughs: 'School's in session, X! Lock in that muscle memory. How you train is how you play!'

One day, frustrated with Evan's evasive movements, the battalion captain smacks him across the back of the head. Jack morphs out of thin air, standing nose to nose with the man. 'Hurt him all you want if you're training him. But if you lay a hand on him again in anger, I will make the rest of your face match your chin. Do you understand me?'

The battalion captain's eyes achieve a sudden clarity. 'Yes, sir,' he says.

Driving home, Evan says, 'Thanks.'

Jack nods. The truck rattles across potholes. The dashboard vent blows hot and steady. Jack seems to be working up to *something. Finally he says, 'I know that details of your background are ... hazy. If it's important to you, we can run a genetic test, find out your ancestry, who you are.'*

The choice awes Evan into silence. Jack seems to sense that this is one time not to push. He waits patiently.

At last Evan clears his throat. 'I know who I am,' he says. 'I'm your son.'

Jack makes a muffled noise of agreement and angles his head away, perhaps so Evan can't see his face.

The pace of training is relentless. Evan learns to breach, to scale barbed-wire fences, to rappel from trees, fences, walls. He works with an old-school surveillance engineer annoyed by his weak grasp of circuitry and with a teenage hacker frustrated with his processing speed. He's taught how to approach people, to find and exploit weaknesses. To eliminate nonverbal tells, he masters the art of remaining still when talking or listening. Every time he lifts his hands, the interrogation specialist raps his knuckles painfully with a metal file; eventually Evan sits as if his wrists are tied to the arms of a chair. A whip-thin psychologist administers batteries of tests with esoteric questions: have you ever cheated or betrayed a loved one? No. *Have you ever had sex with an animal?* No. *Where does loyalty stop?* When someone asks you to have sex with an animal. *In the corner, Jack sprays out a mouthful of coffee.*

Evan shoots standing, kneeling, prone, firing on targets from seven to three hundred yards. After he is trained on conventional targets, his marksmanship instructor moves him to human silhouettes, then full-body photos of women and children. When he hesitates, she says, 'People don't run around with target rings on their heads and chests. Man up, X.' For sniper work she dresses mannequins in clothes, then cores out lettuce heads, fills them with ketchup, and mounts them atop the collars. She walks back uprange to where he waits. 'When you pull the trigger,' she says, 'I want you to see a head explode.'

As he lines up the shot, she lectures, 'We keep death at a distance here, X. Hospitals and nursing homes tuck it away. Our food comes to us neatly packaged. Refrigerators preserve it. It used to be you wanted a chicken, you walked out back and snapped its neck.' Her deodorant carries to him on the breeze, citrusy and surprisingly feminine. It stirs something in his sixteen-year-old body. 'My old man was a colonel, wanted me to understand that slaughterhouses did our bidding for us. When I was about your age, he took me to one. Just us and a machete and the steaming horror of an afternoon, looking Death in its rolling eyes.'

He fires, and a lettuce head downrange turns to red mist. 'Nicely done,' she says.

Later she duct-tapes an orange over her eye, makes him tackle her and punch his thumb through it. 'Good,' she pants, sprawled in the dirt, her breath hot against his neck. 'Now stir your thumb. Curl it like a fishing hook. And pull out what you can.' While he does, she screams and thrashes. He stops, mortified. Her one bare eye glares up at him. 'You think it'll be calm?'

He gathers himself, sinks his thumb back into the pulp.

That night over dinner, Evan fingers the spattering of dried pulp on his sleeve, shoves at his food.

Jack doesn't need to look up. 'What?'

Evan tells him about the orange, the thumb, the screams of his instructor, how he'd been on top of her, holding her down, breathing her breath.

Jack leans back, folds his arms. 'We need to teach you to kill in the heat of the moment. And in the cold calm of premeditation. You have to live with them differently. Which means you have to train for them differently. Not just sniper distance. Not just bayonet distance. But face-to-face, eye-to-eye.'

'So I learn to treat people as objects to be broken?'

'No.' Jack sets his water glass down on the dining table, hard. 'Conventional wisdom is that you should dehumanize the enemy. Dinks, krauts, sand niggers, numbers on the forearm. It may be easier in the short term, but long-term?' He shakes his head. 'Always respect life. Then you'll value yours. The hard part isn't turning you into a killer. The hard part is keeping you human.'

'Is that what the other Orphans are taught?' Evan asks.

Jack twirls linguine on his fork, regards the bulb of pasta, sets it down. He glances over at the picture of his wife on the mantel, the one at some exotic black-sand beach where she's knee-deep in surf, laughing, her wet sundress clinging to her thighs. Jack wipes his mouth. 'No.'

It is a confession of sorts.

'Why not?'

'It's harder.' With the heel of his hand, Jack pushes his plate a few inches away. 'There's a Cherokee legend. An elder tells his grandson about the battle that rages inside every person.'

'The two wolves.'

'That's right. One wolf is anger and fear and paranoia and cruelty. The other is kindness, humility, compassion, serenity. And the boy asks his grandfather, "Which wolf wins?" You remember the answer?'

'"The one you feed".'

'That's right. Our challenge?' Jack folds his cloth napkin,

wipes a smudge of Alfredo from the edge of his plate. Then he looks directly into Evan's eyes. 'Feed both.'

A furious rapping on the front door broke Evan from his meditation. By the time he registered a return to the present tense, he was on his feet on the Turkish rug, pistol in hand, staring down the locked door across from him and whoever waited behind it.

17. Broken Pieces

The angry banging on the door resumed, echoing around the hard surfaces and off the high ceiling. Eight noiseless strides took him to the side of the jamb. He'd filled in the peephole, as peepholes provided scant protection from bullets and awls, but he'd installed a pinhole camera outside in the corridor, using an air-conditioning vent as a concealment host. With a knuckle he nudged aside a hanging silk tapestry of a Thai Buddha on his wall, revealing an inset security monitor.

He took in the high-resolution image. A T-shirt stretched tight across a feminine form. A mass of wild, wavy hair. One fist, the fist not currently engaged in the knocking, placed on an angrily cocked hip.

Mia Hall, 12B.

Releasing a breath, Evan dropped the Wilson Combat pistol into the pocket of an overcoat hung on a brushed-nickel wall peg and reached for the knob.

Before the door was fully open, Mia started in. ' *"Take out a knee?"* Really?'

Evan said, 'Uh-oh.'

' "Uh-oh" is right. "Uh-oh" as in: I spent this afternoon not in court but in the principal's office at Roscomare Elementary.' She crossed her arms, a parental bearing of admirable effectiveness. 'You really informed him that *that's* how to handle a bully?'

'I was kidding.'

'He's *eight*. He looks up to you. You need to come tell him that violence is not the way we solve problems.'

Her expression made clear that this was not a request.

Behind the partially opened door, the matte black handle of the pistol protruded slightly from the pocket of the overcoat. Evan tapped it in all the way and stepped out, meekly following Mia down the hall.

One of Peter's eyes peered earnestly up at Evan, the other hidden beneath a pack of frozen peas. He reclined against a clutch of pillows in a bed shaped like a race car, strewn with mismatched *Harry Potter* sheets. A fray of hair stuck out at an odd angle, still growing in from the pirate-eye-patch/duct-tape mishap. Evan and Mia stood over him as if administering last rites.

Peter lowered the peas, revealing a swollen eye dappled with broken blood vessels. It looked impressive but was not a significant injury. Nonetheless, Mia gasped.

Peter smiled at Evan, flashing a prominent front tooth. '"Next time", right?'

'No,' Mia said. '*Not* next time. This is not what we do, Peter. *Next time* you're gonna make a better choice that doesn't land you — and *me* — in Mrs DiMarco's office. Tell him, please, Evan.'

The room smelled of Play-Doh, toothpaste, and bubblegum. A gold-foil seal of a grinning roadrunner

shimmered on a homework folder on the floor: ROSCO-
MARE ROAD ELEMENTARY. A trio of balloons, each
bearing the logo of a children's shoe store, bumped
along the ceiling. On the desk a Lego figure was under-
going some kind of primeval surgery, lying on a cot of
tissues beside several Q-tips and a tube of superglue. A
crayon drawing of the see-no-evil, hear-no-evil, speak-
no-evil monkeys fluttered from a tack beneath the vent.
Evan might as well have landed on a different planet.

He cleared his throat. 'Fighting is bad,' he said.

Mia regarded him through a fall of hair, seemingly
disappointed and encouraging at the same time. She
gave him a prompting nod.

'A better means of conflict resolution,' Evan continued, 'is to tell.'

Mia issued a noise of consternation that seemed to
encompass her, Evan, the entire bedroom tableau.

The *Jaws* theme sounded. Mia lifted her iPhone from
her pocket and stiffened. 'Sorry. I'm sorry. This is a big
work problem. Can you just . . . ?'

Evan nodded, and she stepped into the other room,
answering. He noted that she left the door open. Peter
stared at him expectantly. What the hell was Evan
doing here? His thoughts drifted to Katrin, holed up in
the motel room waiting for sunrise and Evan's return.
Her father held hostage at this very moment. Was he
bound? Gagged? Had they beaten him?

Evan looked around the room for inspiration, found
none. A family portrait sat framed on the desk, Peter a
fat newborn, Mia with a dated haircut, her bespectacled

husband wearing an easygoing grin. A Post-it adhered to the windowsill issued another directive from that Peterson guy: *'Make at least one thing better every single place you go.'*

Evan closed his eyes and thought back to being a kid. He pictured the way Jack's lips flickered when he sussed out the situation beneath a situation, as if they were searching for words. Evan reached for the wobbly desk chair, swung it around, sat on it backward.

He took a breath. 'Look,' he said. 'I don't know how you're feeling about it, but I'm pissed off that a kid did that to you.'

Peter stared down at his hands, fingers fussing along the hem of the sheet.

Evan said, 'He probably came after you and you tried to defend yourself and got popped in the face. That's unfair, and it sucks.'

Peter kept his eyes lowered. 'I wish I could stick up for myself,' he finally said, his voice on the edge of cracking.

'You can,' Evan said. 'You're just not big enough to do it with your fists. So why don't you use your smarts, keep clear of this kid, stay in eyeshot of a teacher? Nothing wrong with working the situation. Okay?'

'Okay.'

'And if that fails? You can always put drain cleaner in his water bottle.'

Peter grinned and offered a fist. Evan bumped it with his own as he headed out of the room.

The muted TV flickered over a landscape of scattered toys and dirty laundry spilled from a basket that had been dropped haphazardly on to one of the couch's split cushions. A dinner tray lay where it had slid off the couch, littered with pieces of a broken plate and bowl.

Mia, nowhere in sight.

Evan walked down the hall, calling her name quietly. The door to the master was ajar, but when he entered the room, he found it empty. From the dark maw of the walk-in closet, he heard sniffling.

'Mia?' He pushed the closet door further open and saw her sitting with her back to a rise of drawers, wiping her face, one hand clutching the ever-present iPhone.

'Sorry. I just – Sorry. Sometimes . . .'

'May I come in?'

'Please.'

He put his shoulders to the wall opposite her, beside the hanging blouses, and slid down to sit facing her. Her feet, shoved into actual bunny slippers. They were fluffy pink and featured a heart and stitched bubble letters that proclaimed, WORLD'S BEST MOM. The sight of them brought something deeper than just amusement. It surprised him to realize that he liked this home, where knives were for spreading butter and superglue for repairing toys.

'Sorry I was harsh earlier,' she said. 'Upstairs.'

'You were just being protective.'

'I'll tell you this: parenting ain't for sissies.'

'No,' he said. 'Doesn't seem to be.'

'And with work right now . . .' She blew out a breath. Her hair floated back down over her forehead. 'Facing it all by myself feels so fucking scary sometimes. And I know that's pathetic with everything I have, but . . .'

He watched her expression shift.

'I did everything right,' she said. 'Studied hard, worked hard, was a good wife. I know – "Grow up", right? I sound naïve and entitled, but Christ. You'd think it'd work out. Better. Than this.' She fluttered a hand around the closet, the heavy sleeves of disembodied coats, the wire hangers, the crowd of sweaters bending a shelf overhead. 'I have this fantasy notion of myself. Holding it together. But I can't seem to get there. Why not?'

He was unaccustomed to these kinds of problems, significant but not extreme, prosaic but not trivial. Everyday difficulties. A boy without a father. A toilet that wouldn't flush. Frozen peas to bring down the swelling. She was looking at him expectantly, and he realized that an answer was due.

'I suppose everything's a matter of discipline and focus.'

She made a thoughtful noise. 'It might seem that way to you,' she said, not unkindly. 'There's no one else in your life – I mean, in your life *all the time*. People are messy. Relationships aren't linear. They knock you on your ass. Make you detour, reverse, change focus. You can't be perfect unless you're alone, and then guess what? You're alone. So you're still not perfect.'

An image came to Evan: Jack moving through the farmhouse late at night, thumbing up flecks of dust, aligning objects on counters, stacking the place mats and cloth napkins with assembly-line precision. Evan had always viewed those nighttime rituals as displays of mettle, an almost religious observance of setting the room, the house, the universe in order.

'Maybe none of what we think matters really matters at all,' Mia said. 'Maybe it's the *little* stuff that adds up, inch by inch, until you've built something you didn't even know you were building. Driving car pool. Making school lunches. Sitting bedside at a hospital night after night . . .' Her eyes glinted in the dark. 'But that's what takes it out of you, too.' She tilted her head back to keep more tears from spilling. 'I worry that I can't handle everything that's coming by myself. All the mess of life. That I'm too sensitive. Too fragile. That it'll keep coming and I won't have what it takes.'

'You're not fragile,' Evan said. 'You're not afraid to show the cracks.'

'Great.' A hint of a smile. 'I'm cracky.' She stuck her arm out at an upward diagonal. 'Help me up.'

'You sure you're ready to exit the closet?'

She cocked her head. 'There's a mess to be picked up and laundry to be done, and I am again equal to the task.'

He rose, grasped her hand, pulled her up. She rose as if weightless. For a moment they were close, stomach to stomach, in the tight space. Her eyes on his chin, her breath faint against his neck. And then she brushed past him, patting his side. They emerged from the bedroom together. In the living room, she turned off the TV, started folding the laundry on the couch.

Starting for the door, he thought again of that life lesson Mia had written out for her son and stuck to the wall: *'Pursue what is meaningful, not what is expedient.'* The little phrase stopped him there on the floorboards. He looked across at the Post-it and read it again, wondering if the Commandments were immutable and determinate or whether new rules could be added as one pleased. Again he thought of Jack poking around in the dark house, tidying up, making invisible adjustments that he'd make again the next night and the night after that. The farmhouse, so safe and clean and soothingly spare, had always felt somehow outside of time. This home gave the opposite impression. With its smudged handprints and framed family portraits, it seemed to contain within its walls the entire brutal cycle of life – and yet it also contained a comfort of a different kind. Though the specific thought wriggled away before Evan could pin it down, he sensed somewhere that this brand of comfort couldn't exist without the brutal realities.

In his peripheral vision, Evan sensed Mia crouch over the fallen tray. He reversed direction and joined her, helping pick up the broken pieces.

18. Look Closer

Around Evan's seventeenth birthday, a threat arises, acquainting him with the real-life stakes of the profession. News reaches Jack that a file in a classified database somewhere may have been compromised. Drawing on a tenacity forged in his early infantry-sergeant days, he locks up the house and stays awake for seventy-two hours in the dark foyer, facing the front door from a wooden stool, combat shotgun across his knees, moving only to drink from a thermos and relieve himself. A phone call from a blocked number indicates that the threat, if it was a threat at all, has passed.

As Jack returns the wooden stool to its place at the kitchen counter, he calls Evan to his side. He throws some leftover turkey on a plate, then pours himself vodka over ice. Leaning against the sink, drink in hand, he wears a thoughtful expression; his vigil has left ample time for contemplation.

'I need to teach you how all this works, because knowledge is power and I will not have you take the risks you will take unempowered. Our program is a full-deniability, antiseptic operation run off a black budget. The money comes straight out of Treasury. It's printed and shipped, utterly untraceable. Which means, essentially, that we have an unlimited budget. DoD manages this, threads the needle through an outlet in the Department of the Interior.'

'Department of the Interior?'

'Exactly. Land management, national parks. Who's gonna look there?'

Jack proceeds to lay out the arcane arrangements. Bank accounts on various continents. The cash moves through a contracting agent in Aberdeen, Maryland, who doesn't even know what he's contracting, then filters out. PO boxes, traceless wires, currency swaps. Lawyers in closet-size offices rented by the week, concealed in beehive complexes housing jewelers, boiler-room operations, fly-by-night travel agencies. Desks and phones and nothing more.

Evan listens intently, his hand dipping below the counter from time to time so Strider can lap turkey from his palm. Jack pretends not to notice. The only permitted variation in discipline comes where the dog is concerned.

'Are you supposed to be telling me this?' Evan asks.

'No.'

The Sixth Commandment: Question orders.

The following morning Evan returns from a run to find in the driveway a red Acura Integra with a bobblehead Jesus adhered to the dash.

Puzzled, he enters the house. A trace of jasmine perfume lingers in the air, as anomalous in the wood-paneled front hall as a feather boa on a marine.

Jack waits in the study, Maria Callas belting 'Suicidio!' from the record player. When Evan's shadow falls into the room, Jack looks up. 'You can't lose your mind over women, over sex. And that means you need to acclimate to it. She is a professional, she is clean, and you are to treat her with courtesy and appreciation. Do you understand?'

Evan nods.

Jack goes back to the third volume of Churchill's A History of the English-Speaking Peoples.

Upstairs, Evan's bedroom door is slightly ajar, enough to reveal a slice of bedding. The fabric shifts. A woman's bare form rolls into view. He glimpses a thatch of shadow between ivory white legs and feels his blood jump.

The next day Evan does pull-ups on the rusted bar by the log pile, his biceps screaming. Jack sips coffee, his breath visible in the night air.

'Respect for women is essential,' Jack tells him. 'Women's rights and economic development within a country are highly correlated. Treating women properly is not just a moral position – which it is – or an American value – which it is. It's a strategic imperative, and you will always, always lead by example in this regard.'

Evan makes a grunt of consent and drops from the bar. When he goes upstairs, there are two women waiting in his bed.

His education in and out of the sheets intensifies. By the time he turns eighteen, he is five-eleven, 175 pounds of lean, ridged muscle. He is neither too tall nor too big nor too evidently strong. He can vanish in a crowd. Half the men in a given bar might think they could best him in a brawl. This is ideal.

Jack decides to call wind for Evan on the sniper range one crisp fall morning. It's been a long while since it was just the two of them with no instructor.

Evan dials the elevation into his scope, correcting for the ballistic arc.

At his side Jack presses binoculars to his face. 'She says you shoot almost as well as Orphan Zero now.'

'I thought we were only letters.'

'Zero's a nickname for Orphan O.'

Evan exhales through pursed lips, applies steady pressure to the trigger. The stock kicks into his shoulder, and a hole appears centered in the red bull's-eye 600 meters downslope.

'Who's Orphan O?' Evan asks, fitting his eye again to the cup of the scope.

'An active Orphan. Some say the best. Until you.'

Evan fires again.

Jack lets his binoculars drop into the brittle leaves, annoyed. 'Focus, Evan. You missed the whole damn target.'

'Look closer,' Evan says.

Jack lifts the binocs again. There it is, the eclipselike bulge where the second bullet nudged the perforation outward on the left side.

Two bullets, one hole.

Jack bobs that bulldog head, makes a noise deep in his throat. As Evan looks over, some heretofore undetectable filter falls away and Evan sees that Jack has aged since that first meeting when he pulled up to the rest stop where Evan was left seven years ago. His flesh seems heavier, tugging at that broad jawline, and his gaze is more human somehow. The glimpse of this Jack, a man nearing sixty with more traveled road behind him than open road ahead, strikes a vulnerability inside Evan that he didn't know he had.

'When Clara died,' Jack says, keeping his eyes downrange, 'I couldn't see anything. Only the spaces she used to occupy.' He rolls his lips, swallows. 'Until you.'

His mouth firms, and once more he is a baseball catcher, square and armored, impervious to collision. He rises, his boots crunching mulch as he turns back to the truck, his face holding the faintest note of dread.

'You're ready,' he says.

*

Evan's eyes opened in the soft morning light of his bedroom. He lay on his floating bed, stared at the ceiling, Jack's words still echoing in his head.

He'd been ready for a long time. Briefly, he wondered what all that readiness had cost him.

And then he rose.

It was time for him and Katrin to make contact.

19. Advertising Cost

'I'm scared.'

Sitting at the edge of the motel-room bed, Katrin shoved her clenched hands into the already stretched hem of the woefully oversize T-shirt Evan had brought her. Her hair, still wet from the shower, fell at blunt angles into a bob. Her irises, a crystalline sea green, looked even clearer given the absence of eyeliner. She took in his face in darting glances, her knees nutcrackering the union of her fists again and again.

Evan pulled a chair around to face her. 'It'll be okay.'

'How can you know that?'

'It always has been before.'

The air, still humid in the aftermath of her shower, felt oppressively heavy and carried the hospital-hygienic scent of bad motel soap. He'd arrived minutes ago to find her pacing around the cramped space, chewing a dark-painted thumbnail to the quick. Now she rammed her hands again into the belly of the ill-fitting shirt, the V-neck tugging down, showing the top swell of her breasts. Nerves firing, limbs jumping – her anxiety fighting the confines of her body.

His black briefcase rested on the bureau beside the TV, knocking out any surveillance devices that might be in the area. He punched a code into the lock, turning off the wideband high-power jammer.

It was time to make a phone call.

Sensing this, Katrin picked up the burner phone from the mattress beside her. She pressed it to her lips, closed her eyes as if praying.

Evan removed his RoamZone. 'We'll use mine,' he said. 'Untraceable.'

She gave a quick nod. 'Hang on. Just hang on.' She took a few breaths. Opened those wide eyes, brimming with fear. 'Okay.'

He dialed. Hit speaker. Set the phone on the corner of the mattress, between him and Katrin.

As it rang, Katrin squeezed one hand in the other.

A man picked up. 'Who's this?'

'Do you have Sam?' Evan asked.

'Looking at him.'

Katrin muffled a cry in her throat.

'Proof of life,' Evan said. 'Then we discuss terms.'

A shuffling sound, and then came a ragged masculine voice. 'Hello? Katrin?'

'Dad?' Katrin blinked, and tears slid down her ivory cheeks. 'I'm here.'

'Hi, baby.'

'Have they hurt you?'

'I'm all right.'

She wiped her eyes. 'I'm sorry I didn't listen to them better. I'm sorry I went to someone for help.'

'Honey, I want you to know . . . I want you to know I don't fault you for any of this. For anything that happened. Whoever you're with, I hope he protects you. I hope he –'

A clamor of grappling as the phone was ripped away. Then the first man's voice again. 'You didn't adhere to our instructions.'

'That's my fault,' Evan said. 'But I'm prepared to negotiate Sam's release. I have money, and I have –'

'We don't care about money. Not anymore. Our directions were not obeyed.'

'Wait!' Katrin said. 'We can fix it. We can make it okay again.'

'This is our advertising cost,' the man said. 'For the next time.'

A single pop of a gunshot.

The thump of deadweight hitting floor.

Evan came up off the chair, almost knocking the phone from its perch. He stared at the speaker holes in disbelief.

As if from a distance, he was aware of Katrin sobbing. 'Sam! Dad? No. No. *No!*'

The voice came again, slicing through the shock static filling Evan's head. 'The bitch is next. Then you.'

The line cut off.

The static thickened until it drowned out everything. He'd made an operational miscalculation, his first in eight years. That night came back to him as a swarm of sensations – the choppy slate of the Potomac, cherry blossoms wadding underfoot, a hot coppery scent piercing the sawdust-filled air of the dank garage.

Katrin's sobs rang in his ears, drawing him back into

142

his shell-shocked body. Her father's blood was on his hands as sure as if he'd fired the shot himself.

As Evan reached for the dead phone, he realized that his hand was shaking for the first time in as long as he could remember. The room gave a vertiginous tilt, the Fourth Commandment falling by the wayside.

It was personal.

20. Red Hands

He stayed with her all day as she wept but did not presume to hold her. At nightfall she pulled him on to the bed and curled into his chest like a child. Those three tattooed stars peeked out from behind her earlobe. Her fingers, resting on his chest, were laden with rings, and bracelets circled her thin wrist, rippling snakelike when she shifted her hand. Her breaths were broken, irregular from all the crying. He rested his hand on her side over the fragile cage of her ribs. When her arm brushed his knuckles, her skin felt soft as cream.

'They're gonna find me next,' she said. 'And they're gonna kill me.'

'No.' Evan stared at the popcorn stucco of the ceiling. 'They won't.'

'Why should I believe you now?' Her voice held no note of malice.

'Because they're not gonna be around much longer.'

He stroked her hair gently until she fell asleep. Then he slipped out. He'd already told her that he needed to run down a few angles and would be back in the morning.

He drove once again to Chinatown. Thirty-six hours later, the apartment complex was still an active crime scene, too populated for him to penetrate. He was eager to investigate the sniper's perch, eager to stand where the sniper had stood, to breathe the same air and see what it told him.

The pop of that gunshot kept returning to Evan, cycling in his mind. Sam White, with that sun-toughened skin, the crinkles at the temples. His final words to his daughter: *Whoever you're with, I hope he protects you.* Evan filled in the blanks, painting the scene from the other end of the phone. The recoil of the pistol, the snap of the head, the concise black dot of an entry hole. And then that distinctive crumpling of a body once life has left it, the herky-jerky cascade of limbs, the limp neck, the chalk-outline sprawl on the floor.

Once home and in the elevator, he found himself standing beside Mrs Rosenbaum, who clutched her tiny snap purse to her belly with both hands as if to ward off snatchers. 'Two more days,' she said, holding up a pair of pruney fingers in case he required a visual. 'Two more days until my son visits with my grand-children. He'll fix my doorframe, no doubt about it. Then I can tell that useless manager . . .'

That voice from the phone looped in Evan's head, drowning her out: *We don't care about money. Not anymore.*

The elevator groaned upward. Evan sensed Ida's gaze as she craned to look up at him.

'Are you all right?' she asked.

He managed a nod.

'You're just standing there breathing,' she said. 'Not even the usual "yes, ma'am, no, ma'am" nonsense. Are you sure you're all right?'

'Yes, ma'am.'

'At least there's that now.'

'I believe this is your floor.'

'Oh. Well.'

For the rest of the ride up, he relished the silence. Entering his place, he beelined for the freezer, then shook himself an U'Luvka martini for so long that his palms adhered to the stainless steel. He poured the vodka over even more ice in a tumbler, craving the antiseptic chill, wanting his teeth to ache as much as his red hands.

Pop of a gunshot.

Thump of deadweight.

Dad? No. No. No!

The tumbler was at his lips. He could breathe the sharp fumes, taste them even at the back of his tongue.

Sending a high-level kill team in on a $2.1-million marker seemed overzealous, but Vegas was clearly willing to go to extremes to teach a lesson to the next big-ticket loser.

This is our advertising cost. For the next time.

Before he knew what he'd done, he'd hurled the glass across the counter at the back of the sink. It exploded pyrotechnically, shards and ice catching light, throwing rainbow prisms on the muted, blue-tinged paint of the ceiling. The crash sounded unreasonably loud off the tile and metal and concrete.

It'll be okay, he'd told her. *It always has been before.*

An image slotted back into place in his mind: Sam's DMV picture, taken on an ordinary day in an ordinary life. A denim shirt collar poking up into view. Tousled gray-white hair.

Dad taught me pretty much everything.

Evan's legs moved him down the hall, past the row of Japanese woodblock prints and the nineteenth-century katana mounted on the wall. He cleared the doorway, and the master suite sprawled before him.

Pop of a gunshot.

He found himself on his knees before the bureau, tugging open the bottom drawer, sweeping aside his boxer briefs to reveal that carved crescent catch.

Thump of deadweight.

His fingernail caught, and the false bottom of the drawer lifted. He removed the thin veneered particleboard and dropped it on to the floor beside him. On his knees he stared down into the newly revealed depths of the drawer, his breath tight in his throat.

Inside rested a torn blue flannel shirt, stiff with blood that had gone black with age.

A relic.

21. Dead Drop

Armed with only the training he has amassed over the past seven years, Evan finds himself navigating a treacherous new reality in treacherous new lands. There are no faces he recognizes, no safe havens, no conversations in his native tongue. He learns when to drift, when to anchor, when to project a potency beyond his nineteen years. Together in the comforting flicker of a birch fire in the farmhouse, he and Jack had built an operational alias that Evan wears now like a well-loved overcoat. It is composed of more truths than lies, the easier for Evan to align himself with it. Jack taught him the difference between acting his cover and living his cover. Evan does not act. He believes, laying down genuine emotion over the false foundation.

Missions follow, too many to count. Evan and Jack communicate by typing inside the same message saved in the drafts folder of Evan's e-mail account. That way not a word is actually transmitted over the Internet, where it could be detected or captured. From various countries on various continents, Evan gets photographs, addresses, instructions. He reads, replies, saves, or deletes.

For a dormant account, the.nowhere.man@gmail.com has an extremely active drafts folder.

Evan dispatches an Egyptian operative in a treetop lodge in Kenya, a drug lord in a São Paulo bathhouse, a Syrian rebel in the storage room of a lampshade shop in Gaza. In a dreary Lebanese slum, Evan modifies orders by removing a car bomb after his target proves to drive only with his children in the backseat. He winds up infiltrating an armed compound and shooting the man in bed, a dangerous improvisation that draws a rare censure from Jack.

Then 9/11 brings a tidal-wave surge in activity, Evan conducting more denied-area operations than ever and also moving unseen through Spain, France, Italy, lending a little uninvited help to friends. At some point – though it is not a distinct moment – his alias becomes known by three-initial agencies in certain territories. The ever-powerful databases have identified patterns of activity that are ascribed to him. The Nowhere Man: executioner and terrorist, wanted for a variety of offenses by a variety of nations, including the United States of America. But this doesn't concern him, as he doesn't technically exist. No clear photograph of him can be found in any file the world over. As his legend grows within particular shadowy circles, quite a few missions are misattributed to him. Raids are conducted to capture him, often in the wrong hemisphere. At least twice a suitable candidate is killed and the Nowhere Man taken off the rolls until another covert action demonstrates his apparent immortality.

Only Jack knows. He remains Evan's sole link to legitimacy. To the rest of the world and his own government, Evan is a wanted man. Jack takes his orders from people at the highest level, and there they perch, breathing the rarefied air, enjoying the ultimate protection. Evan is plausible deniability personified. He is an enemy of the very state he protects and serves. Ball bearings within ball bearings.

He nearly forgets that there are others like him until one winter morning in his twenty-ninth year. At a dead drop in Copenhagen, he receives the message.

'I am one of you. Would like to meet. The Ice Bar, Oslo.' *A date and time are given.*

It is signed 'Orphan Y.'

He stands for a time, note in hand. Snowflakes land on the paper but do not melt. He already knows two things – that he will go and that he will not tell Jack.

He arrives well before the appointed hour, surveilling the block, the bar, exits and entrances, stairwells and tables. The bar features a long glass-walled encasement running the length of the north wall, kept as cold as a freezer. Near the door of the encasement, fur coats hang, donned by men and women alike before they enter. Inside, slate ledges display innumerable bottles of vodka and aquavit. A bartender serves each chosen spirit in a shot glass made of ice.

The rest of the bar is stark and modern. Waitresses distribute pickled herring and reindeer satay on wooden paddles. Evan chooses a corner booth within leaping distance of the kitchen's swinging doors and sets a revolver on the cushioned bench beside him, the length of the barrel pressing into his thigh, aiming out.

He spots the man the moment he enters, the bearing instantly recognizable even seventeen years later.

Same ginger hair, same ruddy complexion.

He winds through the crowd, peels off his winter coat, stands opposite Evan. They stare at each other. Fine hairs bristle on Charles Van Sciver's arms. Across from them, in the freezer, a group of drunken young people, bearlike in their furs, throw back drinks, hurl their ice shot glasses against the glass wall, and high-five.

'Evan. Holy shit, huh?' *Van Sciver says. He slides into a chair, takes in the upscale decor.* 'We're a long way from the Pride House Group Home, aren't we?'

'How did you find that dead drop to contact me?'

'We're well trained.' A half smile. 'I do appreciate your coming.'

'Why Oslo?'

'I'm here for a mission.' He hails the waitress, orders two glasses of aquavit, then returns his attention to Evan. 'I wanted to see someone else who doesn't exist. Nice to have a reminder now and then that we're really here.'

The drinks arrive, and Van Sciver lifts his in a toast. They clink.

'I heard about you now and then during training,' Van Sciver says. 'Passing references. They used your code name, of course, but I knew. Orphan Zero and you, best of the best.'

The notion of Evan's reputation spreading through the Orphan Program seems to him bizarre. Almost as bizarre as sitting across from someone with shared experiences. And a shared history as well. For most of his life, Evan has operated without a present, let alone a past.

'You had a handler,' Evan asks. 'And a house?'

'Oh, yeah, the whole nine. My dad, he was great. Laid out the Edicts, a way of life. He put me in the world.'

Curiosity burns inside Evan, fanned by every tantalizing detail, and he tells himself to dial it back, to remain on guard despite this sudden, unexpected, hard-to-define connection – if not camaraderie, then at least an uneasy rapport. He sips, the Norwegian aquavit smokier than its Danish counterpart.

They talk for a time, being careful but not too careful, nibbling at the edges of things. Mission stories stripped of proper nouns. Training incidents. Operational mishaps.

The glass-walled freezer opposite them fills up, more men and women in fur coats crowding together in the tight space, raucous cheers, shattering ice glasses, but Evan barely registers the annoyance. His and Van Sciver's dimly lit table seems a haven from the noise and revelry, a quiet place in the world.

Van Sciver gulps his sixth shot, though he seems unaffected by the alcohol. 'What I like best?' he says. 'The glorious simplicity. There are orders and nothing else.'

A discomfort bubbles up from the base of Evan's skull, though he can't put a name to it. ' "Nothing else"?'

Van Sciver shakes his head. 'Just getting it done. I was in and out of the Sandbox for a time, playing some offense. This one day I was tucked into the hillside behind a mansion, got a high-value target in the scope through a kitchen window. Tough shot – two hundred and change, wind factor, narrow vantage. But I had it. Problem was his kid, right? Maybe six years old, sitting in his lap. And there are security patrols working the mountain, so I have to roll in and out of the brush at intervals. I couldn't get the target clean in the scope without that kid. And my window's closing. Dusk coming on.' He wets his lips. 'So I zero in on the kid's eye socket, right? One less skull wall for refraction. I lined it up. Then I thought about it.' His big hand closes around the delicate cordial glass. He sips.

Evan has been there himself, on his very first mission, hiding in a fetid Eastern Bloc sewer, sniper rifle aimed through a curb drainage grate, his scope zeroed in on the eye of an innocent. He leans forward. 'What'd you do?'

'I took the shot.' Van Sciver's thumb and forefinger twist the stem of the glass back and forth. 'Edict Twelve: Any means necessary.'

Evan's head feels slightly numb from the booze and Van

Sciver's revelation, but through it he also feels a swell of affection for Jack. He wonders just how different Jack's rules are from those of the other handlers.

He hears himself ask, 'Did it work?'

'The round didn't kill him, but the bone frags did.' Van Sciver picks up his drink, seems to think better of it, puts it back down. 'I turned a six-year-old's skull into a weapon,' he says, with some measure of dark pride. 'I had to get it done. And I did. We don't question. We take our marching orders. And we march.'

There is a flat shine to Charles's eyes, the certainty of a True Believer, and Evan feels an unexpected stab of envy. What an easier line to walk. With the envy comes a degree of fascination.

'Do you ever wonder . . . ?'

'What?' Charles prompts.

Evan rotates his glass in its condensation ring, strives to reframe the question more specifically. 'How do you know he was a terrorist?'

'Because I shot him.'

Evan does his best to keep his reaction from his face, but Van Sciver must read something in him anyway, because he adds, 'That's how the game's played. You don't like the rules, play a different game.' He tosses back the remainder of his shot and rises, tugging on his coat. 'It is what it is, and that's all that it is.'

Evan remains sitting. They stare at each other for a moment, and then Evan gives a little nod. 'See you somewhere or somewhere else.'

He knows there will be no closing pleasantries, but even so, the abruptness with which Van Sciver turns on his heel and walks away catches him by surprise. In the freezer the revelers pound shots and send their ice glasses crashing to the floor. Van Sciver threads through the tables and slips into the freezer, enveloped in the press of bodies.

Through the big glass wall, Evan watches him loop an arm around one drunken man's neck and peel him slightly away from the others, who are toasting raucously with their next round. Booze trickles down their wrists on to the cuffs of their fur coats. They shoot the vodka. Wearing a loose grin, Van Sciver whispers in the ear of the drunken man, who is nodding in flush-faced agreement – the instant bonding of the inebriated. As the next volley of ice glasses shatter against the concrete, the man jerks in Van Sciver's grasp. High fives are thrown all around them. Someone climbs up on the bar, nearly slipping. Van Sciver leans the drunken man against the glass wall and guides him down so he's sitting on the floor. His back leaves a dark smudge on the pane. His head tips forward, chin to chest, and he is still. Van Sciver lifts a hat from one of the other partiers and sets it on the man's drooping head, tilted over his face. Just another passed-out fool. His friends point at him, laugh, and keep drinking.

As Van Sciver glides out of the freezer room, his ruddy face finds Evan for a split second. He shoots a wink and is gone in the crowd.

He'd said it himself: he was here for a mission. Evan has to admire the cold-blooded efficiency. Two birds. One stone.

He throws down a wad of kroner and takes his leave.

Over the following months, the meeting with Van Sciver weighs on him. Snatches of their conversation return at inconvenient moments. Any means necessary . . . We don't question . . . Because I shot him . . . A moral blurriness has been introduced to the equation that Evan cannot, no matter how hard he tries, pull into focus.

And the missions keep pinging into the drafts folder of the. *nowhere.man@gmail.com.* *The summer finds him in Yemen, on the trail of a financier to radical imams. On an afternoon baked into lethargy by a gravy-heavy heat, he finally catches up to the man on an outing at a park. Hours pass as Evan waits for the man to separate from his young wife. Finally he heads into the filthy public bathroom, where Evan garrotes him beside the stall. A messy, up-close business. The man fights, kicking hard enough to break one of the porcelain urinals. After, Evan's shirt is little more than a torn rag of sweat and blood.*

When he gets cleaned up and back to his hotel, the local stations are lit up with news of a dead human-rights activist whose face happens to match that of the man Evan has just dispatched. He feels a dull thudding in his stomach, the beat of paranoia. Or is it doubt? Doubt is one thing he cannot afford.

He requests phone contact with Jack, and two hours later, it is granted. He reaches Jack per the new standard protocol — burner cell phone to burner cell phone — and Jack immediately jumps into housekeeping. 'I moved another eight-figure sum through the Isle of Man. It'll octopus out to your second-tier accounts, and then —'

'Stop,' Evan says.

Jack does.

'He wasn't a financier,' Evan says. 'I saw on TV he was a human-rights activist.'

'It says news, not truth.'

'Let's skip the maxims this time out,' Evan says. 'This is starting to feel arbitrary.'

Jack sighs across the receiver. Then he says, 'I had to put Strider down this morning. Stopped eating. Belly full of tumors.'

Evan feels the loss in his gut, his throat. 'I'm sorry.'

He hears the clink of ice in a glass. He imagines the handsome dog's creep beneath the dinner table, the feel of the muzzle slurping a secreted handful of turkey from his cupped palm. The closest thing to a brother he ever had.

Jack interrupts his thoughts. 'What are you telling me?'

The feeling of grief still enfolds Evan. He is unaccustomed to it. It takes him a beat to reorient himself. 'Maybe I need a break.'

'You're saying you want to come in?'

'I'm saying I need a break.'

'You can't have one. Not right now.'

'Next mission is set?'

'In your folder already.'

Evan is sitting cross-legged on a bed on the top floor of a crumbling hotel. The room is so small he can reach across and pull his laptop from the wobbly wooden desk. Pinching the phone between his shoulder and cheek, he logs in to his account. The sash window is crookedly open, overlooking blocky beige buildings, strings of drying laundry. The air hangs hot and still in the room.

'Hold on,' he says. 'I'm there.'

He clicks on the drafts folder. He opens the sole e-mail-in-progress. The beach ball spins as the photo loads.

He sees the face, and the breath leaves his lungs. The sounds of traffic fade. There is nothing but a white-noise rush at his ears. He blinks hard around his thumb and forefinger, pinching the bridge of his nose, but when he looks back up, the pixelated photo is the same.

Charles Van Sciver.

Jack reads something in the silence as only he can. 'You recognize him.'

'Yes.'

'From the home.'

'Yes. And.'

'And what?'

Evan stands up, goes to the window, trying to find fresh air. But the air is all the same here – in this room, outside, in the whole bone-dry country. 'We met once. I know. Who he is now.'

'You met? That's an unfortunate irregularity.'

'Call it what you like. If he's an Orphan like me, why is he landing in my e-mail account?'

'He's been compromised. A couple of our guys . . .'

Evan could hear the pain in Jack's voice. 'What?' he pressed.

'They went to the other side.'

'Do you have any more information than that?'

'I don't.'

'Well, if you want me to hunt down an Orphan, you'd better unfuck Washington and get me a specific answer as to why.'

'There are no answers. You know this.'

'That doesn't mean there aren't questions. The Sixth Commandment – or did you forget?'

Evan looks across at the open laptop. He sees Van Sciver staring out, but he also sees the young Van Sciver, circling them up on the blacktopped basketball courts in the shadow of the high-rise Lafayette Courts projects, a huddle of young thugs with nothing but time and nothing better to do.

'I won't do it,' Evan says. 'I won't kill my own. He came up with me.'

'He's dead anyways,' Jack says. 'It'll be you or someone else.'

'That strikes me,' Evan says, 'as a faulty moral argument.'

A silence. Then Jack says, 'Fair enough. Head back to Frankfurt. They'll send someone to clean up behind you there.'

'They always do.'

Evan hangs up.

He initiates another call three days later, dialing the number of the next burner cell phone on the list he has memorized. Jack answers in the kitchen; Evan can hear the tail end of the coffee's percolating.

'I need to see you,' he says.

'No way. You are taking a lot of heat for the Bulgaria job – you could be wrapped in surveillance right now.'

'I'm not.'

'How do you know?'

'Because. You trained me.'

A beat.

Then Jack says, 'This is an irregular contact.'

For Jack there is no word more damning than 'irregular'.

'It's an irregular life. I need to see you. Now.'

'No. Stay in Germany. Get off the radar. You'll never make it into the country right now.'

'I'm calling you from L Street and Connecticut Ave.'

The ensuing silence is protracted.

Jack says, 'There may have been a leak on this end. I don't want to be drawn out. I'm watching my movements.'

The Bulgaria job. A leak. Uncharacteristic excuses from a man who does not make any.

Jack says nothing. Evan doesn't either.

At last Jack caves. 'There's an underground parking lot on Ohio Drive directly south of the Jefferson Memorial. It's closed for construction. I'll be at P3 at midnight. For five minutes.'

He leaves Evan with a dial tone.

After nightfall Evan walks along the choppy slate of the

Potomac, hands shoved in his pockets. The cherry trees are in bloom, and he is surprised, as always, at how little fragrance they give off. The fallen blossoms wad underfoot.

He finds the structure and does a few walk-bys before approaching, threading through orange cones and hazard tape. A makeshift plywood sheet has been nailed too often over the door to the north stairwell, and it unseats readily with a gentle prying. He walks each level, moving between the slumbering cement mixers and construction trucks loaded with equipment. He descends to P3, surveils the perimeter of the dark floor, and tucks in behind a concrete pillar to wait. For over two hours, he makes not a single move, as inanimate as the gear and vehicles surrounding him.

At midnight on the dot, Jack materializes from the far end of P3, where, to Evan's knowledge, there is no stairwell. Then again, it's a magic trick befitting a onetime station chief. Ball bearings within ball bearings.

His footsteps tick-tock across the open. A glowing red elevator sign casts him in severe light, stretching his shadow across the oil-stained floor. He stops in the open, looking directly at the patch of darkness hiding Evan.

'Well?' he says.

Evan emerges. They embrace. Jack holds him for an extra beat. It has been twenty-six months since the last time they saw each other – a fifteen-minute meet in a coffee shop in Cartagena. The years have made Jack slightly more jowly, though he still looks fit, no extra padding. The sleeves of his blue flannel shirt are cuffed up past his forearms, which are as muscular as ever. Baseball-catcher arms.

When they pull apart, Evan scans the parking level. Clears his throat. 'I'm out,' he says.

Jack takes his measure. 'You're never out. You know this. Without me you're just –'

'A war criminal. I know. But I'm going underground. The Smoke Contingency.'

The designation, a joking play on his name, had become a shorthand between them.

'We cannot be having this conversation,' Jack says. 'Not here, not now. Do you understand me? I know you think you're alone out there. But there are protections I afford you. The well-placed phone call. The friend at the passport checkpoint. I am the only person who –'

Emotion crowds Evan's chest – a smothering black claustrophobia. 'I can't do it anymore!'

The sharp words ring off the concrete pillars and walls. He cannot recall the last time he's allowed emotion to color his voice. He wipes his mouth, looks away.

Jack blinks. He is looking at Evan in a way he never has before, a parent noticing for the first time that his child is no longer a child. His eyes are moist, his lips firm. He is not at risk of crying, and yet his expression seems a precursor to the act.

'I wanted you to see more than black and white. I wanted you to remain . . . human. In this, perhaps, I failed you.' He blinks again, twice, his big square head canted, pointed at the tips of Evan's shoes. 'I'm sorry, son.'

Too late, Evan feels the rumble of a moving vehicle through the soles of his shoes. He tenses. An engine roars, and headlights sweep the north wall like a prison watchtower light. At the far end of the parking level, a black SUV careens down the circular ramp from P2, bottoming out, riding a cascade of sparks.

Already two guns are firing through the windshield, flares of light through spiderwebbing glass. Jack hooks Evan's arms and tugs him behind a pillar, rounds powdering the concrete inches from their faces. Evan has his Wilson drawn, and he rolls across the back of the pillar and out the other side, holding a Weaver shooting stance, his bladed body presenting a narrower target. As the SUV barrels toward them, he fires into the shattered maw of the windshield.

A bullet rifles by, close enough that he can feel the heat at the side of his neck, but his hands stay steady, his aim sure. He cannot see through the windshield, not yet, but he places rounds through both front seats and whoever occupies them. The SUV's roar diminishes, the tires slow. Evan dumps a mag, loads another, keeps firing even after the cabin is decimated, even as the vehicle slows, slows, the broad hood nearing, the front bumper kissing his thighs as it finally stops.

The red elevator light illuminates the interior, two riddled bodies splayed forward against the dashboard. Hair and bone.

From behind him he hears a gurgle. Jack, slumped against the pillar, his blue flannel shirt sopped at the shoulder. The blood is bright, arterial. Jack's hand, gripping the wound, is so uniformly coated that it seems as though he has slipped on a crimson glove.

A blip of missing time and then Evan is on his knees, pulling off Jack's shirt. The crimson stripe claims the white undershirt, angled like a sash, expanding through the cotton even now. Jack's hand shifts, and a straw-thin spray squirts between his fingers.

Jack is saying something. Evan has to tell his brain to take in the sounds, to shape them into words, to ascribe meaning to the words.

'I'm already dead,' Jack says. 'It caught the brachial.'

'You don't know that. You don't —'

'I know that.' He lifts a callused hand, lays it against Evan's cheek perhaps for the first time ever.

Wafting down the shafts and the curved ramp, the sound of police sirens. A hot-copper scent cuts through the sweet smell of sawdust.

'I'm going to die,' Jack says. 'Don't blow cover. Listen to me.' A paroxysm of pain racks his body, but he fights out the words. 'This is not your fault. I made the decision to meet you. I did. Go. Leave me. Go.'

Evan thinks he is choking, but then he feels the wet on his cheeks and realizes what is happening to his face. The sirens are closer now, a chorus of warbling screams. 'No,' he says. 'I won't go. I won't —'

Jack's good hand drops to his belt, and there is a clank, and then his service pistol is up between them. He aims it at Evan. 'Go.'

'You wouldn't.'

Jack's gaze is steady, focused. 'Have I ever lied to you?'

Evan stands up, stumbles back a step. He thinks about the warnings Jack gave him. Heat from the Bulgaria job. A potential leak. I don't want to be drawn out.

And yet Evan had done precisely that.

He throws a panicked look over at the smoking SUV, the mystery bodies slumped forward, faceless. Back to Jack, each breath wheezing out of him. Evan wants there to be more time, but there is no more time. It dawns on him that Jack's flannel shirt is still mopped around his hand. His fist tightens around it, moisture spreading between his fingers. Somewhere above them tires screech. Boots on concrete.

'Son,' Jack says gently. 'It's time to go.' He rotates the barrel beneath his own chin.

Backing up, Evan arms the tears from his face. He takes another step back, and another, and then finally he turns.

Running away, he hears the gunshot.

22. Pieces of His True Self

Evan came back to himself kneeling on his bedroom floor before the open dresser drawer, the bloodstained collar of Jack's flannel shirt looped around his hand like a rosary. The gunshot seemed to echo through the doorways of his condo, a ghost sound that filled the air all around and yet had no source. That noise had sent him into a new life. He'd slipped out of that underground parking structure beneath the Jefferson Memorial and into a different existence.

The first weeks after Jack's death he'd spent in a rented cabin in the Alleghenies, alone with the smell of pine mulch and the rustle of leaves. In his entire life, he'd known only one genuine human connection, and the loss of it had left a hole clean through his center. In his bones, his chest, beneath the vault of his ribs, he ached as if the damage were physical. In a way he supposed it was.

Either he'd drawn Jack into the open or he had been followed himself. Two marked men in the same location, a public meet that Evan had insisted on.

This is not your fault. I made the decision to meet you.

No matter Jack's intent, his words conveyed the opposite. Evan replayed them, hearing them as he'd heard Jack's whiskey voice reading him Shakespeare by the light of the fire when he was a kid: *And Brutus is an honorable man.*

In that drafty cabin, Evan hibernated, grief bleeding him of energy. At the month mark, he started to emerge from the etherlike stupor, grasping that Jack's murder had ramifications beyond the emotional. Evan's only tie to legitimacy had also bled out on the concrete floor of P3.

He had no handler, no contacts inside the government, no nation that wasn't actively hunting him, even the one he served. He was, in a word, untethered.

Jack's voice cut through the haze: *Get over yourself, son. There is no emotion more useless than self-pity.*

Evan rose that morning, walked into the crisp autumn breeze, and gazed across the slopes. They were stubbled with red spruce, the Christmas-tree smell sharpening the air. Needles stabbed his bare feet. The wind blew clear through him, and he had a sense of a wider world and his place within it.

He had a virtually limitless bank account, a particular skill set, and nothing to do. He was untethered, yes, but that also meant he was free.

He moved to Los Angeles, the farthest he could get from D. C. without tumbling off the edge of the country. And he rebuilt. A third life, in the open as well as in the shadows. An operational alias built with pieces of his true self. A cover that let him hide in plain sight. He stayed mission-ready. Kept fit and trained up. He never knew who would come looking, what fist might knock on his door.

Several years passed.

He stayed alert, vigilant, kept his ear to the ground to listen for underworld tremors. Word filtered back to him through various sources that the Orphan Program had been dismantled, the operators scattered to the four winds. He never learned the fate of those Orphans who turned, but he imagined that the others now sold their specialized services to the highest bidder or had retired to a beach in a quiet corner of the world. Neither option appealed to him.

And so he decided to put his training to personal use. A pro bono freelancer, helping others who could not help themselves. Either way he had a calling, aligned with the heading of his own moral compass. Five years, a dozen successful missions.

And now he had failed.

Pop of a gunshot.

Thump of deadweight.

The blue flannel shirt stained with Jack's blood seemed an indictment and a testament of the day's loss, his own Shroud of Turin.

Dad? No. No. No.

Evan laid the stiff fabric gently in the false bottom of the drawer, lowered the concealing particleboard over it, and rearranged his clothes. The drawer closed with the faintest click.

He couldn't save his own dad. He didn't save Katrin's.

All he could offer her now was vengeance.

He passed the floating Maglev bed on his way out, padded down the cold hall with the Japanese wood-block prints and the mounted sword.

Shards of the tumbler lay scattered across the counter, in the sink. A sharp alcohol waft reached him, the antiseptic fragrance of overpriced vodka. He swept up the bits of glass. Wet a hand towel and wiped down the counter, the backsplash. One of the reflective subway tiles had sustained a tiny chip. He worked the flaw with his fingernail, as if he could sand it back to perfection.

It remained.

He'd just sat down, exhaled deeply, and prepared to meditate, when a vehement shrill jarred him from his peaceful pose on the Turkish rug. He didn't place the sound right away. It returned, strident enough to make his teeth hurt. Not an alarm but his rarely used house phone, installed only because a local number was required for the HOA Resident Directory.

He'd just picked up when Mia's voice came at him. 'Drain cleaner in water bottles? What were you thinking?'

Evan exhaled quietly.

'Look, I know you were joking. He *told* me it was a joke. But if he repeats that to a teacher? It would be considered a terroristic threat. You don't understand how insane schools are these days.'

Evan rolled his lips over his teeth. Bit down. Told the muscles of his neck to relax. 'You're right.'

'You know what? This isn't your fault. It's my fault. I should've . . . I don't know –'

'I get it,' Evan said.

'Okay.' A brief pause. 'Um. Goodbye, then.'

'Goodbye.'

Well, that was that. Good. No complications. No distractions. He'd made a brief, uncharacteristic foray into a sticky domestic situation, and now he could retreat into dealing with his work and the considerable danger facing him and Katrin.

The bitch is next. Then you.

In the morning he'd regroup with Katrin. He'd run down the people behind the murder of her father. And he'd eliminate them before they could pose a further threat.

Forgoing his meditation, he walked down the hall, the concrete cool beneath his bare feet. He took a hot shower, the steam burning his lungs, then toweled off. The floating platform that held his mattress wobbled ever so slightly as he slipped into bed. He cleared a space inside his mind, a park of his own, and populated it with the oak trees of his childhood, the ones visible from the window of his dormer room in Jack's house. He'd always envisioned bounding across the burnt-orange canopy, forty feet off the ground. He counted down slowly from ten, part of a self-hypnotic technique for falling asleep.

He'd just hit zero and drifted off when the perimeter alarm sounded. A staccato series of beeps – external intruder, windows or balconies.

He flipped off the bed, landing in a four-point feet-and-hands sprawl on the floor. Two shoulder rolls took him through the door into the bathroom. He gripped the hot-water lever, shoving through into the Vault.

His eyes swept the monitors. Nothing, nothing – *there*. Bumping against his bedroom window, a foreign object.

He exhaled with annoyance when he realized what it was.

After silencing the alarm, he walked back into his room and raised the armored sunscreen. Floating outside his window, a balloon.

With the logo of a children's shoe store on it.

Each upper-story window of Castle Heights tilted open only two feet at the top before a locked hinge stopped it for safety. Evan had disabled the hinge on his bedroom in case he needed to exit the building quickly in the event of a frontal assault on the penthouse. Letting the pane yawn wide now, he tugged the balloon inside. Knotted around the mouth was a kite string that tailed down the side of the building to – he assumed – the twelfth floor. A folded note was Scotch-taped on the balloon's side. Evan raised the flap of paper and read.

'I'm sorry I told Mom yor joke. Do you fergive me? Chek Yes or No. Your frend, Peter.'

Taped beside the note on the balloon, a stubby pencil and a sewing needle.

The grinding of Evan's teeth vibrated his skull. He had a team of professional assassins tracking him and the woman he'd sworn to protect. Her father, murdered. Two Commandments and counting already out the window. The last thing he needed was an eight-year-old kid invading his condo and his sleep with schoolroom notes.

Evan closed the window hard on the kite string and went back to his bed. He pulled the sheets up and floated there in the darkness on his levitating mattress, detached from the world. He counted down from ten, but sleep didn't come. He kept his eyes closed, focused on his body, the weight of his bones, his own quiet breathing. From time to time, he could hear the balloon squeaking faintly against the ceiling.

Exasperated, he threw back the sheets and crossed to the balloon. He pulled off the pencil, made an X in the 'Yes' box, and popped the balloon with the conveniently supplied needle. He opened the window and threw the deflated sack to the wind. He started to cinch the window closed again, then hesitated. He stuck his head out in time to see the white string being taken up through a window nine stories below by two tiny hands.

23. Reading the Chessboard

'What are you doing?' Katrin asked. She'd risen from the desk chair to face him imploringly across the drab motel room. More precisely, to face his back.

Evan kept moving, focused not on her but on the room – in fact, on all three adjoining rooms, 9 through 11. They shared an identical layout: blocky furniture, front door, one big window in the front and one in the rear. He'd laid wide the adjoining doors so that standing in Katrin's room – Room 10 – gave him decent sight lines through the space. Now he wanted to obscure those sight lines to his advantage.

'They found us before,' he said. 'We don't know how. Which means we don't know when they will again.' He adjusted the angle of the connecting door to the east so he could see between the hinges to the neighboring rear window. The sheer curtains granted a shadowy view of the industrial trash barrels in the alley beyond and the thin, bobbing branches of a dying white birch. He'd left his businessman-gray Ford Taurus slotted neatly between other sedans in an apartment carport off the alley. After the shooting in Chinatown, he'd kicked his usual precautions into overdrive, retrieving the stashed car from a long-term parking lot adjacent to the Burbank Airport.

Closing one eye for perspective, he swung the door a half inch farther, then another half inch. *There.*

'Every time one of us leaves this room,' he said, 'it increases the risk that they'll find us. Every time we're together, it increases the risk that they'll find us.'

'Can't we just go on the run?' Katrin asked. 'I have my passport in my purse. I've kept it on me ever since this started, and some cash. It's not a lot, but –'

'You can't run from a problem like this,' Evan said, brushing past her. He played with the adjoining door to Room 11 on the other side until it gave him a similar angle through that space as well. Taking the chair Katrin had just vacated, he situated it precisely in the middle of Room 10 so when he sat there he'd maximize the slender vantages he'd created through the hinges of the doors on either side.

'Why not?' she asked.

'It'll catch up to you.' Moving swiftly, he rolled one of the circular nightstands over to the front window. Retrieving his briefcase from the bed, he set it on the nightstand, input the code, and lifted the lid so its inset pinhole lens faced the sliver of a break in the front curtains. 'This team is very good at what they do. We need to bed down, figure out a counterattack, not get drawn out.' On his RoamZone cell, he called up the video feed from the lens and repositioned the briefcase until his phone screen showed a full capture of the parking lot in front.

Then he sat in the chair with his back to the briefcase and propped his RoamZone against the TV in front of him, establishing a more-or-less 360-degree view through the three adjoining rooms and the outside space around them. For the first time since arriving, he looked fully at her.

Her petiteness struck him. She had the finely made build of a dancer – slender arms that still held muscle, delicate wrists, shoulders-back posture. She wore a scarf headband under which her short bangs stuck out jaggedly. Her lashes held mascara – heavy and yet not overdone, and her eyes looked weary, edged with pink. A flush still showed at her throat and the rim of her nose, the tinge pronounced given her milk-white skin. Clearly there'd been a lot of crying and very little sleep, though she'd held it together since he'd arrived.

'You're right,' she said. 'What do I care anymore? They already killed my dad.' Her voice was laced with undeniable grief. 'If we stay . . .' Her eyes welled. 'Will you get them for what they did?' She crouched before him, curled her hands over his, looked up at him with those vibrant emerald eyes.

'Yes.'

She stood, blinking to hold in the tears. 'I always come out on the wrong end. Relationships, cards, finances. I know it's my own goddamned fault. But I never get it right. I always lose. And when it mattered the most, with Sam . . .' When she spoke again, her voice was hoarse. 'I wanted so bad for this time to be different. And it wasn't.' She seemed to come back to the present, regarding him there in the chair with his odd surveillance setup. 'What do I even call you? "The

Nowhere Man" is a little stilted, right?' She gave a dying laugh. 'Watch out for that sniper behind you, *Nowhere Man*. Hey, *Nowhere Man*, can you pass the salt?'

'Evan,' he said.

'Is that your real name?'

'Does it matter?'

'Evan,' she said, trying it on. 'Evan.'

In the video feed on his phone's screen, a rusty pickup pulled in to the parking lot. An old guy with a wispy white mustache climbed out and legged his way to reception.

'We're going to break apart every aspect of what happened,' Evan said, 'and figure out how they tracked us down in the restaurant. But first we need to figure out some protocols. You should keep to the room as much as possible. When I'm not with you, you need to be extremely cautious. Keep your head on a swivel.'

'For what?'

'Anyone who stands out.'

'How am I supposed to do that? How am I supposed to do *anything* if they're as good as you say they are?'

The rumble of an engine came audible through the rear wall. Evan tracked the car's shadow as it flickered past the sheer curtains of the three motel rooms, one after the other. Once the sound faded, he returned his focus to Katrin. 'You play poker.'

'Yes.'

'Tell me how you read your opponents.'

'That's not the same –'

'Tell me.'

She took a deep breath. Held it. Then: 'Perfectionists are easy to pick up. Always polishing their glasses. Clipped nails. They stack their chips just so. They tend to be gun-shy, easier to bluff. When they're close to the felt, they play tight.' She sank on to the bed, curled her feet beneath her.

On the video feed, Evan watched the guy with the white mustache exit reception, twirling a key around his finger. He stepped out of frame, and a moment later Evan sensed the shudder of a door opening and closing far up the row of rooms.

'The eyes are a tell, which is why the pros wear sunglasses and baseball caps,' Katrin was saying. 'The pupils constrict at a bad hand, though it's hard to catch if the lighting's bad. Guys'll stare longer at a *good* hand before flopping. There's some bullshit about liars looking away, breaking eye contact, blinking more, but that's not true with practiced liars. They'll stare a hole right through you. And you have to listen to them, too. Their speech is more fluid when they're confident.'

Another movement on the video feed caught Evan's attention. An SUV turning in to the parking lot from the westbound lane. It idled up in front of reception. He refocused his gaze on Katrin. 'Like your speech now?'

She almost smiled. 'Yes. And when they're tilted, their feet point in.'

'Tilted?'

'Off their game. Lacking confidence. But you can't always see beneath the table, so . . .' A one-shouldered shrug. 'Most important is reading the patterns.'

No one had exited the SUV yet. Through the thin walls, Evan could hear it idling outside. The briefcase lens gave him a nice clear side view on his cell-phone feed but no angle on either license plate. The windows were not tinted, and there were two men in the front, having a discussion. Nothing alarming. Yet.

'Some players go hyperaggressive and bluff hard and often, even when they're card dead. You can scoop a lot of pots if you know when to call them. And sometimes it's smart to bluff – and lose on purpose. It's money well spent if it shows you're unpredictable. Think of it as a business expense that'll pay dividends in future hands. That's the thing about poker. You're not playing your hand. You're playing the *other guy's* hand.'

'And that,' Evan said, 'is what we're going to do with the people who killed your father.'

Her mouth parted slightly, and he watched the realization roll across her face.

A purple Scion now entered the parking lot from the eastbound lane, followed by a second SUV. Evan leaned forward and plucked up his phone, palming it for a better view as they turned in.

Neither had a license plate.

The Scion parked at the edge of the lot near the street while the second SUV crept forward.

Evan stood up.

'What?' Katrin said. 'What?'

'Did you make a phone call from this room?'

'No.'

The SUV coasted past the other one down by

reception and headed through the short drive toward the rear alley.

'You didn't leave? Step out even for a second? Open the door to any delivery guys when you ordered food?'

Evan kept his eyes glued to the video feed. The driver and passenger doors of the first SUV opened, and two men exited. Muscular builds, black T-shirts, light on their feet. Given their bearing and cropped hair, Evan pegged them for ex-military.

'No. *No.* What's going on, Evan?'

The men rested their hands on hip holsters but did not draw. They spread out in the front parking lot just as headlights swept the sheer curtains in the rear of Room 9 next door. The second SUV, arriving in the alley. The men were pinning them in, front and back.

It was impossible that Evan had been tracked – he'd been too careful. Which meant that Katrin had alerted them. And yet there was no denying that sniper round aimed through the restaurant's window directly at her heart.

Her pale skin had grown paler. She stared at him, her lips pressed together, thin and bloodless.

The headlights in the back alley halted, the vehicle just shy of Room 9. The wide perimeter set by the men in the front parking lot encompassed all three adjoining rooms. Which meant they'd likely been tipped.

Evan grabbed Katrin roughly and spun her, frisking her. Whether he trusted her or not, he had to protect her right now. The Tenth and most important

Commandment was seared into muscle memory: *Never let an innocent die.*

He found nothing.

'What are you doing?' Katrin said. 'You're the one who just got here – like last time. You're the one who was probably followed.'

'Under the bed,' he said.

She obeyed, vanishing beneath it, the dust ruffle fluttering into place after her.

Pistol drawn, he stood in position before the chair, peering through the hinge-side gap of the door into Room 9 to his left. A shadow eased barely into view in the lower corner of the rear window, the outline of a gun distinct behind the sheer curtain. The silhouette showed a canister ballooning from the tip of the barrel – a homemade suppressor, likely jerry-rigged from an oil-filter cartridge. Untraceable, intended for one-time use.

An assassin's tool.

A glance at his phone showed the two-man team in the parking lot staying put, holding position. Which meant the assault would come from the rear, through the windows. The men in the parking lot were there to put Evan and Katrin down if they tried to flee through the front door. Exhaust wisping from its tailpipe, the Scion remained at the property's fringe, the overwatch position of whoever was running the mission. The shooter from Chinatown, waiting back at a sniper's distance?

Evan's operational priorities clarified. Which angles to cover, who to take out first, best means of egress.

From beneath the bed, Katrin's jagged breathing came audible, and he shushed her as quietly as he could manage.

The form at Room 9's rear window lowered out of sight. Evan strained to listen for footsteps moving through the alley. He lifted the Wilson, rotating it slowly across the back window directly behind him, gauging the shooter's crawling progress as he passed beneath the sill of Room 10.

At the appropriate interval, movement sparked in Evan's narrow view into Room 11 to his right. The shadowed figure, easing on to his feet again.

A quiet scraping back in Room 9 reached Evan's ears, and then came a muffled pop of the window lock. The partner. A black-gloved hand, ghostly beneath the wind-fluffed curtain, gripped the pane and slid it soundlessly upward.

They were entering the rooms on either side simultaneously.

'What's the point of calling me in if you're gonna keep me in the car?' Candy said.

'Let the field team take the first charge,' Slatcher replied. 'I'm the backstop. You're on cleanup. That *is* your specialty.'

Candy made pouty lips. 'And here I was hoping we'd be getting our hands sticky like old times.'

Wedged behind the wheel of the Scion, Slatcher refocused on the text messages scrolling across his right eyeball. More precisely, at the messages projected from the high-def contact-lens display. Top Dog was talking, and when TD talked, you listened.

Top Dog loved his toys, especially ones that enhanced secure communications. His latest and greatest was wearable technology. The fully pixelated contact lens projected images so they could be perceived with ease. Supposedly molding the liquid crystal cells into a spherical curve had been a bitch, but that wasn't really Slatcher's concern. His concern was keeping the goddamned thing from drying out in the middle of a mission.

TD's last text message scrolled: IS THE AREA CONTAINED?

Slatcher lifted his hands and typed in the air on an imaginary keyboard. His reply appeared in a two-foot float off his face: YES. PERIMETER ESTABLISHED.

He wore radio-frequency-identification-tagged press-on nails to type and send messages literally out of thin air. There was no end to the beauty tech products in Top Dog's bag o' tricks.

Beside him Candy twirled her hair, whistled the chorus from 'Girls Just Wanna Have Fun'.

ARE BOTH TARGETS CONFIRMED?

NOT YET.

WHEN?

One of his men in the front parking lot looked back at the Scion, gave a little nod. Slatcher's fingers danced a few inches above the steering wheel.

NOW.

*

Keeping his eyes on the black-gloved hand reaching through the window of Room 9, Evan reached behind him and lifted the briefcase from the nightstand. He stepped through the adjoining door into 9 and crouched, setting the briefcase quietly on the threadbare carpet just past the threshold. Katrin's sideways face, tight with panic, filled the gap beneath the dust ruffle. She was trembling. Over the bed and through the opposing doorway, the rear curtain of Room 11 billowed up into view, then drifted out of sight again. The window, penetrated.

Evan made a calming gesture to Katrin, a slight sink of one palm toward the floor. Then he pulled back into Room 9.

The intruder readied for entry. One glove gripped the edge of the window frame, braced. A boot rose into sight, slipping through the curtains. Evan gauged the man's position, moving to the blind side. He flattened against the wall next to the window, his back pressed to the drywall.

It had to be silent.

If there were shots, if the intruder shouted or fell back through the window, the team in the parking lot would crash the front doors.

Evan laid his pistol within reach on the carpet and eased open his Strider knife. It gave the faintest click when the black-oxide blade locked.

The menacing bulb of the suppressor sliced through the curtains. A broad shoulder swung into view next, straining beneath the T-shirt.

Evan held position.

The lead boot pointed now, toes feeling for the carpet. Sweat sparkled on the band of the man's neck, in the back of his buzz-cut hair. Veins stood out on his hand and wrist, his grip firm on the pistol.

Evan could have reached out and tapped his shoulder.

The faintest tremble came from the floorboards two rooms across – a boot setting down in Room 11. Evan sensed it more than heard it. He felt a pull to Katrin, hiding one room over, soon to be within reach of the second intruder.

First things first.

He held his focus on the man before him, eliminated all else. Painstakingly, the man drew his upper torso through the curtains and shifted his weight on to his lead leg. He shot a quick glance at the open adjoining door as he drew his other foot through, but Evan remained sunk back in his blind spot.

The man's trailing knee came to his chest, the foot clearing the sill. He eased it to the floor. Straightened. Started to turn.

Evan slid behind him, gripped the back of his head, and whisked the blade across his throat. The man corkscrewed stiffly on to his heels, their bodies aligned chest to spine, a full-body seal to muffle any sounds of struggle. Evan tipped the man's head down hard, chin to chest so the lungs wouldn't suck and give away their position. The gun tumbled from the limp fingers, and

Evan caught it midway to the floor as he sank the man's bulk to the carpet.

Evan deposited him soundlessly on the floor. His heels scraped quietly against the carpet. His eyes rolled up at Evan, the sclera pronounced. His lips guppied, but there would be no sound, not with what had been done to his trachea. The puddle from the severed carotid expanded out and out, wreathing his head like a halo.

Evan moved soundlessly to the brink of Room 10, halting shy of the adjoining door's frame and extracting his RoamZone from his pocket. The briefcase sat open on the floor just back from the threshold, the pinhole lens in the lid feeding his cell screen a tilted swath of the room – seam of wall and ceiling, headboard of the bed, top half of the doorway to Room 11. A head whipped through the frame as the man entered Room 10. The edge of his shoulder remained. He was standing beside the bed under which Katrin hid, but Evan couldn't make out his orientation.

Not the view he needed.

Evan reached toward the threshold with his shoe, nudging the back corner of the briefcase as delicately as he could manage, all the while keeping his eyes on the shifting video feed on his phone.

The side of the man's neck came into the frame. His cheek. One eye. Two. Evan had his head in frame and little more.

The man was scanning the room, not yet noticing

the infinitesimal movement of the briefcase in the shadows beyond the threshold.

Evan's palm was sweating against the hardened-rubber cell case. He watched the feed, debating whether to attack or lie in wait.

Then the man sank from sight.

Evan strained to make out a sound, heard nothing. Was the man searching under the bed? He couldn't afford to wait to find out. With the toe of his shoe, Evan pressed on the briefcase lid, the view in his hand scanning as it tilted down. The bedspread came into sight, one nightstand with a lamp – then the man. He squatted by the mattress, pistol aimed beneath the bed, his other hand reaching for the dust ruffle.

On the tiny screen, Evan made out Katrin's canted head beneath, the flash of her eyes, her open mouth wavering, not yet screaming. The pistol swung, centering on her head.

Evan kicked the briefcase across the threshold into Room 10. It spun on the carpet, rocketing behind the man, the feed on Evan's phone whirling vertiginously. At once the blocky heels of the man's boots loomed large on Evan's screen, the briefcase seemingly stopping right behind him, and his left foot began a startled pivot.

Evan took a single giant lunge through the doorway, grabbing the man's gun hand as it swung to meet him. He caught the inside of the wrist and raked the arm in violent outward rotation, snapping tendon and bone. Already his knife hand was rising, that tanto tip tapping up the man's bared torso – *smack-smack-smack* – each blow placed between a different set of ribs.

The look of surprise on the man's face was pronounced – he was elite, not cannon fodder, and dying clearly wasn't in his playbook.

The gun floated to the bed, bouncing twice, and Evan tilted him down softly on to the mattress on top of it.

Katrin was looking up at him from beneath the bed with an expression he couldn't at first place. Maybe horror.

He held one finger to his lips, extending his other hand to her.

She rolled on to her back, throwing up a hand, and he clasped it around the thumb and whisked her out and on to her feet. A wet gurgling sounded from the bed.

'My God,' she said, too loud. 'Is he . . . ?'

The front window exploded in at them, the pistol reports setting his ears ringing. Evan pivoted to protect Katrin, shards showering his back. Her mouth pressed to his chest, her scream vibrating his skin through his shirt.

He propelled her into Room 11. Sweeping aside the curtains, he half flung her out into the alley and hopped through after her. A crimson feather lay across one porcelain cheek, a stud of glass glittering in the skin.

'Your briefcase,' she said. 'What about –'

He grabbed her hand, yanked her toward the carport and the waiting Taurus. They jumped in, and he pulled

out and down the alley. He accelerated to the first inter-
secting street, then veered right and stopped, idling
behind a Norms Restaurant. A few of the patrons were
hustling out on to the sidewalk, craning in the direction of the gunshots. Others rushed to their cars,
shielding their kids.

'What are you doing?' Katrin said. 'Let's get the hell
out of here. Why'd you stop?'

He took his foot off the brake, letting the car creep
forward, forward, until he could make out the motel
parking lot one block over. The purple Scion remained,
still perched in its spot right off the street.

He pulled the RoamZone out, the feed still active. A
worm's-eye view of the Room 10 carpet, strewn with
broken glass. 'Did you recognize that man?' he asked.

'No.'

'Never saw him before?'

'*No.*'

On the feed, a set of boots approached, and then the
view carouseled, bringing a rugged face into close-up.
One of the men from the first SUV. Behind him,
sprawled across the bed, a pair of legs shuddered.

'How about him?' Evan asked.

'No,' Katrin said. 'I swear.'

The man touched his ear. 'We got two down, Slatch.
Well, shit, one and three-quarters. Gonzalez is fucked.'

The other half of the transmission was not audible.

Behind the man another voice shouted, 'Clear!' His
partner swept by in the background, barreling across
into Room 11. The bark came again: 'Clear!' He ran

back into the main room. 'Looks like they split through the alley. Does he want us to pursue?' The partner cocked his head, looking directly at the lens. 'The fuck?'

'Can we please get out of here?' Katrin said.

Evan shot a look up the block at the Scion, but it gave up nothing, just the glare of the midday sun off the windshield. Whoever was behind the wheel was waiting for the field team to confirm the targets' presence, letting them absorb the higher risk.

They'd absorb more than that.

Katrin again: 'What are we waiting for?'

On Evan's phone the second man approached now, shoulder to shoulder with his partner. They leaned in, peering at the briefcase.

'This,' Evan said, and keyed a code into his phone.

From a block away came a resonant boom. The feed went to static. A few onlookers shrieked. But Evan wasn't watching them.

He was watching the Scion.

At last a tall, bulky man emerged from the driver's seat and stared across the parking lot from behind the open car door. His hands rose and squiggled in the air before him, as if he were playing an imaginary piano.

From the passenger side, a woman emerged. Big floppy hat, sunglasses, shaggy blond hair. The row of rooms was out of view, but smoke wafted across from where Room 10 once was.

The man and woman did not rush to check out the aftermath. Already they were scanning the street, parked cars, the windows of neighboring buildings. Focused not on the explosion or the lost men but on the surrounding area. They were accustomed to diversionary tactics, to secondary attacks, to reading the chessboard.

The big man swept his gaze up the street toward the diner. Before it reached Evan, he dropped the car into reverse, eased back behind the diner, and U-turned for the freeway.

24. Fucked-Up Date

The green freeway signs of the 10 flashed overhead as Evan sliced between two trucks, gunning away from the coast. He had to get Katrin to a secure location, and right now anything beyond his direct control was not secure. Which meant that he was going to do something he'd never done before.

He was going to take a client to one of his safe houses.

He was certain he hadn't been tracked to the motel. So then how had he and Katrin been located? His mind shuffled through possibilities, replaying particular images from the motel as though they were movie clips, slowing them down, freeze-framing to check details. This was an added benefit of mindfulness meditation – it enhanced recall and helped to heighten awareness. That was the aim when meditating or fighting or lifting the latch on his mail slot: to see everything as if for the first time.

He pictured himself climbing out of the car at the motel. Anyone sitting in a parked vehicle in the front lot? No. Any tourists out and about, snapping photos? No, just a mom and two kids waiting on the sidewalk while the father paid the meter. When he'd first checked in, had the receptionist logged his license-plate number? No. There had been a security camera behind the front desk, at a lazy angle across the front counter. Katrin had been with Evan when he'd booked the rooms. Most security footage these days was stored on an online server.

So.

If Evan were the one hunting Katrin, what would *he* have done? Assuming that his target would want to regroup after the sniper near miss, he'd look at every low- to mid-level motel within a thirty-mile radius of the dim sum restaurant. He'd eliminate those without ready freeway access and those that were part of big chains with fixed check-in procedures. Then he'd tap into the security cameras in the remaining lobbies and run facial-recognition software on the resultant feeds. This would require enormous resources and know-how, not to mention a huge amount of luck. Implausible? Highly. But – depending on whom Vegas had hired and how expert they were – not impossible.

If he was going that far, why not consider whether satellite footage had been retrieved from the blocks surrounding the restaurant in the wake of the shooting? His Chrysler would have been lost from imagery in the alley, but it could have been picked up pulling out on to Hill Street. A few blocks later, he'd screeched over into the liquor-store parking lot to wand down Katrin. Had he stayed close enough to the umbra thrown by the building to hide their outlines?

He caught himself, reining his thoughts back to reality. If a mission that grand had been in place, there would've been a full tactical team raiding Lotus Dim Sum, not a sniper in an apartment window across the street. These scenarios were beyond the pale even of his well-cultivated paranoia.

Wasn't it a lot more likely that Katrin had tipped them off?

And yet why would she tip off the people who were trying to kill her?

She faced away in the passenger seat, her feet tucked beneath her, chewing a thumbnail, her forehead pressed to the window. He thought, *What aren't you telling me?*

The blood had dried on her cheek, the glass fragment still glistening in the wound. He'd clean her up when they got to wherever they were going.

He finally decided on his Downtown location, a loft perched five stories above Flower Street with a partial view of the Staples Center. Like all his safe houses, this one was end-stopped, easy to burn in the event something went wrong. The mortgage and all affiliated payments were drawn from a bank fed by a wire from an account owned by a shell corp. His pursuers could monkey up that pole, but they'd find nothing at the top.

Because it was a single room, the loft was the best wired of Evan's places, security cameras capturing the space in its entirety. He needed to watch Katrin when he wasn't with her.

He couldn't trust her.

She didn't speak for the entire drive, not even when he exited Downtown. Pulling in to the subterranean parking level, he felt the cramp of his hands squeezing the steering wheel. He shot a glance across at Katrin, still turned away. No one in the world could connect him to this building. Until now. Every twist of this mission cut closer to his core, knifing deeper into his comfort zone.

The parking rows were crammed – narrow lanes, tight turns, SUVs muscling across the painted lines. Dangling overheads threw dim flares of light. Bicycles plugged into a wall-length metal rack, Kryptonite locks floating in the few empty spots, cinched around front wheels where the frames had been stolen. It was a nice building, but not too nice. Evan found a spot in the back.

When he got out of the car, Katrin still didn't move, so he circled behind and opened the door for her. She emerged languidly, her movements slowed by shock.

Or she was faking it well.

Though the parking level was empty, he adjusted her scarf headband so it crowded her face, hiding the blood-crusted cheek. She stared through him. After grabbing a blocky Hardigg Storm Case from the trunk, he took her up a rear stairwell, and they made it to the fifth floor and into his loft without crossing paths with anyone.

The loft featured only the bare essentials – futon on wooden frame, a few dishes and pans, a set of folded towels on the bathroom sink.

She scanned the room. 'What is this place?'

Evan set down the Storm Case on the floorboards, clicked the latches, and lifted the weatherproof lid.

Various tools and weapons were nestled in the foam lining. He assembled the nonlinear junction detector.

She crossed her arms, flicked her head at the black wand. 'Really? You're gonna scan me *again*? You still don't trust me?'

He stood, the detector at his side. 'I don't know.'

She scraped some of the dried blood off the side of her chin with her fingernail. 'You think I'm . . . what? Wired? Wearing a bug? Implanted with a chip?'

'Maybe.'

'Okay. Okay.' Too exhausted to be angry, she heel-stepped on one shoe, kicked it aside. Then the other. She let her scarf headband flutter to the floor, then tugged her shirt off over her head, careful to pull the collar wide so it wouldn't rub against the cut in her cheek. She reached behind her back, unclasped her bra, let it fall. 'Let's get this over with,' she said. 'For once and for all. I have nothing to hide. No card up my sleeve.' Her hands were at her belt, and then she was stepping out of her jeans, flicking them aside. With her pixie-hipster trappings shed, she was unexpectedly full-figured. She spread her arms. 'I have nothing to hide. Scan me.'

Evan looked at her, doing his best to keep his gaze from her lush form. The cut in her cheek was little more than a nick, though it had bled nicely, as faces did.

She was breathing hard, her ribs rising and falling, her face flushed. But her eye contact remained unflinching. 'Well?'

He stepped forward and scanned her. The swells of

her calves. The curve from hip to waist. The slope of her breasts. The twin strokes of her clavicles. The blunt edge of her hair at her nape.

Then he flattened her clothes on the floor and scanned every seam, every wrinkle. There were new technologies every week – he used plenty of them himself – and he didn't want to miss the faintest wire thread or speck of metal.

The wand emitted nothing more than its customary buzz.

He straightened up from his crouch, and she gestured at her clothes. 'May I?'

He nodded, turning slightly away while she dressed. The day had blended into evening, the lights of the city blinking on beyond the tall tinted window that constituted the south-facing wall.

When she was done, she came around in front of him, held out her hand. 'My turn.'

Though her gaze was intense, her full lips stayed slightly pursed, the first sign of amusement she'd shown since her father was killed. He debated protesting, thought better of it, and handed her the wand.

She scanned him bottom to top, standing on her tiptoes to reach his face. As she passed the circular head of the wand across his temple, he could feel her breath, feather-soft against his neck. She finished and offered up the wand, standing close still, her eyes uptilted.

'Now what?' she said.

'Sit up here on the counter.' He gestured to a spot under one of the recessed ceiling lights, and she hopped up. He retrieved a washcloth and a first-aid kit from the bathroom and returned. After wetting the cloth with warm water from the kitchen tap, he stood in front of her. With her up on the counter and him standing, their faces were about level. She looked from him to the washcloth, then back at him. She parted her knees so he could lean in and work on the cut.

It was superficial, as he'd thought, the glass fragment tiny. With the washcloth he dabbed at the side of her chin, the blood coming off in flakes. As he worked his way up to the cut itself, her wincing grew more pronounced. Her eyes darted nervously to the tweezers, visible in the clear pouch of the first-aid kit.

'Close your eyes,' he said. 'Focus on the pain. What does it feel like?'

The dried blood around the glass was stubborn but gave way under his ministrations. Her closed eyelids flickered. She swallowed hard. 'Like there's a piece of glass embedded in my fucking face.'

'That's a start. Is it hot?'

'Yeah. Hot.'

'Does it have a color?'

'Orange,' she said. 'Orange and yellow.'

'Is it changing?'

'Yeah. It throbs. And then dies down.'

'Pick a part of your body that *doesn't* hurt.'

'My hand,' she said.

Her hand was resting on his shoulder.

'Okay,' he said, reaching slowly for the tweezers. 'Your hand. Focus on that. What's it feel like?'

'It's cool,' she said. 'Steady as a rock.'

'What color is your hand?'

'Cobalt blue.'

'You feel every finger distinctly?'

He felt her hand ripple ever so slightly on his shoulder.

'Yeah,' she said. 'Yeah.' And then – 'You're gonna use the tweezers now, aren't you?'

'I already did.'

She opened her eyes. He gave the piece of glass a jeweler's tilt in the tweezers, and it winked back a star of light.

'That,' she said, 'is magic.'

The cabinet next to the refrigerator held a few basics, and he boiled pasta and heated some sauce. She watched him work at the stovetop.

'This is the most fucked-up date I've ever been on,' she said, and he smirked.

He served her at the counter. She'd slung her purse up beside her, and it yawned open, showing an over-stuffed wallet, a zippered makeup bag, the blue fold of a passport.

While she ate, he walked behind her, squatted above the Storm Case, and started putting away the nonlinear junction detector.

'Can I get something to drink?'

Right on schedule.

The raised lid of the case hid his hand from view as he plucked a tiny glass vial from the foam lining.

'There's a machine in the lobby,' he said. 'Don't go anywhere.'

'Wouldn't dream of it.'

He headed out, took the elevator down, fed a couple of bills into the Coke machine, and chose the darkest shade of Powerade – fruit punch. He took the stairs back up, pausing on an empty landing, and lifted the tiny vial to the light. Inside, a thin layer of what looked like fine black sand shifted as he angled the vial. They were microchips – silicon with trace amounts of copper and magnesium. The technology, developed by the biopharmaceutical industry, had been pirated from a Phase II drug designed to regulate diabetes. Once ingested, the sensors massed, generating a slight voltage when digestive juices were stimulated. This voltage sent a signal to the patient's skin, where a patch relayed the blood-sugar readings to the cell phone of the treating physician. The variation Evan had acquired conveyed instead the GPS bearings of its carrier. If not replenished, it broke down in the body and passed from the system within several days.

Evan poured the particles into the plastic bottle and swished them around, dispersing them until they were lost to the dark red liquid. He continued upstairs.

When he entered the loft, Katrin was behind the counter, cleaning up her dishes. He twisted the cap, pretending to break the seal for her, and offered the bottle.

She shook her head. 'Don't drink that stuff.'

'Stress burns electrolytes,' he said. 'Drink.'

She studied him for a moment, then took the bottle, gulped it halfway down, and left the rest on the counter. Stifling a yawn, she trudged toward the futon. 'I feel like I haven't slept in a month,' she said.

Fully clothed, she burrowed beneath the fluffy white comforter. He put the bottle in the fridge and walked over to her. 'I'll leave a stack of cash on the counter,' he said. 'Same rules as the hotel with regard to ordering food, going out, everything. I will be back sometime tomorrow.'

'Okay, got it,' she said, her voice slurred with exhaustion. She lay on her side, facing away at the tinted window. Across a river of headlights, the Staples Center glowed Lakers purple.

From the inside of the vial's cap, he peeled off a skin-colored patch the size of a dot and readied it on his knuckle so the sticky edge hung halfway off. He crossed to the futon and tucked her in, letting his hand nudge just behind her ear, the patch transferring to her skin beside the three tattooed stars. It was waterproof, thinner than Saran Wrap and just as transparent. It disappeared beautifully.

As he pulled away, she squeezed his wrist and rolled over sleepily. 'I don't know how I'll ever thank you,' she said.

He gave a little nod and adjusted the sheets over her. She rocked back on to her side and let her eyes close.

On the way out, he lifted her passport from her purse.

25. Business of a Certain Type

It was fully dark by the time Evan reached Northridge, the moon a bullet hole through the black dome of the sky. Maneuvering a grid of streets on the flat floor of the Valley, he arrived at the industrial park just off Parthenia. The layout had a movie-studio vibe, blocky buildings scattered like sound stages.

The Taurus's tires crackled across the asphalt between businesses, all of them shuttered for the night. Except one.

A single point of light glowed above the entrance to the last building in the complex. It was a Victorian streetlamp, rising like a prop from a bed of begonias. In place of a light, the streetlamp held a backlit sign that in turn featured a streetlamp illustration, beneath which was written '*CraftFirst Poster Restoration*' in old-timey letters. The Magritte-meta conceit was an appropriate one, as the brick façade housed a business behind a business.

He parked and rang a buzzer on a call box. A moment later the door clicked open and he entered, passing through a brief foyer with periwinkle walls exhibiting Italian noir posters from the forties. Another door, another buzzer, and then he was through into the vast workspace.

Industrial shelving units lined the perimeter, crammed with all order of supplies. Jars of paints, rubber-cement thinner, fine-tipped brushes with tape-padded handles, palette knives and X-Acto blades. Rolls of army duck canvas, Mylar and fine-texture poster backing. Jumbles of corner brackets and frame stretcher bars. The space resembled a factory floor, with various conservators bent over giant square plywood worktables, restoring vintage posters and prints. The rolling tables, positioned haphazardly wherever elbow room was afforded, rose only to the workers' thighs, allowing them ready access to their tasks.

Most of the painters were plugged into iPods, big clamp headphones hugging their skulls. Every last one wore eyeglasses; this kind of work strained the vision. A shiny-haired man adjusted a crinkled British three-sheet of *The Day of the Jackal* between blotter sheets and slipped it into a nineteenth-century cast-iron screw press. Next to him at a wet table, a worker sprayed an olive German *M* poster with a retrofitted insecticide atomizer while his partner sponged at a stained spot gently with Orvus soap, a pure, fragrance-free surfactant used for livestock and posters. It made water wetter, the better to penetrate paper fibers. The two men quickly whisked the poster on to a suction table, which roared to life, a vacuum wicking the moisture from below before it could spread out.

'Evan! Over here! You have to see this.'

Melinda Truong, a lithe woman with a curtain of black hair reaching her lower back, popped up from a cluster of men around a workstation and waved him across the floor. As he wove his way to her, a mounted TV blared the ten-o'clock news. Evan glanced up to see if it was carrying the story of the motel shooting, but it was a feature about some assemblyman gone missing.

The ring of workers parted deferentially as he approached. Melinda took his face in both of her hands and kissed him on either cheek close to the edge of his lips. She wore a fitted sweater, yoga pants and bright-orange sneakers of elaborate design. Tucked behind her ear was a 000 paintbrush – the finest make – with its handle wrapped in pink tape. At her waist, slung in an actual holster, was an Olympos double-action airbrush, which looked like a 1970s take on a ray gun. Its grip was also padded with pink tape. The only woman in the operation, she color-coded her tools to keep her men from borrowing them.

She tugged his hand, turning him toward the table around which the little group had gathered. 'This poor girl was stripped from a cinema display case in Paris. She lay in a dank warehouse for years after the war, then was shoved into a trunk until last June. She came to us in intensive care.'

He stared down at the object of her affection, a Ginger Rogers insert from *Lady in the Dark*, sandwiched between Mylar sheets. It had multiple tears, pinholes and fold wear. 'She looks tattered,' he said.

'You should've seen her before we got our hands on her. She had to be demounted, washed, the tape adhesive residue removed with Bestine. We're patching her with vintage paper now. She'll be worth six figures when we're done – her owner'll be thrilled. Of course, we're only billing him at one twenty-five an hour.' The long lashes of one eye dipped in a graceful wink. 'Not like for our *special* services.'

She seemed to notice the workers around her for the first time. '*Well?*' she said sharply in her native tongue. '*What are you waiting for? Back to work!*'

As they scurried into motion, Evan nodded at a poster of *Frankenstein Meets the Wolf Man* pinned on the neighboring table. 'How about that one?'

'This guy?' She grinned, showing perfect rows of pearl-white teeth. 'He's good looking, right? Been damaged and restored a few times, like most good men.' She freed a corner of the poster, showed off the back side. 'Got all these collector stamps to establish provenance. *But.*'

She barked another order across the room, and a moment later the lights in the building went out with a series of clanks. A black-light wand clicked on in her hand, the greens and whites of the poster suddenly luminescent. 'Fake, see? The glow gives it away. They made an ink-jet printout, glued it on to vintage backing, and intentionally distressed it.' The lights came back on, and she whisked the poster off the table, Frankenstein disappearing into the wide drawer of a flat file cabinet. She smirked. 'I know a good forgery when I see one.'

Slipping her arm through Evan's, she led him down a back hall that smelled pleasantly of petroleum. 'The poster trade, Evan, is the Wild West.'

'Seems to be.'

They entered a dark-walled photography room, its windows blacked out to prevent reflections during shooting. A fine excuse to have an impenetrable back room in which to conduct business of a certain type.

'It's been what – six months?' she said. 'You came because you miss me?'

'Of course. But not just that.'

'You need another license? Social Security card? Travel visa?'

'Haven't had a chance to burn the ones I've got.'

Her lips made a sly shift to one side. 'You brought me a lead on a German *Metropolis* three-sheet?'

Melinda's – and every poster trader's – holy grail, the poster went for upwards of a million dollars. There were three in the world that anyone knew about.

'Alas, no.' Evan withdrew Katrin's passport from his pocket and held it out.

Melinda regarded it a moment, then took it and thumbed to Katrin's photo. A playful tilt of her head. 'Should I be jealous?'

Setting the passport down on the workbench, she opened and closed several letterblock drawers housing customs stamps. 'Do you want her to have been to India?' She removed one of the larger stamps. 'Or how about the Galápagos? This is the elaborate one they give you at Baltra.' She thwacked the stamp on to a piece of scrap paper, took a moment to admire her handiwork.

'No. I don't need it embellished. I need to know if it's real.'

Her thin eyebrows lifted, but even then not a wrinkle appeared in her flawless skin. She crossed to an AmScope binocular microscope hooked into a computer for image capture. All business now, she flipped her long hair over one shoulder and bent to the wide eyepiece mounted on a boom arm. She studied the passport cover, its seams and multiple pages under different specialized lights.

Then she took her time on the computer, sorting through the captured images. Back to the passport itself, now with a loupe, examining the photo page square inch by square inch.

'It's real,' she said.

'Are you sure?'

She straightened up, deleting the images from the computer, then clearing the cache. 'It is very hard to fake a passport, Evan. The paper is impossible to replicate.'

'Even from etched and engraved metal plates?'

She shook her head. 'No way.'

'How about if it was silk-screened from a high-detail Photoshop print?'

'Even *I* couldn't achieve this clarity in the pixelation.'

That answered that, then.

Melinda blew out a breath. 'Look, maybe someone

could re-create the embossment tool for the security images, but these holograms? No way. This is a flawless specimen.' She held his gaze a moment longer, perhaps sensing that he needed more convincing. 'Not a fake. Not a *good* fake. Not a *great* fake.' She offered the passport back with an artful flick of her wrist. 'It's her.'

26. Unnerved

Sitting at his personal command centre in the humid semidark of the Vault, Evan sipped two fingers of U'Luvka over ice and watched the surveillance feeds of the loft. Katrin slept fitfully, stirring in the throes of an unpleasant dream. She had plenty of reason to be unnerved.

He was unnerved himself, and this was not a sensation he was accustomed to experiencing.

He *was* used to missing puzzle pieces, equations that didn't add up in full, but something was more significantly off kilter here. He didn't know how he and Katrin had been tracked – not once but twice. He didn't know who wanted to kill them. He didn't know that he could trust his client.

He rewound the footage to confirm that Katrin hadn't strayed from the loft. She hadn't even left the futon. Next he called up the readings from the microchips in her system to test if he could grab the GPS signal, but none showed. Likely she was too far from her last meal, the digestive juices not stimulated sufficiently to charge the sensor particles in her tract.

His rules required that he zero in on the people who were pursuing them. And, from there, zero in on the Vegas outfit who had hired them.

Aside from the phone number of Sam's killer, as untraceable as his own, his only concrete information was the nickname he'd heard spoken during the motel raid: *We got two down, Slatch.*

The monitor to Evan's left loaded results from NCIC, the National Crime Information Center computerized index, the pride of the FBI. The powerful data-mining engines of the Alias File had been churning for a while now, ever since he'd typed '*Slatch*' into the search field, putting to work all those tax dollars he didn't pay.

Three results popped up now. The first, Julio 'Slatch-Catcher' Marquez, a Mexican-mafia gangbanger currently serving a dime in Lompoc for armed robbery. Beneath that, Evelyn Slatch-Donovan, a Hollywood madam with ties to organized crime. Dismissing them both, Evan clicked on the third. Only a single picture of Danny Slatcher existed on federal record, a surveillance shot of him stepping off a speedboat on to a dock, a panama hat and sunglasses obscuring his features. But his form – that vast, bottom-heavy build – was undeniably that of the man Evan had spotted in the motel parking lot.

A pulse started up in Evan's neck, his heartbeat quickening with the thrill of a lead putting out.

In Slatcher's right hand was an elongated Pelican case, the very size Evan himself used to transport sniper rifles. It seemed extremely likely that Slatcher was the man behind the scope in Chinatown who had fired the shots at Katrin. For now Evan would operate on that assumption.

Two names were listed under Slatcher's known associates. The first, marked *'deceased,'* had been a dirty banker out of Turks and Caicos, the man's file showing about what one would expect for a deceased money launderer. Ball bearings within ball bearings.

The next brought up a few fuzzy photos of a woman with a thick mane of hair – probably a wig – riding helmetless on a green-and-white Kawasaki. *'Candy McClure.'* Maybe she was the woman from the Scion, but it was hard to tell. There was no other information listed for her, just the few blurry photos and a name.

Evan moused over to Danny Slatcher's criminal-record history and pushed the button.

What he saw cut his excitement off at the knees.

Redacted file.

Two words that carried a host of implications. Not to mention complications.

Evan realized he was clenching his teeth. He clicked the next link, for Slatcher's ATF Violent Felon File, knowing already what he'd find.

Redacted file.

And the next. And the next.

Evan set down his highball with a clink, looked over at Vera in her mound of glass pebbles. But the plant had nothing to offer.

Danny Slatcher was not a two-bit gun for hire. Or a high-end hit man for the mob. He was something much more lethal.

Evan didn't like the notion singeing the hairs on the

back of his neck, making the acid crawl the walls of his stomach. He knew now that he had to get to Slatcher's perch in Chinatown to reconstruct the shooting from the other side of the scope. Whether LAPD still had the building sealed off or not, Evan had to infiltrate the crime scene.

27. Cat and Mouse

Lotus Dim Sum seemed back in working order, the windows replaced, the glass swept from the sidewalk. Two days after the shooting, the apartment across the way still remained under LAPD control.

From beneath the glowing pagoda gate of Chinatown Plaza, peering up from the shadows, Evan took in the apartment on the top story of the building. He munched fresh-baked almond cookies, pulling them from their neat stack inside the Baggie. Though he'd covered his fingertips with a thin sheen of superglue, he could still distinctly feel the crumbly texture of the baked flour. He preferred superglue to gloves, as it was less conspicuous and left him more tactile precision. The apartment building Slatcher had used looked to be the nicest in the tight row along Broadway, the neighboring complexes shabby and peeling, the balconies serving as overflow storage for bicycles and surfboards, dead plants and drying laundry.

Evan's previous drive-bys had clarified that Slatcher had fired not through a window, as he'd first assumed, but through the sliding glass door of a balcony. The event itself – a sniper shooting into a crowded restaurant, causing a stampede – had a terrorist-like scope, and LAPD had responded with a commensurate show of force, enfolding the building in a lockdown. Three patrol cars were in evidence, parked at intervals along the curb. Yellow and red neon glowed down from the gate, mapping patterns across Evan's face as he waited and watched, trying to place the locations of the various police officers.

Several remained in their vehicles. Uniformed officers screened the building's residents at the front entrance, the garage, and the rear and side doors. Two more patrolled the interior, popping into view from time to time in the windowed stairwells. He clocked their patterns, noting that they spent disproportionate time on the third floor. One of the officers stepped into the shooter's apartment on her rotation, appearing through the glass sliding door as she checked the rooms, the kitchen, the balcony. There was no getting into the building through any traditional means.

A shift of the wind brought the click of mah jongg tiles from a back room across the plaza. Evan ate the last cookie in the stack, dropped the wrapper into a trash can, and hustled across the street, nodding at the cop sipping coffee behind his steering wheel.

Evan entered the building next door to the one used by Slatcher and rode the elevator up to the fourth floor. From the street he'd scouted the apartment at the end of the hall, noting that all the lights had been out. A plastic holly wreath, muted with dust, festooned the door. The lock was an insult to its name; he got through it with a simple zip of a credit card.

A wheezy snore emanated through the open

bedroom door off the tiny foyer. Ancient carpeting padded Evan's steps as he moved through the apartment and on to the balcony. The chirp of the venerable sliding door in its tracks barely rose above the whoosh of the wind. Without slowing, Evan stepped over the balcony railing, pivoting and sliding his hands down the posts so he was dangling four stories above the street. A slight swing of his legs pendulumed him away from the building and back, and he let go, dropping on to the balcony below, landing in a spot of cleared space between a row of surfboards and a mini-fridge.

Through the pollution-clouded glass of the sliding door, he could make out the dinner party in progress one room over. Wineglasses clinking over a well-set table, feminine laughter, the waft of roast chicken and leaded hot cider.

Evan put his back to the diners and peered across the alley to the building opposite. The sniper's building. It was too far to jump. But he wasn't planning on jumping.

From the stack of surfboards, he slid out a longboard and lifted it, extending it horizontally out over the alley. The tip caught the lip of the balcony across. He set the back of the board down on the railing before him, then climbed gently up on to it, preparing for his tightrope walk. The surfboard wobbled slightly as he inched out over the alley.

One cautious step. Another.

From below carried the sound of a car door slamming shut. He looked down at the police cruiser below him. The heavyset cop – the one he had nodded to as he'd crossed the street – had emerged from his car. Styrofoam cup in hand, he shuffled directly beneath Evan into the alley. Evan froze, his arms slightly extended, a bird debating flight. The board shimmied, threatening to topple, his calves and thighs screaming to hold it in check. The cop hurled his coffee cup into a Dumpster, the wet thunk echoing up the tight alley walls. Hitching his pants, he retreated to the cruiser. The door slammed.

Evan exhaled.

Then he kept on. A few more painful steps brought him to the opposing balcony. He hopped down, drew the surfboard across, and tilted it behind a tall fern, stashing it there for his retreat. Lights glowed deep in the attached apartment, but no one was in view. Evan picked the cheap lock on the sliding door, cut diagonally through the room, and eased out on to the west-facing balcony, the one overlooking Broadway. Using it as a launching point, he hopped across two parallel balconies, passing unnoticed before a make-out session in progress and then two grown men immersed in Grand Theft Auto. One last jump brought him to the sniper's roost.

He shot a cursory glance across Broadway. The vantage gave a nice, clear shooting angle into the restaurant, but the rest of the plaza was mostly blocked from view. Slatcher's follow-up shots had to have been taken from higher ground. The roof.

Evan turned to face the apartment itself. A perfect

circle the size of a Frisbee had been cut into the glass door right beside the handle. The hole had been made by a circular glass cutter with a suction cup, a favorite of thieves. And snipers. Evan knew from experience how much the missing glass helped – no bullet refraction, no suspiciously slid-back door, no crack for the wind to fluff a curtain and draw the eye. The room beyond was clearly unoccupied, neatly vacuumed, prepped to show potential renters. The front door faced him directly across.

Evan was about to reach through the hole and unlock the slider when the front door opened. He pivoted out of view just as the female cop stepped into the apartment, her flashlight sweeping the room. He kept his shoulder blades pinned to the stucco wall beside the glass, hoping she'd head for the kitchen first as on her earlier patrols. But the flashlight beam wagged back and forth, approaching.

She was heading straight for the balcony.

Evan jumped up lightly, grabbing the edge of the flat roof, his palms facing inward. The lever clicked beside him as the cop unlocked the door. It started to rattle open. Evan hoisted his legs up and over his grip, a variation on a gymnast's high-bar rotation. As the cop's boots tapped out on to the balcony, Evan slid smoothly on to his stomach on the roof and pulled his hands back from the edge. His shirt made a slight grinding sound against the graveled tar paper, and the flashlight beam shot up over the roof's edge, a science-fiction effect. He remained motionless, not so much as breathing. The beam played along the concrete lip. He could smell the faintest trace of the cop's perfume.

Finally the flashlight beam lowered. The boots retreated, the door drew closed, and Evan eased out a breath. He lifted his gaze, noting the clear view into the plaza across, the unobstructed angle on to the alley where he and Katrin had jumped into the strategically parked minivan, taking fire.

So once Evan had cleared Katrin from the restaurant, Slatcher had climbed to the roof and cycled his follow-up shots from here. Still flat on his stomach, Evan turned his head. Right beside him, a domed heating vent thrust up from the tar paper. He had a silhouette view of the vent's flashing strip, secured by hand-twist screws. Of the four screws, two were barely twisted on at all.

Someone had removed and replaced the heating vent in a hurry.

Evan rolled over, spun off the screws and lifted the vent. He pulled a small Maglite from one of his cargo pockets and directed the powerful beam down the exposed shaft.

Sure enough, a sniper rifle was caught in a duct junction ten meters down.

It looked to be a McMillan .308-caliber police model – easy to acquire, common enough to make it hard to track. Dumping the gun at the scene was a calling card of the elite contract killer, who knew better than to hold on to a weapon that could be tested for forensics later. A pair of latex gloves rested near the rifle barrel, a keen choice, as leather gloves left unique prints. Beside them a white, cup-shaped object had landed. Evan focused on it until it resolved as a medical mask.

He felt the adrenaline moving through his veins quicken.

Before fleeing the scene, Slatcher had trashed not just the rifle. Not just gloves that would have exhibited gunpowder residue. But the truly professional touch was the medical mask he'd left behind as well after he'd ceased shooting. Had he been arrested leaving the scene and given a nasal swab to detect inhaled gunpowder residue, the mask would have ensured a negative test result.

A noise startled Evan from his thoughts – the vertical access door across the roof banging open. He would have been spotted instantly were the door not facing the opposite direction. The cop had to walk around the concrete framing to bring Evan into sight.

Reacting quickly, he grabbed the dome of the roof vent and clicked it back into place over the shaft. Already rolling for the roof's edge, he swept the loose screws off into space with the blade of his hand. He caught the lip as he tumbled over, also catching a fleeting glimpse of the flashlight lens emerging from around the side of the open access door.

His weight swung him neatly around the roof's edge. He released, bending his knees to cushion his landing on the balcony. He wound up right in front of the hole cut into the sliding glass door.

Way down below he heard the screws tap the

sidewalk as they finally hit ground. Reaching through the hole, he unlocked the door and slid it open slowly, stepping inside and easing it shut just as he heard the cop's footsteps creak the roof overhead. Now the flash-light beam played down along the balcony's edge, though Evan was safely out of view inside.

He was pushing his luck with this little game of cat and mouse. He had to move quickly. Tilting his head, he picked up the angle of moonlight across the neat vacuum stripes. Boot imprints from the cops trampled the space. But in one spot the carpet thread was scuffed up at three points, the corners of a triangle.

A sniper's tripod.

The flashlight beam withdrew from the balcony, and he heard the cop's footsteps moving back toward the access door.

Evan searched the ceiling just in front of the scuff marks, and sure enough he picked up a metal glint. A staple, embedded in the popcorn ceiling. The ceiling was low enough that he could reach it when he went up on tiptoes, and he pried the staple free. Beneath it was a tiny swatch of fabric – a torn bit left pinned beneath the staple, likely when CSI had removed the screen drape. The purpose of a drape, which typically went from ceiling to floor, was to shield the sniper from view. Evan held the bit of fabric up toward the window so it was backlit by the neon glow of the pagoda gate. It was gauzy, of course, for Slatcher to see and shoot through, but not opaque enough to block the glint of a scope in direct sunlight.

His meet with Katrin had been scheduled for high noon. The move to Chinatown had taken them to twelve-thirty, the L.A. sun near its apex.

If Evan had arrived at the restaurant at any other time of day, he wouldn't have caught that reflected glint. He took a moment to consider this fragment of good luck, then exhaled and refocused on the room.

At last he positioned himself behind the spot where the tripod had been set down. The sole picture of Danny Slatcher had shown him carrying a Pelican case in his right hand, so Evan lined up behind the imaginary rifle in a right-handed shooter's orientation, peering through a pretend scope.

What he saw confirmed his worst fear, and he felt his jaw clench until it throbbed.

The view through the circle cut into the sliding glass door gave him a perfect angle down at the restaurant. Based on where he'd been sitting at the table, his critical mass would have blocked any shot of Katrin.

Slatcher hadn't been aiming at her.

He'd been aiming at Evan.

28. Unholy Union

Evan walked the L.A. River to clear his head. The unlikeliest-looking waterway in the county, it was a polluted trickle through a wide concrete channel. Shrubs dotted the water's edge, and graffiti embellished the sloped sides of the basin. The slumbering homeless lay like sacks of grain, dead or drunk or just goddamned exhausted. Downtown was overhead and all around, and yet down here, sunk in a trough beneath the city, it felt like a desolate underworld, isolated from man and God.

The December air whipped at Evan's neck as he sidestepped overturned shopping carts, loose tires from semis, the occasional mossy hull of a wrecked car left behind by some musclehead who'd tried to play drag-racing Danny Zuko when the water dried up.

Traffic hummed all around, invisible save the light-saber headlights scanning the darkness above and the soothing white noise that thrummed the basin walls, a primordial murmur of blood rushing through veins. Evan had come to the stretch flowing beneath the East Los Angeles Interchange, the unholy union of Highway 101, Route 60 and Interstates 5 and 10. He'd read somewhere that this was the busiest highway exchange in the world, daily spinning half a million vehicles through its confusion of cloverleafs.

He realized now why he'd come to this place to make the phone call he was about to make: it was a comforting reminder of his anonymity in this great stacked sprawl of a city.

The bullets fired into Lotus Dim Sum had been meant for him. Someone had set Danny Slatcher on his tail, put him in the crosshairs. And Katrin wasn't the bait. Couldn't be the bait. Because Evan knew how to read people. Jack had taught him that, as had eight different psyops experts over years of training and countless under-the-gun interactions since then. Her tears had been real – as was her fear. Which meant that he'd dragged *her* into this. Devastated her life. Gotten her father killed.

Of the myriad questions scratching at the walls of his skull, one rose above the din: who had hired Danny Slatcher to kill him?

Evan had certainly cultivated plenty of enemies. As a covert operator, he'd put countless notches into his gun belt, and he'd added quite a few more as a free-lancer. His would-be murderer could be anyone from a foreign insurgent leader to a vengeance-bent relative of someone Evan had dispatched. Whoever it was had been working a long, smart play. They'd waited and watched, reading patterns and collecting clues, just as Evan himself had been trained to do.

He reached a patch of darker shadow beneath an overpass, the area cleared of homeless encampments, prostitutes and druggies. A spot of privacy in the beating heart of the city. The water rustled past, its dank scent coating his lungs. He raised his tough rubber phone and dialed the number of the man who'd murdered Sam White.

It rang. And again.

There was a click, but no one spoke.

Evan said, 'Which one are you?'

A silence. And then a familiar voice said, 'What?'

'Which. Orphan. Are. You?'

Somewhere from another dimension came a screech of tires, the blare of a horn. The moon lay rippling on the muddied surface of the slow-moving water. A few bats flurried beneath the overpass, then settled peacefully back into the gloom.

At last the voice sounded in Evan's ear. 'Some say the best. Until you. Now there seems to be some debate on that point, doesn't there . . .' A brief, savored pause. '. . . Orphan X?'

Hearing his alias spoken aloud for the first time in nearly a decade left his head humming. He'd been identified. Named. The moment he'd been dreading for two-thirds of a lifetime.

He pulled the phone away from his mouth, cleared his throat, then brought the receiver back to his lips and returned the favor. 'Orphan Zero,' he said.

'That's right.'

Who better to hire to go after the Nowhere Man than a former Orphan? The person who wanted Evan dead had made inquiries in the right circles, had hired the best. And the best happened to be not only one of Evan's own but one of the few who could connect the dotted trail between the Nowhere Man and Orphan X. Danny Slatcher likely didn't know Evan's actual name, but he understood the shadowy contours of Evan's identity as Evan understood his.

Evan thought of Slatcher's redacted file. He thought of a dismantled Orphan Program, all those trained assaulters out of work, unmoored from purpose and oversight, left to find meaning – and jobs – on their own. He thought of Katrin's face when she'd heard the pop of the gunshot through the phone, the deadweight thump of her father's body hitting the floor.

Evan felt his hand grow tight around the phone. *Never make it personal. Never make it personal. Never . . .*

Blackness pooled in his chest, drowning out thought and reason, drowning out the hum of cars all around, Jack's voice in his head, the Commandments themselves.

He said, 'You shouldn't have killed Sam White.'

He hung up and started back for his car.

Danny Slatcher set down his phone and eased his considerable frame back against the headboard, the box spring groaning beneath him. Candy came out of the bathroom, naked save the threadbare motel towel twisting up her hair, to shoot him an inquisitive glance. He did not look over at her.

She took in his expression and retreated into the bathroom.

Slatcher's arm span was such that he could reach the round wooden breakfast table from the bed with barely a lean. He plucked up the slender metal box and set it in his lap.

Inside, ten press-on, peel-off fingernails and the high-def contact lens display rested in the molded rubber interior like some relic from the future.

He appareled himself with an ease that he found mildly distasteful.

The virtual cursor blinked in space a few feet from his right eyeball as he waited for Top Dog to accept his request. At last the cursor shifted from red to green.

Slatcher elevated his hands like a pensive concert pianist, then typed: WE'VE GOT A PROBLEM.

29. There and Gone

'Wait,' Katrin said. 'Just *wait*.' She circled the tiny loft, running her hand across the tinted glass that made up the west-facing wall. Her fingertips squeaked unpleasantly across the window. '*You're* the target?'

As he'd recounted his discovery in Chinatown, she'd grown tenser and tenser, until he could see the muscles tightening in her neck. Even now she was still trying to sort through the ramifications.

'Let me get this straight,' she said. 'Now we have *two* sets of people after us. My bad guys and your bad guys.'

'I don't think that's the case,' Evan said. 'I believe my bad guys took over from your bad guys. Paid them off to clear them out of the way.'

'Why do you think that?'

'Because it's what I would do.'

'But how would the guys after you even *know* about me?'

'They must have gotten on your tail somehow when they realized you were going to make contact with me.'

'*How?*'

'I don't know yet. Maybe from Morena. Maybe from an intercepted call, though I don't know how –'

'*Then* what?'

'They sussed out your situation, determined that you owed the wrong kind of money to the wrong kind of people.'

'They could find that out?'

'As well as I could. Yes.'

She stared at him a moment, then shook her head in disgust or disbelief and resumed her pacing. While she faced away, he pulled her passport from his pocket and slid it into her purse on the counter. His self-loathing materialized as a bitterness at the back of his throat.

She whirled on Evan just as he withdrew his hand. 'Paid two-point-one *million dollars.*'

'Yes.'

'Just for a shot at you?'

'Yes.'

'How are you worth that much? Who *are* you?' She threw her hands up. 'Right. *Evan.* That's who you are. The Nowhere Man.'

He stood behind the kitchen island, facing her across the loft.

She lifted a hand, pressed it to the side of her head. The cut on her face had all but vanished, the tiniest blemish on the curve of her cheekbone. 'Why do they want to kill you?'

'I don't know.'

'But they bought my marker to draw you in. They bought my *dad.* They're the ones who . . . who killed my dad?'

The word came like broken glass. 'Yes.'

There were tracks on her cheeks, glittering in the winking lights of the city.

'I'm sorry,' he said.

She wiped at her face. 'And your bad guys? They're even *more* dangerous?'

He nodded.

'More dangerous than Vegas hit men?'

He nodded again.

'And I know too much now – what they did to my dad, at the motel, that they're after you. So I can't even run. I'm at *greater* risk now. Because of you.'

Evan put his palms on the Caesarstone counter, dotted with sleek black take-out containers from the robata restaurant next door; she'd been eating when he'd arrived. Mustard portobello caps, tiger prawns with yuzu pesto, filet bites with sea urchin butter – the rich smells made his stomach churn. Nestled in the puffed-up lining of the trash can to his side was the discarded Powerade bottle. At the sight of it, he felt his guilt ride its way up his throat, flushing his face. As if on cue, his cell phone gave a sonar ping.

The GPS signal, now active, transmitted from Katrin's digestive tract to the hidden patch behind her ear to Evan's pocket.

The submarine alert sounded again, and Evan silenced his phone.

'What's that?' she asked.

'Nothing that matters now.'

Mercifully, she'd moved on to another agitated rotation around the loft. 'Jesus Christ, aren't you supposed to *help* me? Wasn't that the deal? The magic phone number. "Do you need my help?" "I have never lost anyone". You were supposed to *protect* me –'

'And I will.' He took a beat to calm his tone. 'If you give me your trust, I will protect you. No matter what. That's all we have. Do you understand?'

She turned, backlit against the window from the distant purple-and-red glow of the Staples Center. From the club across the street rose a cover band going at a Mumford & Sons song, the words blurred but the banjo rising clear and true – *will wait, I will wait for you.* Katrin wore a loose-fitting T-shirt that had fallen off one shoulder, exposing a strap of black bra, and her sleek hair was mussed. The dim light had turned her lipstick dark, dark red, the color of venous blood, and her green eyes shone in a stripe of light thrown from a streetlamp below.

'So it's just me and you now,' she said. 'In the whole big world.' Her glossy lips caught the sheen of city lights through the window, and for a moment they were ruby again. A new tear carved down the perfect skin of her cheek. She turned away. 'I forgive you,' she said.

He wet his lips. 'I don't.'

She was looking out the window. 'Come here.'

He came. When he was close, she reached behind her, made a fist in the fabric of his shirt. Pulled him so he pressed up against her from behind. The pressure was insistent. He breathed the smell of her hair, felt a sudden shift, his focus veering off the rails. She wiggled her hips, the jeans sliding down and down, and then his were, too.

Her pants, her socks were puddled at her ankles, and she kicked one leg free so she could step to the side. Her shirt was pushed up, her back smooth and pale. He placed his hands on her hips and she tilted just so and there was a divine slickness and her elbows and palms were up against the glass and their rhythm seemed to find resonance in the neon pulse of the city below. Her short breaths fogged the glass, there and gone, there and gone.

After, they lay on the low mattress facing the city, Evan running a finger along the cello silhouette of her body, tracing the slope of her hip. Her left shoulder blade sported a kanji symbol for passion, though the third horizontal stroke was too short. They watched the headlights strobe by on the Harbor Freeway.

'All those cars out there,' she said. 'I look at all those people and I think, why me? Why not them? It's shitty to say, I know, but I can't help thinking it since this whole thing started. I just want to give up. But there's no choice, really, with a nightmare like this. When people talk about being tough, maybe that's all it means – when you've got no choices left. You just have to keep going until it's over.'

He stroked her side until she drifted off, and then he gently slid off the futon so as not to wake her. It struck him that he'd more or less shattered the Third Commandment by now. Another violation of an inviolable list. It was becoming a habit.

He crossed to the kitchen area, pulled a bottled water from the fridge. He heard a faint buzz from across the room.

His RoamZone, vibrating in the pocket of his kicked-off jeans.

He stood frozen in the loft. The floorboards were cool against his bare feet, but that had nothing to do with the chill he felt sweeping across his skin.

The Seventh Commandment decreed that there was to be one mission at a time. He'd told Morena in no uncertain terms: *Only give my number to one person. Understand? Only one. Then forget that number forever.*

The phone buzzed again. He crept across, tugged it from the pocket. A caller ID he did not recognize. A few feet before him, Katrin breathed slow and steady, out cold. He retreated to the kitchen, turned on the taps for white noise, pressed to pick up.

His voice was dry and cracked, and he had to start again. 'Do you need my help?'

'I do.' A man's desperate voice. '*Dios mío*, I do more than *anything*. It is true? It is true that you can help me?'

Evan lifted his gaze to Katrin's sleeping form. The tattooed kanji strokes on the bare skin of her shoulder. 'Where did you get this number?'

'The girl. She give it to me.'

Evan felt a pulse beating low in his stomach — suspicion morphing into something harder-edged. 'What's her name?'

'Morena Aguilar.'

'What did she look like?'

'The skinny teenage girl! She have a burn on her arm. She say you help her. She say you save her little sister from the bad man. She say you help me, too.'

The night air seeped through Evan's pores, an instant chill, making his hair prickle. Every aspect of the past four days was thrown suddenly, violently into question.

He thought about how quickly Katrin's call had come, just a few days after he'd asked Morena to locate the next client for him. How her seat in Lotus Dim Sum had in fact been safely back from the sniper's vantage, blocked by Evan himself. How easily she had been tracked, first to the restaurant, then to the motel. Then he considered the man on the other end of the phone.

Which was the impostor?

If it was Katrin, Evan had to clear out of the loft – and quickly – before Slatcher and his team closed in.

He moved swiftly across the room. The door opened silently on well-greased hinges. He looked up and down the hall but saw no one. Yet.

His thoughts jumped immediately to Morena Aguilar, living with her aunt and her little sister in Vegas. Both Katrin and this man had referred to her by name and description. Morena had been the point of entry; she was how Slatcher and the people behind him had gotten on to Evan's trail. They'd connected Evan to her somehow, located her, and woven her into their plant's cover story. Which meant she was at serious risk. If not already dead.

Evan had to get to Vegas and find her.

Keeping an eye on the hall through the cracked door, he fought his focus back to the phone call. 'What's your name?'

had been dropped haphazardly on to one of the couch's split cushions. A dinner tray lay where it had slid off the couch, littered with pieces of a broken plate and bowl.

Mia, nowhere in sight.

Evan walked down the hall, calling her name quietly. The door to the master was ajar, but when he entered the room, he found it empty. From the dark maw of the walk-in closet, he heard sniffling.

'Mia?' He pushed the closet door further open and saw her sitting with her back to a rise of drawers, wiping her face, one hand clutching the ever-present iPhone.

'Sorry. I just – Sorry. Sometimes . . .'

'May I come in?'

'Please.'

He put his shoulders to the wall opposite her, beside the hanging blouses, and slid down to sit facing her. Her feet, shoved into actual bunny slippers. They were fluffy pink and featured a heart and stitched bubble letters that proclaimed, WORLD'S BEST MOM. The sight of them brought something deeper than just amusement. It surprised him to realize that he liked this home, where knives were for spreading butter and superglue for repairing toys.

'Sorry I was harsh earlier,' she said. 'Upstairs.'

'You were just being protective.'

'I'll tell you this: parenting ain't for sissies.'

'No,' he said. 'Doesn't seem to be.'

'And with work right now . . .' She blew out a breath. Her hair floated back down over her forehead. 'Facing it all by myself feels so fucking scary sometimes. And I know that's pathetic with everything I have, but . . .'

He watched her expression shift.

'I did everything right,' she said. 'Studied hard, worked hard, was a good wife. I know – "Grow up", right? I sound naïve and entitled, but Christ. You'd think it'd work out. Better. Than this.' She fluttered a hand around the closet, the heavy sleeves of disembodied coats, the wire hangers, the crowd of sweaters bending a shelf overhead. 'I have this fantasy notion of myself. Holding it together. But I can't seem to get there. Why not?'

He was unaccustomed to these kinds of problems, significant but not extreme, prosaic but not trivial. Everyday difficulties. A boy without a father. A toilet that wouldn't flush. Frozen peas to bring down the swelling. She was looking at him expectantly, and he realized that an answer was due.

'I suppose everything's a matter of discipline and focus.'

She made a thoughtful noise. 'It might seem that way to you,' she said, not unkindly. 'There's no one else in your life – I mean, in your life *all the time*. People are messy. Relationships aren't linear. They knock you on your ass. Make you detour, reverse, change focus. You can't be perfect unless you're alone, and then guess what? You're alone. So you're still not perfect.'

An image came to Evan: Jack moving through the farmhouse late at night, thumbing up flecks of dust, aligning objects on counters, stacking the place mats and cloth napkins with assembly-line precision. Evan had always viewed those nighttime rituals as displays of mettle, an almost religious observance of setting the room, the house, the universe in order.

'Maybe none of what we think matters really matters at all,' Mia said. 'Maybe it's the *little* stuff that adds up, inch by inch, until you've built something you didn't even know you were building. Driving car pool. Making school lunches. Sitting bedside at a hospital night after night . . .' Her eyes glinted in the dark. 'But that's what takes it out of you, too.' She tilted her head back to keep more tears from spilling. 'I worry that I can't handle everything that's coming by myself. All the mess of life. That I'm too sensitive. Too fragile. That it'll keep coming and I won't have what it takes.'

'You're not fragile,' Evan said. 'You're not afraid to show the cracks.'

'Great.' A hint of a smile. 'I'm cracky.' She stuck her arm out at an upward diagonal. 'Help me up.'

'You sure you're ready to exit the closet?'

She cocked her head. 'There's a mess to be picked up and laundry to be done, and I am again equal to the task.'

He rose, grasped her hand, pulled her up. She rose as if weightless. For a moment they were close, stomach to stomach, in the tight space. Her eyes on his chin, her breath faint against his neck. And then she brushed past him, patting his side. They emerged from the bedroom together. In the living room, she turned off the TV, started folding the laundry on the couch.

Starting for the door, he thought again of that life lesson Mia had written out for her son and stuck to the wall: *'Pursue what is meaningful, not what is expedient.'* The little phrase stopped him there on the floorboards. He looked across at the Post-it and read it again, wondering if the Commandments were immutable and determinate or whether new rules could be added as one pleased. Again he thought of Jack poking around in the dark house, tidying up, making invisible adjustments that he'd make again the next night and the night after that. The farmhouse, so safe and clean and soothingly spare, had always felt somehow outside of time. This home gave the opposite impression. With its smudged handprints and framed family portraits, it seemed to contain within its walls the entire brutal cycle of life – and yet it also contained a comfort of a different kind. Though the specific thought wriggled away before Evan could pin it down, he sensed somewhere that this brand of comfort couldn't exist without the brutal realities.

In his peripheral vision, Evan sensed Mia crouch over the fallen tray. He reversed direction and joined her, helping pick up the broken pieces.

knees. Carmen, Morena's eleven-year-old sister. Over her jeans she wore a dirty Disney nightgown with what looked like a blue Popsicle stain down Minnie's face.

'I know you,' she said in a hoarse whisper. 'You're the one who helped us. Mr No-Place Guy.'

Evan came around the side of the house, the baked lawn hard underfoot. Though out of view from the front door, he lowered his voice. 'Morena's gone?'

'She left the third day we was here. We went out to get groceries, and I noticed a man noticing us. I'm good at that.'

Evan remembered Carmen with her crayons in the corner booth at Benny's Burgers, watching him through the window. 'I know you are,' he said. 'Can you tell me where she went?'

'She got scared. She said if someone was watching, it had to do with whatever let us leave L.A. That she had to go into hiding 'cuz if she stayed with me, it wouldn't be safe for me. When we got back from the grocery store that night, she snuck out the window.' Carmen rested her hand on the base of the open frame she'd just jumped through, her face lost to thought.

'Do you have a number I can reach her at?'

'She's freaked out. Too scared to use a phone, anything. She thinks that's how they followed her, by her phone. Like how the bad man in L.A. used to keep track of her. She said she won't use one no more. No matter what.'

'So you've seen her since?'

'Two times.' Carmen held up two fingers. 'She came to see me at the school playground.' She gestured up the dark block. 'You can see it from far away, so if I sit on the swings at recess she can tell if it's safe to come up to me or not. There're lotsa kids around and stuff.'

Her aunt's voice wafted out the open window, calling her to breakfast. Carmen glanced nervously at the sill behind her. 'I gotta go.'

'Did she tell you if she found someone else? She was looking for someone else. For me.'

'No. She didn't say anything about that.' Carmen chewed her lower lip. 'If you saved us, then how come I can't be with her?'

Again the aunt's voice floated through the window. *¡Carmen! Ven aquí. Tu desayuno está listo.'*

Evan crouched, bringing himself to her eye level. 'Listen to me. I have to see her. Her life depends on it. Go to your swings at morning recess and wait for her. Tell her to meet me in the Bellagio Casino at the restaurant overlooking the dancing fountains. I will be there at noon today. I'll stay there all day, tonight, however long it takes for her to get there.'

Carmen rocked back on her heels, literally taken aback by his intensity. 'Okay. Okay. But I don't know if she'll come today. Or tomorrow. Or when.'

'I'll wait. Tell her it's safe there. Lots of people, cameras everywhere. Can you remember this?'

Already Carmen was scrambling for the window. 'I'll wait for her at recess, lunch, after school. I'll remember. I swear.'

She landed inside and shoved down the pane just as her aunt opened the bedroom door and began chiding her for not listening. Evan hustled back to his car, parked up the street.

He had a lot to do before noon.

31. More Truth than Lies

'What the holy hell is going on with you?' Tommy Sto-jack asked, conveying himself about his dungeon-lit armorer shop on his rolling chair, shoving himself off workbenches and desks, plucking up a sticky cup of coffee, a wayward screwdriver, a stray round. Beyond the missing finger, he had all sorts of warhorse injuries – titanium pins in various bones, hearing loss, bad knees from too many hard parachute landings. Though he still got around well enough on his own two feet, he could work his black Aeron like a wheelchair.

Evan sometimes wondered if this was practice for later, when his joints gave out entirely.

Tommy scratched at his arms, which were covered with flesh-colored square Band-Aids. 'You look like someone pissed in your cockpit.'

Evan took a breath, lowered his shoulders, smoothed out his expression. He was unaccustomed to letting stress show in his face and was glad he'd done so only in front of Tommy. After making arrangements at the Bellagio, Evan had embarked on a flurry of research on his laptop. The address that the second caller, Memo Vasquez, had given traced to a slumlord who owned properties all over California and Arizona, seemingly renting them to illegal immigrants. The number

Vasquez had called from belonged to a crappy Radio Shack prepaid cell phone. Good if you were broke.

Or an impostor.

Being illegal was a superb pretext for having no personal information in the system. For now Evan would have to work off Katrin White.

He said to Tommy, 'I need to confirm someone's identity.'

'In the system?'

'She checks out in the system,' Evan said. 'I want it from another angle.'

Tommy scratched at his arms again.

'What the hell are those things all over your arms?' Evan finally asked.

'Nicotine patches.' Tommy slurped coffee over a lower lip pouched out with dipping tobacco. 'I'm trying to get off the smokes.'

'One step at a time.'

'What I'm sayin'.' Tommy creakingly found his feet, his unoccupied chair rolling back into the shadowed recesses of the shop. 'Okay. Who's this broad you're trying to confirm?'

Evan called up the photo he'd snapped of Katrin on the futon, the close-up of her sleeping face, and held it for Tommy to see.

Tommy made a gruff sound of approval. 'Intimate.'

'I'm trying to help her.'

'Looks *like* it.' His hand tugged at the scraggly ends of his horseshoe mustache. 'Helping women who ain't who they say they are seems like a fool's venture to me.'

'A woman who *may not* be who she says she is.'

'Ah.' The stub of a forefinger circled the air, pointing at Evan in warning. 'Tryin' to play hero, huh?' Tommy's laugh came out as a half cough. 'You wanna be a *real* hero? Get old. Peel yourself outta bed every morning with your back like this and your knee like that.'

'Okay. But first let's confirm this ID.'

'That ain't my bailiwick.'

'She's a big-time gambler,' Evan said. 'Which means she's done it before. A lot. At a lot of places. I was thinking, you're a Vegas guy –'

'That I am.'

'– maybe you have a hook at one of the casinos could run some facial-recognition software off this photo. Some places store footage from the floor going back years. See if she's opened a line of credit, what name that line of credit was under. Like that.'

'If she's not who she says she is, why do you believe her if she tells you she's a gambler?'

'The best cover's composed of more truth than lies.'

'That it is.' Tommy gave a terse little nod. 'I know a guy, got a bit of horsepower over at Harrah's. Let's see what rocks we can kick over.'

'I'd appreciate it. Want me to text you the picture?'

Tommy's face wrinkled up in disgust. 'I don't fucking *text*. E-mail that shit. You know the account to use.' His broad, rough hands restacked a scattering of bullet-mold blocks on the bench between them. 'Need anything else? Some Chuck Four?' He reached under the bench, came up with a brick of C4. 'The most effective way to turn money into noise.'

'I'm good on explosives.' Evan turned for the door, double-checking, as always, that the security camera was unplugged. 'Thank you, Tommy.'

'Hey, man. I'll call the guy, that's all. There are no guarantees.' Tommy dug the wedge of tobacco out from his lip and thunked it into a dusty Carl's Jr. cup. 'Only guarantee is we ain't gettin' outta this incarnation alive.'

32. Nowhere to Go

A five-figure cash tip to the manager of the Hyde lounge procured for Evan the premiere table for as long as he needed it. The booth stuck out from the base of the vast Bellagio Hotel over the eight-acre lake like the glass-walled prow of a ship. From his position in the cushioned seats, he could take in the majority of the nightclub, a sliver of the casino floor, and the walkway along the water's brink. He assumed his post at noon.

Right away he noticed a problem. Past a curved stretch of the lake, maybe a quarter mile away, a Chinese restaurant called Jasmine jutted out on to the water. It was new since he'd last been here. His instructions to Morena's sister had been imprecise – *Tell her to meet me in the Bellagio Casino at the restaurant overlooking the dancing fountains.* Now he had two venues to cover. The miscalculation ate at him, a gnawing little worm near the base of his brain that kept him on edge. At least he had a clear view through Jasmine's floor-to-ceiling windows.

He sat for six unbroken hours, keeping watch for Morena even as his hopes for her appearance diminished. He wore jeans, a black jacket and a baseball cap to shield his features from myriad eye-in-the-sky cameras. For Morena to feel safe, he'd chosen a casino as a meeting spot – the only place with more security cams than an airport.

On occasion women dropped by the table to ask if he wanted to buy them a drink. He certainly looked like a man seeking company, and the professionals took notice. He declined politely. His high-profile position here ran against every instinct in his body, but given how fearful Morena seemed to be, he wanted to be front and center so she could spot him before making her approach. Based on what Carmen had told him about her meetings with her sister, this was Morena's preferred method of making contact.

He finally got up to use the restroom, then returned and sat alertly as the sun finished its brilliant chariot arc across the sky, finally dipping behind the Strip. When lavender dusk at last faded into full dark, the world's greatest night-light display morphed into splendid existence, the Paris Hotel's faux Eiffel Tower igniting into a spire of neon gold, overpowering the moon. The dancing fountains exploded into color on the lake surface laid out before Evan, misting the glass around him, a bizarre choreography timed to an Andrea Bocelli–Sarah Brightman duet. Evan eyed the doors, the flurry of activity by the casino entrance, the hall to the bathrooms. The music wailed – *Con te partirò* – as the fountains shattered the still of the lake. Soon enough a DJ with a sideways Celtics cap took up the turntables in his booth inside, remixed and mashed-up Rihanna competing with the pop-opera duet. The dance floor filled up, sauced bachelorettes and boisterous frat boys, cut-loose businessmen and drag queens in heeled thigh-highs, a jam of fluid limbs strobe-cutting the disco beams – *I love the way you lie.*

Evan pictured Carmen sitting on the swings, isolated on the crowded playground, praying for her big sister's appearance. The school day was long gone. Perhaps Morena had decided to wait for cover of night to make her way to the Strip. Or perhaps she hadn't come to the playground at all and Evan would stay here, pinned to this spot tomorrow and the day after that. He searched the crowd again, everyone in full-blown what-happens-in-Vegas mode, talking too loud and too close or snapping duck-faced selfies. Slot-machine payouts *ring-ding-dinged* over Eminem's rap interlude. Across the street fake Europe glowed. Everyone here was chasing a different dream, an alternate version of their same self, freshened-up identities as fake and real as Evan's own, dropped into this fantasy wonderland only to be left behind at the airport departure counter like abandoned baggage.

Amid the masquerade a few simple realities burned through. He needed to find a scared seventeen-year-old girl. He needed to protect her. And he needed to learn whether she'd given his phone number to Katrin White or to Memo Vasquez.

Evan sipped water, craved vodka, scanned the dance floor, the neighboring restaurant, and then scanned them again. He settled back against the upholstery, stretching his neck. When he next looked through the window up along the curve of the lake, a movement inside Jasmine caught his eye.

Through the glittering wall of glass, he watched a feminine figure edge between white-linen tables. Her back was turned, but he read the posture immediately – shoulders lifted in a half shrug, chin tucked, hands lost to long sleeves, the wrists goosenecked in.

Fear.

She turned partway, and he caught her profile.

Morena.

He checked out the restaurant interior around her. It looked clear. He'd just risen to start toward her when his gaze swept the length of four windows, freezing him where he stood.

Danny Slatcher eased into view around a column, moving slowly toward Morena. He wore roomy acid-washed jeans and a Bubba Gump T-shirt, the perfect underdressed Vegas partaker.

Morena kept on, threading between tables, oblivious to the man behind her.

All around them diners chatted and ate, their mouths moving soundlessly as music crashed in on Evan from the lake – *time to say goodbye* – and the DJ – *just gonna staaand there and watch me burn* – the slot machines chiming, coins crashing, the bass speakers on the dance floor *thump-thump-thumping*. He was standing, hands on the glass, watching the tableau unfold across a stretch of sparkling water.

Slatcher kept on toward Morena. Clearly he had no idea Evan was within eyeshot, watching everything unfold.

Morena moved deeper into the restaurant, Slatcher

matching her step for step. Though they remained thirty meters apart, the difference in size between them was astonishing, a grizzly stalking a fawn.

There was no noise Evan could make that would rise above the din of Las Vegas at night, and so he stood on the table and flagged one arm wide, a stab of movement to catch her peripheral vision. It did not, but one of the diners near her looked over, and then another, setting off a flurry of turning heads. Smiles gleamed, and then someone pointed – check out the drunk Vegas idiot standing on a table across the way. Morena picked up on either the diners' movement or the chatter, because she finally turned, her head swiveling, then fixing on him. Even from this distance, he could see the recognition in her eyes. She raised a hand in shy acknowledgment.

Evan pointed violently, stabbing a finger behind her.

She turned abruptly, shooting a look across the restaurant, and went full-body tense. Slatcher noticed her spot him, and he slowed, one hand sliding beneath his T-shirt at the hip.

Evan could never get there in time.

A waitress was at his heels. 'Sir, I'm gonna have to ask you to –'

Focused on the scene across from them, Evan let her voice fade away.

Morena backed up to the window, edging away from Slatcher. He sidestepped a busboy, closing in slowly, cutting off her angles if she decided to run.

A hand clamped on to Evan's ankle, accompanied

by a much deeper voice. 'All right, buddy. I need you to get your ass off the table or I'll have to drag you –'

Evan glanced down as the no-neck bouncer reached for him with his other hand. Crouching to catch the wrist, Evan twisted the meaty arm across itself, locking the elbow, and planted the bouncer's face neatly on the table. He stepped on the wrist, pinning him down, then straightened up again, returning his attention to Morena.

Her shoulder blades were now pressed to the window as she slid along the wall. Nowhere to go. Her palms, down at her sides, flat against the glass. Slatcher closed in. A trio of waiters whisked between them, bearing a birthday cake with sparking candles, and Slatcher used the distraction to skip closer to Morena. They were maybe ten tables apart now.

Beneath Evan's foot the bouncer lurched, his other hand flopping awkwardly over his own head, trying to reach Evan. A few partiers at the fringe of the dance floor took note of the non-scuffle, but for the most part the blaring music and swirling movement provided sufficient distraction to buy him some time.

Slatcher was pursuing Morena only to get to Evan. Evan was the true target. And yet he was stranded here with two windows and a stretch of dancing fountains between them. Helpless.

He stared at Morena, willing her to turn around and look at him again. At last she did, her eyes wide. He pointed at Slatcher, then at his own chest. And then again.

Show him I'm here.

It was all he could think to do.

Beneath him the bouncer bucked and flailed.

Morena's head swiveled back to Slatcher. He was closing in. Six tables away. Now five.

She looked directly at him, then lifted her arm and pointed through the window.

Slatcher's stare turned slowly until it locked on Evan. A frozen moment.

Evan held out his hands. *Come get me.*

Then Slatcher broke away from Morena, running for the door of the restaurant.

Evan watched the air leave Morena as she sagged with relief. He waited for her to look over at him again, then gestured for her to flee.

After this scare he doubted he'd be able to coax her into the open again, but right now he cared only about her safety. He gestured again, more emphatically. Finally Morena burst into movement and sprinted along the far wall, disappearing through the swinging doors of the kitchen.

Footsteps thudded behind Evan – heavy men running. He turned as two more bouncers ran toward him. He held an instant for them to reach the table, then jumped between them, sailing over their broad shoulders. He landed on the neighboring table, careened down and across the dance floor, and shot out into the casino between two high-limit blackjack tables.

A commotion echoed up the wide row of shops to the left, one of the radial corridors feeding into the gambling floor. Evan swung around in time to see two women knocked down hard, as if before a truck, purses wagging up on their arms. Slatcher bulled into view as they parted and dropped to the marble. He barely slowed, sprinting for Evan.

Evan reached past the blackjack players and swept their tall stacks of black chips off the felt, sending them airborne. The hundred-dollar chips rained down across shoulders and slot machines, bouncing through the walkways between tables. The gamblers surged. Chairs toppled, grown men dove, even passersby waded in, scrambling after the rolling chips on their hands and knees.

Evan shot past the ruckus, threading between approaching security guards talking into their radios. On the far side of the scrum, he turned and looked back.

Slatcher had hit a wall of security, closing off the zone from the far side. A head taller than the crowd, he glowered across at Evan. Trapped behind the temporary barricade.

Evan turned and bolted past the craps tables, hitting the next wide corridor, already crowded with security guards and onlookers drawn toward the disturbance. Pulling the brim of his cap low, he jogged through a flock of little-black-dress college girls ornamented with Santa caps. He had to get to an exit before word came down from the eye in the sky upstairs.

A woman with cropped blond hair swung around a roulette wheel and into the corridor. She wore a fitted black shirt tucked into dark blue jeans, showing off her curves. Her hand was in her Louis Vuitton purse, and Evan's brain double-clutched before placing her alluring features.

Candy McClure, Slatcher's associate, captured in a few grainy surveillance stills astride a Kawasaki.

Her hand whipped out of her handbag toward his face. Evan ducked, throwing his weight backward, his momentum carrying him on even as he dropped. An honest-to-God stiletto flashed past, missing his upturned face by inches. He landed in a forward slide on his knees, skating across the marbled surface, rotating around to face her. Her hand was already back inside the purse, replacing the knife. She offered Evan a pert, *Well, I tried* smile.

It was as though nothing had happened.

More security guards and gamblers crashed forward all around them, driving on, and McClure allowed herself to be swept along by them.

Evan shook off his disbelief. Too much time had passed now, so he shouldered into a bathroom, the one public location in a casino where security cameras were not legally permitted. He shoved his hat into the trash bin, then flipped his reversible jacket inside out, the black shell now turned to white. With a paper towel, he wiped the sweat from his brow, then moved back out into the corridor, hustling along once again.

An elevator dinged to his right and ejected a raft of fresh security guards. Evan kept his same trajectory, slicing into their midst. He eased out a breath, caught a whiff of aftershave and hair gel on the inhale. The guards breezed past, jabbering into their radios, enlarging images on their smartphones.

Reaching the end of the corridor, he spun through a grand revolving door into the river of people clogging Las Vegas Boulevard. Bucking through two oblivious policemen, he scanned the sea of heads frantically, looking for a scared seventeen-year-old. As he rushed up one teeming block and down the next, he realized he wasn't going to find her any more than Slatcher was.

Morena was long gone.

33. The Long Haul

On his way home, Evan exited the freeway by Dodger Stadium and cased the address that Memo Vasquez had given him. The ramshackle structure, more shed than house, seemed to be deteriorating into the hillside. Dead ivy clung to the cheap cladding. Plywood boarded one of the front windows. Gangbangers congregated on neighboring front porches, sipping 40s, their plaid shorts tugged low. A group of kids played ball, using a shopping cart hung on a Dumpster as a basketball hoop. Strings of Christmas lights blinked sporadically from various rooflines.

Evan made a cautious approach and walked the surrounding blocks but found no signs of surveillance. He'd repeat it on Wednesday even more thoroughly before the arranged meeting.

He thought about Morena in the wind, more scared than ever. He'd have to wait for her to contact him, if she decided to. But he imagined that after the near kidnapping in Jasmine she would vanish again, far from her sister and Danny Slatcher and Evan himself. The thought of her out there somewhere, vulnerable to Slatcher's next move, grated on him, a metal file working his nerves.

As he headed back to his car, his phone rang. The

caller ID showed the burner phone he'd given Katrin. A sense of betrayal surged in his chest, lava-hot.

He answered, holding the phone to his face.

'Where are you?' she asked.

Paranoia has a taste, an acidity on the tongue as sharp as the side effect of a potent medication. Evan's breath fogged in the midnight chill. The air smelled of mowed grass and car exhaust. Up the street a woman wearing hot pink heels with fabric straps that laced all the way up to her thighs strutted through a chorus of catcalls.

Evan asked, 'Why do you want to know where I am?'

Her laugh was musical. 'I don't, really. I suppose what I really want to know is why you're not here.'

He said nothing.

'So,' she said. 'Why aren't you here?'

'I'm figuring out how to fix it.'

'What?'

'Everything,' he said. 'Don't call unless it's an emergency. I'll be back to you Wednesday night.'

'Okay.' Her tone had cooled. 'Emergency only. That's fine. I hope I didn't . . .'

'What?'

'Nothing. Just – thank you.'

He hung up.

He switched vehicles in Burbank, parking the Taurus two lots over from where he'd left his truck. After driving home he made it upstairs and went straight to the Vault. He checked the surveillance feeds from the loft, picking up the minute he'd left and fast-forwarding to observe Katrin's every move. She'd slept, showered, stretched, ordered groceries in, napped. Everything as she'd been instructed.

He caught up to the present, finding her standing at the big tinted windows, looking out at the freeway beyond. Her shoulders shook slightly. She was crying.

Perhaps she knew she was being observed.

He trudged from the Vault, climbed on to his levitating bed, and fell into a deep sleep.

In his dream Jack came to him, his lips rouged black. Slowly the black liquid rose in his mouth, glimmering, then spilled over on to his chin. Jack tried to catch it in his hands, cupping the blood as if he could scoop it back into his body. His wild eyes looked up into Evan's.

'"The past isn't dead",' Jack quoted through slick black lips. '"It's not even past".'

'What does that mean?' Evan said.

'Hell if I know.' Jack shrugged, the terrible fluid streaming through his fingers. 'Dream interpretations,' he added with disdain. 'I hate that shit.'

Evan woke breathing hard, his flesh clammy, the sheets churned up around him. It was 5:00 a.m. His thoughts were disheveled, scenarios cascading one after another.

The air conditioner blew cool and steady across his drying sweat. He sat up in bed and crossed his legs to meditate. As Jack had taught him, he freed up a space inside his mind and populated it with the oak trees of his childhood. He put a Virginia summer sun in the sky and a carpet of wild grass underfoot. Walking between tree trunks, he breathed the dusty scent of the bark and listened for birdcalls. He came into a clearing, and there Jack waited, his smile still rouged, his chin dripping black, his teeth stained vampirically.

Evan opened his eyes, more annoyed than distressed.

From his nightstand drawer, he removed a Tibetan gong the size and shape of a soup bowl. He ran the wooden baton around the rim, making the bowl sing. And then he struck the bronze side once and closed his eyes.

Feeling the tone against his skin, he attended to every micromoment of sensation within him, cultivating the same hyperawareness he used when fighting or setting up a sniper shot. He let the vibrations travel through him, sounding the inside of his body, defining his shape anew. He waited as the noise faded, until there was not a trace of sound lingering, until even the last shiver in the air had stilled.

He opened his eyes refreshed.

His mission priorities clarified.

He could not trust Katrin. He could not trust Memo Vasquez, the second caller. He was meeting Vasquez tomorrow, which gave him a little more than twenty-four hours to surveil Katrin and see if she tried to make contact with a handler.

If she did not, he'd see Vasquez in the morning and press him hard.

It was all about applying pressure until one of them crumbled.

His empty stomach got him off the bed and moving

toward the kitchen. The living wall had seen better days. The drip system appeared to be balky, herbs browning at the edges. Nonetheless he found two robust red tomatoes, harvested some basil and sage, and made an omelet.

Back in the Vault, he sipped fresh mint tea, forked breakfast from a plate, and watched Katrin sleep. Her straight, shiny hair, laid like a wedge against her flawless cheek, made her look as though she were being rendered in black and white.

At last she awakened, stretching herself into an expansive yawn and heading into the bathroom. She freshened up, changed clothes, and moved to the kitchen, searching the cupboards until she found a frying pan. She made eggs and sat at the counter, pushing them around her plate with a fork.

It was as though they were eating breakfast together.

He remembered how she'd called him over to the window, then reached behind her to pull him to her. Her skin like silk. The lipstick smearing on her plush lips.

If she was playing him, she'd done a spectacular job.

His RoamZone gave off a sonar ping, the GPS signal coming up in response to the food hitting her stomach. The microchips in her system would have to be replenished soon if he wanted to keep tabs on her, and right now there was nothing he wanted to do more.

The GPS dot blipped on his phone, pinning her location even as he watched her in real time on the monitor. Sipping his tea, Evan settled in for the long haul.

34. The Samurai-Sword Incident

Angles of Katrin White filled the monitors, bird's-eye, head-on, profiles – even aesthetic shots from severe angles. It was like some pop-art collage, cubism parted out into Warholian repetition: *Katrin Reading a Magazine on Her Belly, One Foot Dangling in the Air.*

Evan watched her at intervals, exiting the Vault to work out at the stations in his great room, to eat lunch, to run on the treadmill near the south balcony. The treadmill gave him a clean shot down to 19H in the neighboring building, the apartment where the digitized, encrypted conversations for 1-855-2-NOWHERE, after zigzagging through telephone-switch destinations around the globe, emerged from Joey Delarosa's Wi-Fi access point and then vanished again into Verizon's LTE network.

Every time Evan returned to the Vault, he reviewed the footage from the loft. And every one of those times, Katrin showed herself to be doing almost precisely what Evan was himself doing – waiting. She made the futon, paced around the kitchen island, did some half-assed yoga while looking at the view. For one thirty-minute period, she curled up on the couch and sobbed. Evan reviewed every last minute, waiting for the slightest misstep. But not once did she exhibit any behavior he deemed suspicious.

At six-thirty Evan's doorbell rang, the sound muted by the thick walls of the Vault. With a few clicks of the mouse, he switched the feed to bring up the pinhole camera hidden in the air-conditioning vent outside his condo.

Mia waited at his door, holding Peter's hand. Though she stood in place, her legs moved in a faint simulation of running, alternate knees dipping forward, a show of nervous impatience.

Evan felt a stab of annoyance. It took him a minute to extricate himself from the Vault and walk to the front door. As he opened it, he braced himself for some parental complaint, but Mia looked anything but peeved.

Her eyes, puffy from emotion, her nose tinged red, the set of her face severe. What he'd mistaken for impatience was fear.

'Hi, Evan. I'm so sorry to bother you. But I have a work emergency. I have to get into the office now, and since it's last-minute, all my sitters are tied up.'

Peter stared at him, the bruising around his eye now faded to a jaundiced yellow. He wore a backpack, stuffed to the point of bursting. How many things did an eight-year-old require on his person at any given moment?

'Wait,' Evan said. 'What?'

'Please.'

'I can't,' Evan said. 'I'm sorry. I'm dealing with a work situation of my own today. Something I really can't step away from.'

'You wouldn't have to watch him,' she said. 'He could just do homework in another room? Check on him every half hour or so?' She stepped forward, lowered her voice. 'This is a real crisis. As in life or death.'

He matched her lowered voice. 'Is that a metaphor?'

'No,' she said. 'I've got no one else right now. I really need your help.'

If by some long shot they attacked him here in his stronghold, could he protect the boy? Evan bit down on the inside of his lip. Looked over at Peter. Back to her. 'How long will you be?'

'Oh, thank God,' Mia said, propelling Peter forward. 'Just a couple of hours.'

Evan held the door open, and Peter scooted past him. Mia started for the elevator, then halted and looked back. 'I cannot tell you what this means to me.'

Evan gave a little nod and closed the door.

From behind him: 'This place is *so cool*!'

Evan spun around. 'Hang on. Where are you?'

Peter was walking around the kitchen, checking it out. He left fingerprints on the Sub-Zero. Turned on the power blender. Tugged out the spray head of the kitchen faucet and let it snap back into place.

Evan ran over, switched off the machine, wiped down the refrigerator. 'Don't touch anything.'

'Okay. Sorry. It's just . . . this place is all hard and concrete, like the Batcave.'

Evan looked over at the winged patch sewn on to his backpack. 'You're a big Batman fan, huh?'

'Know why?' Peter waited for Evan to shake his head. ''Cuz he's not magic. He's not a alien like

259

Superman with superpowers. He can't fly. He's like you and me. His parents got killed, and so he wants to help people now. That's all.' Peter thunked his backpack on to the counter and hopped up on a stool. 'I'm hungry.'

His mind still back on the dead parents, Evan took a moment to process the transition.

'Do you have mac and cheese?' Peter asked.

Evan opened the refrigerator, scanning the sparse shelves. A jar of gherkins, cocktail onions, two saline bags in the fruit drawer. 'I have caviar and water crackers.'

'What's a water cracker?'

Evan extracted one from the box, set it on a dinner plate before Peter. The boy took a bite, the crumbs landing everywhere but on the plate beneath him. He made a face.

'What?'

'There's no *flavor.*'

Evan found a hunk of Manchego in the back of a drawer, cut off a few wedges, and placed them on the crackers. 'This'll help.' He knocked the counter with a fist. 'Start your homework.'

Peter opened his notebook and set about writing.

Evan hurried back to the bedroom suite, locked the door behind him, then stepped through the shower into the Vault. Settling into his chair behind the sheet-metal desk, he unpaused the surveillance feeds and observed Katrin White being Katrin White. She sprawled on the futon. Drank orange juice from the carton. Dug dark nail polish from her purse and painted her toes. He clicked to speed up the feed, watching closely to see if she made any gesture that could be interpreted as a signal – opening the bathroom window, reaching for the phone, sliding something beneath the front door – but she just whiled away the boring hours on Charlie Chaplin fast-forward. It was looking increasingly likely that nothing was going to break before his meet with Memo Vasquez tomorrow morning.

Evan had caught up and was observing Katrin in real time when he heard a cry from somewhere in his condo, then a clattering as something crashed to the floor.

He leapt up and rushed out, swinging shut the hidden shower door behind him. When he barreled out of the bedroom and into the hall, Peter was standing there, blood snaking down his hand.

Half slid out of its sheath, the katana lay on the floor at his feet, fallen from its acrylic wall pegs.

'I'm sorry.' Peter squeezed his thumb, fighting tears. 'I just wanted to see it for a sec.'

Evan went down on a knee. 'Give me your hand.'

A nick through the pad of Peter's thumb – the blade must have barely touched him. Given the sharpness of the sword, the kid was lucky he hadn't lost a finger.

Evan brought him into the bathroom, washed it under cold water, then applied pressure with a Kleenex. He set the bloody tissue by the sink, then took out a tube of superglue from the medicine cabinet.

'You're gonna *glue* my thumb shut?'

'Yes.'

'What if I scratch my cheek and the superglue glues my thumb to my face?'

'Then you'll look like this for the rest of your life.'

Peter regarded Evan's pose with alarm, and then his face softened. 'Ha, ha. You're sure this is okay?'

'Trust me,' Evan said.

Peter did.

Afterward he regarded the wound. 'Do you have any Muppet Band-Aids?'

'No,' Evan said.

They walked back out into the hall, regarding the fallen blade. The sheath, a wooden *shirasaya*, featured an etched and inked *sayagaki* – the hallmark of a long-dead sensei. The hairline crack ran straight through the sensei's signature. There were three people in the country who could properly make the repair; fortunately, one of them lived in Marin. Evan crouched over the scabbard, fingering the damage. As soon as he completed this mission, he'd take the drive up the coast and have the *shirasaya* fixed.

'I'm sorry,' Peter said. 'Homework is boring.'

'I can imagine.' Evan picked up the sword, slid it back into its sheath.

Peter asked, 'What is it anyways?'

An eighteenth-century katana, splendidly forged, with Bizen-styled *choji-midare* in the *hamon*, or blade pattern. Hand-carved *bohi* and *sohi* for balance, *sashikomi* polish, flawless gold-foil collar at the base of the gleaming blade.

'A sword,' Evan said.

He steered Peter back to the counter, then took the damaged sword down to his Ford F-150 in the parking garage and locked it in one of the truck vaults overlaying the bed. Getting it repaired would be his reward once he completed the mission.

When he came back up, Peter was sprawled on the couch, textbook on his chest, asleep. Worn out, no doubt, from the samurai-sword incident. Evan stood for a moment, unsure what to do. Thankfully, the door-bell rang.

When he answered, Mia looked exhausted. 'God, Evan. I don't know how to thank you.'

'Everything okay?' he asked.

'As okay as it's gonna get,' she said. 'How 'bout here?'

'Everything's fine. He got a little cut on his thumb.'

'Oh? From what?'

Evan cringed a little.

Fortunately, Mia drifted past him into the penthouse without awaiting an answer. Her gaze moved to her son on the couch. 'They're so quiet when they're sleeping,' she said.

She packed up his things, slung the backpack over an arm, then stooped to pick him up. 'He's impossible to wake when he's like this. Just gotta get him down-stairs.' She struggled, his limbs flopping around, the backpack slipping off her shoulder.

Evan stepped in. 'I got him,' he said.

35. Hymn to Freedom

They stepped inside Condo 12B, Evan bearing Peter's slack body like some distorted pietà, Mia bobbling her briefcase and Peter's backpack. She kicked off one heeled shoe, then the other.

'Will you please just put him in bed? I have to get out of these clothes.' She colored. 'Not like that. I just mean –'

'No problem.' Evan carried Peter to his bedroom and nestled him into the race-car bed. He stood a moment in the still of the room, trying to recall if he'd ever slept that soundly.

He walked back out into the living room, hearing Miles Davis playing somewhere deep in the condo. A bright new Post-it called out from the post by the kitchen pass-through: *'Treat yourself as if you were someone you are responsible for helping.'*

He wondered what exactly that meant.

He wandered back to Mia's bedroom, nearly colliding with her on her way out. With a nervous laugh, she skipped back a half step. She wore a long sleep shirt that drooped to midthigh. They stood close enough that even in the soft light of her bedroom he could make out the faint scattering of freckles across the bridge of her nose. Her unbound hair fell across her face, so she took it up in a fist atop her head, her sleep shirt stretching tight across her body. He caught a hint of lemongrass – the smell of her skin, of her.

The tune ended and another started up, a delicate piano riff.

'*Oh,*' Mia said. 'Oh, no. Not the Oscar Peterson Trio.' She swayed a little to the music lazily, one hand still holding up her hair. 'I had this psych class once in college. A lecture on meditation. You ever meditated?'

'Some,' he said.

'The professor, she had us pair off and ask our partner the same question over and over again: "What makes you happy?" Just that, time after time. And then we switched. When it came my turn, my first answer was, "Hymn to Freedom". This song. Listen to the trill right . . . *here.*' She dropped her weight a little, let her hair go. The birthmark at her temple peeked out from a fringe of curls.

Her gaze was very direct. 'Want to play?'

He said, 'Sure.'

'What makes you happy?'

He thought, *Long-range precision marksmanship.*

'Rhodesian ridgebacks,' he said.

She made a soft noise, gave a half smile. 'What makes you happy?'

He thought, *Jujitsu double-hand parries.*

He said, 'French wheat vodka.'

'What makes you happy?'

This time there was no space between his thought and the words. He said, 'Your freckles.'

Her mouth parted ever so slightly. She ambled a few

steps backward into her room. Started to say something. Stopped herself.

'Do you want me to go?' he asked.

'No.'

'Do you want me to stay?'

'Yes,' she said. 'Yes, I do, yes.'

She stepped into him and him to her, her hands rising to his cheeks even as their mouths met. She pressed her body against his, her face tilted back, lips soft, that wavy hair sliding lushly through his fingers. They broke apart, forehead to forehead, their breath intermingling, and then she said, softly, 'No.'

He pulled back from her.

She scrunched up her face. *'Nononononono.'*

He waited.

'This is a huge mistake. *Huge.* I have too many complications to have . . . *complications.*'

'Okay,' he said.

'If Peter saw anything, it would be so confusing for him. I'm sorry, but you should probably go.'

'Okay,' he said, turning for the door.

'It's just really a bad time, and —' Her traffic-monitor hands went up, halting the conversation, her own train of thought. 'God, you're so . . . unflappable.'

'What do you expect?'

'I don't know. Argue with me. Make it my fault. Get angry.'

'Is that what you want?'

'*No,*' she said. She blew out a breath, frustrated. 'Yes? Maybe?'

'That doesn't interest me,' Evan said.

'Mom?'

They both swung their gazes to the doorway where Peter had appeared, grinding the heel of a hand into one eye. He squinted at them, exhausted and confused. 'What are you guys doing in here?'

'Oh, honey, hi, yes . . . um. I was just asking Evan here to help me . . .' Mia's hand circled a few times, looking to pluck a good excuse from thin air. '. . . move the furniture.'

'Why do you need him?' Peter asked. 'Is it heavy furniture?'

Evan said, 'I like to think so.'

Mia stifled a laugh, covering her mouth with a hand. 'Come on,' she said to Peter. 'Let's get you back down.'

''Kay.' Peter looked across at Evan. 'Night, Evan Smoak.'

Evan headed out, ruffling Peter's hair. 'Night.'

When he stepped out into the corridor and closed the door of Mia's condo behind him, he was enveloped in a sudden quiet. The elevator hummed pleasantly as he ascended.

When he entered his penthouse, the ambient light through the armored sunscreens reflected faintly off the door of the Sub-Zero, throwing the edge of a child-size handprint into relief on the stainless steel.

He stood in the near-perfect silence of his condo, staring at the smudge mark, feeling something stir inside, an echo of some ancient battle fought within himself that he'd never known was being waged. In the pristine reflection above the handprint, he saw only himself, wearing an expression of mild vexation. The roll of paper towel, floating on a steel rod beneath the cabinet, beckoned to him.

But instead of wiping away the mark, he walked down the hall toward the master suite. At the edge of the sink sat the red-spotted tissue from Peter's cut. Evan stepped past it into the shower, resting his hand on the hot-water lever and rotating it the wrong way.

Returning to the feeds from the loft, he brought himself up to speed on the ordinary doings of Katrin White. All the while the thought of that dirty handprint, marring the refrigerator, stayed lodged in the back of his thoughts, scratching like a bug fighting its way out.

He refocused on the monitors, pushing his discomfort away. Once he'd caught up to the feed, he exited the Vault, climbed into bed, and lay in the darkness. The bug scratched and scratched, burrowing through his thoughts, an unwelcome guest. An hour passed. Another.

Finally Evan got up and padded down the concrete hall to the kitchen.

He wet a paper towel and eliminated the handprint from the stainless-steel door of the Sub-Zero.

36. Special Girl

Between rickety hillside houses and a run-down school, an ice-cream truck jingled up the tight lane, hailed by a cluster of sprinting kids out for morning recess with their teacher. Evan had checked out the van earlier, buying a water from the elderly driver as a pretext to eyeball the interior. In fact, he'd spent hours surveying the surrounding area, scanning for any sign that a trap was in place. Everything looked normal, or at least Elysium Park's version of normal. Evan waited for the ice-cream truck to pass, then got out of the Taurus and finally started for Memo Vasquez's house.

Evan approached the meet with extreme suspicion, even by his own standards. He'd observed Katrin for more than sixty hours. She'd exhibited not a single sign of deceit. There was the possibility that she was aware that she was being watched, but Evan had installed the loft surveillance himself, ensuring that it was impeccably concealed. For two and a half days, she'd shown no consciousness of the hidden lenses – not the slightest sideways glance or body-language tell – which Evan knew from experience was hard to fake. So now his distrust was sharpened for Memo.

Evan stepped up on to the creaking porch, knocked twice, and pivoted to the hinge side of the door, putting his shoulder blades to the clapboard. He was a half hour early by design, intending to catch Vasquez off guard.

The door opened, and Evan swung into the gap, propelling Vasquez backward into the tiny front room.

Vasquez, a rounded man with a broad graying mustache, held his hands up. 'Please don't hurt me. Please don't.'

Evan heeled the door shut, swept Vasquez's legs, catching his weight to soften his landing on the floor. He flipped him, frisking him even as his eyes scoured the space. Evan produced soft flex-ties from a front cargo pocket; they wadded up much easier than their stiff plastic counterparts, making them easier to carry. He looped a set around Vasquez's hands, cinching the braided nylon fabric tight. Vasquez grunted.

'Stay,' Evan said.

He moved swiftly through the tiny house. The bare-bones interior contained scarcely the basics. One couch. A card table with two plates, two cups, two forks. Empty cupboards save for a pot and a pan, both scalded. Two mattresses on the floor in the sole bedroom, one with a tangled sleeping bag, the other with a pink teddy bear, its ear chewed to a stiff nub. A stack of cardboard boxes in the corner held T-shirts displaying different baseball players' names and numbers. Evan moved on to the bathroom. A four-pack of toilet paper on the chipped tile. Sliver of dried soap in the shower stall. Two toothbrushes on the sink, one pink, one blue.

The house hardly looked lived in, which meant one of

two things: either Vasquez had only the bare essentials, which made sense, since people living below the poverty line didn't accessorize. Or Slatcher's team had hastily staged the place to sell the fact that Vasquez resided here.

From the warped floorboards, Vasquez's breaths grew labored. Evan hoisted him up and deposited him on the couch. Rolling the rotund man to one side, he removed the wallet from the back pocket of his Carhartt work pants. The wallet's plastic window held no ID, a corroboration of Vasquez's illegal status. Instead it displayed a ragged-edged photo of Vasquez with a squat, bowlegged teenage girl hugging him from the side. She had heavily lidded eyes, a flat nasal bridge, her thick lips shaped into a joyful smile, one hand clutching the pink teddy bear. Vasquez embraced her with one arm, his other hand holding a kite string. Their faces, upturned to the wind.

Vasquez looked at Evan through sagging, wounded eyes. 'I thought you were going to *help* me.'

Evan said, 'And if I trust you, I will.'

'Trust *me*?'

Evan took up a post by a gap in the plywood boarding the front window, keeping his eyes on the street. The earth sloped precipitously here, the houses clinging to the hillside, giving Evan a clean view of the road leading up. Dodger Stadium rose in the distance, a great concrete chalice. The smell of weed laced the faint breeze through the gap.

'Tell me your story,' Evan said. 'Make me believe you.'

Vasquez strained on the couch, sweat dappling the front of his T-shirt. 'Can you please cut my hands free?'

Evan cut the flex-ties and returned to his watch at the window. 'Where did Morena find you?'

'I was at a meeting. For the alcoholics.'

'AA?'

'Yes. I drove to Las Vegas to bring *mi hermana* a washing machine. I cannot miss a meeting for one night. Morena – she was there.'

'Why was she there?'

'She said she went to the meeting to find someone like me. Someone who needed help. Who was on the verge of the slipping.'

Evan had to admit, it was an ingenious place for Morena to seek out people on the edge. Even so, he couldn't keep skepticism from coloring his tone. 'You announced your problems? In front of the group?'

'No. But I wanted to drink. And she perhaps sensed how badly I was.' Perspiration sparkled on his forehead. 'I am driven to drink when I feel how useless . . . how powerless I am.'

'Why do you feel powerless?'

'You see I am not a rich man.' He jerked his chin to indicate the humble surroundings. 'But I am an honest man. It is just me and my Isa. From the picture. Her mother passed away during the birth. I brought Isa here for a better life. It is hard for her in Mexico because of her . . . condition. I make *los* Dodgers T-shirts and sell them in the parking lot before the games. I rent a small space in *el distrito de* textiles to make the T-shirts.

One night the bad men come to my shop. They had wrapped the – what's the word? – yes, the packages. Of *la cocaína*. They say *la policía* are on them. They need to hide the packages in my shop. They have the guns and the blade, like this.' His thick fingers measured off a bowie knife. '*El jefe* put the blade in the face of my Isa. If I tell anyone, he say they will take her. He do not say for what. Just – they will take her.'

His eyes glimmered, and his breathing grew wet. 'I did not know what to do. If I refuse, they will take my Isa. If I run, they promise they will hunt me. If I go to *la policía,* I will be deported. So I say . . . I say okay. I will do this.'

Evan focused as much on Vasquez's delivery as on his words. Cover stories tended to sound rehearsed – too smooth, with no hesitations. Vasquez seemed genuine, full of pauses and broken sentences. And he didn't appear to be stalling either, drawing out the story to give his handlers time to plot an approach.

'How many men were there?' Evan asked.

'Three.'

'And *el jefe* – the boss. Where was he standing? To your right or to your left?'

'To my left.'

'And Isa? She was to your left also?'

'Yes. He was near her.'

'What did the man look like *next to* the boss?'

'He was large. With the big muscles. Like a boxer.'

'And the fourth man? What did he look like?'

'There was no fourth man. Only three men.'

'The third man?'

'He was big, too. Tall. But skinny.'

'Skinny like the boss?'

'*El jefe* was not skinny. He had muscles like rope knots.'

'And he was standing to your right –'

'My left. He was over here. *Here*. With my Isa.' Memo lifted his shirt collar and used it to wipe his forehead. 'You try to trick me. You do not believe. You do not believe.'

'I didn't say that,' Evan said.

Memo stared at him from the couch but made no move to rise. It occurred to Evan that he did not feel he was free to move, and right now that was fine by Evan.

'What happened next?' Evan asked.

'When they leave that night, I am closing up and I see that *la policía*, they are coming door-to-door through *el distrito*. They are close. I take the packages and I throw them in the trash can outside the back door and I run. I run with my Isa. I hide and wait for *la policía* to go away. And then I go back. But when I go back' – his breath caught at the memory – 'the packages, they are no there. They are no there.'

Somewhere up the street, the singsong music of the ice-cream truck played, and Evan heard a chorus of children's voices, clamoring in two languages for their orders.

Vasquez was breathing hard, trying to hold back tears. 'The next night these men come again. I explain to *el jefe* what happen. He say this is my fault. That I owe him this money. Five *thousand* dollars.' Vasquez lowered

274

his head and shook it slowly. Drops of sweat clung to the tips of his hair but did not fall. 'This is more money than I have ever seen. They say if I do not bring it to them soon, they will come. They will come for my Isa.'

'Why do they want her?'

At last Memo looked up, and his dark eyes burned. 'They will sell her organs.'

He sobbed a few times, hoarsely. Standing by the window, Evan felt the familiar fury rise in him. The ice-cream truck was on the move again, coasting slowly down the hill toward the house.

Memo said, 'They say this, too, is their business. They say that her heart is no good because she is a special girl. And her eyes – she have the cataracts.' His lips parted in something like a snarl. 'But for the black market, they will take her liver. Her kidneys. Her lungs.' Memo's voice continued to rise. 'Her *bone. Skin. Veins. Tendons.*' Tears ran down his cheeks. 'They will take their profit from her body.'

'Where is Isa now?'

He choked out the words. 'She is at her school. They have the learning program for her.'

Through the gap in the plywood, Evan shot a final look down the long road. Then he walked over to Guillermo. He looked into his face. Believed him.

Memo said, 'I am running out of time. I cannot get this money, and when they see that, they will take my special girl.'

Evan crouched and set his hands on Memo's knees. 'I will help you,' he said.

Outside, the ice-cream truck's music rose louder, and then came a whoosh of tires as the truck passed. Its headlights swept the living-room wall, bringing up a glint in the cracked plasterboard.

Evan's eyes snapped over, locking on the spot. He rose and looked down at Vasquez. 'Do not move. Not a finger. *Comprende?*'

Vasquez nodded, the furrows returning to his forehead.

Walking over to the wall, Evan dug his finger into the crack, plaster crumbling around it. His finger struck something smooth and hard. He hooked it, yanked it out.

A pinhole lens, identical to the one he used outside his condo.

After laying all this exceptional groundwork, they'd sunk a camera blatantly into the middle of a wall? Why?

Slatcher, he knew, was staring at him right now.

In a rage, Evan tore the lens free, the wire ripping through the drywall, powdering the air. Memo watched from the couch, mouth gaping in fear.

Evan shook the surveillance wire tangled around his clenched hand in Vasquez's face. 'What is this?'

'I never see that before in my life. I swear, I –'

The RoamZone phone vibrated in Evan's pocket. His other hand shot down to the phone, pressed it to his cheek. Before he could speak, he heard the shouting.

'Evan? Evan, it's me!'

Katrin. Her voice wrenched high with panic.

'People are here – the ones from the motel. They

pulled up in front in that Scion we saw. I just watched them run inside. Oh, my God! Where are you, Evan? Where are you?'

He felt a heat at the back of his neck, the warm breath of dread. 'Look through the peephole. Can you get to the stairs?'

'I don't know! I don't know!'

'Check. *Now.*'

Memo rose partway on the couch, hands raised placatingly, fingers spread. 'Listen to me, *amigo.* I swear on my Isa's eyes, I never –'

Evan's blow knocked him straight on to his belly on the floor. Pinching the phone with his shoulder, Evan put a knee between Vasquez's shoulder blades, wrenched back his arms, and flex-tied his wrists. Then he secured his ankles.

A sharp intake of breath came through the phone. 'They're in the hall already, Evan. What am I supposed to do?'

'Dead-bolt the door,' Evan said. 'Get to the bathroom. There's a –'

A thunderous boom came through the receiver, the sound of a battering ram meeting a lock assembly. Katrin's scream was so loud that Evan jerked the phone a few inches from his head.

'Stay on the phone, Katrin. No matter what happens, stay on the –'

He heard the sound of a slap, then Katrin's phone skittering across the floor. An instant later there was a rustling and the line cut out.

Leaving Memo bound on the floor, Evan sprinted for the door. He understood now why Slatcher didn't care if the pinhole lens was obvious. The aim of the subterfuge wasn't to lure Evan here to kill him.

The aim was to draw him *away* from Katrin.

37. Sooner or Later

Evan hurtled recklessly across Downtown, running reds, slicing between cars, veering two tires up on to a sidewalk to squeak past a Volvo. He called up the GPS screen linked to the microchips in Katrin's system, but no signal showed. A half block from his loft, he screeched into a bus zone and leapt from the Taurus, sprinting for the building with his hand riding the still-holstered Wilson Combat 1911.

He drew the pistol as he crashed through the glass front doors, scattering a middle-aged couple and their two kids as he bolted for the stairs. Running up, he halted at the fifth-floor landing, cracking the door and peering through. The door to his loft was a few inches ajar, the wood crumpled slightly around the dead bolt.

Easing into the hall, pistol raised, he crept along the carpet. He spread his hand on the splintered wood and swung the door silently inward. Leading with the gun barrel, he inched inside, taking in the open space with a sweeping glance.

One of the barstools knocked on its side. The burner cell phone smashed to pieces. He crouched over the electronic entrails, touching the few dark spots on the floor next to them. When he lifted his hand, crimson filmed his fingertips.

The drops were not excessive – maybe a bloodied nose from the slap? He knew that Katrin was alive. They didn't want *her*.

Since the loft was burned, he wasted no time leaving, reclaiming the Taurus up the street, and racing back to the Elysium Park house he'd just left. He replayed Vasquez's cover story in his head. The elaborate tale – humble illegal alien with no one to turn to, evil drug lords, the Down's syndrome daughter to be parted out for organs – now seemed implausible, hitting all the right marks to tug at Evan's insides. The photo of 'Isa' had even been planted in Memo's wallet in place of a driver's license, the first place Evan would check.

Slatcher had done his research, building a simulation of a Nowhere Man mission with just the right veneer of desperation and helplessness.

A few minutes later, Evan stood in the dusty interior of the ramshackle house, surveying the scene. A pocketknife on its side, blade pried up. Two sets of severed nylon flex-ties on the floorboards. And no sign of Memo Vasquez.

Disgusted with himself and not at all surprised, Evan started for the Burbank parking lot to swap out vehicles. A question smoldered in him: how had Slatcher located the loft? Evan's mind spun, cycling through various possibilities.

Midway to Burbank, an impulse seized him, and he screeched off the freeway and pulled in to an alley behind a strip mall. Arid heat blew through the back vent of a dry cleaner, bagged and hung garments cycling on the track inside like disembodied souls.

From the trunk he yanked out the Hardigg Storm Case and put together the nonlinear junction detector. He wanded the Taurus meticulously, lingering over every spoke and panel, even sliding beneath the car on the rough blacktop to check the undercarriage. He ran the circular head over the inside upholstery, decapitated the headrests, yanked every item from the glove box. Tearing out the floor mats, he scanned them as if wet-vaccing the fabric.

The detector gave out only its customary crackle of static.

A few people exiting the dry cleaner offered him curious stares, but he ignored them, focused on his task, his sweat-heavy shirt clinging to him. He tugged out the spare tire and checked it, then disemboweled the first-aid kit, scattering its pieces across the ground. The tire iron was clean, as was the carpeted trunk mat, which he ripped out and exposed inch by inch. He shredded the black foam inside the Hardigg Storm Case, strewing it like wads of cotton across the alley.

Sitting among the wreckage of the car, he breathed hard, catching his breath, at a loss.

His stare pulled to the wand itself. A terrible suspicion pulsed to life in his chest.

Rising, he picked up the detector. Then he hurled it against the asphalt, shattering it to pieces. Stomping with his heel, he fractured the plastic handle.

Inside was a tiny digital transmitter.

Crouching, he plucked up the pea-size tracker, held it between his thumb and forefinger, and glared at it.

Hiding a transmitter within the very wand designed to detect it was an unrivaled piece of tradecraft.

He walked over to the dry cleaner's delivery van parked beside him, unscrewed the gas cap, and dropped the transmitter inside the tank. That should keep Slatcher and his team running circles around the city for a while.

In the ravaged car, Evan drove to the airport-adjacent parking lot and picked up his truck. He drove home, trying to piece together when Slatcher's team could have bugged the wand.

The first time Evan had used the Taurus was just before Slatcher's assault on Katrin's motel room. The car had been clean then – there was simply no way they could have known about it before. And once Evan and Katrin had fled the motel through the back window, he'd watched Slatcher with his own two eyes. Slatcher had no tracking intel – he was waiting on comms from his field team in the room, and then he'd turned to study the street. No, there had been no transmitter hidden within the car when Evan had first taken Katrin to the loft.

Which meant that Slatcher had planted it when Evan returned to Chinatown to sneak into the sniper's nest. The scene of the attempted shooting was the most logical place to stake out. Slatcher would have known that Evan would return there eventually.

That burned every location Evan had driven to after Chinatown.

He ran through them in his head. He'd gone to the loft later that night when he and Katrin had sex, though he'd left precipitously after getting the call from Memo Vasquez, likely before Slatcher could scramble his team and set up for the kill. Next Evan had taken the Taurus to Vegas, putting Slatcher back on Morena's trail at the aunt's house. Though Slatcher had followed Morena to the Bellagio Casino, he'd been aware that Evan was somewhere on the premises, which is why he'd put Candy McClure into play on the casino floor.

Evan had visited Tommy Stojack as well, but Tommy demanded that his clients park miles away and bus to see him, so his workshop was safe. On the way back from Vegas, Evan had stopped by Memo Vasquez's house, giving Slatcher notice that Evan had taken the bait on the fake caller. Because Evan had switched vehicles in Burbank before coming home, Castle Heights was still presumably clear.

When he'd returned to the Elysium Park house this morning, Slatcher had probably tracked him by the transmitter the whole way there, then waited to get real-time visual confirmation from the not-so-hidden pinhole camera that it really was Evan. That location put Evan too far away to get to Katrin in time, so Slatcher knew he was clear to crash the loft and take her.

It was pretty goddamned obvious why Orphan Zero was considered the best.

Once home, Evan went immediately to his loft and checked to see if Katrin's GPS signal had magically reappeared despite the fact that he'd received no alert. It had not.

Until she ate and her digestive juices charged the microchips in her tract, the signal would be dormant. This carried with it a silver lining: if Slatcher wanded her down for a signal – and Evan had little doubt he would – nothing would show up unless he happened to scan her immediately after a meal. Something told Evan that feeding Katrin was low on Slatcher's list of priorities. But there was a deadline on the signal as well. Katrin likely had one more day, maybe two, before the minuscule sensors passed through her system.

Then she'd be lost for good.

Next he called up the surveillance footage from the loft. He watched Katrin pacing around the kitchen island as she was prone to do. A creeping unease found its way beneath Evan's skin, the slow-burn horror of observing a person unaware that something terrible was about to happen to her.

Katrin moved to the tinted wall of glass, and then her body stiffened with terror. She scrambled for the cell phone, half slipping on the slick floor.

Evan watched her dial with trembling fingers. Watched her mouth move frantically, the conversation branded in his memory. The sound, fuzzy yet audible: *People are here – the ones from the motel.*

She listened to him, ran to the door, glanced through the peephole. Her hands were fumbling at the dead bolt when the door flew in violently, knocking her back. She staggered but managed to keep her feet.

Slatcher flashed inside, backhanding her. Though his blow seemed almost an afterthought, Katrin's head snapped around as if her neck were a well-greased swivel. The phone skittered away.

The woman, Candy McClure, was at Slatcher's heels, a battering ram swinging playfully at her thigh. With a casual, hip-swaying gait, she crossed to the phone and smashed it with one of her chunky heeled boots. Slatcher gathered Katrin up. She lolled in his grip. Candy went to her other side, flipping Katrin's arm so it slung drunkenly over Candy's shoulders, and they sailed out the door.

The entire intrusion took eleven seconds.

Evan watched it through again. And again.

Oh, my God! Where are you, Evan? Where are you?

He rewound. Hit *play.*

Where are you, Evan?

Rewound.

Where are you, Evan?

He listened to Katrin's plea until it became a mantra of rage, firing his insides.

His thumb punched in the remembered number. It rang and rang, but Slatcher did not pick up.

He was likely trying to backtrace the number and would return the call only once he'd made some headway. As a former Orphan, Slatcher would have considerable skills and resources to run down Voice over IP protocols and digitized switchboards. It would be interesting to see how far along the trail he could get.

Keeping the lights off, Evan walked the perimeter of

his dark penthouse, RoamZone in hand. His shoulder scraped along the walls as if marking the boundaries of his fortress, delineating safe ground. The sunshine charcoaled by degrees, and then a postcard orange bled through the sky, and soon enough only man-made lights prevailed, pinpricks in the black sea of the city.

As expected, the phone rang. Evan clicked TALK, put it to his ear. 'Orphan O,' he said.

'Orphan X.'

'Let me talk to her.'

'Of course,' Slatcher said.

A moment later Katrin came on the line, her voice husky from crying. 'I'm sorry, Evan. I'm so sorry I dragged you into this.'

'What are you talking about?'

'I couldn't get the dead bolt locked. I couldn't get to the bathroom.'

'There are two things I need you to remember. None of this is your fault. And I will find you. Repeat them to me.'

She jerked in a few breaths. Then she said, 'None of this is my fault. And you will find me.' She stifled a cry. 'Promise me?'

'I promise. Now, hand the phone back to the man.'

Slatcher came on the line again.

Evan said, 'You're happy to let us talk, aren't you?'

'I am.'

Evan paced along the hall, letting his fingers trickle across the space where the mounted katana once hung. 'Because you're tracing this call. Right now.'

'Trying to.'

'Good luck,' Evan said, not insincerely.

'Nice diversion with the dry-cleaning van,' Slatcher said.

'Thank you,' Evan said. 'Beautiful move planting the digital transmitter in the wand. You put it there in Chinatown?'

'I did,' Slatcher said. 'While you were in the apartment getting on to my trail, I was in the trunk of your car getting on to yours.'

'But you didn't want to take me out there. Too many cops.'

'That's right. The place was inundated. As you saw. Impressive gymnastics on the balconies and the roof. I didn't think you were gonna pull it off.'

Once again Evan's mind scrolled through various potential enemies. A successor to a Hezbollah arms chief he'd zeroed out during the security-zone conflict in Lebanon. The bitter widow of an oligarch who'd trafficked in fissile material. An uncle of a serial rapist he'd put down in Portland.

He said, 'I don't suppose you care to tell me why you're after me?'

'I'm afraid that's not my call.'

'Right. Gun for hire.' Evan walked the edge of the kitchen, letting the living wall tickle his arm. 'Does your employer wish to reveal himself?'

'No.'

'How'd you get on to me? To begin with, I mean?'

'Oh,' Slatcher said, 'I'm good at what I do.'

Evan crossed the poured-concrete stretch of the great room, leaned against the treadmill, looking out at the glowing yellow squares of the apartment windows opposite him. 'You started with Morena?'

'We could've started with someone before that,' Slatcher said. 'You never know who we know. Maybe we've got someone in place in your building right now.' His tone was conversational, but Evan felt the barbed words twisting in his gut.

A disinformation tactic? Evan decided it was. If Slatcher knew where Evan was, his door would have been kicked in by now.

'What makes you think I'm in a building?' Evan asked.

Slatcher laughed in reply. That part of the conversation was closed.

'I watched surveillance from the loft,' Evan said. 'Two former Orphans working together. Now I've seen everything.'

'Well,' Slatcher said. '*Almost* everything. Just wait.'

Evan had only been guessing at Candy's provenance, but he took Slatcher's words as confirmation. 'I wasn't aware they made a female model,' he said.

'Oh, a few.'

Evan drifted past the treadmill and stopped before the periwinkle sunscreen, gazing over the south balcony at apartment 19H in the facing building. The fine interlocking chain mail of the screen fuzzed his view only slightly. He could see Joey Delarosa reclining on his faux-leather couch, remote control resting on his thigh,

a scoured Weight Watcher's tray sitting on the foot-
rest. From the angle of Joey's head and the regular rise
and fall of his shoulders, Evan gleaned he'd fallen asleep.
The light of the TV mapped patterns on the walls
around him, turning the room into something living.

'You don't want Katrin,' Evan said. 'She's just bait.'

Slatcher's voice, loud in his ear: 'This is true. We
want you.'

'I'll be happy to oblige.'

'Confident, aren't you?'

'We both want the same thing,' Evan said.

'What's that?'

'To kill each other.'

'Right,' Slatcher said. 'So how do we approach this?'

Down below in the neighboring building, Joey Delarosa's front door burst open. A balaclava-masked man
flew in, the momentum of the battering ram carrying
him several steps into the apartment. Two more men in
matching black-job gear and Candy McClure poured in
on his heels. Joey's hands exploded up into view, a
heretofore hidden bag of popcorn showering its contents across the couch. Candy was on him instantly,
pouncing like a great cat, frisking and securing him.

'Well,' Evan said. 'Now that you have Katrin, you'll
want to hold a beat. Get any information that she'll
give up. She doesn't have any. It's a waste of time, but
you'll have to do it. Perhaps you could spare her some
harshness by having faith that my operational judgment is sound. I'd never expose myself by trusting her
with anything useful.'

He could hear Slatcher breathing. Down below, the men began clearing the apartment, room by room. Evan watched them vanish, then appear again in the different windows of 19H. He lifted his hand, set it gently on the fine mesh of the titanium screen.

'Leaving Katrin aside, you'll want to see what angles you can run down,' Evan said. 'You'll want to exhaust every resource trying to pick up my trail. In fact, you're probably doing that right now.'

Candy remained in Joey's living room, peering at a handheld device. She followed it to a spot in the wall next to the TV. She punched a fist through the drywall and came out with the mobile phone that Evan had entombed there, sucking its charge from a spliced wire. The phone had mobile Wi-Fi hot-spot enabled and it served as a bridge for the very call he was on, picking up the digital packets sent through Joey's router and bridging the signal into the LTE network, the trail literally vanishing into thin air.

Candy stared at the phone in disgust, dangling on its cords and chargers, and then she let it sag against the wall.

Wearing a fed-up expression, she punched something into the handheld device. A text message?

'Right you are,' Slatcher said.

Sure enough, Evan heard a brief hum over the line, Candy's message coming through to Slatcher.

Slatcher exhaled faintly with annoyance. Then he said, 'I can't give you the meet spot this far in advance. You'll have too much time to set up your counterattack.'

'Right,' Evan said. 'Better to wait so we don't both have to waste time moving it around.'

'We'll be in touch,' Slatcher said. 'When we are prepared for you. You're too dangerous.'

'I understand,' Evan said. 'I'd do the same.'

Slatcher had the upper hand now. Rather than risk going after Evan in a high-profile operation as at the restaurant and the motel, he had switched tacks. He'd make Evan come to him.

In the other building, Candy and her men vanished through the door, and a moment later Joey struggled up on to his feet and stumbled red-faced for his telephone.

'In the meantime you're gonna try to locate her,' Slatcher said. 'You're gonna try to get to us first.'

Evan thought of the ace up his sleeve, the microchips in Katrin's stomach. 'Yes,' he said, at last turning away from the twinkling city lights and heading into the dark heart of his condo.

'Well, I suppose we'll be seeing each other, then,' Slatcher said.

'Sooner or later,' Evan replied, and severed the connection.

38. A Shield of Killers

The sound of a woman sobbing never failed to get under his skin.

Danny Slatcher remained one hall over from the empty office where Candy had secured Katrin White, but still the whimpering carried. They'd set up in an unrented and seemingly unrentable building off the 101 near Calabasas. The isolated structure, situated back behind a big, empty parking lot, had an impractical V-shaped design. The two long halls led to various offices, the meeting rooms tacked on to the rear, facing a scrubby hillside.

A kitchen-atrium, suffused with the reek of dead ferns, was wedged gracelessly in the junction, caught in the throat of the building.

Standing now in the miasma of rotting plants, Slatcher wore the RFID-tagged press-on nails and the fully pixelated contact lens seated on his right eyeball.

The blinking virtual cursor finally turned from red to green.

Top Dog texted a single symbol: ?

Slatcher's fingers moved in a flurry through the air. WE'VE SECURED HER. WILL USE HER TO LURE HIM IN.

TD texted, HOW IS ORPHAN V PERFORMING?

TD loved the code names, the pedigree.

Slatcher typed, FINE.

THE FREELANCERS?

NOT SO FINE.

RUNNING THROUGH THEM, AREN'T YOU?

THERE'S A REASON THEY'RE FREELANCERS, Slatcher typed. WE NEED THEM TO CORRAL THE TARGET.

TD texted, ORPHAN X IS SMARTER THAN THE AVERAGE BEAR.

YES, SIR. HE IS.

The cursor converted back to red.

TD wasn't big on sign-offs.

Danny peeled off the comms gear, placed it back in its slender metal box, and left the stink of the forsaken atrium, heading down the hall toward the sobs.

The cluster of new hires had gathered in the lobby. With their squared-off heads and PED-swollen muscles, they were all military-gone-bad, though this didn't bother Slatcher in the least. He'd long ago learned that the dishonorably discharged were often the meanest and sharpest assaulters. Slatcher wanted a shield of killers in place around Katrin White and Candy McClure until Orphan X lay dead at his feet.

The conversation ceased as Slatcher cut through the men and headed down the adjoining hall. The door to the utility office was ajar. Candy squatted inside the dank concrete rectangle of a room, lovingly checking her plastic jugs of hydrofluoric acid concentrate. She stepped out to join Slatcher as he kept on.

'Should we tell her?' Slatcher asked.

Candy nodded. 'Let's tell her. It'll motivate her to behave.'

They entered the last office on the left. Katrin, blissfully quiet at last, remained where they'd left her, shackled to a desk. Beside her, an untouched bag of McDonald's. The window that looked out on to the hill was nailed shut. Sweat matted Katrin's sleek bangs to her forehead, and her face was swollen from crying. Slatcher's backhand had ballooned her left cheek, a red-wine spill creeping into her eye.

'You're not gonna eat?' Candy asked.

Katrin's eyes barely lifted. 'I'm not hungry.'

Slatcher crouched over her. 'Sam is alive and well,' he said. 'We needed to scare you. We needed you to cry real tears. In front of Evan.'

Katrin's lips parted, but she made no sound. 'No,' she said. 'No. You're lying. You're lying to me.'

'We did what we had to do to get Evan where we needed him. Emotionally. We needed him reckless. Willing to take more risks.'

Katrin's eyes were running. Her thin arms shook uncontrollably. 'You did that to me just to convince him . . . to convince him . . .'

'Look at me. Look at me.' Slatcher's huge hand clamped down over Katrin's chin. He jerked her face to his. 'If you cooperate fully with us, Sam will live. Do you understand me?'

Katrin nodded in his viselike grip, her tears dampening his knuckles. 'I just want it all to be over.'

'It'll be over when Evan is dead.'

Slatcher released her, and Katrin's muscles went slack. She melted to the floor, her cheek pressed to the thin carpeting. Grease spotted the fast-food bag by her face, the smell turning her stomach.

As Slatcher came off his haunches, he seemed to keep rising and rising.

He exited.

Candy remained behind, leaning back on the desk and examining her nails, her pert pretty face wearing a look of mild boredom.

Katrin sucked in one shallow breath after another but couldn't seem to find any air.

'Shitty Russian hit men,' Candy said, 'focus on destroying dentals. Then they chop off their victims' fingertips and put them in a glass of beer to erase the prints. But me? I'm not a shitty Russian hit man. I don't go for that penny-ante crap.' With a fluid motion, she pulled herself off the desk, her body seeming to roll forward on to her feet. Her boots planted themselves delicately in front of Katrin's face, and then she leaned down, bringing a waft of girly perfume. 'I prefer to erase the entire person. We may not have done that to Sam yet.' She nestled her lips against Katrin's ear. 'But I'm *dying* to.'

She stood over Katrin, those shapely legs sturdy and spread, Colossus of Rhodes with a bleach job. 'So please,' she said, *'don't* cooperate.'

Even after she walked out, Katrin couldn't catch her breath.

39. A Noise that Kept Not Coming

Lying on the floating slab in the inky darkness of his bedroom, staring at the void of his ceiling, Evan concentrated, replaying his and Slatcher's conversation word for word.

You never know who we know. Maybe we've got someone in place in your building right now.

Slatcher was trying to psych Evan out, put him on the run where he'd be more visible.

Here he had sundry alarms and weapons, basejumping parachutes and tactical rappelling rope, reinforced walls and windows. He was safe enough right now.

But Katrin was not.

He pictured how they'd lain together on the futon, his finger tracing the slope of her hip. Those three asymmetrical stars tattooed behind her ear. The kanji strokes on her left shoulder blade. Those spots of blood on the floor of the loft. The promise he'd made: *I will find you.*

Two feet from his ear, the RoamZone charged on the nightstand. He'd been waiting for the sonar ping to announce Katrin's location, bracing himself for a noise that kept not coming.

The night suddenly felt colder than it was.

Promise me. Crimson filming his fingertips. *Where are*

you, Evan? The shattered burner phone. The sob tangled in Katrin's throat. *Where are you, Evan?*

Where are you?

He threw back the sheets, dressed, and made his way to the Turkish rug. He sat cross-legged, veiled his eyes, and tried to meditate.

For the first time in his life, he could not.

40. Blind Spots

By first light of morning, Evan had already run a full check of his security systems, fine-tuning the motion detectors' sensitivities, testing the alarms, assessing the surveillance camera angles and searching out blind spots.

Right now he could not afford any blind spots.

Still no GPS ping from Katrin's microchips. Had they already broken down and passed from her body? Was she not being fed? Had she sweated off the hidden patch behind her ear? Perhaps she was being held underground, the signal muffled by concrete walls.

He kept moving. He extracted the SIM card from his RoamZone and dropped it down the garbage disposal, letting the blades whir until he heard only bits tumbling. He pulled them out and trashed them, then jumped online, moving his phone service from the outfit in Bangalore to one in Marrakech. No longer could he rely on domestic-violence-inclined Joey Delarosa. After Joey had called 911 last night, the cops had arrived and removed the excavated mobile phone from between the studs, puzzling over it as if it were an artifact from outer space.

After slotting a fresh SIM card into his phone, Evan grabbed a Pelican case from a cabinet beside his weapons locker and took it up on to the roof. He selected a hidden spot behind the metal shed protecting the generator. Despite the Southern California blaze overhead, a December wind numbed his fingers as he worked.

From the top of the case, he telescoped out a yagi directional antenna, then plugged in a coaxial cable with an omni stubby antenna mounted on a tripod. He pointed the yagi at the horizon and – *voilà*. His very own rogue GSM site. The little base station dodged all authentication between itself and the nearest cell tower, making it untraceable – literally off the grid. Next Evan enabled the Wi-Fi hot spot on his RoamZone, forming a gateway to the LTE network. Ordinarily he would power up the base station only when making a call, turning it off immediately afterward, but he'd have to leave it running until he received Slatcher's call.

'Evan? Is that you?'

He rose quickly in time to see Hugh Walters approach. 'What are you doing up here?'

'Oh,' Evan said. 'It's a hobby of mine. Trying to track comets. I always hoped to discover one, have it named after me.'

Hugh brightened with an inner light that Evan hadn't thought him capable of. 'I was in the shortwave-radio club at my prep school,' he said.

'Were you, now?' Evan said.

'I was indeed.'

'Look, I know it's outside of regs for me to –'

Hugh waved him off. 'Hey, let's call it a secret between amateur scientists.'

'I'd appreciate that,' Evan said. 'It's a bit embarrassing.'

Hugh offered a hand, and they shook on it.

Evan asked, 'What are *you* doing here?'

'Checking the roof. I need to be mindful of any and all repairs before going into an HOA meeting. Today's is right about . . .' A gold Rolex shot out from beneath Hugh's cuff. ' . . . *now*. I assume you'll be in attendance this time?'

'Today's not the best for me,' Evan said.

Hugh punished him with a well-directed frown. 'Why? You're off for the holidays, aren't you? What's so pressing that you can't attend?'

'Just some personal issues.'

Hugh nodded soberly. 'Well, I can tell you *one* person who'll be disappointed you won't be there.'

'Who's that?'

'Mia Hall.' Hugh mistook Evan's expression of surprise. 'That's right, fella. I know there seems to be some interest between you two. But this morning she seemed . . .'

'What?' Evan said.

'I don't know. She just wasn't her usual self. She seemed really upset about something.'

'I'd imagine being a single parent isn't a breeze.'

'It's not that,' Hugh said. 'She seemed *scared*.'

Evan felt the breeze cut right through him.

Hugh wet his lips. 'Maybe you could drop by the HOA meeting and check on her?'

Evan's mind assembled snippets of his conversations with Mia over the past couple of weeks. *As a DA*

I sometimes get threats. I have a work emergency. This is a real crisis. As in life or death.

He pushed the thoughts away. He didn't have time for this. This wasn't the mission. It wasn't his concern. There was Katrin to consider and the Seventh Commandment and a whole lot more.

'I'm sorry,' he said. 'I can't.'

Evan took a seat halfway down the length of the imposing conference table, perpendicular to Mia so he could watch her without being obvious. She'd offered him a cursory nod as he'd entered, averting her eyes. Odd. Peter was nowhere to be seen.

Piped-in 'Jingle Bells' played softly through hidden speakers, Hugh's pleased grin leaving little doubt that the cheery Muzak stylings were his handiwork.

Most of the usual suspects were in attendance, except for Johnny with his martial-arts warm-ups. Johnny's father, with the strained pride of a parent accustomed to inflating his child's achievements, explained that he was belt-testing today. For the *next* black stripe.

Several measures had been robustly voted on already – enhancing the porte cochère with outdoor carpeting, new boxwood hedges for the north wall of the building, amending the morning beverage initiative in light of the kombucha disappointment. Selecting the new cushion colors for the lobby had pitted Mrs Rosenbaum and Lorilee Smithson against each other in a vicious battle. Throughout the proceedings Evan kept his attention on Mia, who held her gaze tensely downward, her mouth set.

Ida Rosenbaum was yet again irritated. '– with what we pay in fees, the manager can't fix the frame to my front door? It's falling to *pieces*.'

'Again with the doorframe,' Botox-riddled Lorilee said. 'I thought your son was handling that for you.'

Mrs Rosenbaum's cheeks quavered – a flash of emotion she tried to cover. 'He can't make it this year. He's very busy, very important. He wanted to be here for the holidays, said he's coming *first thing* in the New Year.'

Lorilee chewed her gum triumphantly. 'We've heard that before, haven't we, Ida?'

Mrs Rosenbaum seemed to deflate in her chair. Her lips parted, but no response was forthcoming. The remark had cut the legs right out from under her.

Even Hugh took pity on her. 'I will speak to the manager for you, Ida,' he said. 'As soon as things settle down in the New Year, we will get your door fixed.'

Clearly devastated, she managed only a quick jerk of a nod.

Evan peered across at Mia to see if she noticed the exchange, but she was uncharacteristically oblivious, lost in the haze of her thoughts.

'Moving on,' Hugh said, directing a stare at the twenty or so weary souls in attendance, impressing upon them the gravity of the upcoming matter. 'As I've intimated for some time, everyone will need to be assessed three thousand dollars for the new earthquake policy.'

A chorus of complaints erupted. Pat Johnson clutched his chest as if to contain a bout of angina.

Hugh rapped his empty coffee mug on the fine-grained tabletop a few times to restore order. 'I know,' he said. 'Hear me out. Hear me out, people . . .'

Evan watched Mia, the only one not responding. Her gaze was low, aimed beneath the lip of the table, presumably fixed on the iPhone in her lap. She chewed her lip anxiously.

The muscles of Mia's face tensed, and then, faintly over the commotion, Evan heard the theme from *Jaws*. Mia held the phone to her face silently, her expression implacable, then slipped it secretively back into her purse, pushed away from the table, and rose to leave.

Evan stood as well, following her out.

He caught her at the elevator, waiting for the car, drumming her hands impatiently on her thighs.

'You okay?' he asked. 'Rushing out of there?'

'Yeah, yeah. I'm fine.'

He watched her eyes and knew her to be lying. 'Where you headed?'

'My brother's,' she said. 'He just called. I have to pick up Peter.'

Her brother's ringtone was *Peanuts*, not *Jaws*.

She pulled a tangle of curls off her forehead, exposing that birthmark on her temple. Her faint freckles were barely visible across her nose.

'You know,' he said, 'if something's wrong or you need help . . .'

Her gaze darted back to the illuminated floor

numbers. 'Thanks, Evan. But this isn't the kind of problem you can solve.'

He thumbed the UP button and waited silently at her side.

The down car arrived first, and he let the doors close behind her.

He squeezed his eyes shut. Katrin. The mission. Upstairs.

He thought of Peter's husky voice, that sloppy Gonzo Band-Aid on his forehead. *Thanks for covering for me.*

Goddamn it, kid.

Evan jogged for the service elevator. It arrived promptly, and he rode it down to the parking level.

It let out near the trash bins, and he stepped unseen on to the dim floor. He heard Mia's footsteps before he saw her. A clipped, fast walk to her car, the iPhone out again and at her cheek.

Moving toward his truck, he cut behind the trunks of various German sedans, holding parallel to her across the parking level. She climbed into her Acura, pulling out fast enough that the tires chirped on the slick concrete. He emerged from cover, reaching for his driver's door, when he heard heavy breathing behind him.

Slowly, he half turned, Johnny Middleton coming visible in the shadows to his side. Brass knuckles laced one of his fists; the other held a T-handled fighting knife. He stepped toward Evan, his face flushed, his stocky form wrapped in that martial-arts sweat suit.

'I'm sorry, Evan,' he said.

41. Emotional Centers

Evan squared up in the narrow space between vehicles as Johnny shuffled forward. His eyes were bloodshot; one lid throbbed spasmodically. Evan's own eyes stayed on the fighting knife, waiting for it to rise, but Johnny held it low at his belly. Only secondarily did it strike Evan that he'd brought nothing but fists to a knife fight.

He gauged the angle to collapse Johnny's throat with a finger-thrust strike, but then Johnny's arms went loose at his sides. Unexpectedly, he started to cry. 'I don't know what to do,' he said. 'I don't know what to do.'

Johnny's parking space was two slots over, the trunk of his BMW open. He hadn't been lying in wait, Evan realized, but he'd been interrupted from something.

'What happened?' Evan asked.

'It was in the combat-training room last week,' he said. 'I broke a guy's nose. It might have been after the whistle. He's got older brothers. They're serious fighters. Grew up with it, I mean. It's a bad fucking scene. I thought we were cool, but I showed up today for belt testing and they were waiting. All three of them. I took off, but they followed me back here. I don't want my dad to know. Jesus – if he found out . . .'

Evan exhaled, frustration seeping in. First he'd made

a quick exception to help Mia, and now here Johnny was, whining like a slapped bully. Maybe that's what real life was, one problem bleeding into the next. How had Mia put it? *Life would be boring if we didn't have other people around complicating everything.* He had Mia to worry about now in addition to Katrin. The last thing he could do was add Johnny to the mix.

'Listen,' Evan said. 'I have to get back to work.'

Johnny lowered his head and began sobbing.

Evan looked at the ceiling.

Fuck.

'Where are they?' he asked. 'These guys.'

Johnny pointed up the ramp. 'Outside. Just waiting.'

'Put the knife away.'

'Look, man.' Johnny wiped at his cheeks. 'This is seriously dangerous, street-level shit. Be grateful you don't deal with this kind of stuff.' The flush had crept up his face, turning his forehead shiny, making the hair plugs stand out. 'I'm not really a tough guy. If I don't bluff 'em down, they'll fuck me up bad.'

'Call the cops.'

'I can't do that. That's a pussy move.'

'You're gonna talk yourself right into a body bag.'

'You don't understand these guys, Evan. They'll just wait. They'll just wait and come back for me later.'

Evan took a breath. Exhaled through clenched teeth. 'Then I'll go with you. To talk to them.'

Johnny's laugh turned to another sob halfway through. 'Evan. This isn't some . . . some *business* dispute like whatever you're used to. These guys are savages.'

306

Already Evan was walking toward the slope. Johnny followed him up, still pleading with him. Evan waved his foot in front of the sensor, and the gate rattled open.

'Oh, Jesus Christ,' Johnny said. 'Oh, Jesus Christ.'

They emerged into the midday sun. Up on the side-walk, three men in their twenties waited, wearing sleeveless shirts despite the cool weather. Wiry builds, compact muscles, gelled hair. They looked to be of Indonesian descent. The smallest wore a protective nose splint.

Evan gestured to the loading-dock area behind the building, and the brothers drifted in that direction, keeping a good distance ahead, disappearing around the corner.

'You don't want to do that,' Johnny said. 'You *really* don't want to go back there where no one can see us.'

They stepped around the corner. Midway down the rear façade of the building, the brothers had assem-bled. Arms crossed, matching scowls, like something out of a bad import rap video.

As Evan approached, Johnny lost a half step, edging behind him. The men stood in formation, stone-faced.

Evan said, 'I understand my friend here screwed up.'

The oldest-looking brother's lips pursed, anger pier-cing the mask. 'He broke Reza's fucking nose. I'd say that qualifies as screwing up.'

Reza, his lips twisted in a scowl, lifted a hand to the splint, his chest rising and falling rapidly beneath the thin shirt. His shoulders were glossed with perspiration.

Evan looked from brother to brother, taking his

time. 'You're hoping for fight or flight,' he said. 'But there are other options here, and to be honest, I don't have time for this right now. Let's find an easier solution.'

A vein pulsed in the middle brother's arm. 'We're not here to fucking *talk*.'

Johnny's voice, husky with fear, came from behind Evan's shoulder. 'I *told* you.'

Evan stared at the oldest brother. 'I know you think you've got this under control. But you're breathing hard. Your heart rates are up right now. Blood pressure, too. You're sweating, all three of you. The emotional centers of your brains are going haywire. Your stomachs are tightening as we speak, all those stress hormones coursing through you.' He stepped forward. 'You're not in control as much as you think you are. If a fight breaks out, you won't be happy with the result. You've got numbers, yes, and you're hoping I'm as nervous as you are, that I'll fight rashly, that I'll make mistakes. But I want you to look at me. And tell me: do I look scared?'

The siblings' heads swiveled as they regarded one another, some unspoken communication passing between them.

'Andreas already told you,' the oldest said. 'We're not here to talk.'

They fanned out, forming a semicircle around Evan. Their hands came up, open, ready to throw.

Evan released a breath, annoyed. 'Really?'

He oriented toward the oldest, knowing he'd be the

first to engage. He watched the man's feet shuffle, read the positioning. He anticipated the low, sweeping kick before it came, a test-the-waters first strike, and he simply raised his own leg and pivoted it outward. Evan's shin shield hammered the driving ankle, sending a painful vibration up his attacker's leg. The oldest brother skipped back on his good foot.

The lesson would be simple: every time one of the brothers struck, he would feel pain.

Andreas threw next as predicted, a right cross, but Evan shot his elbow up into a spear and leaned into the punch. As Andreas swung, the soft union of his pec and shoulder impaled on the bony tip of Evan's ulna, and Andreas gave a cry of pain, his arm dangling numbly at his side.

Reza was in motion already, pivoting into a round-house kick. Evan caught the leg softly with both of his hands and slammed it down into the top of his own rising femur, the knee smash bruising the tibia and gastrocnemius, stunning the limb into uselessness.

The oldest had rebounded to attack again, Evan stepping into his punch, driving the heel of his hand hard into a shoulder post before the arm could swing around. The brother staggered back, then recovered, countering with a tight jab. Evan's hands moved like horizontal buzz saws in a kali deflection, clapping the arm from either side, his palm slap-guiding the fist, his knuckles digging into the soft meat of the biceps. The oldest brother grunted and spun away, Evan letting him tumble into Reza, knocking him over.

Andreas had already wound up for a high kick, but Evan shot his lead leg up and straight out, letting Andreas's momentum carry his crotch into Evan's foot.

A clod of air left Andreas in something like a bark. 'Ouch!' he said, and sat down next to his brothers.

Evan had responded only with blocks and deflections, making not a single offensive move.

From somewhere behind him, he heard air hiss through Johnny's teeth.

The brothers cradled various limbs and breathed raggedly, more stunned than injured.

Now Evan stepped forward and offered Reza a hand. Reza looked to his oldest brother, who nodded, and then Reza grasped Evan's hand and allowed himself to be helped to his feet. The other brothers stood on their own.

'Okay,' Evan said. 'Let's try this again.' He turned to Johnny, who was watching, mesmerized, his mouth slightly ajar. 'Johnny?'

No response.

Evan snapped his fingers in front of Johnny's face, and Johnny reanimated. 'Yeah? What?'

'Apologize to Reza for punching him after the whistle. It was a dishonorable thing to do.'

'I'm sorry,' Johnny said. 'Really sorry.'

'Shake his hand.'

Johnny held out his hand, and Reza took it.

'That nose has been properly reset,' Evan said. 'By a doctor. You will pay all his medical bills. Agreed?'

'Agreed,' Johnny said. 'I agree.'

Evan looked at the oldest brother. 'Are we done here?'

The brother stared at him for a time, trying for implacable, though everyone knew it was already over. 'Yeah,' he said. 'We're done.'

Evan gave him a nod, then turned and hustled back for the garage.

Johnny followed at his heels. 'Holy shit holy shit *holy-shitholyshit*. How'd you *do* that?'

They rounded the corner of the building, moving toward the porte cochère.

'I fought some as a kid,' Evan said, giving the valet an affable nod.

'Who the fuck *are* you?'

Evan halted, Johnny bumping into him from behind. Evan turned, his eyes inches from Johnny's. 'This never happened. Understand me?'

Johnny held out his hands. 'I understand.'

Evan slipped through the glass front doors, leaving Johnny in the shade of the drive-through.

42. The Inside of a Conspiracy Theorist's Mind

Five-twenty and still no ping from Katrin White's GPS signal.

Locked down in the Vault, Evan raked through the databases, scouring every corner of the universe for trails that might lead to Danny Slatcher or locations he'd used in the past. He dug and pried, trying not to watch the clock.

His mistrust of Katrin might have cost her her life.

With ex-Orphans on his trail, Evan had had to doubt everything and everyone, see the lie beneath every sentence, betrayal beneath every smile. Over the past two weeks, he'd been pulled increasingly into the ordinary world with all its human complications, real people with real problems, and it was harder and harder to tell what was authentic and what was a strategic simulation of authentic. He'd charted connections and coincidences, creating webs of partial logic that resembled nothing so much as the inside of a conspiracy theorist's mind. Assessing the genuine in the everyday was his particular blind spot, as he had never lived in the everyday. Katrin did. And his inability to decipher the language of the everyday, to read her correctly, might prove to be the tear in the fabric that would unravel them both.

This mission had been a death trap from the start, the foundation caving in beneath his feet, the Commandments crumbling one after another. Only one mattered anymore, the Tenth and most holy Commandment: *Never let an innocent die.*

He pounded at the keyboard, hacking through files as if forging through brush with a machete. But Slatcher lived up to his reputation. Traceless. Invisible. A ghost.

Six-oh-seven and still no ping from Katrin White's GPS signal.

Evan cocked back in his chair with an aggravated sigh. Only now did he realize that Vera had died. The aloe vera plant, companion through so many adventures and witness to his sins, had turned brown and brittle. He lifted her from her bed of pebbles. The size of an artichoke, she fit neatly in his palm, as light as a bird's nest. She deserved more of a send-off, but she got only the trash compactor. When he looked up, he saw that the living wall, too, was expiring, a wide swath of the herbs long gone, the floor beneath dusted with fallen leaves and sprigs. The drip system looked to be clogged, another repair to add to the list along with the katana's scabbard. He stared into the malnourished rise of plants as if it were a mirror.

The wall and Vera were the only lives fully in his care, and he hadn't even managed to keep them afloat.

Seven-sixteen and still nothing.

He debated reviewing his own past assignments and missions to determine which had given rise to someone seeking vengeance in the form of Danny Slatcher, but there were too many, and every last one had left a vapour trail of lethal enemies.

Three past eight. Nothing and nothing.

And then he spotted something.

But not on the monitors he'd been focused on.

One of the south-facing outdoor surveillance cameras picked up two men approaching the loading dock where Evan had squared off with the brothers earlier in the day. These men were big specimens in dark, loose-fitting clothes, tattoos showing on their hands and necks. Evan initiated the facial-recognition software, but it was too dark behind the building for a clean capture.

They wouldn't be outside long.

As they approached the security door next to the giant roll-up loading gate, one of the men pulled out a pick set and the other went up on tiptoes. As the second intruder reached up, a thin piece of metal flashed in his hand. Evan knew what it was immediately – a magnet shaped like a stick of Wrigley's chewing gum. Each exterior door of Castle Heights was alarmed with a mag strike in the gap between the top of the door and the frame. Sliding a magnet to cling to the top strike would ensure that no broken-connection alert would be sent when the door opened.

Which it promptly did under the ministrations of the pick set. The two men vanished inside, holding their total time in the outdoor camera's field of vision to under ten seconds. A skillful team.

This was not their first entry.

A few inches from Evan's mouse pad, the matte black Wilson 1911 waited in its holster.

He clicked to locate the appropriate interior camera, picking up the two-man team hustling through the rear service corridor. There was enough light inside to capture their features, the facial-recognition software scrolling the results across the screen.

Michael Marts and Axel Alonso.

Evan's eyes swept their criminal histories. They'd worked together since their late teens, a string of petty B&Es culminating in the robbery of a taxi driver. That bought them five years in Chino, but they'd been released early – four months ago – for good behavior.

They were in the service elevator now, riding up.

Keeping his eyes on the screen, Evan reached across the desk, his hand claiming the holstered gun. He clipped it at his hip and rose, leaning over the monitors, setting his knuckles on the sheet metal.

He moused over to the sentencing report for the robbery in the first degree and clicked to bring up the name of the prosecutor.

District Attorney Mia Hall.

The confirmation sent a prickle through the nerves of his back. The men were coming after her for putting them away.

Sure enough, the service elevator stopped at twelve.

Evan brought up a hall camera just in time to catch the men strobing by en route to Mia's place. He could no longer pick them up. Castle Heights had no eyes on the door of 12B, which meant that Evan didn't either.

His heart was hammering. Impatience simmered, a low boil.

He stared at the blank RoamZone. Nothing from Katrin. He had to be ready to move the instant that ping came in. That was his contract. His law. The sole thing he'd been honed to do for two and a half decades.

But Mia. And Peter.

What could he do? What could he *not* do?

He realized that – for the first time – the answer would lie neither in his brain nor in his training, but somewhere else.

A security alert sounded on one of his screens.

A balloon, bumping against his bedroom window. Magic Markered across it in bold letters: SKARY MEN R HERE. HELP.

The men were inside her apartment already. Their focus would be on guarding that front door.

Evan started out of the Vault. Then froze, agitated, his hand pressed to the hidden door.

A lifetime of training told him he couldn't reveal himself to Mia. That would risk not just the mission.

It would risk *everything*.

And yet.

Could he risk *not* doing this?

It wasn't really a choice.

He'd go, all right.

Just not through the building.

43. Scary, Scary Man

Evan stood on the side of Castle Heights, invisible against the dark exterior, his feet planted on the stone. The view, twenty-one stories straight down. The wind was less powerful than *loud*, roaring across his eardrums, all but drowning out the traffic sounds below.

He paid out black rappelling rope from the mechanical descender, straps biting into his torso as his weight strained the harness. The improvised abseiling system was not designed for him to lower himself from his bedroom window in controlled fashion.

It was designed for him to run down the side of the building.

He tested the holds once more, then began his sprint down the dangling length of black rope, his boots tapping across windows and stone. The bluish glow of 20B's television blurred underfoot, then the aquatic green of the fish tank in 19B, followed by the pitch-black windows of 18B. Way below, streetlights blinked from red to green and car horns bleated, the river of headlights lurch-stopping along Wilshire Boulevard. Next 17B whipped by; the sixteenth floor passed in a flash, and then the fifteenth too was a memory. High-tensile-strength nylon cord zippered through various figure eights on Evan's torso, frictioning through his gloves as he slowed, slowed, the twelfth floor flying up at him.

Peter's bedroom window was open, kite string still tailing up to the balloon above, and Evan kicked off the stone, swinging out from the building, turning in a slow half rotation, his Original S.W.A.T. boots aimed at the two-foot gap at the top of the pane.

He swung through the window, landing on his feet on the bright-blue area rug beside the race-car bed, already unclipping from his harness. Peter cowered against the footboard, covering his ears, his eyes squeezed shut. His desk chair was jammed beneath the doorknob. One of the men was knocking on the door – hard, but not too loud. They didn't want to alert the neighbors.

At the sound of Evan's landing, Peter's eyes opened. He did a literal double take, one hand sliding up across his blond hair, leaving it askew.

'Holy crap,' he said.

Evan held a finger to his lips.

A raised voice carried through the door: '– what you can do is give me the last four fucking *years of my life* back.' And then a harsh whisper: 'Get the kid outta the bedroom. *Now.*'

The knocking persisted. Then a new voice came, muffled against the wood. 'Listen, kid. You gotta open up. Or I'm gonna kick down the door.'

The first man again. 'We're not kicking down any doors. Open the door or we'll break your mom's fingers.'

There was a sound of a brief struggle, and then Mia shouted, 'Don't you do it –' before her words were stifled.

Footsteps moved away from Peter's bedroom, the second man seemingly going to help with Mia.

Evan quietly pulled the chair from the doorknob, setting it down gently on the rug. As he turned back, Peter grabbed his arm.

'I'm scared,' he said in that rasp of a voice.

'Don't be.' Evan twisted the knob slowly, retracting the latch. 'Everything's fine now.'

He eased the door open and peered through the crack. Mia was struggling violently, both men doing their best to restrain her. Marts tried to hold her from behind, one tattooed hand clamped over her mouth. His other hand held a .45, but it was aimed at the floor, not at Mia's head, which Evan took as a good sign regarding his intentions. The lack of a suppressor was another positive. The last thing Marts would want to do was fire a gun inside the building. It was also the last thing Evan wanted to do in close quarters with hostages present. Keeping his Wilson holstered, he slipped through the doorway.

Mia bucked and thrashed, Alonso trying to rein in her kicking legs.

Evan slipped up behind him and tapped him on the back. 'Excuse me,' he said.

Surprised, Alonso turned.

The shoulder joint is largely a myth. It's less a joint, more of a bony fit held together with musculotendon tension and a modest bit of cartilage. It is extremely mobile. And highly vulnerable.

Alonso was still rotating around, his mouth frozen in an O of shock, when Evan threw a right hammer-fist punch, clubbing the fragile left collarbone. The destruction blow shattered the collarbone, the sound like the pop of a dinner plate dropped on an anvil. Alonso simply went limp and went down, striking the floor like something inanimate. As he fell away, he cleared Evan's view to Mia's wild rolling eyes, her expression more shocked even than Marts's.

Marts flung her to the side, his gun hand coming up, but Evan caught the inside of his wrist and snapped it palm-up, supinating the elbow, which gave way with a muted crackling. The .45 popped loose from Marts's limp fingers, and Evan snatched it from the air, his hands field-stripping it even as it fell, its momentum barely slowing until it rained down in pieces on the stained carpet – slide, operating spring, barrel, frame, magazine.

Marts got off a jab, but Evan scooped it to the outside, spinning his body open. With spear-straight fingers, he drove a *bil jee* strike into Marts's eyes, and Marts gave a cry that sounded neither human nor animal, but like a wet structure caving in on itself. As Marts reeled back, Evan grabbed his flailing arm and spun him in a half rotation, seizing him from behind with a single snakelike strike that locked him in a police choke hold. Marts's neck was pinched in the crook of

Evan's right elbow, crowded between the biceps and the meat of the forearm, Evan's left hand palming the back of his head.

At their feet Alonso groaned into the carpet, a sheet of tendons standing out in his neck. Mia had scooted herself across the floor so her shoulders were pressed against the base of the couch. Her legs were still churning, propelling her nowhere as she watched with a mixture of horror and fascination.

Marts struggled in Evan's grasp. 'You motherfucker, do you have any –'

With his left hand, Evan applied a hint of pressure, forcing Marts's head into the pincerlike vise, cutting off the flow of the carotid arteries. Marts went marionette-limp in Evan's arms.

Evan let off the pressure, and a moment later Marts snapped back to life.

'We done?' Evan asked.

'No, we're not fucking –'

Pressure on.

Marts tilted forward again, limp in Evan's arms.

Pressure off.

Marts woke up again.

'Are you ready to listen?' Evan asked.

'I'll listen as soon as you –'

Repeat.

This time when Marts's head rolled back atop his shoulders, he said hoarsely, 'Okay, *okay*. I'll listen.'

'I need you *both* to listen. Got it?' Evan set a boot on

Alonso's wrecked shoulder, and the man arced on the floor as if an electrical current had been run through him. He nodded furiously.

Evan said, 'There are two choices. You ride down in the service elevator to the parking level with me calmly and quietly. Or I will drop you down the trash chute. We are on the twelfth floor. What's it gonna be?'

Marts said, 'Service elevator.'

Evan hoisted Alonso up, and he stood beside Marts, shuddering in pain.

Mia's legs still cycled, though now in slow motion, trying in vain to move her through the couch. Evan said to her, 'Don't call the cops. Please. I'll come back.'

Though her stomach was undulating, racked with silent sobs, she stared at him blankly.

He said, 'Okay?'

Her nod looked like a tremor.

As he propelled the men toward the door, she scrambled for Peter's bedroom. Evan peered through the peephole, checking that the corridor was clear before steering the men out. Closing the door behind them, he heard the sound of Peter's muffled crying and the low murmur of Mia's soothing voice.

He got Marts and Alonso into the service elevator and down to the parking level without incident. With every step Alonso jerked in a shallow breath. Marts had sweated through his shirt. They demonstrated the cooperation of broken POWs.

Evan removed a set of keys from Marts's front pocket. 'Your car,' he said. 'Where'd you park?'

'Two blocks that way.'

They crossed the parking level and exited up a rear stairwell. Marts and Alonso drag-walked up the steps with their torsos contorted against the pain, a *Walking Dead* bearing.

Lights shone from various apartments, but the neighborhood was pedestrian-free, one of the advantages of car-centric Los Angeles. They made it to the car, a beat-to-shit Buick, without incident. Evan popped the trunk, then yanked out the spare tire and tossed it on to the weedy sidewalk buffer.

'No,' Marts said. 'Oh, no.'

'Please,' Alonso said.

Evan just looked at them.

They climbed into the oversize trunk, adjusting themselves with slow, excruciating movements.

Marts's voice floated up, reedy with exertion. 'Can you maybe just —'

Evan slammed the trunk.

He drove up the 405, exiting at Mulholland, and curled west, turning off where the famous drive gave over to dirt. He forged up into the canyons, passing the defunct Nike missile facility, wending along the tortuous trail. The tires hammered over uneven ground, and more than once pained whimpers emanated through the backseats. Evan reached a clearing overlooking the Valley, the Sepulveda Basin a puddle of black spilled on the blanket of lights below.

He parked and opened the trunk, helping the men climb out. Their tattoos shiny with sweat, they stood gingerly, craning their necks to take in the surroundings. Tall chaparral and oaks rose all around. Dust from the tires textured the air, drifting ghostlike through the darkness. An owl hooted from somewhere overhead.

'You're gonna kill us,' Marts said.

In the light of the moon, Alonso's face looked bloodless. His fragmented collarbone had not broken the skin, but a shaft poked out his shirt in the front. 'We weren't gonna hurt her bad,' he said. 'We just wanted to rough her up, scare her. Let her know what she cost us.'

'If I didn't believe you,' Evan said, 'you'd already be dead.'

'Then . . .' Marts's words faded into a dry cough. He tried again. 'Then why are we here?'

'Mulholland is three miles back that way.' Evan pointed. 'I'll leave your car where the blacktop picks up.'

With glazed eyes the men stared into the darkness where he was pointing.

'I know you know tough guys,' Evan said. 'Guys above you. And they have guys above them. But the people you can get to? They won't rise to a level that will be a problem for me. Do you understand what I'm telling you?'

Both men nodded obediently.

'Consider me Mia Hall's personal guardian angel,' Evan said. 'If she ever so much as hears your *names* again, I will put you in the ground.' Spinning the keys around his forefinger, he started for the car.

He turned the Buick around in a tight three-point, the headlights sweeping the men's wan faces. They stayed rooted to the ground, shuddering. Kicked-up dirt gusted across their scarecrow frames.

Evan hit the brakes beside them, rolled down his window. 'Start walking,' he said.

Painstakingly, they turned to face the gloomy hike back.

Marts said, 'You are a scary, scary man.'

Evan drove off. He watched their stooped forms diminish in the rearview. It seemed they couldn't yet muster the energy to move.

44. Self-Fueling Engine

Katrin sat in the empty office, her back to the wall, regarding the untouched fast-food bag beyond her feet. Her window, her sole luxury, had been taken from her, boarded with plywood and reinforced with steel bars. When she moved, the thick plastic zip-tie bit into her ankle. It was hooked to the metal leg of the desk above a sturdy crossbar, and in the hours she'd passed here alone, she'd made zero headway on the heavy screws. Truth be told, she'd given up after several attempts and a broken thumbnail. The screws weren't going anywhere, and neither was she.

Stress was taking her apart, bit by bit. Her slow-burning terror had materialized as nausea, swelling at intervals, then receding. The thudding at her temples competed with bouts of light-headedness. She knew that she was dehydrated and calorie-depleted, but the thought of food brought on a fresh wave of queasiness. The smell of carpet cleaner choked the air and seemed to coat her mouth, her lungs.

She could hear heavy boots thunking around down the hall and the grumble of deep voices. Once in a while, she heard Candy as well, a feminine murmur and then bursts of laughter from the men.

Slatcher had stripped Katrin of her possessions,

including her watch and phone, so she had no way to keep track of the time, but it seemed that Candy came every few hours to take her to the bathroom.

Which is why now, only twenty or so minutes after her last trip to the toilet, Katrin was confused to hear those hefty boots tapping up the hall.

Confused and not a little scared.

Candy entered now on a breeze of perfumed air. In her hand swayed a fresh McDonald's bag. Replenishments.

'Your Gandhi hunger-strike routine isn't gonna get you anything but weak,' Candy said. 'And I don't think you wanna be weak. For you or for Sam. So what say you grow the fuck up and deal a little, 'kay, partner?' She flashed her dimples and lofted the new bag across the room. It landed with a wet thud at Katrin's side.

Candy turned around, her hips somehow playing an outsize role in the simple act, and vanished through the door.

Katrin stretched for the bag, static fuzzing her vision. She was weaker than she thought. But when she unfurled the greasy cheeseburger wrapper, the rising smell forced her to lay it aside. She breathed the carpet-cleaner air for a time.

Then she reached for a french fry. Trying to fight her stomach into place, she held it before her face.

For the entire taxi ride back from Mulholland, Evan kept his RoamZone open to Katrin's tracking screen. It remained infuriatingly stagnant.

He asked the driver to drop him several blocks from

Castle Heights, then jogged back and went straight to the penthouse, hauling up his rappelling rope and harness before anyone noticed them blowing in the wind. The act brought to mind pulling up a drawbridge, a metaphor Jack might have appreciated – Evan, alone in his fortress once again.

He pit-stopped in the Vault to fuzz out damning intervals of the building's surveillance footage from earlier in the evening. The footage, sparingly monitored in real time by Joaquin over the top of his *Maxim* magazine, was rarely reviewed after the fact, but Evan preferred never to rely on luck. Exiting the penthouse with his recharged RoamZone in hand, he rode the elevator down to Mia's place and tapped gently on the door, having no idea what to expect.

A darkness occluded the peephole, and then the door swung open. Her curled hair tamped down from a shower, Mia looked at him, then gestured to the couch. Peter's door was closed, the boy presumably asleep.

Evan walked to the couch and sat. Mia took an armchair opposite him, pulling her legs in under her. The pieces of Marts's gun had been collected in a Ziploc freezer bag, which rested on the coffee table between them, positioned like a conversation piece.

Which, Evan supposed, it was.

Mia's voice was husky from crying. 'Did you . . . kill them?'

'No,' Evan said. 'But they'll never bother you again.'

'Thank you for protecting me. Thank you for protecting Peter. And I mean that – deeply and sincerely.'

'But?' he said.

She leaned forward, lifted the Baggie a little, and let it clunk back on to the table. 'You took this gun apart so fast I couldn't even see your hands move. You beat those men – seasoned violent offenders – like nothing I've ever seen. You swung in through Peter's window like friggin' Spider-Man. What *are* you?'

Evan broke eye contact, looking away. It was a conversation he'd never had before, and there was no way to begin it now. On Peter's door the pirate-themed KEEP OUT! sign was torn from Alonso's banging, and Evan considered the boy sleeping safely in the room beyond.

When it became apparent that he had no ready answer, she said, 'No one knows anything about industrial cleaning supplies.'

'No.'

'So no one can ask you anything about your job.'

'I suppose not,' he said.

'Evan Smoak. Is that your real name?'

'Yes and no.'

Her mouth opened and closed a few times. 'You do understand what my job is, right? I can't know that you . . . that you . . .'

He waited.

'I can't know whatever it is that I don't know about you.' She smacked her forehead with a palm. 'Jesus, this is *insane*. I sound *insane*. But whatever you did with those men . . .' Angrily, she blew a wisp of hair off her forehead. 'I am a district attorney, Evan. I took an *oath*.

329

Several, in fact. That job is how I support my child. And it's contingent on – no, it's *predicated* on my not breaking the law.'

'So you want to try to prosecute me?'

'If I said yes?'

'I'd be gone.'

'We'd find you.'

Evan slowly shook his head.

'I'm going to call my boss right now.' She stood. 'See how we can untangle this mess. See how we can make it right.'

But she made no move for her phone. They looked at each other. The silence stretched out and out.

Evan asked, 'Who called you when you left the HOA meeting today? You said it was your brother. But it wasn't his ringtone.'

She blinked slowly, from exhaustion or confusion. 'My boss. Telling me that the threats from those guys had escalated. We've been tracking them these past few months.'

Evan thought about that *Jaws* ringtone sounding on Mia's phone, again and again. All those agitated conversations, her pacing intense circles on her brother's front lawn. He remembered washing dishes side by side with Mia at her sink. *The idiots these days, they brag about everything on Facebook. What they've done, what they're gonna do.*

Evan said, 'That's why you just moved here, even though your husband's life-insurance money cleared years ago. Better security.'

Her weary gaze sharpened. 'How do you know that? About when I got the money from Roger's policy?'

He hesitated. There were so many things he couldn't tell her, and yet he owed her something. 'There are a lot of people who would like to kill me,' he began cautiously. 'So I have to keep my eyes open.'

She coughed out a note of disbelief, sinking back into the armchair. 'And you question *me* about lying?' Hunching forward, she rested her elbows on her knees. 'Wait. You knew about Roger's cancer. His life-insurance policy. So that means . . . that means you know everything about me, too? Peter's adoption. My income. Where I work. You *spied* on me?'

His silence was answer enough.

'You were faking? The whole time?'

'No.'

'With Peter –'

'No.'

'– my freckles –'

'*No.*'

'– about being surprised. When I told you things about myself. That my husband had died. You already knew.' Her lower jaw sawed back and forth, her teeth grinding. 'You *knew.*'

'I did.'

A tear spilled over the brink of her eye. Just one. 'How sad for you that you see everyone this way. As potential threats. As liars. When it's you. It's really you.'

His hands were off his lap, trying to shape the air, but into what he was not sure. He lowered them.

'People build trust, Evan,' she said. 'That's how relationships *work*. That's what they *are*.'

It spread through him like something physical – a pervasive sadness that this was something he had never learned and did not know.

That was the curse of paranoia. It became a self-fueling engine, heating up the more it consumed.

Evan started to reply when a sound cut him off.

A sonar ping.

At first he thought he'd hallucinated it. But no, there it was again, Katrin's GPS coordinates chiming in his pocket.

He was standing already.

Across from him Mia's head remained turned away. She was studying the cordless phone on the counter.

'I'm sorry,' he said. 'Do whatever you have to do. But I have to leave now.'

She gave a faint nod without looking at him. He hesitated a moment, then picked up the Ziploc bag containing the field-stripped .45 and started out.

The Post-it beside the wall-mounted phone had been replaced. The new one read: *'Make friends with people who want the best for you.'*

He thought, *What a goddamned luxury* that *would be.*

45. Human Hive

Slatcher's voluminous form was crowded between the metal plates high above the ground. Though the hum of electricity filled his head, the phone connection remained pristine, an earbud receiver collecting Evan's voice.

Evan had been breathing hard when he'd picked up, as if he were rushing somewhere. Slatcher had made it clear that he was controlling the board now, telling Evan where he needed to rush *to*.

'Universal CityWalk,' Slatcher said. 'The plaza by the movie theaters.'

'Nice choice,' Evan said. 'Hard to imagine a more crowded location.'

Slatcher spoke using a microphone patch over his larynx that pulled his voice directly through the skin, filtering out all ambient noise. 'Thank you. I assume you're close enough to make it by midnight.'

'I can make it by midnight.'

That was good. Slatcher wanted to provide Evan with enough time to case the area. But not too much time.

'Good. I'll take you to Katrin from there.'

'It's not gonna go down that way,' Evan said. 'I will approach you once I've made sure I'm safe. In the plaza you will show me FaceTime footage of Katrin – proof of life in real time. On your cell phone, I will watch your men release her in a public place. Then I'll go with you.'

'You're willing to die for her?'

'I am,' Evan said.

Slatcher felt a grin tug at his mouth. 'That's what it'll take.'

'Unless I kill you first.'

'Sorry, Orphan X. You're not that good.'

'We'll find out,' Evan said. 'I have one condition: no field teams. Just me and you. That's the rules. If I see that you brought *anyone* – and you know I'll identify them – I'm in the wind. You'll miss your shot. And I will not surface again.'

'I thought you said you were willing to die for her.'

'I didn't say I was willing to commit suicide for her.'

Neon flashed dizzyingly all around Slatcher's face. He hoisted his bolt-action Remington M700, manipulating it carefully in the claustrophobic space, and checked the Leopold variable power scope. Too much light for the night-vision attachment. 'Fair enough,' he said.

'Talk to you soon.'

Click.

But Slatcher wasn't planning on talking. From his roost inside the two-story-high guitar outside the Hard Rock Cafe, he was planning on ending the conversation before it began.

The clamor of the crowd rose up to him, a continuous mob streaming past, pouring in and out of restaurants, bars and nightclubs, queuing for the Cineplex, tracing glow bracelets through the air. From this height he could hear the clacking of roller coasters in the amusement park behind.

He stuck the tip of the rifle through the sound hole of the giant suspended guitar, peering through the scope up the length of CityWalk. With its escalators and leaping fountains, tourists and street performers, brewhouses and sing-along piano bars, it hummed with movement, a human hive and grand temple of capitalism. Enough flashing signage bathed the monstrosity of a promenade to shame Times Square. One block down, a glowing blue King Kong hung off the side of a building. Beyond the iMax line, a teenager fluttered above a giant fan in a sky-jumping tube as his friends looked on, slurping Jamba Juice and chewing Wetzel's Pretzels.

Slatcher switched comms to the radio channel and keyed the primary channel. 'Big Daddy to Field Teams One and Two. Abort. Abort. I'm gonna fly solo.'

A moment later a crackle. 'Field Team Leader One. You sure? I thought your employer requested body recovery.'

'Can't risk it,' Slatcher said. 'Target's already late to the dance. I'm in position, holding high ground. He can scout all he wants, but he won't stand a chance.'

Slatcher spotted the team leader, dressed in a paramedic uniform, on the second deck of the food court by Tommy's Burgers. He watched the man's lips moving on a slight delay. 'Confirm, Big Daddy. Team One out.'

Another voice chimed in: 'Team Two out.'

'Go back to base,' Slatcher said. 'Watch the package and provide backup to Hot Mama.'

The sweeping scope captured the second team leader on the patio of a Mexican joint, slurping a fishbowl-size margarita. 'Confirm, Big Daddy.'

In the green-tinted night-vision wash, he watched the freelancers disperse. Slatcher couldn't risk having Orphan X identify one of his men.

Evan would arrive as soon as possible and scrutinize the central plaza from every angle. But against the backdrop of all the lights and motion, a sniper scope would vanish like a blue sequin dropped into the ocean. Slatcher had miscalculated once before in Chinatown. It would not happen again.

He dialed back the magnification and moved the crosshairs from one face to the next as they floated across the plaza beneath him.

Now all he had to do was wait.

46. Pyrotechnic Horrors

The blinking dot of Katrin's GPS had long since vanished, but Evan had it locked in the RoamZone's memory. In his Ford F-150, which he'd taken for muscle, he'd looped several times past the unrented building off the 101. After killing his headlights, he found a spot past the edge of the dark parking lot where he could observe the place through a head-high hedge of night-blooming jasmine. The accent lighting in the halls threw enough glow to turn the faintly tinted windows transparent, though it was hard to make out anything but shadows from this distance.

Somewhere behind those windows, Katrin White waited, held against her will.

He played the Fourth Commandment in his head until he felt a healthy tactical remove.

A few minutes past eleven, a pair of midnight blue SUVs pulled in to the lot and four men spilled out of each.

The field teams returning to base, as he'd hoped.

Above all else, Evan had two things going for him: he'd separated Slatcher, the greatest threat, from the rest of the crew. And no one was expecting him *here*.

In his lap rested a Benelli M1 combat shotgun, black as night. It had more robust internals and faster cycling than an M4, the higher capacity giving him seven shells plus one in the chamber, a bonus round ghost-loaded on the lifter. He eschewed the trendy pistol grip, the classic stock better for going around corners. The first three shots were seven-eighth ounce shells, each holding a single solid lead slug, the better to focus the total energy dump on wiping out a door hinge. Beneath those were nine-pellet buckshot loads, ready to go once he'd breached the building. The pellets would inflict multiple traumas, expanding into a blow radius that could turn a rugby scrum into pink mist. A Jack-ism sprang to mind: *You don't want all the holes in the same place.*

Given the numbers he was facing, Evan had gone with the Benelli over his Wilson pistol, choosing brute power over precision. A shotgun was a fight-stopper, a hit even to an extremity usually proving fatal.

Evan shouldered through the jasmine hedge and did a surveillance pass around the building's perimeter, noting the layout of rooms and halls. The men had substantial firepower – Glocks and AK-47s – but they weren't patrolling in any formal fashion. They milled around in the lobby and meeting rooms, eating and bullshitting. Candy McClure kept her distance, tending to something in what looked like a utility room in the western hall, emerging from time to time to take a breezy lap through the admiring men. Slatcher, nowhere to be seen, was likely teed up in a sniper's nest somewhere above Universal CityWalk. But he'd be back once it was clear that Evan had no-showed.

With his back to the hillside, Evan crept along the

rear of the building. Five or so rooms down the corridor from Candy's utility closet, one window had been blacked out. Risking a closer peek, he saw that it had been fortified from the inside.

Katrin's cell.

He'd counted eight men and Candy. To get in and out cleanly, he needed them spread throughout the bird-in-flight V of the building. He located the breaker box near the terminus of the eastern corridor. Through an atrium of some sort at the juncture of the two hallways, he watched the guns-for-hire comparing weapons in the lobby. He wanted to get some of them moving down the eastern corridor – away from Katrin's room.

He'd brought only stun grenades, not wanting to risk the collateral damage caused by frags. He lifted the metal lid of the breaker box and let it clamp back down over the body of the flashbang, an upside-down alligator clamp that held the grenade in place. Slotting a finger through the pin, he pulled it. Then he sprinted across to the rear of the western corridor.

He raised the shotgun, aiming it at the top hinge, and waited. The night breeze blew slow and steady. In the side of his neck, he felt the pulse of his heartbeat like the tick of a clock's second hand.

Across the way the flashbang detonated, the building going black.

Evan fired the three hinge-removers – *boom, boom, boom* – the door sagging open, and then he was inside, barreling along the corridor. Down by the junction of the lobby, four of the men appeared, heading toward

Katrin rather than toward the explosion, a savvy tactical move.

Though Evan was out of range, he shot a warning blast up the hall to push them around the corner. He sprinted for the utility closet, each jarring step rocking the doorway back and forth.

He was ten meters away when Candy burst out, her raised fist firing muzzle flares. With no time to lift the shotgun, he slid on to his back, rocketing forward on the slick floor, on a collision course with her legs. He scissor-kicked for her Achilles, but she leapt over him, her hand swinging to aim as he popped to his feet. He lunged inside her reach, grabbing the gun as it grazed his cheek. Her hand blocked the rising shotgun. For an instant they were nose-to-nose, locked up, and then her lips pursed in a smirk and she yanked the trigger, the pistol report sounding inches from Evan's head. The noise filled his skull, his field of vision tilting violently out of frame, a painting knocked askew. He jerked back, and she drove her face forward, hammering his temple with a head butt, her teeth-clenched screech laced with the scent of strawberry bubblegum.

He spun away from her, barely holding on to the shotgun. Her stainless-steel pistol shimmered as she raised it for the kill shot. Rather than fight his momentum, he threw himself into the rotation, whipping his leg up and around, his shin striking her square in the sternum. Her gum ejected from her open mouth as she flew back through the doorway into the utility closet.

The utility closet, filled with plastic jugs.

They broke her fall.

Liquid flew up around her, sloshing freely from the cracked jugs, and she gave a piercing scream. Evan heeled the door shut, firing again down the hall to drive the men back into the lobby. The spent case ejected from the Benelli, spinning to the floor. With the side of his boot, he swept it across the tile, wedging the plastic end beneath the utility closet's door, trapping Candy inside.

Her screams continued, rising to inhuman decibel levels. She banged on the door, the sounds getting wetter. Vapor crept from beneath the door, not wood smoke but the smell of sulfur and flesh.

At the corridor's end, an AK held in a gloved hand made a puppet appearance, firing rounds off the walls and ceiling. Blind cover fire as the field teams readied to make their charge.

Evan would not give them that chance.

Combat shotgun cinched between his shoulder and cheek, he sprinted toward the lobby.

This was not going to go well for them.

The corridor sounded like a hall of pyrotechnic horrors – blasts and shrieks, splintering wood and bellows of pain. Katrin fought to press herself up against the wall, though the zip-tie around her ankle held her leg straight out in front of her. It was impossible to separate her own shuddering from that of the building.

The bloodbath continued in sound and vibration only.

Boom.

A warbling cry torn off midstream.

Boom.

A heavy thump and then a death rattle of leaking air.

She covered her ears, closed her eyes. Even through the walls, she could smell smoke, the scent burning the back of her tongue.

A sob-warped pleading penetrated the walls. *'Hang on – just hang on, let me – !'*

Boom.

One kneecap pressed into her chin. Still she tried to draw her other leg to her chest, but the plastic tie sliced the flesh of her ankle. She was crying, but she couldn't hear herself.

A thunderclap of the door being kicked in. Her mouth opened, and this time she heard herself screaming. When she opened her eyes, the upper hinge was already knocked clear of the screws, the lower one snapping free as the door cartwheeled inward.

A black boot materialized from the dust-filled haze of the corridor, and then Evan melted into sight.

'We gotta move,' he said.

She looked a mess, her choppy bangs sweat-matted to her forehead, her face blanched, her lips dry and cracked. Wearing a thin tank top, she curled forward as if striving for the fetal position, her collarbones pronounced. Evan moved to her, letting the shotgun drop to the carpet, his hand in his pocket, digging for the Strider knife. The black-oxide blade flicked up with a snap, and he sliced through the plastic zip-tie, her freed leg retracting into her body as if spring-loaded.

He'd killed five of the eight operators and taken Candy out of commission. Which still left him outgunned.

Deep in the building, he heard running, shouts, bursts from radios. For now the remaining men were diverted to the eastern wing near the breaker-box explosion, bracing for a second-front attack. He let out his breath. The first moment of respite since his entry.

'Katrin, listen to me.' He cradled her face in his hands, one fist still gripping the Strider, the blade sticking up next to her cheek. 'We have to move quickly.'

'Did you kill the big guy?' she asked.

'No. He's not here. But other men are.' He sensed he was talking too loudly over the ringing in his ears. 'Stay behind me, touching distance. We're gonna head to the hillside, then loop back around.'

She nodded, tried to stand, her legs failing her.

In his pocket the black phone vibrated. After an instant of frozen shock, he yanked it free, tearing the lip of his cargo pocket. He glanced at the screen, expecting Slatcher's untraceable number. Instead the screen announced a pay phone with a 702 area code. Las Vegas.

Morena Aguilar.

Had Slatcher gotten to her, claiming another hostage even as Evan freed Katrin?

Still in a crouch, he snapped the phone to his face. 'Morena? Are you safe?'

'Yeah, no thanks to you.' Her voice came rushed and angry. 'Why can't you all just leave me and my sis alone? You said we'd be *done*.'

From the eastern corridor, he heard doors banging open, the men searching room by room. It wouldn't be long until they realized that their western contingent had been demolished.

With his free hand, he dropped the locked-open Strider and grabbed the shotgun, training it on the doorway. 'I have to go. Call back. Leave a number. Your life depends on it.'

As he pulled the phone away from his ear, he heard her fading voice: '– did what you said, okay? I found a guy. That was the deal.'

The ringing in his head amplified. Everything decelerated – the throbbing at his temple, the dragon swirl of smoke in the doorway, the guttering blue of the emergency light from the hall. The phone drifted back up to his ear, also in slow motion.

'*Guy?*' he said.

The realization was still rattling through him, making its way to his brain. Awareness hit, and he whipped around in time to see Katrin slip his own knife into his abdomen just beneath the ribs.

47. One Breath

Blood spurted through his shirt, matting the fabric to his flesh. The pain, merged with the ringing in his ears, shut out the world, a few seconds of mind-numbing overload. Her bird-thin shoulders hunched inward, Katrin backed away from him in seeming horror, one fist pressed over her sobbing mouth. Her pixie-round face, flushed red in near-perfect circles at the cheeks, looked even more doll-like. He stared at her uncomprehendingly. The phone trembled in his hand, lowering, lowering, until he dropped it into his gaping front cargo pocket. His fingers drew to the warmth spilling from his body.

'I'm sorry.' She was shaking her head, as if to negate what she'd just done. 'I didn't want to do any of it. But they . . . they made me. They made me do all of it.'

He staggered back a step, the weight of the shotgun tugging his arm downward until the barrel tip struck carpet. He leaned on it like a cane. His other hand came off the wall of his gut, a red palm spread before him.

Katrin's voice, wobbly with emotion, was still coming at him. 'Slatcher said he won't stop, that Sam won't be safe until you're dead. And the call, Morena – you were gonna find out.'

Morena's final words over the phone had saved him.

If he hadn't jerked away at the last minute he'd be down on the floor, bleeding out. When it came to a stomach puncture, every millimeter brought a fresh hell.

Nonetheless, he was hurt badly. Just *how* badly remained to be seen.

The ringing in his head fuzzed out all sound. Katrin half turned away, the strokes of that kanji tattoo spreading like spider legs from beneath the rear strap of her tank top. Her lips moved, shaping words: *I didn't want to, Evan.*

Still she held the blood-streaked Strider knife, but there seemed no risk she'd use it again. Turning his back on her, he staggered for the doorway. Fumbled along the wall and out into the corridor, still aswirl with Sheetrock dust, the shotgun low at his side, the tip trickling along the floor. He picked his way through the trail of bodies, this one propped against the base of the wall, that one lying in a glossy puddle, its three remaining limbs spread in a snow-angel sprawl. A fire sprinkler doused Evan's left side. He no longer sensed Candy's pounding on the jammed utility door behind him, but shadows flickered across the lobby at the end of the corridor ahead.

He veered into the first office to his left. To raise the shotgun at the window, he had to kick the barrel, the effort releasing a cry of pain. The recoil almost knocked the Benelli from his grip, but his aim was close enough. The shards flew away, sucked outside as if by a vacuum.

Somehow he rolled over the jagged sill and on to the

marshy weeds. Rather than move toward the hill, he headed for the lobby, charting the straightest line to his truck. The back door of the atrium stood open, the grass around it trampled from some earlier search. Evan stumbled inside, assailed by the odor of dead plants.

He moved through a neat industrial kitchen and peered into the lobby. Empty. The glass doors waited ahead and beyond, the promise of the parking lot and his pickup.

As he stepped from cover, running sounds echoed down the corridor, more than one set of boots. Gasping for air, he shouldered hard into the wall by the doorframe. It took everything he had to hoist the Benelli. He couldn't hold it properly, but he seated the stock against his shoulder and rested the barrel on the crossbar of his forearm. Firing it would hurt. The boots grew nearer, nearer, and then Evan swung around the jamb and pulled the trigger.

The recoil knocked him backward, spinning him down on to one knee. Heat crept over the waist of his pants. He drooled a little. From the corridor he heard wet gasping. When he managed to look back up, two bodies lay still.

He forced himself to his feet and banged out through the glass doors. A neat line of SUVs faced outward from the near curb, an offensive line in formation. He tottered between two of them, his shoulders knocking the sideview mirrors.

The parking lot played visual tricks on him,

stretching out like an asphalt football field. Through the full-body ache, he sent out a hope that the remaining operator would stay with Katrin rather than pursue him. Trudging across the open blacktop left him wildly exposed; he'd be gunned down here without a fight. Each breath seared his lungs; every step radiated a sense-memory echo of the stabbing through his torso. He told himself to keep walking, and his legs somehow stayed under him.

At last he fell through the jasmine hedge, his shoulder striking the wheel well of his trusty Ford. He tossed the shotgun into one of the truck vaults between a tray of ammunition and the cracked scabbard of the katana, then smeared himself around to the driver's seat.

Squeezing the wheel, he tore out of the spot and lurched into the parking lot, circling for a pass at the row of SUVs. He aimed his rugged bumper assembly at the line of shiny hoods, clipping the grilles one after another, jarring him painfully in his seat. The mini-collisions would activate inertia-sensing switches in the SUVs' bumpers, shutting down the power to the fuel pump and ensuring that no one could pursue him.

Rather than U-turn to use the lot exit, he hammered over the outer curb directly on to the overpass, bouncing high enough for his hair to skim the roof. Swiping sweat from his eyes, he rode the wide sweep of the lane up and around, veering on to the freeway. As he merged, he looked across the divider to the opposite lanes and spotted a purple Scion peeling up the exit toward the building. Odd that Slatcher hadn't yet ditched the car. As it flashed by, Evan caught a glimpse of the big man overflowing the driver's seat, one meaty arm pressed to the window.

He did not look happy.

The red taillights ahead blurred together into a stream, traffic slowing, and Evan braked abruptly, barely avoiding a rear-end. His face contorted, braced against the throbbing. Staying this tight was no good; it compounded the agony. He cast his mind back through the years to his first instructor, the bearded man in the barn. Those lessons taught with the tip of a knife.

Expectation of relief from pain would increase the opioids in his brain, an analgesic effect. Mind over reality.

He fought to move his focus away from the pain, to find the anchor of his breathing.

One breath.

There is no more pain to handle beyond this moment. Get through this moment and this moment only.

One breath.

There is only this moment. There is not the next moment or tomorrow.

One breath.

In this moment there is no pain.

Static crowded his vision from the edges, and he blinked against it, the black strip of the freeway fading in and out, a TV show that refused to come into focus.

48. Shot-to-Shit

Slatcher stood in the lobby, sparks from a shot-to-shit overhead light cascading across the yoke of his shoulders. He drew in a deep breath, rising into a rare moment of perfect posture, a grizzly on hind legs.

He moved into the west corridor, knowing already what he'd find.

White walls smeared with dark streaks. Tattered cargo pants. The sticky floor tugging at the soles of his boots.

He stepped across a prone form and then another. Corkscrewing away from a body at an exotic angle, an arm shone fish-white in the guttering glow, the fingers upthrust like some rare underwater creature.

He passed the boarded-up room and saw where the door had been kicked clear off the frame. The White woman stood backed into the corner, trembling violently, gasps escaping her bloodless lips. She held a folding knife in her limp grasp, the blade still wet. Her eyes were blank, holes in a mask with no face behind it. The mask tilted forward and dry-retched a few times without so much as a change of expression. There'd be no answers from her right now.

Slatcher brushed past the doorway, surveying the wreckage. From the meat-and-fabric bulks sprawled beneath the flickering lights to the hinge-blasted rear door lying flat on the floor, the damage was comprehensive.

Slatcher wasn't wearing a hat, but if he had been, he would have tipped it to Orphan X.

Not the best. But maybe – at last – an equal.

A faint scratching noise reached him. He cocked his head. Pulled his boot free from a black slick and headed for the maintenance closet.

There it came again, a desperate sound, almost plaintive. Fingernails against wood.

He opened the door, the smell hitting him in the face. Looking at the sight within, he felt his dark admiration transform into rage.

49. Scarlet Trail

The static haze lifted, Evan's vision clarifying in time for him to recognize that he was pulling through the ridiculous porte cochère. Yawning in his director's-chair perch, the valet started to rise, but Evan dismissed him with a nod. Fighting the wheel, he pulled down to the parking level and into his spot, barely missing a concrete pillar.

The dark stain enveloped the left side of his shirt, saturating the belt line of his cargo pants. He couldn't afford caution. He was, as the corpsmen were wont to say, bleeding like stink. If he didn't get upstairs immediately to stop the flow, he'd die. Wobbling toward the stairs, he almost lost his footing on an oil slick.

He didn't even register them until they were on top of him.

Mia and Peter.

She clutched a pharmacy bag, her son standing glumly beside her wearing a bathrobe over Riddler pajamas. Though she stared at Evan in shock, Peter was focused elsewhere, gazing anxiously up the stairs, tugging at her hand. 'C'mon, Mommy. My heart's still *pounding.*'

Instinctively, Evan turned away, hiding his bloody side from the boy.

Mia's expression stayed frozen, but somehow she managed to answer her son. 'The Ativan should kick in soon, sweetheart. It'll help you settle down. It's been a horrible night.'

Peter looked up at her, then across at Evan. His mouth popped open.

Evan white-knuckled the railing, pulling himself up step by step. He tugged the sleeve over his other hand, trying to wipe off the blood as he went, but it was no use.

Mia broke from her trance, moving up the stairs at his side. 'Jesus Christ, Evan,' she said. 'What happened? Are you okay?'

His head swam from the blood loss, his skin clammy and trembling. His heart redlined, each pulse reverberating through his chest. A dizzy spell staggered him, Mia shouldering some of his weight.

'Yes.' He pulled himself upright. 'Good.'

'Is this from Marts and Alonso?'

The pain stole the word from his mouth, so he shook his head no.

Mia tucked Peter behind her, trying to block his view. 'You've got to get to a hospital.'

Evan moved hand over hand along the wall toward the service elevator, leaving bloody prints. No time to clean, to cover his tracks. 'No. No.'

'This isn't a choice.'

'I'll be killed.' One breath. 'Men after me.' One breath. 'Go.' Breath. 'Away.'

The car arrived, and he tilted into it. Blood dripped off the hem of his shirt, tapping the floor.

Leaning heavily on the elevator rail, he looked back at her. Her forehead furled with concern. One tooth pinched her bottom lip. She looked like she might cry.

'*Please*,' he said.

The doors wiped her face from view.

Moving on autopilot, he let his breathing blot out everything. Muscle memory guided him to his front door.

A cold gust rolled up his torso, cooling his sweat-drenched face, and he realized he was inside his condo now, standing at the open refrigerator.

He pulled a saline IV bag out of the fruit drawer. From the butter shelf, he grabbed a bottle of Epogen, nearly dropping it. He battled his legs to get him across the poured-concrete expanse, down the hall. His sock squished inside his boot.

At last he spilled on to the bathroom floor. Flinging open the cabinet beneath the sink, he yanked out the First Responder kit. The magnetized buttons on his shirt gave way readily beneath his weak tug, an ancillary benefit. He doused a washcloth and wiped at his stomach, getting his first clear look at the wound.

The knife had penetrated his stomach two inches left of the midline, level with his rib cage, slicing the superior epigastric artery. The artery was just shallower than the abdominal wall muscles, which looked to be unscathed. A centimeter or two deeper would have added a host of untenable complications, puncturing his stomach, intestines, or diaphragm. Through the gash he watched blood spurt finely from the artery at intervals.

Doing his best not to anticipate what was coming, he pulled out the suture kit and readied the needle. One breath. One breath. One breath.

He entered a tunnel of torment, lost to time. Electricity jolting up nerve lines. Sweat tickling his jawline. Fingertips pulsing like crimson slugs.

And then it was done, or had been for some span of time, an ugly stitched seam of skin staring up at him. Somehow he'd thrown silk whipstitches around the bleeder and sutured off the slice above.

He breathed for a few moments, wanting to give himself a break, but then he started to drift off and knew he had to snap to. One-handed, he started an IV in the bend of his elbow. He spiked the bag of saline and started it feeding into his arm to up the fluid volume in his circulatory system until he could replenish his blood. Grabbing a syringe, he drew up a dose of Epogen from the bottle and sank the needle into his thigh, the injection burning as he depressed the plunger. An anemia med, Epo stimulated the marrow to produce more red blood cells, something he sorely needed given the quantity he'd left behind on the floor of the office building, in the footwell of his truck, on the walls of Castle Heights.

He stared longingly over at the hidden door in the open shower enclosure, but he knew he'd never make it into the Vault to scrub the surveillance footage. Even if he did, there was no way he could clean up the blood in the parking level, the rear hall, the service elevator.

The scarlet trail led right to his door, but he could do nothing about it right now. He'd have to add Castle Heights to his long list of burned locations and move on as soon as he was able. The pain in his chest at the thought of this wasn't physical; it was something deeper, buried close to his heart. Unable to base-jump, to abseil, even to drive away, he found himself in that rarest of places – at the mercy of chance, powerless to help himself.

He dragged himself to the floating platform of his bed. With a final effort, he hung the IV bag from his reading lamp. Then he collapsed into blackness.

50. The Ghost of Her Lips

*In the cold, pale light of morning, Evan rides in the passenger seat of the dark sedan. He is a boy, early in his training with Jack, and they are headed to another surprise session. Acclimatized to the vicissitudes of stress and adrenaline, Evan has learned not to brace himself. There is no point. In twenty minutes he might be shoved off a bridge on to a landing pad (*fun*), drownproofed in cold water with his hands and feet bound (*not fun*), or shot full of sodium pentothal (*disorienting but ineffective*).*

A Volvo pulls up alongside them, and as he is prone to do, Evan watches the family inside. The kids are three across in the back, quarreling and coloring and pigging their noses against the windows. The car falls behind them.

The next block accommodates an elementary school. Parents are dropping off kids with backpacks and crumpled bag lunches and bright-colored thermoses. The students run to and fro and talk in animated cliques.

Evan wonders what they talk about.

*After the day's session (*mace-spray training – not fun*), they return home. Bleary-eyed, Evan stacks firewood by the side of the house, the rough bark scraping his forearms. He hears no rustle behind him, but when he turns, Jack is there in his 501s and flannel shirt with each sleeve cuffed twice, neatly.*

'You need to talk,' Jack tells him.

357

Evan thrusts the logs atop the stack, scratches at his arms. 'Just me, huh? Alone? Always? That's how it'll be?'

The setting Virginia sun frames Jack's broad form, bestowing on him a celestial grandeur. 'That's right,' he says.

'Who said that thing about one twig can break? But a bundle is strong?'

'It's attributed to Tecumseh,' Jack says. 'But who the hell knows.' He studies Evan, his lips twitching. Evan has come to know that this means he is processing, rooting out the situation beneath the situation. Jack gestures to the brush along the side of the house. 'Gather a bunch of twigs.'

Evan does.

Jack crouches, unties his shoe, yanks the lace free and uses it to fasten the bundle. Then he unfolds his pocketknife, thumbs up the blade, and hammers it through the twigs. They crack uniformly at the midpoint. Jack grabs a single twig, lays it on the ground by itself, hands Evan the knife. 'Have at it.'

Evan tries, but the solitary twig pops free from the steel point, scarred yet intact. He stabs and stabs but the twig keeps skittering away, unwilling to be pinned down. Evan finally looks up, defeated. 'Okay,' he says. 'I get it. But . . .'

'Talk.'

'Won't it be lonely?'

'Yes.'

In his head Evan grasps for something to hold on to, a brass ring he can carry out of today's journey past the Volvo and the school, through the clouds of mace, into the promise of solitude. In the face of the unknown, as always, he tries to be game. He polishes off one of Papa Z's old chestnuts: 'What doesn't kill you makes you stronger, I guess,' he says.

Jack's eyes are as doleful as Evan has ever seen them. 'Some-times,' he says. 'But the rest of the time, it just makes you weaker.'

The knocking inside Evan's head became a knocking in the outside world.

Someone at the penthouse door.

Palming sleep from his eyes, he swung his legs over the side of the bed with less effort than he anticipated. Scattered on the floor, various syringes, depleted saline bags, wads of gauze. A glance at the clock showed that it had been two and a half days since he'd stumbled home. Ample time for his spilled blood to be discovered, surveillance footage reviewed, officials alerted.

He'd healed up quickly, the Epo working its modern medical magic. The shiny skin at the wound's edge remained tender, and he still felt a nasty sting in his gut when he bent over, but the pain had mostly lifted. He wouldn't be doing sit-ups anytime soon, but as of this morning he was generally mobile.

He pulled on a loose T-shirt and a pair of jeans, picked up his Wilson Combat pistol, and trudged up the hall. If it was the cops, he'd keep the front door bolted and rappel gingerly out the window.

The time had come, perhaps, to leave everything behind.

The inset surveillance screen showed Hugh Walters bristling in a Fila tracksuit. Evan tucked his pistol into the back of his jeans and opened the door.

'You have some explaining to do,' Hugh said.

'I understand,' Evan replied. 'Before you do anything, can you just give me –'

'You precipitously left the HOA meeting before voting was completed. As a result I reviewed your attendance record, and do you know what I found?'

Midsentence, Evan froze. Poleaxed, he managed to shake his head.

'Your attendance record falls below the requirements – *requirements*, not *suggestions* – of the HOA guidebook.'

Evan stepped out into the corridor. No blood drops on the carpet, nor finger streaks along the walls. It had been cleaned already? Without Hugh's finding out?

'As such,' Hugh said, 'you'll be assessed a fine, per the regs, of six hundred dollars.'

'A fine,' Evan repeated.

Their amateur-scientist rapport had clearly evaporated, but that was the least of Evan's concerns. He needed to find out if he'd been compromised – and by whom.

With a sigh, Hugh pulled off his black-framed eyeglasses and rubbed his eyes. 'Look, Evan. I know this stuff isn't a priority for you. Believe it or not, it's not for me either. To be frank, I don't really give a shit about revamping the carpets or a new noise ordinance.'

Evan blinked at him.

'But for a lot of us, a sense of community is important. And here in the big city? For some of us? This is all we have. So just . . . think about it, okay?'

Caught off guard by Hugh's sudden detour, Evan nodded. 'I will.'

A ding down the hall announced the elevator's arrival. Mia and Peter emerged, Mia with a bag of groceries clutched in her arms, the requisite French loaf poking out of the top.

'Ah,' Hugh said. 'Perhaps I judged too soon.' Offering Evan a sly tip of the head, he moved off down the corridor, acknowledging Mia and Peter as they passed.

Evan waited in the doorway for them to approach. Peter tugged on the straps of his backpack, seating the weight higher on his shoulders.

'Can we come in?' Mia asked.

Evan stepped aside, letting them enter. Peter scooted around the kitchen island, Mia spinning in a slow three-sixty to take in the great room. 'Wow. Serious digs.'

It occurred to Evan that no one had been inside his place socially. Ever.

'We wanted to bring you this.' She set the grocery bag down on the counter. 'And to make sure you're not . . . you know. Dead.'

Peter was leaning with both hands and his forehead against the Sub-Zero, exhaling in an attempt to fog the stainless steel. Mia and Evan moved farther into the condo, edging into a relative privacy. She drifted by the kickboxing station and gave the heavy bag a little poke.

'So how exactly did you wind up with your stomach . . . ?' Her hands came up. 'Wait. I don't want to know. I *can't* know.'

He walked over, leaned against the opposite side of the heavy bag. 'It was you. You cleaned up the blood for me.'

'Yes,' she said.

'Why? You didn't owe me anything. What I did for you and Peter –'

'It's not because I *owed* you, Evan. It's because I wanted you . . .' She wet her lips. 'Well. Maybe you'll know what it means to need someone now.'

A sensation tugged at him, decades old. Something he'd seen in the faces of those kids he used to watch in passing cars. The bundle of sticks, vulnerable to Jack's knife. Bright thermoses and bag lunches. He thought about that moment in Mia's bedroom, the softness of her lips, the piano trill that straightened her spine. *What makes you happy?* How different from Katrin with her passion tattoo and blood-red mouth, all allure and high stakes and porcelain skin, intoxicating right up until the moment she slipped a knife beneath his ribs. *What makes you happy?* What if that moment with Mia, laced with a hint of lemongrass and scored by 'Hymn to Freedom', had taken a different course? *Argue with me. Make it my fault. Get angry.*

'Consider it a parting gift,' she said.

His face must have shown more than he wanted it to, because her eyes welled and she said, 'I'm sorry, Evan. But I – *we* – can't have you around. It's too dangerous.' She reached out, her fingers resting lightly on his chest. 'I'd be an irresponsible parent if I –'

'Thank you,' he said. 'For what you did.'

She inhaled, her chest rising. 'This is it, then.'

'Okay,' he said. 'This is it.'

She turned to go, then paused. 'Your forehead,' she said. 'It's cut.'

He lifted his fingers. A nick from the blowback when he'd shot out the window. 'It's nothing.'

'Nope,' she said, digging in her purse. She came out with a colorful Band-Aid and stripped off the wrapping. Kermit with his gaping grin.

'Really?' Evan said.

''Fraid so.'

He bent to her, and she smoothed it on to his forehead with her thumbs. She hesitated, then kissed his forehead. 'Goodbye, Evan.'

'Goodbye.'

He heard her shoes tap over to the kitchen and then two sets of footsteps moving to the front door. It opened and closed.

For a time he stood there, the ghost of her lips lingering on his face.

51. *&^%*!

The ten RFID fingernails overlay Slatcher's own, though since the press-ons had been designed for normal-size hands, they looked more like painted stripes. They always made him feel like a girl playing dress-up in a too-small gown. The fully pixelated contact lens, seated on his right eye, scrolled the virtual-messaging session with Top Dog, rendering the texts midway to the dashboard of the purple Scion. He sat in the shoved-back driver's seat, his fingers tickling the air, giving answers he did not want to give.

Top Dog was angry, and when Top Dog was angry, you typed faster.

YOU STILL HAVE NO LEADS ON ORPHAN X. HOSPITALS, ERS, MORGUES.

Slatcher noted the lacking question mark. Nonetheless he replied. NO.

The green cursor barely had an instant to blink before TD's next text sprang up: WHAT IS ORPHAN V'S CONDITION?

The car hugged the curb on an idyllic suburban street lined with willows. Fallen silver-blue leaves collected on the windshield wipers. Using the back of his hand, Slatcher blotted sweat from his brow. The windows magnified the midday Vegas sun, turning the car desert-hot even in cool December.

The movement inadvertently rendered some symbols: *&^%*!

IS THAT SUPPOSED TO BE A JOKE?

NO. SORRY. TECH MALFUNCTION.

ORPHAN V?

HOSPITALIZED. OUT OF COMMISSION. HER BACK LOOKS LIKE SOMETHING OUT OF A CREATURE FEATURE.

HOW ABOUT 'KATRIN WHITE'?

A drop of sweat trickled down the bridge of Slatcher's nose, making it itch, but he didn't dare scratch it. I LET HER GO. SHE SERVED HER PURPOSE. SHE DID RIGHT BY US.

SHE'LL NEED TO BE CLEANED UP.

He regretted the implicit order. He preferred to play by fair rules, but Top Dog had no such moral qualms. Slatcher typed: IMMEDIATELY?

NO. SHE GOT CLOSE TO HIM. I WANT HER WATCHED. ANOTHER LINE IN THE WATER.

COPY.

ORPHAN X TOOK OUT ALL YOUR FREELANCERS?

EXCEPT ONE. BUT IT DOESN'T MATTER. I WILL HANDLE EVERYTHING PERSONALLY FROM HERE ON OUT.

YOU'D BETTER, TD typed. OR I WILL.

Another implicit threat. A second drop of sweat forged down Slatcher's forehead. The itch on his nose grew in intensity. He forced his fingers to type. COPY.

WHAT'S YOUR PLAN?

Laughter and shouts carried from the school playground across the street.

MORENA AGUILAR. SHE'LL LEAD US TO HIM.

I WANT HER WRAPPED IN SURVEILLANCE. WHATEVER IT TAKES.

Slatcher lifted his gaze to the little girl sitting on the swings. A teenage girl crouched in front of her, her hands gripping the chains. Almost lost in the sea of playing kids, they spoke closely, intimately.

THAT'S WHY I'M HERE, Slatcher replied.

The teenager stood, kissed the younger girl on the cheek, and turned. Watching Morena walk away, Slatcher reminded himself not to reach to turn the ignition key just yet.

Instead he finished typing: SHE WON'T LEAVE MY SIGHT.

52. The Other Guy's Hand

On the third day, Evan finally entered the Vault. Within twenty minutes he'd cleaned up the Castle Heights surveillance footage. It was odd watching himself zombie-stumbling through the corridors, smearing charcoal along the walls. An entire seven minutes of his life that he had little memory of, operating unconsciously on the training drilled into his body. He fast-forwarded to find whatever else would need to be deleted. A short while later, Mia appeared in the corridor of the twelfth floor. On various monitors he followed her to the elevator, up to the twenty-first floor, then along his corridor. She paused outside his penthouse. He'd left the front door ajar.

She entered and moved tentatively toward his bedroom. He was lying on the bed, unconscious. Going quickly to him, she checked his pulse. Then his forehead. For a time she sat beside him and held his hand. He watched the minutes tick by.

Then she left the penthouse, closing the door firmly behind her. She returned to her condo and emerged a minute later, bucket and brush in hand. It was the middle of a night in which she'd already endured a home invasion. She'd only just gotten her traumatized boy put to bed. And yet there she was, scrubbing the floors, walls and elevator for nearly two hours.

Protecting him.

He was standing to leave when he spotted an icon that an e-mail had arrived, after a long journey of auto-forwards around the globe, into the inbox of the. nowhere.man@gmail.com. He couldn't remember the last one he'd received.

Two days old, it was from one of Tommy Stojack's accounts. And the subject line read: *'Katrin White.'*

A chill moved through Evan's stomach, making the scabbed wound tingle.

He took a moment, then sat down, rolled his chair back to the desk, and read Tommy's message.

'Bad news: my hook at Harrah's left. Good news: he moved over to Caesars. Your girl's in the databanks over there. They couldn't pin nuthin on her, but she had a run on a poker table that JDLR.'

Stojack slang for 'just didn't look right.'

Evan opened the attachment, an internal report from Caesars. A scanned copy of a gambler rewards card featured a photo. There was that milk-white skin, the emerald gaze, her choppy hipster hairstyle rendered here not in black but a rich auburn. The name beneath: *'Danika White.'* A header written in party streamers read: *'Vegas. Be whoever you want to be.'*

His throat was dry enough that it took some effort to swallow. He read on.

Danika was a high roller, working the no-limit tables at Caesars and racking up serious debt, which had been mysteriously paid off on 7 December. Two days after Evan killed William Chambers and three days before Katrin White had set the meeting at Bottega Louie. Shared intel with other casinos showed arrears all up and down the Strip, similarly wiped off the books two weeks ago.

The lies compounded. There had been no covert poker circle. No Vegas hit men skinning indebted Japanese businessmen. No trust-baby husband who'd left her in the financial lurch. Danika had simply gotten in over her head gambling too hard for too long. Slatcher – or whoever was behind him – had stepped in and purchased her casino markers; they'd paid their money and bought her outright.

But they wouldn't have been able to if she hadn't been willing to make the deal at the outset. In his sordid career, Evan had seen plays like this dozens of times. Reach out to a desperate mark. Offer her the shot of a lifetime. Then once you own her, tighten the screws.

By the time Danika White understood the nature of the pact she'd entered, it would have been too late.

Armed with her real name, Evan's virtual excavations grew drastically easier. Danika's parents were alive and well, retired to a planned community in Boca Raton. She had no husband of record and one daughter, twenty years of age.

Her name was Samantha.

In his head, Evan replayed Danika's reaction in the motel when the gunshot had sounded over the phone: *Sam! Dad? No. No. No!*

In her state of panic, her first reaction had been a tell. She'd used the proper name of who she'd really thought had been hurt before catching herself.

As each fabrication toppled, it knocked over the next, a domino chain of deception. Vowing to follow it to the end, Evan breached the DMV's database. Samantha's driver's license showed her to be a beautiful kid, the resemblance to her mother striking. After a two-year stint at Santa Monica City College, Samantha had gotten a financial-aid package at UCLA. Though she held down two work-scholarship jobs, her tuition account showed multiple interest charges for late payments. Evan unearthed a cell-phone number for her and dialed.

The voice, young and breezy: 'Yeah, it's Sam?'

In the background Evan heard a bustle of activity, someone calling her name. It sounded like classes letting out, or maybe she was walking through the quad. He exhaled, relieved that she wasn't being held hostage. A good strategic move on Slatcher's part – he could get to her readily, so why deal with the complications and risks of detaining her?

'Hi, Sam,' Evan said. 'I'm a friend of your mom's and –'

'Wow. Almost ten months this time. Impressive. I thought she'd finally given up for real.'

'Sorry?'

'What's she need now? More money? Like I'm not working enough to pay for my own life? I told her – I don't want to see her or talk to her. And that includes any lame go-betweens.'

'No, it's not that. It's just . . . She stopped returning calls the past few weeks –'

'Get used to it. Look, dude, I don't know who you are, but let me save you some years of your life. At the end of the day, when it comes to Danika, all that matters is Danika.'

Evan approximated a crestfallen tone. 'Okay. Thank you.'

'Hey,' Sam said. 'I'm sorry, okay? I'm just trying to help so you don't have to go through what I went through.'

She hung up.

Evan cocked back in his chair and closed his eyes, letting the picture resolve more clearly. Danika – probably at Slatcher's command – had fashioned Katrin from pieces of her true self. She'd kept her last name and her gambling habit. She'd appropriated Sam's name for her fake dad. Her fictional husband invested in planned communities in Boca Raton, just as her real parents lived in one.

Evan recalled building his own first operational alias with Jack, toiling by the light of the birch fire in the farmhouse. Jack had taught him to assemble the cover story using more truth than lies, giving him less to remember and less to forget. Evan had learned to align himself with his false persona as closely as possible, forging a true emotional attachment so his instincts would respond accordingly. He'd learned to fall into a role and forget the part of himself that did not believe it.

Slatcher and his crew had done this for Katrin. After acquiring her in Vegas, they'd traumatized her, coercing her into a damaged state that matched what they needed her to display. After Slatcher had seemingly shot and killed Sam, Evan remembered holding Danika on the motel bed, how she'd wept herself hoarse against his chest. Slatcher and his crew must have threatened Samantha's life, promising to hurt her if Danika didn't come through. They'd ensured that the guilt and terror thrumming through her body were real. They had to be to allay Evan's suspicions.

A former Orphan, Slatcher had tailored her cover story to suit Evan. A terrorized woman up against impossible odds, in desperate need of his help. The father with his life on the line, dying because of Evan's miscalculation. Katrin had laid Evan's own secret guilt bare. *I made a stupid fucking mistake, and my dad's paying for it*, she'd said. *Do you have any idea how that feels?*

Yes.

This indicated that Slatcher – and his employer – knew about Jack. Had they been behind his death? Evan followed the chain of logic all the way down to the depths and did not like where it led him.

Danika had all but dared him to check her passport, pointing out that she had it on her, leaving it in clear view in her purse at the loft. The salient fact that Slatcher's employer could generate a real passport as well as a full network of backstops in the databases was not lost on Evan.

He set his elbows on the sheet-metal surface of his desk and rubbed his eyes.

Sam's dying words to his daughter over the phone had only set the hook deeper: *Whoever you're with, I hope he protects you.* Through his suspicions, against his judgment, Evan *had* protected her. Though their location had been tipped off to their pursuers time and time again, though the Commandments had crumbled away one after the other, Evan had stuck with her right up until she'd skewered him with his own knife. Who better to fill that role than a poker player, skilled at analyzing others, reading scenarios, bluffing for gain? Ultimately, Danika had summed it up best herself.

You're not playing your hand, she'd told him. *You're playing the* other guy's *hand.*

Dangling from his pull-up bar, Evan practiced knee raises to break up the fresh-forming scar tissue in his stomach. He moved slow and steady, breathing through the pain. He was focused so intently that he didn't at first hear the RoamZone ringing.

Jogging to the kitchen counter, he snatched it up.

Vegas. Pay phone.

'Morena?'

'You okay?'

He was genuinely confused. 'What?'

'Last time I called you, you sounded hurt. Bad.'

He breathed, felt the scar tissue strain. 'I was,' he said. 'Not bad.'

'Okay. I thought you might be dead or something. I just wanted to check.'

Evan restrained his urge to press her, trying to imagine how Jack would've played this out. He'd always had that knack – when to take up space, when to give it.

Evan walked along the row of sunscreens, patches of muted light rolling across him. 'Is that the only reason you called?'

'At first I thought it was his cop friends, you know? Coming after us for revenge. You and me, we're the only ones who knew anything about what happened to

William Chambers, so I knew I had to get away from my sis and my aunt.'

'That was brave. And wise.'

'But these aren't his cop friends, are they?'

'No,' Evan said. 'They're much worse.'

'They think I know something. I don't know nothing. My life, it's over. But Carmen, she can have a good life, maybe.'

'You will, too,' he said.

'I can't go near you again. If I stick my head up, they'll get me.'

Evan fought an urge to argue with her. Walking a lap around the great room, he did his best to channel Jack. *I will never lie to you.* If there was not trust, there would be nothing else.

'Yes,' Evan said. 'They will.'

Wet breathing. A hiccup of a sob. 'I'm scared. I should be scared, right?'

'Yes. You should.'

'It's hard living like this. Invisible to the world. Apart from everyone. Like I don't even exist.'

He thought of Mia in her bedroom, swaying to the Oscar Peterson Trio. 'Yes,' he said. 'It is.'

She cried some more, muffled gasps. Seventeen years old, targeted by a world-class assassin. Rage rose in Evan's throat, but he choked it off.

'If you don't tell me where you are,' he said, 'I can't protect you.'

When Morena spoke again, her voice was heavy with sadness. 'I know,' she said.

53. A Backstroke with No Water

Excitement pulsed to life in Slatcher's spacious chest when he saw Morena Aguilar switch buses. Slowing the Scion, which had been trailing the northbound Downtown Express, he noted that she wasn't catching a connection but crossing the street to hop on to a southbound bus. Reversing course back to the Strip. A basic diversionary move that would have been advised by Orphan X prior to a meet.

For three days and nights, Morena had remained under Danny Slatcher's watchful eye. She'd visited her sister once more on the playground and slung chips and guac at a shitty fast-food joint accustomed to paying under the counter. But until now there'd been no break in her routine that indicated that Evan was back in play.

Flipping a U-turn, Slatcher immediately roused his remaining man in the field, who through some cruel parental oversight was actually named Don Julio. 'Big Daddy to Tequila One. Pull off the little sister and track my location.'

With a giant thumb, he enabled a phone app that sent his coordinates.

'T-One to BD. Be to you in . . . seven minutes.'

Even around lunchtime the logjam leading to the

Strip rivaled rush-hour L.A. Angling all the air-conditioning vents toward himself, Slatcher patiently hung three vehicles back from the bus, making sure at each stop to account for all the passengers as they got off.

How dull and achromatic Vegas looked by daylight never ceased to surprise him, a collection of odd-shaped buildings smeared in a vague row like a line of dusty Lego that had been crushed underfoot. Sahara Avenue crept by, the Stratosphere looming like an alien antenna from a seventies sci-fi flick. In the rearview Slatcher noted the slate gray SUV swing around behind him.

Again he keyed the radio. 'You take point when she moves. She'll recognize me.'

'Copy.'

The bus came up on Sands Avenue, approaching Treasure Island with its skull-and-crossbones marquee, the pirate ship slumbering in Siren's Cove waiting for its nightly shows. Another Strip meeting seemed in the making for Evan and Morena – plenty of activity, plenty of witnesses, plenty of cameras. The bus veered east, carving between the Wynn and the Palazzo, hugging the edge of an extravagant golf course. Just before Paradise Road, the bus halted and ejected Morena through the yawning doors, her head lowered. Hands balled in the pockets of her coat, she moved at a rapid clip, shooting nervous glances all around. She passed in front of a giant outdoor parking structure, rising seven stories from the pavement like a concrete corncob, and skipped through the automated doors into the lobby of

La Reverie. A purple glow uplit the soffits of the new hotel-casino, reflecting off the shimmering glass and competing with the Nevada glare.

Parking tickets be damned, Slatcher left the Scion at the curb in front of the corncob structure, positioned for a quick post-kill getaway. The SUV drifted past him, and a half block ahead he saw Julio valet at La Reverie, hop out, and slice through the smoked-glass doors. Above Slatcher's head an open footbridge forged across from the parking structure's top level, plugging into the side of La Reverie. For an instant he debated taking that route to come at the meet from a different angle, but having no idea where Orphan X was set up, he bolted for the casino lobby instead.

As he spun inside, he noted the elevator doors closing. On cue, a text chimed into his phone.

Ti: 8ᵀᴴ FLOOR.

Julio had made it into the car and was riding up beside her.

Slatcher banged through the wide door into the stairwell and lunged up three stairs at a time. Despite his giant frame and extra girth, he was well conditioned, a physiological marvel. Near the fifth floor, a few spindle-legged party girls clomped their way down on improbable stilettos, and he bowled past them, flattening them to the wall. By the time he reached the eighth-floor landing, his breath burned in his chest. He waited behind the door, heard the elevator doors rumble wide. A moment later, through the tempered-glass panel above the lever handle, he watched Morena dart by, less than three feet away. Behind her, Julio ambled, light on his feet, his blend-in biz-casual suit holding the contours of his basic-training body with nary a rumple.

Easing the handle down, Slatcher leaned out of the doorway. Morena kept on with a charged walk, her hands forming fists at her sides, seemingly too focused to check behind her. Though Julio held a relaxed pace, his long legs kept him a few steps off her heels. Slatcher stepped clear of the stairwell and moved swiftly behind them both, using Julio's breadth to block Morena's line of sight should she decide to shoot a look over her shoulder. If he and Julio timed this right, they'd stack the doorway all at once, Morena serving as a shield for any return fire.

Midway down the hall, she tapped on a door, then turned the handle and entered. Slipping a hand beneath one impeccable lapel, Julio drew a pistol and accelerated the final two steps to the door. His own pistol now in hand, Slatcher turned on a sprint, closing on Julio, his momentum carrying him into perfect position.

They aligned to crash the room in tight order, a three-car train pulling in to the station at last.

Eight stories up from the balcony window of the gaudily decorated hotel room, Evan had watched the sluggish convoy lurch along Sands Avenue – first the wheezing bus, then the purple Scion, then a dark SUV. He'd tied a length of rappelling rope around the balcony post, letting it dangle above the open-air footbridge one story below. He'd parked his Ford F-150 on the roof of the parking structure across the bridge, backed into the space to allow for speedy egress. From the window he could see the rear of the waiting pickup, its truck vaults gleaming in the bed.

The high vantage had allowed him to watch Morena hop off the bus and scurry out of view toward the lobby. He'd noted Slatcher unpack himself from the illegally parked Scion, the SUV gliding by to pick up Morena's tail. Then he'd walked to the door of Room 8124, unlocked it, and backed midway to the balcony. Given Slatcher's size, Evan had debated bringing the Benelli combat shotgun, but this plan called for greater precision. Jack's voice came to him: *Shot placement trumps all calibers.*

Drawing his Wilson 1911, Evan assumed a modified isosceles stance, aiming the tip of the suppressor at the door. Slatcher had been hoping that Morena would lead him to Evan.

He was about to get his wish.

Evan waited, reading vibrations through the floor. In his stomach the healing wound glowed, an excited heat spreading out beneath his rib cage.

The lever handle clicked down, and it all went live.

Morena flew through the door, immediately diving into a somersault, moving along the path Evan had cleared through the furniture. As she whipped past his calf, the bulky freelancer filled the doorframe and Evan shot him twice in the chest and put a third bullet through his nose. He dumped right there, clearing the view to Slatcher.

Behind him Evan heard Morena scrambling over the balcony, seizing the rope, starting her one-story descent to the footbridge.

Unlike the freelancer, Slatcher had barreled into view with his pistol not just raised but ready to fire, so Evan's first round went to the gun hand. Slatcher's pistol pinwheeled to the side, and then the big man kneed his collapsing operator forward, forcing Evan to skip back to avoid being toppled by him.

The scar tissue tugged in his gut as he raised the gun, a slight hitch that cost him. Slatcher's eyes were locked on the barrel of Evan's Wilson, assessing the precise line of fire, and he lifted his massive arms as he charged, catching the bullets as Evan fired.

The first round deflected wetly off the meat of Slatcher's forearm, raised to cover the bridge of his nose, the second stigmataed his right hand, buying him a millisecond to whip his forehead out of the path.

He did not slow.

His bullet-torn forearm hammered Evan's wrist like a steel pipe, the shotokan blow knocking Evan over. He rolled with the blow, grabbing a whirligig view of his Wilson 1911 skittering off the edge of the balcony and, far below, Morena's form darting across the footbridge to safety. Even as he spun back up on to his feet, he recalculated. He'd trained once with a shotokan master who'd toughened his hands, feet and shins into iron, pounding nails into the floor with his fists. The master had spoken of executing one-punch kills, and Evan knew from Slatcher's opening salvo that he was capable of the same. The last thing he could afford was to be in this tight with a man this big.

They circled each other in the arena of the suite, both striking open-hand guards, palms turned in, fingertips floating above the upper temples. Given the size disparity, Evan had to disrupt Slatcher's nervous system, going for the centers – eyes, nose, ears, throat. But the biggest organ was the skin. He needed Slatcher to feel pain now, not tomorrow.

He attacked with pencak silat, an open-hand Indonesian fighting style, feinting left, then thunderclapping Slatcher's right side with a palm-heel ear smash. The big man's eyes showed mostly white until the pupils rolled back into view, a robot reanimating. Evan waited for Slatcher to lash out defensively, then sidestepped, parrying with a dagger thumb to the eustachian tube at the hinge of the jaw. He felt his thumb sink pleasingly into the soft skin at the target, but he'd slipped too far inside Slatcher's reach in order to get off the shot and knew instantly it would cost him.

Slatcher's hands blurred, the wrecked one throwing flecks of blood upon impact. Evan did his best to cage his head, drawing the bars of his forearms together, but he was getting rained on. Despite the battering, he fought to stay inside the range of the devastating hook.

There was no break to capitalize on; Evan would have to create one. He rotated his elbow as he whipped the blade of his forearm upward like a greaser slicking back the side of his hair. The tip of his ulna, positioned like a cutting diamond, split Slatcher's chin to the bone.

Blood ribboning from the wound, Slatcher tilted back and sucked in a breath.

They were fighting in different languages, an around-the-world street brawl, Filipino deflections countering Japanese double-hand parries. They careened back through Indonesia, open-hand slaps and bone-grinding arm-break holds, Evan's front kick finally shoving them back to standoff distance.

Crimson snakes curled around Slatcher's arms, the bullet gashes glittering. Evan felt his right cheek swelling and prayed it wouldn't obstruct the eye. The luxurious carpet, spotted and trampled, might have been pulled off an auto mechanic's floor. Someone darted by the open door, shrieked, and kept on. With one foot Slatcher flipped the dead field agent's corpse to the side, clearing space. His rocklike shoulders bulged beneath his shirt. Despite the gunshot wounds, he barely looked winded. If Evan didn't get out soon, Slatcher was going to take him to pieces.

He charged Evan now with a shotokan lunge punch. Evan intercepted it with a muay thai *teep*, the ball of his lead foot clawing forward to thrust into the tendons of the lower abdomen. Given Slatcher's substantial gut, this had little effect, but it did shift Slatcher's weight forward, putting his head within reach.

Evan threw an arm clench over the big man's head, his hands locked in a lace hold across the back of the impossibly broad neck, his forearms squeezing to crimp the carotids. Yanking Slatcher's face downward, Evan threw *tangs*, knee strikes hammering through

Slatcher's raised, tattered forearms into his cheeks, his nose. At the same time, he torqued Slatcher from side to side, trying to keep him off balance by rocking him on to one leg, then the other.

No such luck. Slatcher was too strong – he simply picked Evan up and bulled him through the dressing mirror. Evan's stomach screamed, the wound reopening, scar tissue tearing. The glass shattered around him, shards cascading over his shoulders.

Evan hit the carpet, and Slatcher reared back, allowing a tiny window of freedom. Evan bolted, leaping across a toppled armchair and out on to the balcony. Slatcher struck him from behind, power-driving Evan into the balusters, but Evan let his body flip over the handrail, grabbing for the rappelling rope. He caught it, lost his grip, caught it again, slid a few palm-burning yards before his hands released of their own volition. The last six feet were a free fall, the footbridge flying up to bludgeon his tailbone and shoulder blades. Before the pain could announce itself, Slatcher blotted out the sun, dangling from the rope and then letting go, size-seventeen boots growing larger by the instant.

Evan rolled up over his shoulders, shot a quick look around for his fallen Wilson – no such luck – and lurched off for the parking structure and his truck. Slatcher's landing shook the footbridge. Within seconds the thundering steps behind Evan had quickened to a drumroll.

Despite the dagger of pain in his gut and the full-body ache from the drop, Evan stayed in a sprint, trying to dig in his pocket for the key to the truck vault. He skidded sideways on to the roof of the parking structure, nearly losing his footing as he made the turn for his truck.

Morena was long gone; Evan had told her to keep running, that he'd make sure no one came after her. That was a long-term promise. Way across the roof, an elevator opened, the family of four inside jolting cattle-prod upright at the scene before them. The father leaned forward, jabbing at a button, and the elevator swallowed them back up.

With bruised and aching hands, Evan fumbled out the keys, dropped them, picked them up, all the while sensing Slatcher's rolling-boulder approach. He fought the key into the first vault and grabbed the stock of the combat shotgun, swinging it free and scattering the sheathed katana and the tray of shotgun shells across the roof.

Slatcher was on him.

There was no time to bring the Benelli around, no time to do anything but lean to dodge the hurtling mass. Slatcher clipped him, knocking the shotgun away and crushing himself into the lowered tailgate. The collision was seismic. Bone crunched, but Slatcher gave up only an understated grunt. Evan dived for the shotgun, but it skittered out of reach toward the metal bars guarding the broad concrete overhang. The ammo boxes had burst open, red shells spraying everywhere. Bouncing off the truck, Slatcher nearly slipped on them, but he regained his footing and squared to Evan.

Breathing hard, Evan pulled himself unevenly to his feet.

Slatcher stood stooped, favoring his broken hip. His split chin had painted a bib of crimson down his shirt. Blood trickled down his arms, dripped from his fingers. The collision with the truck had stunned him, and Evan had one shot to capitalize on that.

Slatcher lumbered toward him, hands coming up into fighting position. Evan sidestepped, forcing him to circle the wrong way and set his weight on to that broken hip. Slatcher gritted his teeth and took a quivering step. Bone crunched. Before he could set himself, Evan stepped forward, planting his left foot, and delivered a Wing Chun oblique kick with his right, pivoting to piston his heel forward, aiming beneath the pillar of Slatcher's lead thigh. He hit the knee squarely, shattering it backward, and the big man bellowed and sagged, somehow keeping his feet. For an instant Evan wobbled off balance, time enough for Slatcher to hop forward, rotating the immense base of his hips and driving a reverse punch into Evan's solar plexus.

Pain exploded in his wound, torpedoing through his insides. The force of the blow knocked him off his feet, and then he had only a sideways view of the rooftop as he slid back and racked into the guardrails. The back of his head clanged off the metal, concussion flares hazing the world. The sun-baked concrete cooked his cheek, and he felt a curious detachment as he watched Slatcher drag himself across the sideways roof, growing larger.

Evan blinked, snapping to. He turned his head.

Through the guardrails was only the concrete slab of the solar-paneled overhang, a ten-foot ring around the structure, petals of green-black glass. Beyond that a seven-story drop. He blinked again, harder. There was more, if he could just see it. His bowling-ball slide into the rail had knocked the katana beneath the bottom metal rung, as well as a number of shotgun shells, still spinning like tops. But he wasn't focused on them. He was focused on the Benelli combat shotgun just beyond, the barrel come to rest several inches off the rim.

Evan pulled himself up the guardrails, a boxer climbing the ropes, and spilled over the top. Slatcher's fist skimmed overhead, missing by inches. The shells clattered; the sword finished a lazy half rotation, then fell, slotted into the space between solar panels.

Evan crawled along the curved eave toward the shotgun, hands and knees sliding on the slick solar panels. He heard Slatcher shatter a panel behind him, landing hard. Evan's fingers strained, inches from the shotgun stock.

Slatcher lunged for him, grabbing his calf, knocking Evan's hand forward into the Benelli.

It skimmed soundlessly off the rim. For a moment it floated against the pretty glass backdrop of La Reverie. Then it vanished. The breeze ruffled Evan's hair, and he felt the soothing warmth of the sun on his cheek. A poetic moment of ordinary life.

Then Slatcher ripped him backward. Evan fell from all fours on to his stomach.

Rotating on his hip, he hurled his weight into a turn

and kicked Slatcher with everything he had left. The top of his foot struck just below Slatcher's jaw, hooking the big man's head and spinning him toward the brink.

Slatcher's broad fingers scrabbled for purchase across the sleek silicon, sending shotgun shells scattering. His legs drifted off the lip, and then his hips went, that low center of gravity tipping him over. His elbows ledged the rim. Then slipped. Slatcher's bloody hand flailed up over his head.

And caught something.

The sheathed katana, stuck in the gap between sets of solar panels.

It protruded from the roof's edge like a bracketed flag from the side of a building. Slatcher's downward weight wedged the long sword handle tighter into place, pulling it horizontal until it locked between the panels and the concrete lip of the roof.

His mighty arm trembled. The hand tendons were frayed from the bullet wound, his fingers not clenching fully.

A suspended moment. And then his other hand flew up, clamping on to the scabbard beside the first.

He started to draw himself back toward the rooftop.

A pull-up, one hundred feet above the sidewalk.

The sheath slid an inch off the hilt. Slatcher froze. If the sheath went, he went with it. The equilibrium held. After a moment's pause, he began inching his way up again.

Biting his cheek against the pain, Evan pulled himself toward Slatcher and the sword. Slatcher's face strained, a vein popping in his temple. Still, he made headway.

Evan came within range. He positioned himself to kick Slatcher off, but Slatcher watched him intently, ready to react even from his compromised position. If any part of Evan's body came within reach, he had little doubt Slatcher would latch on to it and bring Evan with him.

Evan turned to the sword instead. He fought to free it from between the panels, but Slatcher's weight pinned it in place. He grabbed the base of the scabbard and attempted to force it off the length of sword, but the same was true, the downward pressure too strong.

Slatcher kept rising, his elbows hovering just off the concrete rim, nearly able to set down.

A crackling sound turned them both to statues.

Evan's eyes dropped to that hairline crack in the sheath from when Peter had dropped it. The crackling noise resumed. The fissure expanded. Then forked. The fracture lines spread beneath Slatcher's hands.

Evan's breath snagged in his throat. Slatcher's eyes, level with Evan's, widened, bloodshot lines pronounced in the sclera. His lips trembled, his Adam's apple jerking.

Both men watched, motionless.

The sheath broke into pieces beneath Slatcher's fingers, his grip slipping, his weight tugging him downward again.

He jerked his hands off one at a time, letting the fragments fall away, his palms slapping back on to the metal itself, acquiring a new grip.

Evan waited for the cutting edge to ribbon his hands, but no – in a stroke of luck, Slatcher was hanging from the dull back of the sword.

Through clenched teeth Slatcher released a hiss of amusement at his good fortune. His neck sheeting with muscle, he coiled his arms, those cantaloupe biceps bulging, raising his giant frame again.

The two-century-old *tamahagane* steel flexed, the edge grinding on the concrete lip. The metal, used for cannonballs in the Meiji era, would not break.

Slatcher rose another few inches, his face lifting above the lip of the roof.

The sword grip was elongated, designed for a two-hand samurai hold. Beyond the length wedged beneath the solar panels, four extra inches protruded. Just wide enough for Evan's fingers. The cord wrap gave him a good grip, the round *tsuba* guard pinching the edge of his hand.

Gripping as hard as he could, he tried to free the sword. No such luck.

A few feet past him, he sensed Slatcher rising, his shadow creeping across the rooftop, centimeter by centimeter.

The sword jogged slightly in Evan's hand, and he realized: he couldn't loose the sword, but he might be able to turn it.

With all his strength, he twisted the handle like a

motorcycle throttle. At first nothing happened, but then the sword spun barely in its makeshift housing.

The tiny movement knocked Slatcher down six inches.

Evan kept on, turning the cutting edge upward. The sword rotated jerkily, Slatcher losing ground, his huge form swinging from the blade. His giant hands, torn and bloody, trembled violently.

With a roar Evan ripped the sword in a quarter rotation, the sharp edge now pointing at the sky.

There was an instant of surface tension, Slatcher's wild gaze flying up to land on Evan, and then the katana did what it was designed to do.

The blade lopped Slatcher's fingers off at the first knuckles. His arms began cartwheeling, a backstroke with no water.

He and Evan locked eyes, and then Slatcher fell. Evan watched him plummet in the reflection off the glass of La Reverie until that, too, was cut from sight.

He did not see Slatcher hit the purple Scion, but he heard it.

54. No

Evan looped the Ford down seven stories of ramp, reaching the street. The police sirens were still a few blocks away, the cops hung up in constipated Strip traffic. Encircled by a ring of horrified onlookers, Slatcher's body was crumpled into the roof of his car, the damage from the fall leaving him nearly unrecognizable. Several of his fingers littered the pavement around him, confetti decorating the gruesome spectacle.

Pulling on a sweatshirt to cover his bloody shirt, Evan shouldered through the crowd, moving briskly and tilting his head downward in hopes no one would note his bruised face. 'Excuse me! I'm a doctor!' Under the guise of checking for a pulse, he searched Slatcher's pockets, finding only a slender metal case in the front pocket of his pants. The onlookers seemed too horrified to take notice of Evan, sneaking glances and snapping iPhone pictures. One young woman cried into her boyfriend's chest, stamping her feet in agitation.

Evan slipped away, finding his shotgun in a hedge at the base of the parking structure. His Wilson 1911, on the sidewalk across the street by La Reverie, was being staked out by several workers, so he left it behind.

Hopping back into his truck, he pulled out and drove

away just as the screaming cruisers screeched on to the scene. As he waited on the clogged freeway ramp, he pulled up his shirt to check his stomach. The sutures had torn through the skin, the wound gaping, but the artery had not ruptured.

He ran the freeway for a solid hour before pulling off and checking the silver box.

Ten fingernails. A contact lens.

He poked at the lens, and it animated, shimmering with a computer screen glow.

Okay, then.

He drove to a CVS pharmacy and bought contact solution. Back in his car, parked at the edge of the lot, he soaked the lens thoroughly in case it had been poisoned.

Then he popped it into his eye.

The fingernails pressed on with ease.

He waited.

A cursor appeared. It blinked red for a time.

And then green.

Evan waited, motionless.

A single line scrolled into existence. ORPHAN O?

NO, Evan typed, and logged off.

55. Silent Work

Later that night, after restitching his wound at home and cleaning himself up, Evan exited the elevator at the sixth floor of the Kaiser Permanente Medical Center on Sunset Boulevard. Smiling at the charge nurse posted at the station, he lifted two weighty bags filled with mediocre food from the cafeteria downstairs. 'Just coming back in with chow for my fellow car-crash victims.'

She noted his black eye and nodded him past.

A research session in the Vault had fulfilled his worst expectations, leading him here.

Strings of silver tinsel adorned the halls, Christmas decorations that felt more like an afterthought. Room 614 came up on his right, and he snatched the chart off the door and shouldered through the curtains, unsure how bad it would be.

A man lay unconscious, his head mummy-wrapped, his right arm in a cast, one leg in traction. A tracheal tube disappeared down his throat, but a quick glance at the screens showed him to be breathing above the ventilator.

Memo Vasquez had finally landed in the system.

Evan eyed the charts, noting the fractures, contusions, the collapsed lung, the intestinal perf. The drug dealers had exacted a payment for their missing drugs from Vasquez's body. But had they also fulfilled their promise?

Evan set a hand gently on Memo's arm, and a moment later the man stirred. Dark eyes peered out from beneath the bandages. His hand lifted an inch above the sheets, and Evan took it. Memo squeezed weakly. His head was cocked back at an uncomfortable angle.

Evan said, 'I'm sorry I didn't believe you.' He braced himself, then asked, 'Did they take Isa?'

The ventilator shoved air into Memo's lungs. Memo released Evan's hand and made a small writing gesture. Evan brought him a pen and pad.

In a trembling hand, he wrote, '*sí*.' Then, painstakingly, he wrote, '*yor face?*'

'You should see the other guy,' Evan said. 'Now, can you tell me where to find the bad men?'

The hand moved again. It took the better part of five minutes for Memo to write out the location of a warehouse. Not an address but a rough set of directions, a mix of Spanish and phonetic English. It would be sufficient.

Evan tore off the top sheet of paper. 'Everything will be fine now.'

Memo gestured again for the pencil. With a loose grip, he etched a few more words. '*they will deport us. i hav no kard i am ilegul.*'

Evan set down the pad by his hand. 'Not anymore,' he said. 'Your name found its way on to the approved list in Immigration Service's database. They'll be mailing a green card to your house in the morning. A gift for the holidays.' He gave the chart a last glance and set it down on the tray. 'They really worked you over.'

The stubby pencil scratched some more. *'U shud see ather guy.'*

Evan smiled. He sensed a glimmer of amusement in Memo's eyes before they darkened with concern.

'Rest up,' Evan said. He patted the wrapped hand and turned to leave. 'I got this.'

From the asbestos roof of the condemned warehouse, Evan slipped through the high, double-hung window, pivoting to grab the inside sill. His boots dangled ten feet above the concrete floor. He pushed off and landed on bent knees, letting his body collapse to the side so it wouldn't absorb the impact all at once.

Though there was a torn twin mattress in the corner, the girl was sleeping on the floor. The small storage room was vacant, an excellent makeshift cell.

Bare walls conveyed the sounds of men arguing from the dilapidated manager's office down the corridor. Through a skylight Evan had observed the three of them squabbling over digital scales – teardrop tattoos and prison ink and a security camera that possibly streamed to an off-site location. The rest of the former sweatshop was abandoned, one wall of the main floor collapsed, rubble strewn across rusted industrial looms.

Rising to his feet in the tiny space, Evan walked quietly to Isa, not wanting to startle her. As he drew near, he saw that she had forsaken the bed so her stuffed animal could sleep there. The pink teddy bear with the chewed ear was tucked in cozily beneath the sole sheet, its head resting on a pillow.

Evan rested a hand gently on the girl's shoulder.

She roused. She might have been fourteen or fifteen, but it was hard to tell given her condition. The upward slant of her eyes, like they were smiling.

'Your father sent me,' Evan whispered.

She nodded, her tongue protruding slightly over her bottom lip.

He gestured to the pink teddy bear. 'What's her name?'

'Baby.'

'You're taking care of her well.'

The words came soft and slurred. '*Sí.* She get scared easy.'

'She's lucky to have you,' Evan said.

A bright, proud smile and a stubby thumbs-up.

'I'm going to go,' Evan said. 'You stay here with her and make sure she feels safe, okay?'

'Uh-huh.'

Evan reached into his cargo pocket. 'I'm gonna put this mask on now. Don't let it frighten Baby. It's not to frighten her.' He pulled on one made of black Polartec that covered his face, save for the band of his eyes.

'A mask.' She beamed up at him. 'Like a superhero.'

'Like a superhero.' Evan unfolded his monocular night-vision headgear. It fit snugly, hugging his scalp, the high-res lens positioned over one eye, leaving both his hands free.

'Are you okay here alone for a little while?'

She pointed to the bed. 'I'm not alone.'

'Of course.'

The sheathed combat knife pulled reassuringly at his belt. Gunshots would scare her. His work was going to have to be silent.

He set his hands gently on her shoulders and looked down at her with his Cyclops eye. 'The lights are going to go off. But the cops will get here really soon after that. I'll make sure of it. Okay?'

'Uh-huh.'

He drew the lock pick from his back pocket and tapped it against his knuckles. 'You are a very brave young woman,' he said, turning to focus on the door handle.

'*La puerta*,' she said. 'It's locked.'

'That's okay.' He jiggled the torsion wrench, sliding the rake pick home. 'I can go through doors.'

She blinked, and he was gone.

Later that night, back home in the open enclosure in his master bathroom, Evan set his palms against the tile, leaning into the punishingly hot blast. Water poured from the rainfall showerhead, washing dried crimson flecks from his face. He scrubbed at his hands and forearms, freeing rivulets of red. There was a lot of blood.

None of it was his.

56. The Tenth Commandment

Evan was enveloped in a deep, satisfying sleep when the buzz of his cell phone pulled him to the surface. He rolled off the floating ledge of his bed and reached for the RoamZone, fresh sutures straining in his stomach.

Before he could speak, Danika's voice came at him. 'Help me. Evan, *please*. I know I betrayed you, but I didn't have a choice. I didn't have a choice.'

Her words came in bursts, and she was breathing hard, as if she were running.

'There are always choices,' Evan said.

'I don't have anyone else.' Her footsteps grew louder, echoing off tight walls. A stairwell? 'They don't need me anymore. I'm expendable now.'

'Who's after you?'

'The guy above Slatcher, I think. The guy behind everything.'

The chill of the concrete floor numbed his bare feet, and he realized only now that he was standing.

'I'm at your place,' she said.

Slowly, he turned his head to the bedroom door. 'My place?'

The sound of a door slamming shut, and then she was panting in his ear. 'The loft.'

He eased out a breath through clenched teeth.

'I came looking for you,' she said.

He moved through the bathroom, into the shower enclosure, through the tiled wall. 'They know that location.'

'I've got nowhere else to go.' She was sobbing. 'They paid off my loan. They owned me. If I didn't deliver you, they were gonna –'

'I know all this.' Evan's fingers were a flurry across the keyboard, and then the loft surveillance feeds came up.

There was the woman he still thought of as Katrin, her back to the closed front door, one arm flattened at her side as if she could hold off a battering ram, her other hand pressing what looked like a cheap prepaid phone to her cheek. Her chest surged with breaths, a flush creeping up the ivory skin of her neck.

'They promised me that every gunshot I heard would be a bullet through one of my daughter's limbs.' She was crying freely now. 'When we were in the motel, I thought they'd started already. I thought that's what I was hearing. They were going to *maim* her. She may not want to see me, but she's my daughter. My *daughter.* The only good thing I ever did. I fucked up and fucked up being a mom, but I couldn't let them do it. No matter what, I couldn't let them hurt my daughter.'

She moved off the door into the loft. And then, keeping the phone to her ear, she looked directly up into one of the surveillance cameras. An icy fingernail skimmed up Evan's spine. She'd known about the cameras all along. For the three days he'd observed her, she hadn't shown a single tell, those thousands of hours at poker tables serving her well.

'The man after you,' Evan said. 'He gave you the passport?'

'No,' she said. 'I never met him. Slatcher took me to pick it up.'

'Where?'

'The Federal Building. In Westwood.'

That fingernail returned, skimming the back of Evan's neck, tightening his skin.

The Federal Building confirmed everything.

The cold of the Vault seeped into Evan's bones, and he had to fight the urge to shudder.

'They told me what to do,' Danika said. 'They told me everything to do. But now I don't know what to do anymore.'

'You know too much,' Evan said. 'They will find you as surely as I would.'

A few silent sobs racked her chest. 'Please, Evan. I never made it right with Sammy. I don't care if I die anymore, but I just want that chance first. I need you. I need your help.'

The Tenth and most important Commandment looped in his head: *Never let an innocent die.* She wasn't innocent, but she was still *an* innocent. Every instinct in Evan's body fought him. Decades of habit, muscle memory.

He had to force the words out. 'I can't help you.'

She was staring at the lens as if she could see him

through it, though of course she could not. '*Can't* or *won't?*'

He stopped fighting the cold and let himself shiver. 'Yes,' he said.

She stepped closer to the camera embedded in the hanging kitchen cabinets, peering up dolefully. 'You're gonna just leave me to them?'

Milk-white skin.

The curve of her hip.

Those plush, blood-red lips against his.

'I would've helped you,' he said. 'If you'd trusted me, I would've fixed everything.'

'I know. I know that *now*.' Tracks glittered on her cheeks. 'But they got me first.'

Over the line he heard a screech of tires, and then her gaze shot over to the giant glass wall.

'Oh, my God,' she said. 'He's here now. He's pulling up. Evan, what do I do?'

Terror emanated off her.

Emotion welled in his throat. 'I'm sorry, Danika.'

'Evan, tell me what to do. What do I do?' She ran across to the window, straining on her tiptoes to look down. Then she darted to the front door. She opened it, shrieked, slammed it closed again. 'He's in the hall, Evan!' She scrambled to the middle of the loft, craning her neck to look up, seemingly into his eyes. 'Please. Goddamn it, Evan – help me, *please!*'

Never

let

an

innocent —

The front door rocketed open, a suppressed report sounded, and her head snapped to the side. She collapsed to a hip, her hands catching the floor, her stiff arms sliding her down gracefully, and then she lay on her side, expired.

A broad form eased into the room, shutting the door quietly behind him, shoulders turned to the main surveillance feeds. A few splinters cactused out where the dead bolt had torn through the inner frame. Though both locks were shot, the door could still close. From the hall nobody would notice anything amiss. Keeping his head lowered, the man walked over and put another suppressed round into Danika's chest, her torso bucking. The pistol spun, clipping up into a tension-hold underarm holster, and then the man crouched to pick up Danika's still-live prepaid phone.

As he stood, Charles Van Sciver lifted the phone to his face, looked into the main surveillance camera, and smiled.

'Hello, Evan,' he said.

57. Another Lit Window

A few more pounds on the frame, his cheeks even fuller, the ruddy complexion more pronounced.

Evan's words came out hoarse. 'Hello, Charles.'

Van Sciver strolled leisurely around the loft. 'There are 367,159 people in the United States alone who share your given name,' he said. 'That's one in every 854 Americans.' The words came across the line on a slight delay, unhitched from the movements of Charles's mouth, lending the conversation an otherworldly effect. 'Of course, you lost that clunky last name of yours years ago. Well before Oslo. So it's been a challenge.'

'I'm glad I'm not named Ignatius.'

Charles smirked. He stopped before Danika and looked down at her corpse. The dark puddle beneath her head slowly expanded. 'They're so helpless, and you're so strong,' he said. 'That's your weak spot, Evan, always has been. Your soft, soft heart.'

Evan thought about that authentic fake passport properly issued through the State Department. About being tracked through those fifteen telephone-switch destinations around the world. About why Slatcher never bothered to swap out the Scion — because no authorities were tracking him.

'You're not freelance,' Evan said. 'You're government-sanctioned.'

'At least as much as we ever were,' Charles said. 'But yes, I'm still inside, if that's what you mean.'

'Who's running you?'

'Who's running *me*?' Again Charles gave that cocky grin, the one that brought Evan back to cracked asphalt basketball courts, mac-and-cheese dinners, the over-populated bedrooms of the Pride House Group Home. 'No one runs me. It's mine.'

'What's yours?'

'*Everything.*'

The realization struck Evan, roiling his insides. Lies stacked on top of lies until the tatters of his past avalanched down on him. 'The Orphan Program. It was never discontinued.'

'Its purpose has shifted. But I'm the top dog.'

'How many of us are left?'

'Enough,' Charles said.

'How'd you get on my trail?'

'Oh, you wouldn't imagine how hard it was to track down the Nowhere Man. We designed a data-mining program to parse crime-scene reports. It hit on William Chambers's murder. We got on to Morena Aguilar from there.'

'What tipped you?'

'The target raised a red flag. Dirty cop, lotta allegations – right in your wheelhouse. Then the forensics. The rifling showed he'd been shot with a 1911, your preferred pistol for years, though the ammo threw us off at first. You generally use hollow points, but you were throwing 230-grain hardball that night. Then I realized – the crowded neighborhood, you wanted to go subsonic so the bullet wouldn't have a sound signature. But what really gave it away was the money left behind to pay the girl's rent. What's a broke Salvadoran girl doing with hundred-dollar bills?'

Careless, Evan thought.

'We wanted to keep her in the dark in case we needed to use her later,' Charles said. 'We just never expected her to toss a real client into the mix so fast.'

'Because that interfered with the fake client you set up.'

Charles toed Danika's body. 'That's right.'

'You wanted to position somebody close to get an inside line on my location.'

'You know how it is with someone like you. We needed to control your position so we could execute a coordinated attack in a well-scouted location.'

'Like at the motel.'

'That's right. And even so, look how that went. That's why we switched it up, grabbed a pawn so we could move you around the board.' His eyes flicked again to the body at his feet. 'We needed plenty of notice for mission planning. We were hoping you'd spend the night at the loft, but you're like a shark. Always moving.'

'Where'd you find Danika?'

'Oh, we had an eye on a number of candidates, but we were waiting until we got a bead on you. We'd been watching Danika for some time. She seemed the best fit.'

It took a moment for Evan to process that one. 'So that's why you're after me?' he finally asked. 'My pro bono work?'

'Of course not.' Charles pinched his eyes, a show of frustration. 'We are after you because of the information in your head. You're not a safe asset to have out there in circulation.'

'Neither are you.'

'I'm not out there in circulation.'

'I was told you turned.'

Charles looked genuinely taken aback. 'I *never* turned.'

'The summer after Oslo, I was assigned to kill you. I refused.'

'Two of us were assigned to kill *you* that summer. It was the first time they ever let Orphans work together. Your handler lied to you. You were always the target. We just couldn't find you. Until now.'

'Then why . . . ?'

It struck Evan there in the dim glow of the monitors. Jack had sent Evan the picture of Charles knowing that he'd recognize him, knowing that he would go underground before he'd kill a fellow Orphan. The Smoke Contingency.

Jack had given him the fake assignment to warn him and get him off the grid. If Evan had known the truth, he would have gone up against the Orphans and the whole goddamned government. He would've gotten himself killed.

Realization flickered across Charles's face, and then

that smile sprang back into place. Phone to his ear, he paced around Danika's corpse. 'Oh, that's rich. You didn't know. Why did you think Jack Johns went down? For trying to protect *you*.'

Evan reached behind him for the chair, lowered himself into it. He thought of Jack at the dinner table, twirling linguine around his fork. *The hard part isn't turning you into a killer. The hard part is keeping you human.* His tense voice before their fateful meet beneath the Jefferson Memorial. *There may have been a leak on this end. I don't want to be drawn out. I'm watching my movements.*

Jack had broken countless protocols to protect Evan. He'd known the risk he was taking. And he'd taken it.

Evan's grief over Jack's death had never left; it remained, woven through his core. It shifted now, fissuring the foundations, stealing the breath from his chest. His mouth opened, but no words came out.

The only glimmer of gratitude he could find was that Charles could not see his reaction. But Charles sensed it. He turned neatly on his heel, eyeing the hidden camera in the hanging cabinets.

Evan forced out the words. 'Why did they want to kill me?'

'You don't get it, Evan. It wasn't *personal*. The drones changed everything. Anytime the State Department wants, they can click a button and a truckload of extremists explodes halfway around the world. Why deal with human error and all the diplomatic risks that come with a program like ours? They don't need us anymore. They haven't for years. They started wrapping us up.'

'You mean letting us wrap one another up,' Evan said.

'That's right. And they still are. Having us eliminate the ones who are high-risk.'

'We're *all* high-risk, Charles. That's what we are.'

'Right,' Charles said. 'But some personality profiles predicted higher likelihood of defiance.'

'Like mine.'

'Like yours.'

'So if I were the type who'd agree to kill you and if you were the type who'd refuse to kill me, we'd be on opposite sides of this camera right now.'

'Well, you can't argue they got it wrong, can you?'

'The new purpose of the Orphan Program is assassinating Orphans? Can't you see where it's headed, Charles? They'll have us keep killing one another –'

'Until there's one left,' Charles said.

'Doesn't that concern you?'

'No.'

'Why?'

'Because' – Charles stepped closer yet to the camera – 'I'll be the one.'

'Then what?' Evan asked.

For once Van Sciver had no reply.

Evan waited, and sure enough Van Sciver took another step toward the camera. Evan willed him to take one more, but Charles remained there, glaring resolutely into the lens.

'No matter how long it takes,' Charles said, 'I will find you.'

'Goodbye, Charles,' Evan said.

Charles's face changed, and he flinched an instant before Evan clicked the mouse, detonating the charge hidden in the camera.

The screen went to static, the entire circuit of hidden cameras fried by the explosion. For a long time, Evan sat and watched the snow as if it were a code he was meant to decipher.

He thought about Charles's distance from the small charge and wondered if the kill radius had been sufficient.

When at last he stood, his legs felt weak. He urged them to carry him into the kitchen, where he shook two jiggers of Jean-Marc XO until his hands stuck to the aluminum shaker. He poured the vodka into a glass, dropped in a stick of manzanilla olives, and drifted across to the balcony facing Downtown.

The questions – and possibilities – were endless. Evan shared a secret most-wanted list neither with armed robbers nor men who wore turbans and beards, but with individuals who had training and skills given to them by the very government now seeking to eradicate them. Which meant he might have allies in addition to foes. Who else was on that hit list, and who else was behind it?

Charles had claimed that the Orphan Program lived on under him in some new form, downsized but deadly. That much Evan believed. Right now it was devoted to terminating former Orphans considered to present a risk. Evan believed that as well. But what other uses

Charles might have for the program once he was sitting behind the controls, that was anyone's guess.

Sipping his vodka, Evan leaned against the railing, peering across Los Angeles. Evan's hunters were out there somewhere among those glittering lights, and he was here, and they couldn't find him. Not tonight.

Tonight he was just another lit window among millions.

58. Parting Gift

It had been just two days since her mother's body was found in Griffith Park in a wooded creek behind the old-fashioned carousel, and though Samantha White had expected a variation of that middle-of-the-night phone call for years, a part of her was still in shock. And a part of her had finally accepted defeat. Of her own path in life. It was as if her mother had cleared the way for Sam to step up and take the miserable spot she'd left behind.

With a stack of student-loan late notices in hand, Sam legged across campus to the financial-aid office. Her adviser had left her three messages, and the fact that she was willing to come in on this of all days to meet Sam meant that something was truly amiss.

She passed a crew of frat boys in Bruins-wear, still abuzz from last weekend's football game. The pre-med students scurried out of Boyer Hall with their color-coded notebooks and stacks of textbooks. Who was she kidding anyway? She'd never belonged here. She'd always been an impostor – a loser from a loser past. And finally it was time to give in and accept her loser future.

She had a friend who worked as a banker at the Hustler Casino in Gardena. It was sleazy, sure, but the girl made decent cash, enough to cover rent on her place and lease a Civic. Maybe Sam could score a job there, start paying down the UCLA loans from the semesters she'd managed to get in. Eventually she could make her way to Vegas for bigger money. Like her mom. *Ouch*, she thought. *There's the rub.*

After an upbringing that saw Sam sleeping in station wagons outside Indian casinos and all-night diners, she'd craved the straight and narrow. Her mom had always been in and out, more trouble than help, but she'd made gestures when she could. A gift card here. Some gas money there. Until it had gone the other way.

Once the coroner released the body, Sam was going to use what was left in her emaciated checking account to pay for a burial. A funeral-home bill wasn't the parting gift she'd hoped for, but Danika was still her mom and she deserved a resting place.

Sam paused outside the financial-aid office, late notices fluttering in the breeze. So this was how it ended, not with a bang but a whimper on a cold-ass December morning.

She entered, stepping into a rush of warmth and the smell of pine. No one was working reception, of course, not today, but Geraldine's door was open, and she called Sam back.

Sam entered the office, and Geraldine glanced up with those sympathetic eyes. 'I'm sorry for your loss.'

'How do you know about that?'

Geraldine gestured to the chair before her desk. 'Why don't you sit down?'

'Look, I get it,' Sam said. 'I have to withdraw. Just give me some time to line out a real job, and I'll start –'

'Sam,' Geraldine said. 'Sit down.'

Sam flopped into the chair.

'It seems your loans have been repaid.'

'It's been a long couple days, Geraldine. This isn't funny.'

'I was contacted by an estate lawyer for your mother. It appears that she'd been paying into some sort of education fund for you.'

'A fund? What fund? From *where*?'

'Out of the Balearic Islands of all places.'

Sam felt a rush of heat behind her face, and she was worried she'd start crying and that Geraldine would think it was because of the money.

She swallowed. Bit her lower lip. 'She did?'

'There's enough left over to cover your final two years of tuition,' Geraldine said. 'You'll still have to work to pay for housing.'

Unable to find her voice, Sam nodded. She had to get out of there or she was going to start bawling like some reality-show moron who'd had a surprise family reunion sprung on her. She stood up quickly, and across the desk Geraldine matched her.

Geraldine offered her cool, slim hand above her blotter.

'Merry Christmas,' she said.

59. Next Time

Evan woke up with a sense of peace for the first time in months. It had been eight days since Danika's body had been discovered in the park, nearly six miles from where she'd been shot. The *L.A. Times* had reported on a gas explosion in the Downtown building, but there'd been no mention of a body – Danika White's or Charles Van Sciver's.

Someone had cleaned the location.

Either Van Sciver himself or, if he had in fact been killed, others in his orbit. They'd be searching for Evan.

And he'd be searching for them.

As he'd done first thing every morning and last thing every night, he reached for Slatcher's slender silver case and put on the contact lens and fingernails.

He powered up the system and watched the cursor blink red, red, red.

No sign of Van Sciver.

After a full minute, moderately reassured, Evan put it away.

As he dressed, he thought about what was next. His missions as the Nowhere Man would certainly continue, but there were some complications he'd need to sidestep. His connection to Memo Vasquez was known, just like his connection to Morena Aguilar. The best thing he could do for them now was to never go near them again. Because of that, Evan would be identifying his next client himself.

But first perhaps he'd take a little break.

He drove to the hardware store and bought a few lengths of premium red oak, wood putty and paint. Back in the Vault, he watched Castle Heights' internal surveillance cameras, waiting for Ida Rosenbaum to emerge for her post-breakfast walk. Then he headed down to Condo 6G.

Once he'd finished, he spent the rest of his morning driving his circuit of safe houses, altering the autolighting schedule, clearing junk mail, checking the upkeep of his stashed backup vehicles.

The southbound 405 looked like a parking lot, so he detoured to take a canyon route back over the hill. Twenty minutes later he was inside Wally's Wine & Spirits, perusing the offerings. A single bottle of Kauffman Luxury Vintage vodka remained.

A point-of-purchase spin rack on the counter held reading glasses, corkscrews and bottle openers. Waiting to be rung up, Evan gave it a little twirl. Coming into view, a pack of Muppets-themed Band-Aids.

'Sir? Sir? *Sir?*'

He looked up.

Peering over her spectacles, the clerk pointed at the bottle. 'Will that be all?'

'Yes,' he said. 'That's all.'

When he got home, he pulled in to the porte cochère. 'Wow, Mr Smoak,' the valet said, eagerly scrambling for the keys. 'You're actually gonna let me park your truck?'

'Just don't run anyone over,' Evan said, and the kid grinned.

Inside, Hugh Walters, crowned with a Santa hat, finished trimming the lobby tree. From his high ladder perch, he lowered a bagel on top in place of an angel. Seeing Evan, he shrugged. 'It *is* L.A.,' he remarked.

Over at the bank of mailboxes, Johnny Middleton turned to offer a too-vigorous high five. Ever since they'd faced down the brothers together, his attempts at bonding had intensified. Feeling vaguely foolish, Evan returned the high five and checked his mail.

Inside, a rectangular box from GenYouration Labs. He'd been waiting on it.

He opened the package and read a bit as he strolled to the elevator. 'Twenty-first floor, please,' he called out to the security desk.

'Yes, Mr Smoak.'

Evan paused. 'And happy holidays, Joaquin.'

'You, too.'

Evan climbed in. As the doors slid shut, a wizened hand slithered through the gap and clicked the bumpers, knocking them apart. Mrs Rosenbaum got in. Leaning back, she studied him.

'Healing up from your motorcycle accident, I see.'

'Yes, ma'am.'

'My Herb, may he rest in peace, always said he'd lock our children up in the basement before he'd let them get on a motorcycle.'

'Your kids were lucky to have you.'

She made a muffled sound of agreement. They rode up a few floors in silence.

'That good-for-nothing manager finally got around to fixing my doorframe this morning. Can you believe it?'

'That must make you happy.'

'I suppose he just wanted to get it out of the way so he could tell everyone he did it this year.' They reached the sixth floor, and she plodded out. 'Well, goodbye, then.'

At the twelfth floor, Evan exited and headed down the corridor. As he passed 12F, he sensed an eavesdropping eye at the peephole. 'Afternoon, Your Honor.'

Pat Johnson's muffled voice came through the door. 'Afternoon.'

Evan paused outside the last door in the hall. From inside he could hear raised voices: 'You *gotta* let me stay up till midnight. We have to watch the thingy in New York.'

'That's on at *nine* here.'

'They rerun it! And I wanna see *fireworks*. How 'bout we watch half?'

'I don't negotiate with terrorists!'

Evan knocked.

A few footsteps, and then Mia's face appeared, split by the security chain. She drew her head back slightly. 'Evan?'

'I have a late Christmas gift for Peter. Or, I guess, a goodbye gift. Like we discussed, I won't come by anymore after this.'

'Oh,' she said. 'Okay.'

The door closed, the chain lifted, and then she stepped back and let him in.

'Your eye,' she said. 'What h—' Her hands came up, palms out. 'Wait. Never mind. Nothing.'

He smiled. Given even the little she knew about him, he should have packed up and left Castle Heights by now. But he hadn't. By staying put he had accepted back into his life the faintest sliver of trust.

From over on the couch, Peter waved, and Evan walked toward him. Mia returned to the kitchen, giving them some space.

Evan crouched before him, and Peter clicked off the TV. Evan held up the thick folder from GenYouration Labs. 'Do you know what this is?'

'Dinosaur DNA?'

'Close. It's *your* DNA.' Evan opened the printed report. 'You're fifty-eight percent Mediterranean, thirty-one percent Northern European, and eleven percent Southwest Asian.'

'Asian!'

'Yeah. Look here.'

Peter sat at the edge of the cushion, captivated. 'Cool.'

'Very cool. Your earliest ancestor migrated out of Africa sixty-five thousand years ago, crossing the Red Sea into the Arabian Peninsula. His people were nomadic hunters, with tools and weapons. Unafraid to face new lands and challenges.' Evan turned the page. 'When drought hit, your ancestors chased herds of wild game through modern-day Iran to the steppes of Central Asia.'

'What's a steppe?'

'Big flat grasslands,' Evan said. 'They're beautiful.' He turned the paper sideways. 'Look at this map here. See how your people migrated up through Europe? They were big-game hunters.'

'Whoa.'

'Whoa is right.' Evan flipped through the colored pages. 'Then there's an Ice Age and more migrations, and you have a strain in you from agriculturalists of the Fertile Crescent. But you can read all this yourself.' He handed over the report. 'You said you wanted to know where you came from.'

'Thanks. I love it. Mom said you're not gonna be around much.'

The sentences, strung together as if they were of a piece. Maybe they were.

'That's right,' Evan said.

'She said I won't understand till I'm older, but I think that's just what grown-ups say when they don't know what to do.'

'Grown-ups don't know what to do more often than you might think.'

'That sucks,' he said. 'It gets lonely sometimes. Being the only kid.'

Evan considered this. Then he said, 'Someone very close to me taught me to build a space in my head. You can put whatever you want in there. You don't have to let in anyone you don't want to. But you can let in anyone you want.'

'Like Batman. Or Captain Jack Sparrow.'

'That's right.'

'Or you.'

Evan nodded. 'Or me.'

'Bye, Evan Smoak.'

'Bye, Peter Hall.'

Peter flipped to the beginning of his DNA report and started reading.

Evan stood and started for the door. Mia ducked down and peered out the pass-through at the paper bag in his hand. 'Finally got that vodka, huh?'

'I did.'

'Ready to celebrate tonight?'

'A version of that.'

'Made your resolutions yet?' she asked.

'Not yet.'

'You don't have much time.'

'No,' he said. 'Guess not.' He paused. 'Happy New Year, Mia.'

She brushed back her hair, bit her lip. 'Happy New Year.'

That Post-it remained, stuck to the side of the pass-through right in front of him. *'Treat yourself as if you were someone you are responsible for helping.'*

Evan wondered if maybe now he had an inkling of what that meant.

Once he got back upstairs, he worked out hard, then cleaned around his sutures. He took a hot shower and read for a while. Sometime before midnight he poured a few fingers of the Kauffman over ice. Standing behind the sunscreens, he let the vodka warm his mouth, his throat. Silky texture, clean aftertaste.

Sporadic fireworks ushered in the New Year, distant bursts on the horizon. Sipping his vodka, he watched the splendid cascades of fire and light. When nothing remained but the clinking of cubes, he rinsed out his glass in the kitchen sink.

A flash from the fireworks illuminated a child-size palm mark on the Sub-Zero. He pictured Peter the last time he was here, leaning against the fridge and huffing his breath to fog the stainless steel. Evan stepped to the side, bringing the handprint into relief.

He decided to leave it there.

He walked down the long hall, past the blank spot where the katana used to hang. After getting ready for bed, he sat on the edge of the Maglev platform and donned the high-def contact lens and radio-frequency-identification-tagged fingernails as he had each of the past nine nights.

The cursor blinked red, red, red.

Relieved, he peeled off the gear and put it in its silver case for the morning.

Turning off the light, he lay floating in the dark, detached from others, from the world, from the very floor beneath him. Adrift in the possibilities of a fresh year, he closed his eyes.

He counted down from ten and had just dozed off when a distinctive alarm sounded. Wearing a faint smile, he opened his eyes. Reaching across to the remote on his nightstand, he silenced the alarm. There was no need to check the monitors.

Rising, he clicked on the light and crossed to his

window. Against the pane a balloon floated, bearing two words messily Magic Markered in a child's hand.

NEXT TIME.

He opened the window, corralled the balloon inside, and cut the kite string with a replacement Strider knife, one that hadn't yet been used to stab him. Letting the balloon bump along the ceiling, he got back into bed. Reaching to turn on the lights, he paused. His hand hovered over the silver case.

One more try.

He donned the gear again. The cursor appeared in its virtual float a few feet off his face. It blinked red, red –

Green.

Evan stared at the live connection for a few moments, his heart making itself known in his chest. He made no move to type, and no text appeared. Ten seconds passed, then thirty. Finally, with careful movements, he powered down the device. He removed the nails and the lens.

Carrying the silver case as gingerly as an explosive, he entombed it in the Vault and went to bed.

Epilogue: Loss

In a desolate stretch of the snowy Allegheny Mountains, a fire burns in a cabin, smoke spiraling from the chimney. Through the single-pane windows carries the sound of grunting. Inside, a three-hundred-pound water-filled heavy bag hangs from a ceiling joist. A scrappy twelve-year-old boy beats at it with all his might – fists, forearms, knees. A stocky man stands behind him, holding a stopwatch.

The boy's blows become weak and infrequent, and finally the man clicks the stopwatch. The boy keeps his feet, panting.

'Albuquerque, molecular, thirty-seven, Henry Clay, grand slam, X-ray, loss, nineteen, Monaco, denoted,' the man says. 'What is item nine?'

The boy's thin chest heaves. 'Monaco.'

'Item two?'

'Molecular.'

'The sum of items three and eight?'

'Fifty-six.'

A series of low beeps draws the man's attention. He walks over to the counter where a blocky satphone rests. He ratchets up the stubby antenna, pointing it through the roof, and clicks to pick up.

'Jack Johns,' he says.

The voice comes through, scratchy with static. 'He's in the wind again.'

'Safe?'

'Yes. For now.'

Jack closes his eyes, lowers his head, exhales. Reaching over the top buttons of his flannel shirt, he scratches at the silver dollar of taut, shiny skin near his shoulder. This many years later and still it itches like sin in the winter.

The voice squawks through again. 'You copy?'

'Copy,' Jack says.

He removes the battery, then tosses the phone into the fireplace.

The boy is at his side, sensing the shift in emotion.

'Did I say to stop?' Jack asks.

'No, sir.' The boy returns to his post by the heavy bag behind Jack.

On top of the burning logs, the phone blackens and melts. Jack keeps his eyes on the dancing flames. He has to clear his throat twice before he can continue the test. 'Item seven?' he asks.

'Loss,' the boy answers.

Acknowledgments

It takes a village to launch a book. To launch a new series, it takes a small municipality. Given that, I'd like to acknowledge:

— Sensei Brian Shiers, for teaching me mixed martial arts. I attained much wisdom on the receiving end of his various choke holds, eye jabs and leg sweeps. My primary-care physician and I thank you.

— Billy S_____, shadow serviceman and master armorer. If ever there's a man who fills the combat boots, it's you. Thanks for lending me your brain and your weapons.

— Jeff Polacheck and the delightful Pearl Polacheck, for giving me a behind-the-scenes look at high-altitude living on the Wilshire Corridor. Thanks for braving my questions as I poked around back halls and crawl spaces, figuring out how to build Evan his Fortress of Solitude.

— Geoffrey Baehr, Knower of Arcane and Invasive Technologies. Thanks for teaching Evan how to creep unnoticed through the virtual universe.

— Professor Jordan Peterson of the quoted proverbs. Thanks for giving Mia a road map for how to raise her son and for giving me a road map for how to raise myself.

— Melissa Little, Queen Restorer of Vintage Movie

425

Posters, for showing me the tricks of the trade when it comes to forged art and documents.

– Melissa Hurwitz, M. D., and Bret Nelson, M. D., for patching up my injured characters or permitting them to expire with the dignity of verisimilitude.

– My editor, Keith Kahla of the keen eye and tireless ethic, for helping hammer Evan Smoak into shape. The rest of my team at Minotaur Books – Andrew Martin, Kelley Ragland, Paul Hochman, Jennifer Enderlin, Sally Richardson, Hector DeJean and Hannah Braaten – for giving him a home.

– Caspian Dennis of the Abner Stein Agency, and Rowland White and his fine team at Michael Joseph/ Penguin Group UK for taking care of Orphan X on his OCONUS operations.

– The unimprovable Lisa Erbach Vance, as well as Aaron Priest, John Richmond and Melissa Edwards of the Aaron Priest Agency.

– My superb crew at Creative Artists Agency – Trevor Astbury, Rob Kenneally, Peter Micelli and Michelle Weiner for giving Evan a sensational boost.

– Marc H. Glick of Glick & Weintraub and Stephen F. Breimer of Bloom, Hergott, Diemer, et al., who have had my back for two decades and change.

– Philip Eisner, for his writer's eye and dark sensibilities.

– Dana Kaye, publicist extraordinaire.

– And of course Maureen Sugden, my dream copyeditor.

– Thing One (Simba) and Thing Two (Cairo), who accompany me into every chapter.

– Daughter One and Daughter Two for making me happy to come out of the book every evening.

– And Wife One. For that thumbs-up you flashed on 26 September 2013.

'Safe?'

'Yes. For now.'

Dying to know what awaits Evan Smoak?

Well, here's a taster.

Read on for the first chapters of

The Nowhere Man, the next Orphan X thriller.

Available for pre-order now
in hardback and ebook

1. What He Needs to Know

A naked selfie.

It starts with that.

Hector Contrell sends a seventeen-year-old kid to troll middle schools in East L.A. The kid, improbably named Addison, makes for fine bait. Seedily handsome, starter mustache, pop-star cheekbones, dirty blond hair flipped just so. He wears a hoodie and rides a skateboard, the better to look like he's fifteen. He says he's a pro skater with a contract. He says he's a rapper with a deal at a major label. He's really a pot-smoking dropout who lives in a rented garage with his older brother and his friends, spends his nights playing *Call of Duty* and hitting a green glass water bong named Fat Boy.

He hangs out near campuses at lunch, after classes, his skateboard rat-a-tat-tatting across sidewalk cracks just barely past school-ground limits. The girls cluster and giggle, and he chooses one to peel off the herd. He tells her to snap pictures. He tells her to get a secret Facebook account, one her parents don't know about, and upload them there. He tells her that everyone does this in high school, and he's mostly right, but not everyone is hooked into a scheme like this. He targets Title I schools, broke girls, easily impressed, looking for a dream, a romance, a way out. Girls whose parents lack the resources to do much if they disappear.

The secret Facebook page links go to Hector Contrell.

The genius of it is, the girls create the sales catalog themselves.

From Contrell the links go to all sorts of men with unorthodox tastes. Austrian industrialists. Sheikhs. Three brothers in Detroit with a padlocked metal shed. Online they can peruse the merchandise discreetly and, if need be, ask for more product information – different photographic angles, specific poses. They make their selections.

Given immigration confusion, gang influence, and splintered family trees, disappearances aren't rare when you're dealing with broke ethnic girls. They're a renewable resource.

Hector Contrell comes in the black of night, and another girl vanishes off the streets and wakes up in a stupor in Islamabad or Birmingham or São Paulo. Some of the girls are kept. Some are designated for onetime use.

Anna Rezian is the next prospect. Her father is a plumber, works hard, comes home late and tired. Her mother, a cocktail waitress, comes home later and more tired. Only fifteen, Anna takes care of her younger brothers and sisters, tries to remember to look at her textbooks after she gets the kids down. It's a hard routine for a girl her age.

One day after school, Addison's blue eyes peer out

from beneath his scraggly bangs and pick her and only her. That night she touches up her eyeliner, sheds the flat-front Dickies with the worn knees, checks the lighting. This choice, this moment is going to be a portal to a Whole New Her.

But after she uploads the selfie, nothing magical happens. Staring at the image she has released into the world, she feels an unease begin to gnaw at her.

She decides to stop after the one photo. But Addison needs more; they've been requested from a buyer in Serbia. In a ganja haze, he catches her in the alley outside her family's one-bedroom apartment. When his low-rent hipster charms fail him, he tells her what she'd better do. Big-shotting in the Crenshaw night, he lets fly that he works for someone who will hurt her and her family if she turns off the tap.

She stays up all night, trembling in the glow of her ancient laptop, clicking her way through the infinity of Facebook and chasing threads. Friends of friends have heard of friends who have disappeared. Over the top of her laptop, she looks at her sleeping siblings and contemplates what it will feel like if harm befalls them because of her stupidity. She looks at her sleeping parents, exhausted after their long work days. The chasm of guilt inside her widens by the second, pushing her further and further away until she is on an island of her own making, until her family members seem like specks on the horizon. Something awful is coming, either for them or for her. She makes the choice.

She sends new photos.

She stops sleeping. She starts plucking out her hair in patches. She cuts herself at school, hoping the pain will wake her from this nightmare. Maybe it's a cry for help instead, each crimson line across her forearm a smoke signal released in hopes that someone will ride to her rescue.

Someone does see the signal. One of her classmates' father, an older man with a cane and a fresh limp, finds her sobbing in the bathroom of a 7-Eleven when she's supposed to be in homeroom. He gives her a phone number: 1-855-2-NOWHERE. A magical fix-it line.

She dials.

Evan Smoak picks up.

'Do you need my help?' he asks.

That's how it works.

Fourteen hours later Evan is standing outside Addison's rented garage. The air tastes of car exhaust. The streetlights are broken, the stars smeared by smog, the night dark as tar. Evan is a wraith.

Addison's brother, Carl, and his crew of friends are out scoring black tar at a park in Boyle Heights. Evan knows this. Addison is alone. Evan knows this, too.

He has done his research.

The First Commandment – *Assume nothing* – demands it.

The wraith raises a single knuckle, taps the garage door.

A moment later it creaks upward.

Stooped, Addison emerges from an effluvium of day-old bong water. He rocks on his heels, gauging Evan.

By design, Evan is hard to gauge. Thirty-something. Fit but not muscly. Somewhere around six feet. An average guy, not too handsome.

Addison underestimates him.

This happens a lot, by design.

The kid's lips twitch to the side. He jerks his head, flips his hair out of the blue eyes that have landed many a young woman on a container ship heading for uncharted waters.

'The fuck you want?' he says.

'Hector Contrell's address,' Evan says.

The pretty-boy lashes flare, but Addison covers quickly. 'No idea who that is. And no fucking way I'd tell you if I did.'

Evan looks through him. This tends to make people uneasy.

Uncertainty washes across Addison's face, but he blinks it away. 'I know people, you tool,' he says. 'People who can make you disappear like that.' The snap of his fingers, sharp in the crisp air. 'Who the fuck you think you are anyways?'

'The Nowhere Man,' Evan says.

The kid's Adam's apple jerks once. Up. Down.

The moniker is not widely known. But dark rumors have spread through certain streets like trash blown down graffitied alleys.

Addison takes a quick step to the side to stabilize

himself. His voice comes out husky, pushed through a constricting throat. 'That's just a bullshit story.'

'Then you don't have to be scared, do you?'

Addison didn't say anything.

'You do know what happens to the girls,' Evan tells him.

It takes a moment for Addison to relocate his voice. 'They disappear.'

'To where?'

'I don't know. Guys.'

'Who use them for . . . ?'

The kid shrugs. Actually muffles a snicker. 'Whatever guys do.'

'The address.'

'I can't tell you. Hector will kill me. *Literally* kill me.'

Evan's gaze is steady.

Addison falters. 'No,' he says, a new realization dawning. 'Oh, no. Look – I'm just a kid, man. I'm seventeen. You're not gonna kill me, are you?'

There is a punch Evan was taught in his early teens by a gruff marine close-quarter-combat instructor.

It is called the palate breaker.

A nonlethal blow that fractures the bridge of the nose, the sinus bones, and both orbital sockets, splitting the skull horizontally temple to temple. It leaves the upper jaw floating, unattached.

Evan's gaze narrows. He picks his spot.

You wouldn't have thought the kid could keep his feet, but there he is, upright on the curb. Something like drool leaks from his lips, the holes of his nose.

'No,' Evan says. 'I won't kill you.'

Addison makes a wheezing noise. With his new face, it will be hard for him to troll for girls anymore.

'The address,' Evan says again.

What is left of the mouth tells him what he needs to know.

2. The Social Contract

Evan slipped through the plastic tarp into a new-construction McMansion, the spoils of Hector Contrell's war on the broke families of East L.A. The house, distanced from its neighbors, topped an inclined driveway at the edge of Chatsworth.

Evan drifted through doorless frames, making silent progress toward the heart of the house. Studs framing the wide halls and exposed ceiling beams gave him the impression that he was walking into a massive rib cage, into Hector Contrell himself. Sawdust chalked the back of Evan's throat. Nails protruded from the floor, poking the soles of his Original S.W.A.T. boots. The aggressively checkered gunner grips of a custom Wilson Combat 1911 pistol bit the flesh of his palm.

He found Contrell in the living room-to-be, ensconced like a pilot within a cockpit of computer monitors and servers from which he ran his flesh empire with impunity. A burly, bearded man wholly unhooked from the social contract, who took what he wanted because he wanted it. The high-tech station with its bluish glow and snaking cables seemed anomalous, sprouting up like a mushroom from the exposed subfloor.

Hector noticed movement in the shadows and

stood, revolver quickly in hand. For a time, it seemed, he kept rising.

Standing just past the semicircle of pushed-together desks, Evan looked up at him. A FUCK YOU tattoo on the front of Hector's neck indicated that nuance was not the man's strong suit.

Hector said, 'I don't know who you are or why you're here, but I'm gonna give you five seconds to leave before I aerate your torso.' For emphasis he kicked one of the monitors off the desk, which went to pieces at Evan's feet, sparking impressively.

Both men kept their guns down at their sides.

Evan watched the monitor give off a dying spark. Then he lifted his eyes.

'One of the functions of anger is to convince people of the seriousness of your intentions,' he said. 'To signal that you're out of control. Unpredictable. Willing to do damage. To evoke fear.'

Hector drew himself even taller. No minor feat. Backlit by the monitors, his meaty left earlobe showed a missing slot where an earring had been ripped free.

Evan took a step closer. 'So look at me. Look at me closely. And ask yourself – do I look scared?'

The big man leaned in, the glow of the computers turning his face into a shadow-ravaged land-scape – empty eye sockets, pronounced jowls, the curve of one cheek. His thick lips pulsed, the first show of hesitation.

Evan's gun remained at his side, just like Hector's. They faced each other across the desk.

When Evan was fourteen, Jack had trained him how to fast-draw. It wasn't with *High Noon* theatrics – unholster, lift, and aim. It was a two-millimeter tilt and 3.5 pounds of index-finger pressure.

The shadows shifted across Hector's face. His beefy hand twitched above his gun. He moved first.

The plywood walls gave off a good echo.

Later that night Evan eased into the alley that ran behind the dilapidated apartment that accommodated Anna Rezian's family. A sheen of blood had hardened on his left forearm, cracking like dried mud when he moved. He'd washed his hands and his face but could feel the leftover flecks on the side of his neck.

There'd been backspray.

He lifted his black phone from his pocket. It was a RoamZone model, encased in fiberglass and tough black rubber, the screen protected by Gorilla Glass. He kept it on him.

Always.

It was a lifeline. Not to him, but to those who called it.

He sent a text to Anna: OUTSIDE.

As he waited, a concern niggled at the base of his skull. He had seen something in Hector's house – he didn't know what it was, but it was wrong. Was his client in danger? No. He'd been thorough. Not a threat to her. Not a threat to him. Something else. Something important but not immediate.

Anna's backlit silhouette appeared at the mouth of the alley about ten yards away. She wore a nightie, her spine hunched, her dry hair sticking out. The alley formed a wind tunnel, the October air whipping at her brunette tufts, making them wag stiffly.

'You're safe now,' he told her.

Her feet were bare. He could see the tremble in her knees.

'I thought you were one of them coming to get me,' she said. 'I thought walking down here would be the last thing I ever did. But then . . . but then it was you.'

'I'm sorry I scared you,' he said.

'What does it mean? That I'm safe?'

'You don't have to worry anymore,' he said.

'About what?'

'Any of it.'

'Addison?'

'Has other concerns now.'

'And his boss? The guy behind it all?'

'He died.'

Anna trudged forward, her scalp shiny in the spots where she'd plucked out her hair. Her face held the same look he'd seen in his other clients, a worn-through, hollowed-out expression that came from falling out of the slipstream of life.

'Albert is safe?' Her voice cracked. 'And Eduard?'

'Yes.'

Anna came closer yet, her cheeks glinting. 'How about Maria? They won't hurt Maria?'

'There's no one left to hurt Maria.'

Openly sobbing now. *'Mayrig? Hayrig?'*

'Your mother and father will be fine.'

He thought of her family in their beds and wondered at the serenity they might offer her. At her age he hadn't had much, which meant he'd had nothing to leave behind. As a twelve-year-old, he'd stepped off a truck-stop curb into a dark sedan and blipped off the radar. Back then any gamble was worth the taking. This one had gotten him out of East Baltimore. He'd been to Marrakech and St Petersburg and Cape Town, and he'd left his mark in blood at every stop. But he'd never had what Anna had waiting for her upstairs. The chill breeze brought with it the realization that he'd devoted his life to preserving for others what he couldn't have himself.

'The pictures of me,' she said. 'They'll be so ashamed.'

Before leaving Hector's place, Evan had safed the house, finding little more than construction materials, empty beer bottles, a few hefty dumbbells in the garage. Fast-food wrappers layered a mattress thrown on the floor in one of the bare-bones rooms upstairs where Hector was living during the construction. Evan had gone back down to the comms center and dragged the considerable body out of the way. Once the cockpit was clear, he spent a few stomach-churning minutes navigating the databases, clicking through the files of past 'eligibles' to locate the matching buyers. Client information was sparse and coded, but he forwarded it on to the local FBI field office. But not before wiping all information about Anna Rezian off the servers.

'The pictures are gone,' Evan said. 'No one will have to know anything.'

Anna took an unsteady step to the side and lifted a hand to the cracked stucco wall. 'Eduard. He's safe now. He's safe.' Still working it through, thawing out of denial. 'You're all safe.'

Anna's face wobbled, and for a moment it seemed she might come apart entirely. 'I don't know how I can face them. Knowing what I almost did to us all. I'll never forgive myself.'

'That's up to you.'

She looked stung by his response. Tears clung to her lashes. She bit her lips. Her chest rose, her nostrils flaring. Deep breath. Exhale. The tears did not fall.

'You're not to call me again,' Evan said. 'Do you understand? This is what I do. But it's all that I do.'

'Albert and Maria are okay now.' Her lips barely moved. Her voice, little more than a whisper. '*Mayrig* and *Hayrig*. And Eduard. Eduard.'

'Anna, I need you to focus. Look at me. Look at me. I have one thing to ask of you before I leave.'

Her eyes found a sudden clarity. 'Anything.'

'Find someone who needs me. Like you did. It doesn't matter if it takes a week or a month or a year. You find someone who is desperate and has no way out. Give them my number.'

'Yes. 1-855-2-NOWHERE.'

Every call was digitized and sent over the Internet through a series of encrypted virtual private network tunnels. After pinging through fifteen software virtual telephone switch destinations around the globe, it came through his RoamZone.

'Yes. You tell them about me.'

'Like Nicole Helfrich's dad when he found me in the 7-Eleven?'

'Like that. You find someone. Tell them I'll be there on the other end of the phone.'

That was the final step for his clients. A task, a purpose, an act of empowerment that transitioned them from victim to rescuer. Evan knew all too well that some wounds never healed, not fully. But there were ways to contain the pain, to take ownership over the scars, and this was one of them.

Anna lunged at him and wrapped him in a hug. For a moment his arms floated a few inches above her thin back. He was unaccustomed to this kind of contact. In the moonlight he could see the wine-colored streak on his forearm, the dark half-moons beneath his nails. He didn't want Hector Contrell's blood on her clothes, in her hair. And yet Anna's embrace tightened, her face pressed into his chest.

He lowered his arms. She was warm. He felt the wetness of her cheek through his T-shirt. She clung to him.

Her voice came muffled. 'How do I thank you?'

Evan said, 'Be with your family.'

He'd meant it as the next instruction, but it struck him that it was also the answer to her question.

She stepped back to wipe her eyes, and he took the opportunity to slip away.

3. War Machine

Lurching from stoplight to stoplight, Evan dreamed of vodka. He had a new bottle tucked into the ice drawer of his Sub-Zero, waiting to greet him when he got home. From the outside his Ford F-150 pickup looked like any one of the millions on the roads of America. But with its laminate armor glass, self-seal tires, and built-to-spec push-bumper assembly, it was actually a war machine.

Up ahead, his building came into view. Branded with the inflated title of Castle Heights, the residential tower pinned down the easternmost spot on the Wilshire Corridor, giving his penthouse condo an unbroken view of downtown Los Angeles. Castle Heights was posh but dated, as easily overlooked as Evan's truck. Or Evan himself.

Recruited out of the projects of East Baltimore as a kid, he'd spent seven grueling years training under the tutelage of his handler. To say that Jack Johns had been like a father to him was an understatement. Jack had been the first person to treat Evan like he was human.

Evan had been created by the Orphan Program, a deep-black project buried inside the Department of Defense. It had identified the right kind of boys lost in the system of foster homes, covertly culled them one by one, and trained them to do what the U.S. government could not officially do in places where it could not officially be. A fully deniable, antiseptic program run off a shadow budget. Technically, the Orphans did not even exist.

They were expendable weapons.

As Orphan X, Evan had been given bursting bank accounts in nonreporting areas. His assignments spanned more than a decade. Rarely sighted, never captured, he was known only by the dead high-value targets he left in his wake and the alias he'd earned for moving unseen among the shadows.

The Nowhere Man.

At one point, though, he'd wanted out. It had cost him dearly. But it had left him with virtually unlimited money, a rare skill set, and time on his hands. And while he was done being Orphan X, he'd discovered that there was still work he should do as the Nowhere Man.

Pro bono work.

He'd lost the government designation but kept the alias given to him by his enemies.

Evan had heard that the Orphan Program had been dismantled, but last year he'd discovered that it was still operational. The most merciless of the Orphans had taken over the program. Charles Van Sciver. His new directive: to track down and eliminate former Orphans. According to those holding Van Sciver's leash, Evan's head contained too much sensitive information to remain connected to his body.

One thing had been made clear in their last bloody confrontation – Van Sciver and his Orphans would not stop the hunt until Evan was dead.

In the meantime Evan stayed off the grid and stayed vigilant.

At last he finished the gauntlet crawl through Wilshire Boulevard traffic. Turning in to Castle Heights, he whipped through the porte cochere past the valet and descended to the subterranean parking lot, drifting into his spot between two concrete pillars.

He grabbed a black sweatshirt from the back, tugged it on to cover the dried blood on his arm, and headed across the floor. He always took a moment outside the lobby door to close his eyes, draw in a breath, and ready himself for the transition into his other persona.

Evan Smoak, importer of industrial cleaning supplies. Another boring tenant.

Given the hour, the lobby was quiet, the air fragrant with the scent of lilies. Evan crossed briskly to the elevator, nodding at the security guard. 'Evening, Joaquin.'

Joaquin looked up from the bank of monitors running live feeds from the building's perimeter and hallways. Castle Heights prided itself on its security, an additional selling point to attract moneyed middle-aged tenants and flush retirees.

'Evening, Mr Smoak. You have a good night?'

'Typical Saturday,' Evan said. 'Burgers with the guys.'

Joaquin controlled the elevators from behind the

high counter – another safety measure – and his shoulder dipped as he pressed the button for the car. Evan lifted a hand in thanks, noticed the flecks of dried blood beneath his fingernails, and lowered it quickly. He stepped inside, the button for the twenty-first floor already lit.

The doors were just sliding closed when he heard a familiar voice call out, 'Wait! Hold the elevator, Joaquin – *please*.' The patter of footsteps. 'I meant the "please" to come first so I didn't sound all ordery, but –'

The doors parted again, and Evan came face-to-face with Mia Hall. Her sleeping nine-year-old was slumped in her arms, his chin resting on her shoulder.

Mia's eyes rose to meet Evan's, and she froze.

She was rarely caught off guard, but now her mouth was slightly ajar, a flush coming up beneath the faint scattering of freckles across the bridge of her nose.

They'd had an almost-relationship last year. He'd saved her life, and she'd saved his ass. In the process she'd learned more about him than she should have. Which would have been a problem even if she hadn't been a DA for the City of Los Angeles.

They blinked at each other.

She shifted, straining under Peter's weight.

'Want me to take him?' Evan asked.

There was a time when that would have been normal.

'No,' she said. 'Thanks. I got him.'

They rode up to her floor in silence. Remembering the traces of blood beneath his nails, Evan curled his hands into loose fists. He caught the faintest whiff of lemongrass – the scent of Mia's lotion.

Peter's cheek was smooshed into a half pout, his blond hair stuck up on one side, his lips blue with lollipop residue. When the doors parted with an arthritic rattle, Peter lifted his head sleepily. The smile touched his charcoal eyes first, then his mouth.

'Hi, Evan Smoak.' His voice, even raspier than usual. Before Evan could answer, the boy's lids drooped shut again.

Mia carried him out, and Evan watched them walk up the corridor until the closing elevator doors wiped them from view.

4. Clean as a Scalpel

When Evan turned the key, the lock to Condo 21A unbolted with a clank, various security bars releasing within the steel door concealed behind the homey wood-paneled façade. As Jack used to say, *Ball bearings within ball bearings*.

Evan muted the alarm and walked to the kitchen area. He passed the living wall, a drip-fed vertical garden that sprouted mint and sage, parsley and chamomile. The pleasing scent and splash of green were the sole aspect of the corner penthouse that could be described as cheerful.

The floorplan was largely open, seven thousand square feet of poured concrete split by workout stations, sitting areas, a freestanding fireplace, and a steel staircase that twisted up to a loft. Countless safeguards hid inside the sleek, modern space. The windows and sliding glass doors that turned two walls into a city panorama? Bullet-resistant Lexan armed with shatter-detection software. The periwinkle retractable sunscreens? Woven titanium armor. The quartz-rock-layered balconies cupping the sides of the condo? Secondary alarms rigged to detect the audio signature of an unwelcome guest's boots compressing the stones.

Evan slipped around the island to the Sub-Zero.

Nestled among the ice cubes, a fat bottle of Karlsson's Gold beckoned. The handcrafted Swedish vodka, comprising seven kinds of potatoes, was uniquely made, distilled a single time through a copper-lined still. Evan poured a few fingers into a rocks glass over a spherical ice cube and garnished the drink with a single twist of ground pepper from a stainless-steel mill.

Clean as a scalpel up front. Hint of mineral on the finish. Lingering bite of pepper.

Perfect.

Evan walked to the fireplace, fired up the pyre of cedar logs, then peeled off his mission clothes and fed them to the flames. With the rocks glass dangling at his side, he padded naked across the vast space and down the brief hall, passing the spot where his dear departed nineteenth-century katana used to hang. The bare wall hooks reminded him that he'd recently won an online bid for a replacement samurai sword, one that dated back to the Early Edo period. The shipment was due to arrive soon from the Seki auction house.

He stepped through his bedroom into the bathroom and tapped the frosted-glass shower door, which recessed into the wall on silent tracks. Turning the water up as hot as he could stand, he ducked into the stream. He scrubbed. The water ran dark, a crimson swirl circling the drain.

It took a wire brush and some effort to get his fingernails clean.

After drying off he headed into the bedroom and dressed in the same outfit he'd worn before. Dark jeans, gray V-necked T-shirt. Before turning away from the dresser, he hesitated over the bottom drawer.

Emotion came up under his skin, a flush of heat.

He tugged the drawer open and used his thumbnail to lift the false bottom.

Beneath, a blue flannel shirt, blackened with old blood.

Jack's blood.

There wasn't a night in the past eight years that Evan didn't turn off the light, close his eyes, and watch Jack bleed out in his arms.

Evan shut the drawer and rose, trying to dissipate the tightness in his chest. He sat on his bed, a Maglev that literally floated two feet off the floor, the slab held airborne by neodymium rare-earth magnets. Closing his eyes, suspended between floor and ceiling, he focused on his breathing, dropped inside his body, felt the weight of his bones inside his flesh. It usually helped him find tranquillity.

But not tonight.

Images strobed through the darkness behind his eyelids. Hector Contrell's shoulders jerking back as if yanked by strings. Ink pooling in the hollow of his neck, a punctuation mark for the FUCK YOU tattoo. Those mighty legs collapsing, a slow-motion avalanche crumble. The mess on the floor upstairs around the mattress — residue-stained Styrofoam ramen bowls, empty burrito wrappers, crumpled protein packets. The ribcage of the house, bare studs scrolling by as Evan crept inside. The hall telescoping out like some

Kubrickian horror, each empty doorframe replaced by another and another.

Evan's eyes flew open.

No doors. Which meant no door handles. That was what had been nagging at him. The house was open to the world, fluttering tarps in place of walls.

No locked area for the kidnapped girls.

The logistics of moving them around the world were complicated. There had to be a holding area somewhere off premises.

Which meant the possibility existed that another young woman remained in it.

Evan hopped off the bed and moved back into the bathroom, stepping into the shower. He squeezed the lever handle for the hot water, and a moment later came a faint click. The lever, keyed to his palm print, doubled as a concealed doorknob. He turned it the wrong way, and a door, disguised by the tile pattern of the shower wall, swung inward.

He stepped into the Vault.

Four hundred asymmetrical square feet crowded by the underbelly of the public stairs to the roof, the walled-off storage space served as Evan's armory and ops center. From the weapon lockers to the sheet-metal desk burdened with monitors, servers, and cables, it contained all the tools of his trade. The screens displayed pirated security feeds of Castle Heights. Every hallway, every stairwell, every access door.

He breathed in the smell of damp concrete, dropped into his chair, and rolled to the L-shaped desk to access the law-enforcement databases. All the major criminal and civil records, forensic files, and ballistics registers – anything that the local police could dig up on the Panasonic Toughbook laptops wired into their patrol cars – Evan could access.

His training had consisted of learning a little bit about everything from people who knew everything about something. He was hardly an expert hacker, but he'd broken into a few cruisers and uploaded a piece of reverse SSH code into their laptops – a back door for him to get into the system anytime he beckoned.

He beckoned now, searching Contrell's known associates, past residences, former cellmates. Nothing raised a red flag. A few hours later, the watered-down vodka sat forgotten beside the mouse pad, pepper grinds floating like ash.

Through the DMV site, Evan grabbed the license-plate number of Contrell's Buick Enclave. Another series of backstage maneuvers got him into the vehicle's GPS records. He printed out the data captures – longitudes and latitudes listed in an endless scroll.

As the LaserJet spat out page after page, he started breaking down the pauses between the Enclave's movements.

Contrell's destinations.

Evan's work was not done.

The Tenth Commandment: *Never let an innocent die.*

5. The Eyes of the Data-Mining Beast

The room could have been anywhere. Midway up a high-rise. At the distal end of a mansion's wing. Underground, even.

It was big.

The size of a movie theater, but without the rows of chairs. There wasn't a screen.

There were *hundreds* of them.

Lining three walls, stacked top to bottom, the most elaborate display of computing power this side of DARPA. Each monitor scrolled an endless stream of code. The screens were the eyes of the data-mining beast; the banks of servers bunkered behind the bomb-resistant fourth wall were the brain.

Guttering light from the monitors strobed across the dim room, living camouflage. It was hard to see anything aside from the screens. Everything melted together – the rugs, the consoles, the sparse furniture. Even the few visitors with clearance to enter – usually a not-fully-read-in engineer making tech adjustments – seemed to disappear, a fish blending into rippling water.

Charles Van Sciver liked it in here. Liked it for the darkness, through which he could drift alone and unseen.

There were no windows. No mirrors either, not even in the adjoining bathroom. He'd covered them up. The occasional visitor was made to stand at a distance so Van Sciver could stay bathed in the protective anonymity of the flickering lights.

It was safe and contained in here. Just him and his algorithms.

It wasn't fair to say that *all* the computing power was directed at locating Orphan X.

Only 75 percent.

Or 76.385, to be precise.

After all, as the head of the Program, Van Sciver did have other mission responsibilities.

But none as important as this.

For better than a decade, Evan had been the top asset in the entire Orphan Program. He didn't merely know where the bodies were buried. He had buried most of them.

Though the naked eye couldn't process a sliver of the information whipping across the monitors, Van Sciver liked to watch the large-scale data processing in real time. Though he knew the buzzwords – 'cluster analysis', 'anomaly detection', 'predictive analytics' – he couldn't even comprehend what was before him. But he could grasp the output reports, which he checked meticulously on the hour, searching for filaments in the ocean of cyberspace. These threads of the Nowhere Man had to be delicately backtraced. If Van Sciver allowed the slightest quiver showing that he had something on the hook, the line would snap.

Lately his team of engineers had been focused on data warehousing, piecing together bits of information from offshore bank accounts, trying to reconstruct enough of the mosaic to point them in the right direction. They had leads on Evan, of course. A few floating strands on the water. But every time they tugged slack out of the line, they came up with more slack, a money transfer zigzagging off into the depths, a shell corp vanishing behind a mailbox corporation, another trail ending at a disused P.O. box off some dusty Third World dirt road.

Van Sciver paced the perimeter of the room, his ever-paler skin drinking in the antiseptic blue glow of the screens. The lack of human contact ensured that he would never be deterred from his goal. Ultimately it would come down to discipline and abstinence, and so he had cleared out any distracting clutter from his existence. His willingness to deny all pleasure and warmth was why he would win. That was why he would beat his nemesis. Victory would be pleasure enough.

Van Sciver halted. Facing the horseshoe of the rippling walls, he basked in the power represented before him. Time was meaningless in here. The present was spent reconstructing the past and extrapolating the future, a dragon ever swallowing its tail, an infinity of numbers that summed to zero.

But one day they would add up to everything.

One day they would search out the right thread of ones and zeros that would lead to Orphan X.

It was only a matter of time.

6. Struck Oil

Evan noticed everything when he drove. Especially gray Ford Transit Connect vans with no side windows and dealer plates. Like the one that had been hovering in his rearview mirror for the past few blocks.

He threw on his right-hand turn signal. The van did not. Either it wasn't following him or it was driven by a pro unwilling to take the bait. Evan drove straight past the entrance of the Norwalk FedEx office, and the van kept right on behind him. Evan muted the signal, keeping his head down but his eyes nailed to the rearview. He waited a few beats and then abruptly veered off onto a side street. The van coasted by, not even slowing.

He could never be too careful.

He'd spent the morning completing a circuit of the safe houses he kept in the Greater Los Angeles Area, testing his load-out gear, checking the oil on his alternate vehicles, changing up the automated lighting. At his Westchester place, a crappy single-story beneath LAX's flight path, he'd switched out his usual rig for a mud-spattered 4Runner with a scuba flag sticker in the back window.

On the side street now, Evan sat behind the wheel and watched the road for a while. Finally he dropped the transmission back into drive. Backtracking to the FedEx office, he entered, signed a series of customs forms, and left with an elongated cardboard box.

His new katana. This blade had been forged relatively recently, in 1653, by Heike Norihisa, last smith of the five-layered smelt. The katana was decorative, as Evan had intended the last one to be, and he was eager to mount it on the empty hooks in his hall.

But he had another location to check first. He'd spent hour after excruciating hour parsing the data from Contrell's GPS, checking the man's frequent stops, looking for the location where he stored the girls before shipping them out. With every passing day, more sand trickled through the hourglass.

Evan drove to Fullerton. A sheaf of papers rested in his lap, much of the data on them already crossed out with red pen.

The next place on the list proved to be a humble residence, semi-isolated behind a stretch of soccer fields gone to dirt. Detached garage, new shingles, fresh paint, curtains drawn. A security gate guarded a concrete front walk hemmed in by flower beds. A Stepford house writ small.

Evan parked several blocks away and doubled back. He vaulted the fence, put his ear to the door, heard nothing. The lock gleamed, a shiny Medeco. He raked it with a triple mountain pick, feeling for the rhythm of the wafers inside as they lifted to different heights. At last he felt the pleasing click of the release.

The well-greased door swung in on silent hinges. He

drew his Wilson from his Kydex high-guard hip holster and eased inside. The interior, dim from the drawn curtains, stank of cleaning solution and unventilated air. Though he sensed that the place was empty, he moved silently from room to room. It was cheaply constructed and surprisingly clean. Dishes neatly stacked on a spotless counter. Sparkling linoleum floors. IKEA-looking slipcovered couch and chairs, calming taupes, distressed blues. In the living room, he parted the curtains with a hand.

The windows were nailed shut.

He ran his fingers over the heads of the nails, the metal cool against his prints. His heart rate ticked up with anticipation.

He moved on.

The master bedroom featured two double beds, sheets neatly made. Men's clothes in the wardrobe. *Big* men's clothes. One of the jackets looked like it could cover a deck chair.

Evan stopped, breathed, listened.

Then he started down the tiny hall to the rear room. Three door bolts. On the *outside*.

Pistol drawn, Evan stood perfectly still outside the room for a full ten minutes. No sounds of breathing within, no creaking of the floorboards.

Finally he threw one bolt. The muted clank of metal against metal might as well have been a clap of thunder.

Standing to the side of the door, he waited.

Nothing happened, and then more nothing.

The next two locks he unbolted in rapid succession. He bladed his body. Let the door creak inward. Leading with the 1911, he nosed around the jamb. A nicely made bed, lavender comforter, brand-new TV on a stand.

A lovely room, aside from the plate of sheet metal drilled over the window. When Evan shouldered the door to step inside, he felt it to be heavier than the others. Solid core.

The holding pen.

No one inside. The room – bare, pristine, equipped with only the basics – seemed like a diorama. In fact, the whole place had a dollhouse feel.

It had been designed with one purpose in mind: comfortable functionality.

Hector Contrell had to ensure that the merchandise wasn't damaged before delivery.

The bathroom door remained closed. Evan tried the doorknob, but it didn't budge. Seating the pistol in his holster, he took out his tension wrench again. The cheaper lock required only a hook pick and a few jiggles.

As the door swung inward, the smell hit him first.

A smooth leg, mottled blue-purple, hooked over the brim of the bathtub. A mass of tangled black hair covered the face, leaving only a delicate ivory chin exposed. He put the body as older than most of Contrell's 'eligibles'. Late teens, early twenties. Probably designated for a buyer looking for variety.

Until Contrell's operation had been blown and his middlemen decided to liquidate the inventory.

She'd been alive when he killed Contrell. She'd been alive when he went home and poured himself a glass of vodka and drank to a job well done.

Evan lowered the pick set.

That was when he heard the footsteps behind him.

Two men, no doubt the inhabitants of the roomy clothes in the wardrobe of the master bedroom. The one nearest Evan gripped a snub-nosed Smith & Wesson Chief's Special and gripped it well. Firmed wrists, locked elbows. A second pistol hung in a cheap nylon holster under his left armpit, semiauto backup in case five bullets weren't sufficient.

The man behind him carried a healthy gut and a SIG Sauer. His gun was also raised, but he could afford to be less on point given that his buddy had Evan pinned down. Evan couldn't get a clear look around the front man's barrel chest. The man seemed to block everything out. It wasn't just his girth but the way he canted in aerodynamically at Evan. Thrusting chin, ledged brow, chest and biceps tugging him forward on his frame so it seemed that only the balls of his feet were holding him back – a bullet train made incarnate.

'Who's been sleeping in our beds?' he said.

Evan lowered his hands slightly. The S&W followed the motion, stopped level with his heart.

'Goldilocks?' Evan said. 'Really?'

'I gotta agree, Claude,' the man by the door said. 'Not your finest work.'

Claude's features rearranged themselves. His cheeks

looked shiny, as if he'd recently shaved, but stubble was already pushing its way through again. His face, the target demographic for five-blade razors.

'I just thought, you know, the whole breaking-and-entering thing,' Claude said. 'Us coming home, catching you. Plus the Goldilocks reference, it's demeaning.'

'Because she's a girl,' Evan said.

Claude nodded.

Evan held his hands in place. 'You know what they say. If you have to explain the joke . . .'

The man in the back flicked his SIG at Evan. 'Gun on the ground.'

Evan complied.

As he squatted, he gauged the distance to the tips of Claude's shoes. Maybe five feet. Evan could close the space in a single lunge. Easy enough, if he didn't have two guns aimed at his critical mass.

Rising, he eyed the barrel of the Chief's Special. Since Claude was muscle-bound and right-handed, Evan's first move would be to juke left, make him swing the gun inward across that barrel chest. The compression of delt and pec might slow his arm, buy Evan a half second.

That would be all he'd need.

His stare dropped to Claude's second gun, the one slung in the loose-fitting underarm holster. A Browning Hi-Power. It was cocked and locked – hammer back, safety engaged. The safety lever peeked out beneath the retention strap of the nylon holster. Good presentation.

The odor wafted from the bathroom over Evan's shoulder, precipitating on the taste buds at the back of his tongue. Just past the threshold in the hall, he saw the bright red of a few plastic gasoline jugs; the men had set them down quietly. 'You guys cleaning up the operation?'

'Contrell was the CEO,' Claude said. 'We're just workaday guys. Glorified babysitters, really. Sit around, eat pizza, watch the tube. Beats digging ditches.'

Evan flipped the tiny hook pick around his thumb, pinched it again. 'Those were the only options, huh? Sell girls or dig ditches?'

Claude smiled with sudden awareness, his magnificent jaw jutting out all the more. 'You're the guy who put us out of work.'

With a flick of his wrist, Evan flipped the hook pick at Claude's eyes, lunging left just before the gunshot. The bullet cracked past his ear. He dived not so much *at* Claude as *into* him, using him as a shield, getting inside the range of the revolver. Evan's right hand flew at that Browning in the underarm holster, and then he smacked into the big man, pressing chest to chest, a dance move gone wrong.

It happened very fast.

Evan's thumb shoved the safety lever off as his forefinger curled around the trigger. He rode the gun back in the sling and fired straight through the holster from beneath Claude's armpit. The man behind them took the shot through the cheek, blood welling like struck oil. The pistol in his fist barked twice as he flew back.

Evan felt both impacts ripple Claude's flesh, friendly-fire smacks to the spine.

Claude dropped fast and lay still.

The other man had wound up sitting next to the bed, slumped forward over his gut, one hand clutching the lavender comforter. A perfect stillness claimed the room.

The whole thing had gone down in about a second and a half.

Evan picked up his gun and started out. Though the neighboring houses were far, the noise of a firefight would carry.

As he stepped over Claude, he noticed a yellow slip peeking from the inner lapel pocket of the laid-open jacket. Instinct halted him there above the body, told him to crouch and reach for it. He teased it out.

A customer copy of a shipping bill, rendered on thin yellow carbonless copy paper.

All at once the air felt brittle, as if it might shatter if he moved wrong.

His eyes pulled to the bed. Queen-size.

Big enough for roommates.

He looked back at the form, taking in the data.

Origin: Long Beach, CA
Destination: Jacksonville, FL
ETA: Oct 29, 11:37pm
Distance: 5141.11 miles (8273.82 km)

That was not the distance a package would travel by

truck or plane. Not even close. That distance would be two thousand miles and change. This package was traveling down around the bottom of the continent and through the Panama Canal.

He scanned further down the form.

Sure enough, a twenty-foot ISO-standard container had been secured on a midsize bulk carrier called the *Horizon Express*. An additional port fee of $120 was to be paid upon delivery to the Jacksonville Port Authority.

At the bottom of the form, something was written in pen, the blue ink distinct from the black dye pressed through from the other sheets. A name. And an age.

Alison Siegler/17 yrs.

Seeing the casual scrawl fired something at Evan's core.

He wondered about the seventeen-year-old girl locked inside Container 78653-B812.

It seemed that Claude and friend had managed to fulfill one last order this morning before shutting down the assembly belt. Which meant that Evan had one last head to sever from the hydra of Contrell's operation to put it down for once and for all.

He had sixteen days until that container ship reached Jacksonville. He would meet the buyer there. But he didn't plan on leaving Alison Siegler alone until then.

Folding the yellow form in his hand, he headed out, stepping past the trio of gasoline jugs in the hall and through the front door. Jogging up the front walk, he vaulted the security gate.

His boots had just hit the sidewalk when he heard the screech of tires.

Two Ford Transits flew in at him, one from either side, a narrowing V. Familiar gray, no side windows. As Evan reached for his hip holster, their doors rolled open, exposing a row of eyes peering out through balaclava masks. Inside each van a line of shotguns raised in concert, like a gun turret.

Neon orange spots floated within the dark vehicle interiors. The shotgun stocks, color-coded for less-lethal.

Evan had a moment to think, *This is gonna hurt,* and then the twelve-gauges let fly. The first beanbag round hit him square in the thigh, knocking him into a 180, a volley of follow-ups peppering his right side. A rib cracked. Another flexible baton round skimmed the side of his head, a glancing blow, but given the lead shot packed inside, it was enough. No pain, not yet, just pressure and the promise of swelling.

He spun with the blow, wheeling to round out the 360, somehow managing to draw his Wilson in the process. The black-clad men had already unassed from the vans in shooting-squad formation. These men were expert assaulters, leagues beyond Hector Contrell and his sorry assemblage of freelancers.

An enormous man in the middle held a bizarre gun, its conical barrel flaring to accommodate a balloonlike plug. It looked like a basketball stuck in a snake's craw.

It discharged with a whoosh. Evan watched it unfurl at him with detached and helpless wonder. Durable nylon mesh, steel clamps weighting the four corners, the whole thing yawning open like the maw of some great beast.

A wildlife-capture net.

It cocooned him, his wrist smashed to his nose, one knee snapped up into his chest, his feet pointed down like an Olympic diver's. This must have been what the Neanderthals felt like when the lava flow caught up, fossilizing them in all their awkward non-glory.

His gun hand, pinned to his left ear, was as useless as the rest of him.

The pavement smashed his cheek. For a split second, a dot of dancing yellow grabbed his focus – the shipping slip catching a gust of wind, riding an air current into the gutter. The last trace of Alison Siegler, whisked away.

Evan pegged his pupil to the corner of his eye, straining to look up. A massive dark form loomed, a needle held vertically in latex-gloved hands.

The form leaned in.

A prick of metal in the side of the neck.

Then searing darkness.

He just wanted a decent book to read ...

Not too much to ask, is it? It was in 1935 when Allen Lane, Managing Director of Bodley Head Publishers, stood on a platform at Exeter railway station looking for something good to read on his journey back to London. His choice was limited to popular magazines and poor-quality paperbacks – the same choice faced every day by the vast majority of readers, few of whom could afford hardbacks. Lane's disappointment and subsequent anger at the range of books generally available led him to found a company – and change the world.

'We believed in the existence in this country of a vast reading public for intelligent books at a low price, and staked everything on it'
Sir Allen Lane, 1902–1970, founder of Penguin Books

The quality paperback had arrived – and not just in bookshops. Lane was adamant that his Penguins should appear in chain stores and tobacconists, and should cost no more than a packet of cigarettes.

Reading habits (and cigarette prices) have changed since 1935, but Penguin still believes in publishing the best books for everybody to enjoy. We still believe that good design costs no more than bad design, and we still believe that quality books published passionately and responsibly make the world a better place.

So wherever you see the little bird – whether it's on a piece of prize-winning literary fiction or a celebrity autobiography, political tour de force or historical masterpiece, a serial-killer thriller, reference book, world classic or a piece of pure escapism – you can bet that it represents the very best that the genre has to offer.

Whatever you like to read – trust Penguin.

'Guillermo Vasquez – Memo. Memo Vasquez. I am in very bad trouble. I don't have my green card – I cannot go to *policía*. My Isa – my daughter – she is at risk, too.'

'When do you want to meet?'

'Right away. *Por favor*, right away.'

'Where do you live?' Evan asked.

Vasquez gave an address in Elysium Park, a gang-intensive working-class neighborhood in the shadow of Dodger Stadium.

'Wednesday morning,' Evan said. 'Ten a.m.'

'It might be too late for us by then,' Vasquez said. 'That is two and a half days away!'

Evan would need two and a half days. At least.

'Please,' Vasquez said.

He was rushing the meet. Which was either suspicious or – given the circumstances under which people usually called Evan – completely normal.

The hall, still empty. The elevator, visible past the neighboring loft, whirred into action, but the car passed his floor without stopping. Evan shot a glance over his shoulder at Katrin's sleeping form. 'It'll have to do,' he said, and hung up.

He walked back to the futon and stood over her, staring down. She moaned lightly and rolled over, one arm flung across her forehead, a Roy Lichtenstein maiden in distress. Her closed eyelids fluttered.

Guillermo Vasquez.

Katrin White.

One of them was lying.

Squatting a few feet away, he confronted her. Bringing up the camera feature on his phone, he clicked the night-vision option, squared up her face, and snapped a picture.

At the kitchen counter, he jotted a quick note: *'Running down some angles. Stay put. Contact me if emergency. – E'*

He took the stairs down, pausing at each landing to listen for footsteps. The garage was clear. He got into the Taurus and drove out of the parking level without incident. He drove circles around Downtown, his eyes on the rearview mirror, until he was certain he was alone. Then he got on to the freeway and headed for Vegas.

He pictured Morena Aguilar on the day he met her. Wearing her stiff Benny's Burgers work shirt, coiled on her chair like a fierce animal, trapped but unbroken, ready to go to any lengths to protect her sister. *That kid? She never done a wrong thing in her life.* He thought about the flash of optimism in her eyes when she talked about her aunt's place, the fresh start, and then he pictured Danny Slatcher's big fist knocking on that front door.

He'd never contacted a client after a mission was complete. With Morena, as with the others he'd helped over the years, he'd had an understanding – that she wouldn't contact him and he wouldn't contact her. But the Tenth Commandment loomed above all else.

Never let an innocent die.

30. The Calling Song

Morena's aunt, a block of a woman ensconced in multiple layers of nightwear, opened the door but addressed Evan through a locked security screen. Fair enough, given that it was just past six in the morning, the stars holding their radiance even through the lightening sky.

She lived not in Vegas proper but in a cluster of trailer homes in a low-end district of Henderson, the neighboring city. Fastening the sash on her bathrobe, she drew her head back even farther behind the ledge of her bosom. 'Morena? She is not here.'

'I know that you want to protect her, ma'am,' Evan said. 'But she's not safe right now. I'm –'

'I understand who you are.'

'Do you?'

Her impassive eyes gave off only an obsidian gleam. 'Perhaps. But that doesn't change the fact that I know nothing.'

'Can you at least tell me if they arrived here safely?' Evan asked. 'Her and Carmen?'

One lonely cricket was at it in the cluster of dead shrubs at the property line, shrilling its calling song at the dead desert air.

Evan's gaze lowered to a battered trumpet case lying

beside a pile of footwear. Noting his stare, Morena's aunt cinched the door shut another few inches, restricting his line of sight, her bulk filling the gap. Thin blue veins streaked her pronounced upper eyelids. Her mouth, frozen in a downturned expression, seemed at once maternal and stern, the combat mask of a roused mama bear.

'Wherever she is, she is safe,' she said.

'Ask her to call me. She knows my number. Please.'

'She is safer not being found.'

'I don't believe that's so,' Evan said.

'You are entitled to your opinion,' she said, and closed the door gently in his face.

He stood in the morning chill, him and the mateless cricket beneath the wide-open vault of the Nevada sky. He had a laptop in the trunk and could access the databases remotely, maybe pull phone records from the house and go from there. It would be a long investigative slog, running down leads and hitting dead ends.

Time he did not have right now, given the threat to Morena.

He started to walk away when he heard a child's whistle – not a whistle at all, in fact, but a whooshing of air through pursed lips. A side window rattled open, and a small form tumbled out, landing gracefully in a manner that suggested that the move had been tested a time or two.

The little girl straightened up and dusted off her

ensures that even if the magazine scraps the column for which you were writing, or the new editor decides that there shall be no more humor in his pages, you'll still get something.

The ideal arrangement is to ask that the kill fee apply only to situations where the article is rejected, not just when it gets bumped through no fault of your own. "Lately, I've heard more and more reports of articles being killed because the assigning editor left and a new editor or entire regime came in and wanted to start off with a clean slate," says top freelancer Bobbi Dempsey. "I always request the full fee if an article is killed for reasons beyond my control."

There's a higher risk of having an article killed at a magazine with a long lead time, because there's more of a chance that the staff will change, a competitor will run a similar article, something in the news will make it inappropriate to run (for example, an article about a terrific nonprofit organization could be killed if that organization does something unethical or takes a public stance on an issue that the magazine disagrees with), and so on.

After the magazine kills your piece, you're free to sell it elsewhere. The only situation in which this is not true is when you've been paid in full and have sold more than one-time or reprint rights; in that case, you'll have to ask the editor if you can have the rights back so you can sell it elsewhere. Otherwise, technically, they still own rights to your piece; your contract may say that they're buying the right to be the first magazine in North America to print it. Therefore, you must double-check to make sure that they're giving up this right.

Bios

We like bios. Those are the little blurbs that often follow an article, giving short biographical information about the writer, and sometimes an email

---

Etiquette for Killing

If a contract arrives and says nothing about a kill fee, ask the editor about it casually: "I notice there's nothing about kill fees in this contract. What's your policy on that?" The editor may pleasantly surprise you and tell you that they don't mention kill fees because they pay in full even when a piece is killed, or she may tell you they don't pay kill fees because they want to retain the right to leave you in the dust if they decide not to print the piece. (Of course, she won't say it quite so honestly.) In this case, say something like, "Although I'm sure you'll be happy with my article, I just want the reassurance that I'll be paid for my time even if the piece gets cut for some reason. Can we agree on a 50 percent kill fee?"

> ### *Multiple Bio Personalities*
>
> *You may have different bios that you use, depending on the type of publication it'll be in. I have several variations:*
>
> *For health magazines: "Jenna Glatzer is the editor of* Conquering Panic and Anxiety Disorders, *an anthology of success stories from people who've beat anxiety disorders. Reach her through her web site at www.absolutewrite.com."*
>
> *For writers' publications: "Jenna Glatzer is the editor-in-chief of Absolute Write (www.absolutewrite.com) and the author of* Outwitting Writer's Block *(Lyons Press, 2003) and other books for writers. Read about her work at www.absolutewrite.com/jenna/books.htm."*
>
> *For others: "Jenna Glatzer is a full-time writer from New York with nine books and hundreds of magazine articles to her name. Read about her books at www.absolutewrite.com/jenna/books.htm, or visit her popular web site for writers at www.absolutewrite.com."*
>
> *You might want to include personal facts (such as "Kristen is the single mom of two teenagers," or "Kristen is a cancer survivor"), where you're from, where you went to school, why you wrote the article, your former profession ("Kristen is a personal-trainer-turned-fitness-writer"), your hobbies, or your goals ("Kristen is training for the Boston Marathon"). Always try to include a way for readers to contact you (an email address or web site): You never know who might be reading! I've had a film producer, a television celebrity, and editors contact me with work after reading my bio elsewhere.*

address or phone number. Ask to have your bio included in the article, or if you didn't discuss it during your initial negotiations with the editor, include a sentence or two at the bottom of your completed article. If the editor wants it, he'll run it. If not, no sweat off your back. It's worth trying.

You generally don't have to skimp on your word count in a bio for an e-zine article, but in print, space is always an issue, so don't get too presumptuous. Some editors will give you a word count (*Physical* asks for 25- to 35-word bios, for example), while others will assume you'll be reasonable.

Sidebars and Photos

If you didn't mention these in your query, now is the time to bring them up. Does the editor want sidebars? Think visually: charts, graphs, bullet lists, short quotes. How about photos? If it's a major magazine, don't bother asking: They have their own photographers, or will hire a professional freelancer in your area.

Your Follow-Up Letter

It's a very smart idea to send off a letter reviewing the terms if your negotiations took place in a phone conversation. This way, if the magazine fails to send you a contract in a timely manner, you can still feel safe starting the work because you have, in effect, written your own contract. Here's a sample of what I mean:

> **Dear Ms. Editor:**
>
> **I enjoyed speaking to you on the phone today, and I'm looking forward to writing the piece we discussed.**
>
> **I'd like to make sure I understood the terms of this assignment before I begin working, so I would appreciate it if you could take a moment to review this and let me know that it's accurate.**
>
> **Per our conversation, I will be writing a 1,000-word profile of Jan Schmoe, the owner of Jan's Cookies. The article will focus on the tactics she used to start and market this cookie-delivery business. I will turn in the completed article via email by August 6.**
>
> **Payment will be $0.50 a word, totaling $500, payable on acceptance. There will be a 40 percent kill fee, and I will be provided with a 20-word bio. Your publication is purchasing the first North American serial rights. If the article is used on your web site, I will be compensated an additional 20 percent of the purchase price. If it is archived, I will be paid 10 percent of the original purchase price per year that it appears online.**
>
> **Thank you for taking the time to review this. I look forward to working with you.**

Even if it seems like overkill, it's always wise to spell out the terms of your agreement, as soon as possible, in writing. This begins the paper trail, and as much as you may not want to think about it while you're basking in the glow of an assignment, paper trails are important! You'll kick yourself later if you failed to establish the terms of your assignment in writing. Plus, in case you did misunderstand anything, this clears it up before you set out working.

Do I Spec After the First Clip?

Write without pay until somebody offers to pay you. If nobody offers
within three years, sawing wood is what you were intended for.

—Mark Twain

As a novice writer, you are likely to be asked to write an article on "spec" (short for "speculation"). This means that you'll have to write the whole article and submit it without a contract, or any promise of payment. It's a bone of contention among professional writers, because almost no other field works this way: You don't get to pick up a roll of stamps at your post office and tell your friendly postmaster, "I'll just take these, and then if I decide to use them, I'll pay you later."

That said, I advise you to take spec assignments in the beginning when necessary. Once you're established, you shouldn't need to do this, but in order to build up your résumé and your clips, you need to get published. So go ahead and submit on spec, and go ahead and do a few free/nearly free pieces for the experience.

Washington, DC-based writer Carole Ashkinaze, who writes for magazines such as *Business Week* and *Moment*, warns that writing on spec does come with a stipulation. "You must not assume you will get paid something, anyhow, *ever* [for that article]. If the rewards of never receiving a cent for X article or project seem to outweigh the sacrifice—and they often do—go ahead. If you will feel like you wasted your time or were taken advantage of unless you get paid, don't do it."

Writing on spec or for non-paying markets is a very controversial topic among writers: Many will advise you never to write for free, no matter what. "I am a strong believer that writers should never write for free or almost-free except for volunteer services for organizations you want to support," says freelancer Bobbi Dempsey, who has written for magazines such as *Parents*, *Penthouse*, and *Twist*.

My stance is this: In the beginning, you're in training. If you wanted to be a professional actor, would you expect to be paid for high school or church plays? No, you do that to build up your credentials and learn more about your craft. The equivalent of this in the literary world is working for bylines, clips, and exposure from publications that cannot afford to pay, such as many e-zines, some local publications, and some small-circulation magazines. Make sure, if a publication isn't paying you in cash, they're paying you in publicity. Once you've "paid your dues," then it's time to go after the paychecks.

Steve Outing, columnist for *Editor & Publisher*, says, "I'd urge writers considering this to create their own web sites to showcase their writing, rather than earn money for someone else. Some web sites publish quality content and are not in it for money, and it's appropriate to write for those for free if you believe in their cause. I just wouldn't recommend writing for any online venue that earns money and takes writing for free."

If you are lucky and talented enough in the beginning of your career to score an assignment with a magazine that can afford to pay you, then, by all means, expect fair payment. Don't worry; just because you're new, that doesn't mean *Reader's Digest* won't pay you. If the editor thinks your idea is good enough to use, then you are a valuable commodity and should be treated as such. Even most local women's magazines earn enough to be able to pay you *something*, so don't let them get away with running your work for free just because they know you're desperate to see print.

If you are going to submit something on spec at an editor's request, though, make sure you know in advance what the terms will be if the editor does use your piece. How much will you be paid? What rights will they buy?

Even many of the big markets have adopted the practice of requesting pieces on spec, and not just from unpublished writers, either. They sometimes have the nerve to ask experienced writers to write a first article on spec for them, too. They do this because they can get away with it, and because there are thousands of wannabe writers out there who will beg, borrow, and steal for the chance to be published. So, if you want to compete, sometimes you'll have to suck it up and accept this. Once the publication runs one of your spec pieces, you'll be a much more likely candidate for an outright assignment next time.

Two Weeks

Employ a bit of negotiating even when submitting on spec. How so? Agree to submit on spec if the editor will give you a decision within two weeks of submission. That's plenty of time for the editor to look at the piece and see if it fits his needs.

Otherwise, you can often run into the "in limbo" situation: You've submitted something on spec and are left hanging for months, wondering whether or not the magazine will run your piece. Rather than setting yourself up for the uncomfortable situation of having to nag for an answer, make sure you've established this in the beginning. This way, if they aren't going to run it, you can submit it elsewhere.

And sometimes you'll know that it's an unreasonable request that you'd rather turn down. If a magazine wants you to spec a 2,000-word feature that'll require you to travel and do several interviews, well, that's a big gamble. To me, it's also disrespectful; an editor who expects a writer to spend weeks on something that the editor may or may not decide to pay for probably isn't someone you want to work for.

The Case Against Writing for Free or on Spec

If you read discussion lists on the Web, you'll find heated arguments from many professional writers who are upset with the fact that some writers will work for free or on spec. Why? Because it enables publications to keep the practice. It's a case of supply and demand: As long as hundreds or thousands of writers vie to fill each open slot in a magazine, the editors have the upper hand. They outline the terms, and it's quite likely that they'll find someone, somewhere, who is desperate enough to agree to anything.

Just last week, I found a web site for college students that had guidelines stating that not only did the web site pay nothing, but it demanded all rights and required writers to sign a contract promising that they would never use the same research or interviews to write another article ever again.

I sent off a letter to the editor explaining that her terms were terribly unfair. She told me it was "company policy," and that she had no shortage of writers. I wasn't surprised—just a bit sad.

Every time a writer allows herself to be taken advantage of, all writers take a collective step backward in establishing their value. Likewise, when a writer fights back and demands to be treated and compensated fairly, she wins a battle for all of us.

Steve Outing says, "Don't let online publishers have exclusive rights to your work, unless they're willing to compensate you adequately for that. Many web publishers are new to publishing, and they don't seem to understand the concept that a writer should own copyright to his/her work. It's up to writers to educate these 'newbie' publishers."

Consider the Tasini vs the *New York Times* case.

This was a lawsuit brought by members of the National Writers Union against The New York Times Company, Newsday Inc., Time Inc., Lexis/Nexis, and University Microfilms Inc., charging copyright violation regarding the electronic reuse of work produced and sold on a freelance basis.

Before the advent of the Internet, the standard practice of assigning first North American serial rights to a publication wasn't contested. It was generally understood that writers allowed newspapers and magazines to publish their work in print one time. Writers would retain all other rights, a crucial point to surviving as a freelancer, and therefore, have the ability to sell secondary rights to other publications.

However, the companies named in the lawsuit began selling freelance-written material to electronic databases such as Lexis/Nexis without any additional compensation or the purchase of electronic rights from the original authors. Some even required authors to sign contracts granting them electronic rights retroactively.

Many writers fought back, and issued a group action lawsuit. They won, and the companies had to make back payments to the affected freelancers. The case was appealed, and the Court of Appeals upheld the original decision.

This makes the freelancing climate better for all of us: If no one had fought the system, any one of us could just as easily have had our rights ripped off. Notice that the companies named here are not small potatoes; they represent some of the biggest newspapers in the United States. Neither are they the only companies that have adopted this practice.

Since writers work in isolation, it's very important to talk to other writers and report unfair practices to writers' groups and organizations.

This is why you may get some flak from writers for working for nothing. It lets editors know that it's not essential to pay for our words, which may devalue the work of a professional writer.

But there's also the practical matter for you: "If you're writing for places that pay $25, you'll have to work a tremendous amount of hours to put food on the table," says Bobbi Dempsey, who writes for the likes of *Redbook* and *Muscle Media*. "This will leave you no time to even think about approaching bigger markets. As I like to say, 'If you spend all your time eating low-hanging fruit, you won't have a chance to climb the tree and get a better view.'"

So What Do I Do?

I know. It's a dilemma, and one you'll have to think through on an individual basis, depending on the magazine and the assignment. What I offer you is simply my own policy: When I feel it's reasonable and provides a benefit for me, I do it, and when it feels like a drain, I don't. In earlier parts of my career, I did some spec writing on editors' requests. I regretted it once, because the editor never responded to my article, even after repeated reminders (that's why I now advise the "two-week response" agreement). That was the only wasted effort; the others paid off.

To break into and survive in the freelance writing world, you do need to find a way to build your credits and experience so those bigger markets will take you seriously. Sometimes that entails free and spec work. It's up to you to decide if you'd prefer to hold out for payment or go for the credit-only assignments in the beginning. Either way, I promise to respect you!

On Standing Your Ground

Earlier in this book, I mentioned that I had submitted a reprint to several bridal magazines. Yesterday, *Contemporary Bride* called me. They wanted to use the article in their January issue. I was thrilled—right until the publisher said, "We don't pay for articles. I just wanted to make sure we're on the same page."

"Uh, no, we're not," I said. "I am a professional writer, so I do need to get paid."

"Well, there are other advantages. We'll run your bio," he started.

But, no. *Contemporary Bride* is not a nonprofit magazine, nor a tiny, no-budget operation. It's a beautiful glossy magazine with plenty of advertisers. I knew they could afford to pay me, and I knew I wasn't letting them get away with feeding me a line about the great exposure.

We wound up negotiating a price. A small price, mind you, but a price nonetheless. And it was a reprint, so it was a quick buck. By the end of the conversation, he had asked me to send him more reprints whenever they became available, and I had myself a new potential regular market.

On the other hand, an editor at a small web site for writers asked me for a reprint once, and I didn't think twice about payment. I knew the bio would be valuable to me: I could plug this book, for example! And I knew she couldn't afford to pay me. So it was a very cool surprise when she offered up a barter: She said she'd send me a homemade candle if I let her use the article. It reminded me of the time freelance writer Madonna Dries Christensen got paid for an article with three jars of honey. Money's great, but bartering is fun, too.

"I Am an Asset"

I was working part-time as a film publicist when I was offered a major editing job at a magazine. I explained the situation to my producer, who said he'd counter their offer because, in his words, "You are an asset and we don't want to share you."

I'd thought about it before, but it wasn't until I heard those words that the full impact of writing as a business set in for me.

You are not a desperate writer trying to hock your words at a five and dime. If you're good at what you do, and knowledgeable about the publishing industry, then you are a valuable asset to the companies who hire you.

Your work is a product. It has inherent value to the markets that run it. It's your job to sell that product. It's not personal, it's business, and you should earn an appropriate wage in proportion to the value of the product and the rights granted.

Magazines make money off of advertisers and subscribers. With no articles, no one in their right mind would subscribe, and, in turn, no one would advertise. Magazines need writers, desperately, so they can attract and hold onto subscribers. They need good-quality writers who will be consistently interesting enough to warrant precious minutes of readers' busy lives.

If that's you, then *you are an asset.*

The magazine will be paid by the advertisers and the subscribers.

The printer will be paid.

The editor will be paid.

The design team will be paid.

The post office will be paid.

Why shouldn't the writer?

Once you've done a few "practice runs" and sold your work for little-to-nothing, just to get a sense of the business, it's time to get your hard hat on and become a militant negotiator. There is just one rule to negotiating for a better contract: ALWAYS ASK FOR MORE.

Here's what you want:

➤ The most money possible

➤ The fewest rights sold

➤ Payment on acceptance

➤ A bio

➤ A high kill fee

➤ A reasonable deadline

➤ Another assignment

How will you get these things? Simple: You'll ask. You probably won't get all of them, but you can use each one as a negotiating point. If an editor says she can't pay you as much as you'd like, then you should be able to negotiate for fewer rights or more prompt payment. Negotiating for your work, as in every other area of life, is about compromise. You give, they give, and eventually, you come up with a deal that's satisfactory to both of you.

When I began freelancing, I was too much of a chicken to ask for anything. The editor would tell me the terms, and I would say, "Okay! Thanks! I'll get right on it!" One day, after reading yet another article from a professional writer who urged neophytes to work on the skill of negotiating, I decided to do it one small step at a time.

I had just received a second assignment from a publication I liked. The editor was friendly, and it was a national publication. The first contract was a writer's nightmare: all rights, low pay, and payment on publication.

This time, when she offered the assignment, I said, "I'd love to. Can we work a bit on the contract this time to stipulate first rights instead of all rights?"

To my great surprise, she didn't argue at all. She just faxed over a new contract with the amended clause.

It made me realize that she'd gotten away with something the first time: that if I'd just made the effort to ask, I would have kept the right to reprint that first article, too. Because I was a chicken, I lost out on several potential paychecks from resales of that article. This time, I didn't make that mistake. All I did was ask.

This opened a new door for me. If it was that easy to get better terms for retaining my copyright, maybe it wouldn't be so hard to ask for more money, or prompt payment.

That's when I set a new goal: No matter what the editor initially proposed, I would ask for 25 percent more.

Here's the shocker: In every case except for one, I got exactly what I asked for. And in that final case, I did manage about an 8 percent raise above what was initially proposed.

"If you take $1 a word, they'll pay you $1 a word," says Kristen Kemp, freelancer for magazines such as *Seventeen* and *Glamour*. "I won't write for any major people for less than $2 a word. They never say 'no.' If they need something, they need something."

Editors *expect* you to negotiate. They plan for you to ask for more, so their first figure is usually a lowball: a jumping-off point. It's up to you to call their bluff, figure out what they can really afford, and go after it.

If an editor won't budge on price, don't be discouraged. Do whatever you can to ensure a better contract, in any of the areas I mentioned, or more.

For example, if you write for a web site, and they can pay only a minimal amount, trade off for more exposure: Get them to give you a free two- or three-line ad in their newsletter, or a small banner ad for your web site.

Remember: You are an asset. Treat yourself and your work as such.

Militant Negotiating

Now comes practice time.

An editor calls you on the phone, hot for the idea you pitched in yesterday's e-query. It's a mid-sized market. Here's the phone call. Fill in the blanks with your responses.

> **She says: Hi, this is Madge from Mid-Sized Magazine. I'm calling regarding your query about throwing a creative birthday party for pre-teens. I like the idea and would like to assign it for our May issue.**
>
> **1. You say:** _____
>
> **She says: Okay. We'll need about an 800-word piece, and we buy all rights.**

2. You say: _____

She says: **We'll pay you 20 cents a word, on publication.**

3. You say: _____

She says: **When can you have it ready?**

4. You say: _____

She says: **You can send it via email, and a hard copy with your invoice. Any questions?**

5. You say: _____

She says: **Can you provide photos?**

6. You say: _____

She says: **Okay, so I'll expect your article on the 15th. Any other questions?**

7. You say: _____

Score yourself!

For each response in which you strengthened your negotiating position, give yourself a point.

How Did Your Answers Stack Up?

Response 1. You are now at the most powerful point of negotiations: You've just learned that the editor wants to buy your piece. How do you react? Yes, it's fine—and even preferable—to show a little enthusiasm here. "Great! I'm so happy to hear that" is a fine response. So is, "Thanks. I was hoping to hear from you." The only responses to avoid at this point are the ones that sound overeager, desperate, pathetic, or unprofessional. Under no circumstances should you use this moment to announce, "Yay! This is my first sale!" or "Thank God! That query was rejected all over town—I was wondering what I did wrong," or "Man, it took you so long to respond that I was figuring you'd rejected me." It's not the time for small talk, nor is it the time to start negotiating. Wait for her to propose the terms first. Then move in for the kill.

Response 2. "All rights" is a swear word. This is the very first thing you want to hack out of there; however, you don't have much to negotiate with yet, since they haven't offered a price. You might say, "800 words sounds fine, but I don't typically sell all rights. Can we agree to first North American serial rights or exclusive rights in your market/state only?" If you'd rather, you can wait for her to announce a price first, or you can make a statement like, "I don't generally sell all rights, but it depends on the fee. What are you proposing?" If she's hesitant about the "all rights" policy, offer to sign a limited non-compete clause (preventing you from reselling the piece to any direct competitors, who should be listed in the contract). If she says she'll have to talk it over with someone, the conversation ends there. You say, "Okay, great. I'm looking forward to speaking with you as soon as you've spoken to so-and-so." Don't keep going with terms, because then the editor will believe that you're not serious about retaining your rights; she'll think that you're going to do this assignment regardless of whether or not she ever speaks to so-and-so about changing the terms. Even if it's true, don't let it show. Let her think you and your article could walk away—straight to a competitor's arms—if she doesn't try to fulfill your terms.

Response 3. Twenty cents a word isn't thrilling. An 800-word piece will earn you $160 in this case. Is it worth it? How much research will you put in? Will you have expenses? Mention these things. "Well, considering that this piece will require me to interview several subjects in different states, can we agree to 35 cents a word?" Or, you can try, "I'm willing to do it for 20 cents a word" (or 25, or 30, or whatever you think is fair) "if you'll agree to first rights and payment of phone expenses."

Response 4. The proper response here is, "When do you need it?" Asking you to set your own deadline is a double-edged sword. If your answer is too soon, it'll appear that you either (a) do a rushed job, or (b) the article is so simple that it doesn't warrant high pay. If the answer is too late, it'll appear that you can't fit in with the magazine's fast turnaround time. Just let the editor talk on this one. If she really won't commit, try to figure out approximately how much time you'll need. Take into account, if you need to do interviews, that people may be on vacation or otherwise busy for several days, that people may wish to send you material in the mail to supplement their interviews, and that you may have to ask follow-up questions after you've written a draft.

Also keep your research time in mind, and the time it will take to get feedback and edit. Then add a few days to that time to be sure you can deliver on time. My general rule of thumb: For first-person essays and short articles, I propose two weeks. I know I can deliver within a few days if necessary, but if the editor doesn't care, two weeks gives me plenty of breathing room. For feature articles or pieces requiring heavy research, I usually propose a month, and I won't accept less than three weeks (because I know what it's like to have to wait for returned phone calls, and email).

Finally, if the editor proposes a deadline you can easily beat, say so. Use this to negotiate other points. "I can have it to you two weeks earlier if you'll work with me a bit about your payment schedule." No matter what terms are agreed upon, stick to them. Miss a deadline, and you can kiss the next assignment goodbye. Don't make the editor stick her butt on the line for you. It's your job to make the editor look good.

Response 5. Time for some specific questions. You want to know: Does she want it as an email attachment, or pasted within the body of an email? If an attachment, what program? (Microsoft Word is the most standard, but some will request plain text or .rtf files.) Should you send it to her email address only, or should you send copies to anyone else? Do they have a style sheet? (A style sheet will tell you the magazine's preferred way of handling things like serial commas, whether they want the "I" in the word "internet" capitalized or lowercase, whether they want your article double- or single-spaced, and if there are any words or phrases that are taboo.) If not, ask how they would like you to handle punctuation and other textual markings such as italics, underscores, long dashes, bullets, and sidebars. Most publications have their own way of marking emphasized words, as the italic and underscored fonts don't always translate properly when your article is sent off to the printer. Some will ask you to put asterisks or other symbols around emphasized words.

You can, of course, study the heck out of the magazine to learn most of these things, but it's easier if they give you a style sheet. And, yes, you will score extra big brownie points for getting it all right, though a couple of mistakes won't wreck your chances of writing for them again. I failed to notice that *Prevention* used first names when repeating someone's name in an article (so I spent a whole article calling my subject Brimhall instead of Brit), and that they didn't use periods in M.D. or Ph.D. Did my editor freak? Of course not, but I did miss a chance to be teacher's pet by getting it all perfect.

Response 6. You say, "Yes." It's quite simple. *If* they'll pay you extra, then you most certainly can take photos, or find someone who can. If you aren't going to meet your subject in person, ask him or her for any sharp pictures you can have. If you don't have a good camera, or a good eye, then subcontract this work to a photographer. You can keep a percentage of the money for the photograph, since you got him the job. If the pay is very low, you can find a stock photography service that will allow you to use photographs they already have in their catalogue. Many of these services offer a surprising variety of subjects. If they tell you they won't pay extra, then at least require that they pay for your expenses in buying the film and developing the roll.

Questions to ask: Black and white? Color? Digital? (If so, what resolution?) What subject/s would they prefer? If your photos will feature people, do they have a standard model's release they'd like you to use?

Response 7. Now is your chance to clear up any questions you may have about the focus of your article, the tone, where it will appear in the magazine, etc. It is also your time to thank the editor for the assignment and express your enthusiasm to work with her again. Finally, it is your time to ask for a written contract.

Negotiating does get easier as you get more experienced, but do your best to secure the best possible terms for yourself even on your first assignment.

Ready, Set, Go!

The art of writing is the art of applying the seat of the pants
to the seat of the chair.

— Mary Heaton Vosse

So, you've negotiated your contract, have your due date, and are wondering what to do next? Well, get writing, silly!

It's fantastic to show an editor that you can meet or beat deadlines, so get to work as soon as possible. But, don't turn in that piece too early. If you're so overeager that you finish your article the day after it's assigned, you probably haven't given yourself enough time to be objective: to look back over the piece, edit, check and re-check for typos, and maybe even get some feedback.

So, even if you do complete your article draft right away, resist the urge to mail it out. Hang onto it for a few days. The difference between good writers and great writers is often found between the words "first draft" and "final draft." Great writers are great rewriters. Great writers have the humility to know that they aren't so brilliant that perfect prose drops out of their brain on the first try. They're also patient enough to keep tweaking until there's nothing left to tweak.

When you are ready to submit your article, check for a few things. If you're dealing with a caveman editor who still wants your work in hard copy, be sure your manuscript is in standard format: double-spaced, with the title, your name, social security number, and word count on top. Word count should be rounded to the nearest unit of 10. (Word count is generally in the top right corner, and the rest of it is in the top left.) Each page should have a number, and any sidebars should be included on a separate page. At the end of the article, type this on a new line:

-30-

That signifies the end of your article.

In addition to your hard copy, it's a nice idea also to submit a copy of your work on disk so it doesn't have to be retyped.

Most editors these days don't require a hard copy at all. You can just email that article straight to the editor, followed up by an e-invoice. Be sure to check first to make sure that format is acceptable, and if so, find out how your editor wants you to send the article: as an attachment or pasted into the body of the email. If she wants it in the body of an email, forget about trying to double-space and indent. The formatting will never hold up. Just single-space it and put a blank line in between paragraphs. If you send it as an attachment, stick to the standard formatting rules.

Also, remember to send a source sheet. What's that, you ask? It's a compilation of any notes you've taken from interviews or research. Most major mags have fact-checkers who must go through your article with a fine-toothed comb to be sure that the magazine isn't going to get sued for misinformation. Therefore, if you're going to quote people, you must include their credentials and contact information in your source sheet.

You don't always need to neatly type every word of every interview you do. Some magazines—usually the bigger markets—will insist that you send a typewritten transcript of every interview and piece of documentation you've used. Some don't want any of this paperwork, but prefer a short list of sources and attributions. Again, be sure to know in advance to avoid a hassle later.

Prevention and *Physical*, for example, want all articles to be footnoted, including a source for every fact. You must include experts' contact information, plus full citations for any printed material you used in your research. Then you must compile the materials you listed in your footnotes: photocopies of medical journal articles, interview transcripts, correspondence with experts, print-outs of web pages, etc., and mail them in with your article.

I do tend to type out all of my transcripts even if the magazine doesn't ask for it, for two major reasons. First, you never know when you'll need a quotation you hadn't planned to use. Rather than fast-forwarding and rewinding and trying to find the exact spot where your expert told that anecdote about the couple she counseled in 1988, you can just scan your transcript. Second, you never know when you're going to find this interview relevant to a different article somewhere down the line.

If you're including photos of people, you need to include a signed model release form (a simple letter that states that the person in the picture is giving his/her permission to appear in the magazine). You can ask the editor for a copy of their standard model release form.

Finally, when you submit the article, now is the time to propose the next article. Strike while they're happy with you. In your cover letter, be sure to thank the editor for the assignment, and mention that you're enclosing a proposal for your next piece. Positive wording like this shows your self-confidence—go into this assuming that there will be a next piece. That's how regular contributors are born.

Chapter 12

VIEWS ON INTERVIEWS

Inside This Chapter

- **Phone, in person, or email?**
  - **Practicing beforehand**
- **Managing the conversation**

Before the Approach

It can be intimidating to call high-ranking "experts" to ask them to spend their time helping you with your article. But remember that experts and even celebrities are just people, too, and will likely be glad to hear from you.

Most professionals absolutely love to be interviewed, usually because it's free publicity and gives their work more credence (it was good enough to be mentioned in a magazine), sometimes because it's a personal honor to be considered an expert, and sometimes because they genuinely want to share what they've learned and help other people.

Before you approach experts, make sure you already have your questions mapped out, at least briefly. What exactly do you need to know from this person? What could this person tell you that no one else can? Avoid "yes" or "no" questions. Ask open-ended questions that could lead to lengthy responses chock full of great quotations. Also, have a synopsis of your planned article ready, so you can tell your experts what you're writing and how they can supplement your knowledge.

Making Contact

Get on the phone. Condense your idea into two to three sentences, so you can quickly explain yourself to whoever answers the phone.

"Hello. My name is Jenna, and I'm writing an article about the rise in vegetarianism among young women in Nevada for *Youth in Nevada Magazine*. I'm hoping Dr. Spuds would be willing to answer a few questions on this subject."

At this point, the secretary will say, "Please hold," and make you listen to elevator muzak while she summons the boss. Or she'll take down your number and have Dr. Spuds call you back. Or it will be Dr. Spuds herself, and she'll say, "What do you want to know?"

You have a few options at this point. You could: ask questions over the phone, right then and there (make sure you check to make sure your expert is not pressed for time before you begin); set up a "phone date" to conduct the interview; or ask if you can meet in person. A face-to-face interview is good—almost necessary—if the person will be the focus of your article. If the person is being used just to add a few quotations, you don't have to meet in person, because it's unlikely you'll ever need to write, "Dr. Spuds wrinkled her brow and stared into her pea soup as she explained that young women are becoming more health-conscious."

Whether you conduct the interview on the phone or in person, it's a good idea to send over at least a barebones idea of your line of questioning. Email or fax your expert a list of questions or topics before your planned interview date so she can think about her answers. This way, your expert will be prepared, and may even notice something you've omitted before you make a final list of questions.

Another interview option is to trade email addresses and send over a list of questions. This approach isn't usually the best, because it doesn't allow you to react to, and build from, information you gain in answers to previous questions. However, if the publication will not reimburse you for long-distance phone calls and you have to conduct a lengthy interview, email or chat room exchanges are usually acceptable.

Other cases may also justify an email interview. For example, I recently needed to interview a dairy scientist for an article about a nutritional supplement. I needed to ask only a few short questions, and most of the questions were just verifying facts I'd already read elsewhere; I wasn't looking for juicy quotations. Could I have done it by phone? Sure, but it was more expedient just to zip him the questions by email rather than setting up a phone interview, recording it, and transcribing it.

Sites to See

If you prefer digging around the Internet, try www.whorepresents.com (that's "Who Represents"), which will give you agents, managers, and publicists for lots of actors. At www.imdb.com (The Internet Movie Database), you can look up the actor's name, then scroll down to the link marked "agent."

> **Sneaky Secret**
>
> *When writing a letter to the celebrity's agent/manager/whomever, hand-write the envelope and mark it "confidential" or "private." It is more likely to be opened by the right person this way. Otherwise, it will often be trashed as "fan mail" by a secretary or other gatekeeper.*

If you're going the email route, make sure you specify a due date for the responses. Be reasonable: Try to give the expert a week to answer all your questions. At the same time, be sure you'll have enough time to integrate the quotations into your article (and send follow-up questions if necessary).

Celebrities

Don't ever query a magazine with a letter saying you'd like to interview a particular celebrity. That is, not unless you know that celebrity and are already sure he or she will agree to an interview. The kinds of magazines that can command big celebrity interviews aren't about to hand over a risky assignment like that to an unknown writer.

If you have a very specific reason to interview a particular celebrity, or you just can't live with knowing you never tried, then go ahead and give it a shot—but try to line up the interview yourself.

Looking for an actor? Use the Screen Actor's Guild hotline (323-549-6737) to locate his or her agent. You can call this phone number, and, without question, the person on the other end of the line will give you the name and phone number of the agency that represents your celebrity.

If you're looking for a famous author, write to the author's most recent publishing house. If you're looking for a musician, write to the record company's publicity department.

Go through whatever channel you can think of: Find your celebrity's agent, public relations manager, secretary, or fan club president, then write an impassioned letter explaining *why* you simply must interview him or her. It's not good enough to request an interview. There must be a specific reason why you think that celebrity would be the perfect person to speak to about a certain topic for a certain magazine. Mention which magazine you plan to pitch to, and summarize your credits and qualifications.

Celebrities' careers hinge on publicity, so if you can convince them that you can offer good press, you might just score.

Practicing for Interviews

One of the reasons I write is because typing doesn't make me blush. Speaking, however, does. If I can conduct interviews (and I do, all the time), then you sure as heck can, too.

To practice, enlist the help of a friend. Pick a topic in your friend's life that you know very little about, such as a trip she took before you met, a hobby you don't share, or something specific about her job.

Now, make up a topic you might write about, using your friend as your key expert. (Example: "Work-at-Home Moms: How do they do it?") With this topic in mind, think through the information you'd need to write this article effectively. How can this person enhance your article? Ask yourself these basic questions before you write this interview:

- ➤ **WHO** is this person? What is he/she known for? General stats: job title and company, other relevant info (age, credentials, family, background information).
- ➤ **WHAT** has this person done that's relevant to my topic? What can the readers and I learn from this person? What is remarkable about this person's experience?
- ➤ **WHERE** is the person from? Where is the company/school/organization he or she represents?
- ➤ **WHEN** did this person start doing what he or she is doing? How long does the project/program/job/event last?
- ➤ **WHY** is this person unique? Why is he or she the person I'm interviewing for this particular market, audience, and article?

You may want to have a rough outline of your article completed ahead of time so you know what topics you'll need to cover in the interview and where your own research is coming up short.

Establish a time to conduct the interview, and make sure she understands that this is going to be a serious conversation. Tell her approximately how much time you'll need. You may choose to email or fax her a short list of questions—an approximation of what you will ask—but leave out any particularly personal or probing questions, because you don't want her to "rehearse" answers for those. She's more likely to censor herself and give you canned answers, and when you're looking for something juicy, it's far better to get off-the-cuff responses.

Make sure to have a pen and paper nearby when you call. Pretend she's a total stranger. Remind her who you are and for which magazine you write. Ask if she is ready to speak to you. Then ask away, and take careful notes as you go. Don't be afraid to ask her to slow down or repeat something; if you can't ask your friend, how are you going to ask a stranger?

You may notice how difficult it is to jot down every word of the conversation. Do your best quickly to scrawl all major points and beats of the conversation. If the interview is in person, get a pocket recorder.

If you plan to be a professional freelance writer, you should also get a phone recorder. I have had a Sony Cassette Corder TCM-929 for several years, and it has never failed me.

Most states require permission from your interviewees in order to tape them. The best way to attain this is to ask first, then press "record," then ask the subject to state his or her name and confirm that he is aware you are taping the conversation.

Even when you use a recorder, be sure to take notes. Tapes get eaten, batteries run out, and machines malfunction. Your notebook and pen should be much more dependable.

Freelance writer and editor Karen Roman suggests, "Counter as many replies as you can with 'how?' How did they decide on that location? How is it that a particular event took place at that point in time; what events led up to it? This gives the interviewee a chance to recall anecdotes related to the subject, which in turn will give great quotes and breathe life into your article."

Remember that you, as the interviewer, are in charge of leading this interview where you want it to go. If it helps, you might want to pretend you're Barbara Walters or Diane Sawyer, or even a talk show host, and recall how they keep their interviews flowing. If a question isn't properly answered, they ask it again until they're satisfied. If a subject is going off onto a pointless tangent, they direct the person back to the subject.

Now for one of the most valuable uses for interviews: verifying facts. One of the tenets of good journalism is that you must do primary research. What that means is that you can't regurgitate things you read in other magazines, books, on the Web, and so on. Primary research means you've based your story on interviews you've conducted and/or events you've witnessed, company memos you've seen, speeches you've heard or read, and so on. Articles in peer-reviewed professional journals are also acceptable sources.

You can't tell readers that Madonna said, "I plan to have 18 more children" unless you heard her say that yourself. If, instead, you read that quotation elsewhere and you simply must use it, then you must attribute it to the source. That is, you could write, "As reported in *XYZ Magazine*, Madonna said she planned to have 18 more children."

The same goes for "facts" that may or may not be facts. It is a fact that there are 12 inches in a foot, so you don't have to tell us that such-and-such encyclopedia said so. But what about that "fact" you read in a book that said 75 percent of all men cheat on their girlfriends? Can you personally prove that fact? Is it common knowledge? No? Then either find the study the author was quoting (preferable) and directly quote the study, or at least quote the book and author, as in, "In *Why Men Stink*, Jane Haugenblatt says that 75 percent of men cheat on their girlfriends."

Or do it a little better. Ask your interviewees.

You might just interview Jane Haugenblatt herself and get her to say it to you directly so it becomes a primary source, or, if she's not available or you don't feel like talking to her, ask another "expert." Maybe you're interviewing a relationships counselor for this article. You might say, "I read elsewhere that 75 percent of men cheat on their girlfriends. Would you say this is accurate?" Or, if you want to elicit original quotations from her on the matter, ask, "In your experience, what percentage of men cheat on their girlfriends and why?"

She might just rattle off a figure, she might quote other studies, or she might not want to be tied down to a figure, in which case you can always go back to attributing the quote to good ol' Jane and her book. You must include the title of the book, by the way. You can't say that Jane said such-and-such, because again, she didn't say it directly to you, and you're misleading the editor and your readers into thinking she did if you fail to mention *where* she said it.

Chandra Czape, deputy articles editor at *Ladies' Home Journal*, remembers a very good article that fell apart in fact-checking. The writer had based most of the article on things she read in various newspapers. "It was impossible for us to find what the original sources were. We spent a lot of time digging through that because it read really well—that's what was so upsetting about it. When the fact checker was trying to research it, she came up empty on so many different points. That writer is not going to write any more fact-based stories for us."

Interviewees can confirm or negate any of your non-primary research, so don't be afraid to ask "stupid" questions. Sure, you want your expert to realize that you've already done your homework and aren't completely clueless about the subject matter. However, you also have to make sure you have your facts straight, and you need quotations from them.

Let's say I'm doing an article about agoraphobia. I was agoraphobic for several years and I know darn well what agoraphobia is. Despite this, magazines won't consider me an expert on this subject and I won't be allowed to give my own definition of agoraphobia for the readers. So I'll probably ask a mental health professional, "What is agoraphobia?" Then I can give the definition and attribute it to an expert, whether I note this attribution in my article or paraphrase it and footnote it for the editorial staff's eyes only.

If I want this professional to know that I'm not clueless, I might preface the line of questioning with something like, "I'm going to ask you some basic questions, and I don't want you to think I haven't done my homework—I do know the answers to these questions, but I need your take on them/I'm looking for answers in your own words/I need to verify my research with you."

Remember that dairy scientist I mentioned a few pages ago? I had read extensively about how cows who feed on grass produce more healthful milk than those who eat grain and conserved forages. I had some stats that I thought were accurate, and I wanted to run them by him so I could attribute those facts to him in my footnotes, rather than having to attribute them to non-primary sources within the article itself, which tends to slow down a read if you do it more than once or twice in an article. Mostly, he just told me that everything I read was accurate. He was the scientist who had conducted most of the studies that others in my research were referencing anyway, so he was a perfect person to give the "yea" or "nay."

But he also corrected me on one or two points, and gave me further information that I hadn't even considered. I found myself strangely fascinated by his research, and wound up coming up with a spin-off article based on his tangents. His research was supposed to be only a small paragraph in an article I was writing about a nutritional supplement, but he gave me an idea for a brand new feature article about grass-fed cows and how their milk and meat are better for us than feedlot animals—and how grass-feeding is more humane for the animals themselves.

Managing the Conversation

There's a big difference between letting an interviewee ramble about nothing in particular and letting him talk about a possibly interesting tangent. When you catch him doing the former, gently and politely steer him back on track, and if all else fails, say, "That's a great story and I hate to rush you, but I have another interview scheduled in 10 minutes." The second case, however, is stopping to smell the flowers along the path. Maybe he'll steer you in a new direction for this article, or maybe he'll inspire your next article (or 10).

One more possible interviewing pitfall: Not all interviewees are good speakers. And I don't just mean that they may not be eloquent; I mean they (a) may mumble, have thick accents, speak too quickly, or have speech impediments, or (b) may clam up and not give you any useful information at all.

I have learned the hard way to speak up about situation A. I conducted a lengthy and terrific interview with a researcher who dropped all of his sentences. Each sentence would start out at a normal volume, lose steam around the middle, and completely peter out at the end, like so: "Well, when we were researching the carcinogens in hammbu me gr mmmmmmmm." I knew he was doing this, and I was struggling to hear him on the phone. Although I was able to make out almost everything he said, somewhere in my head, I was thinking, "This is going to be a nightmare to transcribe."

And, oh, it was. The tape recorder wasn't as good a listener as I was, and it didn't pick up about one-fifth of his words. As I was transcribing, I had to keep writing "inaudible" in important spots. I knew I couldn't turn that in, so I emailed this researcher and showed him all of the "inaudibles" that mattered and asked him to fill in the gaps. Lucky for me, he did, in a timely manner. But had I not been so lucky, that might have been a wasted interview. Don't let that happen to you. If you can't understand what an interviewee is saying, speak up. Tell him to speak louder, slower, or repeat himself as often as you must. Remember that a tape recorder may not be as clear as you hope.

Other people just get nervous when they're being interviewed, or might be rushed, having a bad day, are generally shy, or any other number of reasons why they might give you quick, unquotable responses to your wonderfully probing questions. In these cases, I usually give the person another shot by email before giving up. I might write, "Thanks so much for the interview. As I was looking back on my notes, I realized there were some spots that needed expanding. Could you tell me a little more about X?" If this fails, it's time to move on to a new interviewee.

When you're doing the interview with your friend, remember to practice speaking up to her, too. If she's mumbling or not giving you helpful answers, this is a great excuse to get some confidence in interrupting and helping your subject to be a better interviewee.

At the end, thank her for her time and let her know that you may need to call back at a later time for clarification or to verify quotations. Assure her that she can call you back if she thinks of anything else she'd like to add.

Once you've done the interview, go ahead and write a draft of the article. See how you can intersperse the quotations and use them within the structure

---

Quoting From Press Releases

Some writers use quotations directly from press releases. This is not illegal; those who write press releases do so in the hopes that people will quote from them. But most editors will be furious if they find out you've done so.

Editors want you to use press releases as background; learn what you can from them, then conduct interviews to get fresh quotations for their magazines. Aside from the fact that quotations in press releases are usually rehearsed statements, you risk that lazy or time-pressed journalists all over the place will use those same quotations in their stories. Editors don't want their readers to find quotations in their magazine that their readers have already read elsewhere.

of your piece. You may even find that your interviewee's words help you to structure your article. I had planned an entirely different lead for an article before that mumbling researcher drew me a mental picture about fat loss that was perfect for the magazine's readers.

Careful of Over-Quoting

You don't need to literally put in quotation marks every idea of your friend's you may use. In fact, if you're using every word, you probably haven't done enough work.

When I write an article, I typically use about 10–20 percent of my interview notes, and pieces from about half of my research material. Sometimes a particular interview will produce only one usable quotation, even if the interview was 45 minutes long. If you try to cram in everything you have on any particular topic, you're going to have a very messy, stuffed-to-the-gills article that will be difficult to read.

A reader needs transitions. She needs "breather" sentences. When you have a lot of quotations, facts, statistics, or information, it's important to break it up into organized sections, with sentences that lead the reader comfortably from one thought to another. Otherwise, a reader may get bogged down and lose track of your overall themes and points.

Take a look at this example and see how you could rework it. (This is an excerpt from the first draft of an article I wrote for *Adaptz*, explaining why people with Down syndrome are denied heart transplants.)

> **"I am greatly concerned about Dr. Radley-Smith's ability to gauge quality of life," says Dr. Len Leshin, a pediatrician in Texas who specializes in Down syndrome health issues. "I understand the concern about organ shortages, but granting transplants should be based on who would most likely tolerate the operation better . . . Once you get into measuring quality of life, then you are one step away from deciding between a famous athlete and an obscure mother of two children. It's a dangerous ethical matter."**

> **Dr. James B. Young of the Cleveland Clinic Foundation raises the most frequent argument for exclusion: "Down's patients range widely in their independence, compliance with treatment recommendations, and educability. Some may be excellent transplant candidates; most will not because of these later issues." Indeed, adherence to strict post-operative regimens and medications are an important factor in a successful transplant. However, this does not explain how infants and children are often transplant recipients. To this, Dr. Young responds, "Children have the potential and**

> **probability to end up taking care of themselves; in some Down's cases this might be likely, but in most, unfortunately, it will not."**

This excerpt is very quotation-heavy, as was the entire first draft of this article. I had to go back and find ways to express the same sentiments accurately without such long stretches of quotations. How would you do it?

Here's how the final copy looked on this piece:

> **Whenever a medical decision is based on life value judgments, it is open to debate, says Dr. Len Leshin, a pediatrician in Texas specializing in Down syndrome health issues. Although he understands the concern about organ shortages, he believes granting transplants should be based on who would most likely tolerate the operation better. "Once you get into measuring quality of life," he warns, "you are one step away from deciding between a famous athlete and an obscure mother of two children."**

> **The most frequent argument cited for excluding a patient with Down syndrome is their inability to take responsibility for their own strict post-operative regimens and medications. However, given this criterion, how are non-handicapped infants and children ever transplant recipients? "Children have the potential and probability to end up taking care of themselves," says Dr. James B. Young of the Cleveland Clinic Foundation. "In some Down's cases this might be likely, but in most, unfortunately, it will not."**

Ask simple questions first, while you're building a rapport with your interviewee, then build to your juicier ones. Using whatever research you've drummed up about this person (from his bio, quotations in other articles, studies he's conducted, etc.), begin with the short facts: "How old are your children?" "What year did you start your business?" "Have you always lived in Atlanta?"

It's okay to share a bit about yourself, too, to help the subject feel comfortable with you. Remember that the interviewee is likely more nervous about how he'll come off in print than you are about asking the questions. The more you can put him at ease, the likelier it is that you'll get honest, candid answers. Strong interviews are often the backbone of strong articles, so make excuses to practice and hone your interviewing skills.

Chapter 13
ON BECOMING A FAVORITE FREELANCER

Inside This Chapter

- **After-assignment etiquette**
- **Getting the details right**
- **What editors really want**
- **Keeping editors interested**

Working With Editors

When I write for a magazine, my aim isn't to turn in an acceptable article. It's to thrill everyone in the whole office.

My first job, of course, is to thrill the assigning editor enough to hire me in the first place. But the assigning editor isn't always the same person who will actually work with me on the piece once it's in motion. Often at larger magazines the person assigning articles pretty much disappears after the contract is signed, and a different editor does the "grunt work" of helping me get the article in shape.

I have to thrill that editor, too. So let's say I already have the contract and have discussed the article with an editor named Joe at *Big Fat Magazine*. But now Joe has turned me over to another editor named Uma. If this is done right away, before I've written the piece, I now have a great opportunity to speak to Uma for further direction before I put in many hours of work on something she'll end up axing. So that's what I do: I email or call Uma and tell her I'm happy to be working with her, and want her input before I begin.

I'll run down everything that Joe told me he wanted and make sure it's the same material that Uma wants. If there's a discrepancy, Uma can take it up with Joe and they can decide together how they want the article handled. Then I'll ask Uma if there's anything else she'd like to add, or any other questions she'd like answered in the article.

Sometimes I'm not told about the second editor until after I've turned in the article: Sometimes I will email an article to the first editor and he'll write back, "Thanks, Jenna! I'm sending this to Uma and she'll be in touch with you soon with notes." In that case I must simply hope that both editors were on the same page and see what the notes look like when they come.

How Much Contact?

Now that I've emphasized a few times that you can and should talk to your editor to get notes about the focus and direction of your article, just how much should you be in contact with your editor from the time of assignment until the article is turned in?

Not much. "Editors love headache-free writers, so reassure them that you'll be a dream to work with. Don't be a pest, or demand constant hand-holding," says Bobbi Dempsey, who specializes in celebrity profiles.

Hand-holding means that you'll call on this editor every time something goes wrong, or every time you have a minor question. That's what you don't want to do. Solve all the problems you can on your own, and call on the editor only when you're really stuck. For example, if an interviewee backs out, don't trouble the editor with it unless you have no possible way of finding a new one on your own. And if you're way over word count, don't ask the editor if it's okay (unless you've worked with her several times already). Just cut it down and make it work. And if you didn't get a style sheet and don't know how to handle the serial comma, for goodness sake, just look in the magazine before bugging your editor about it.

"Last week I had 80-something stories in the works at one time," says Chandra Czape of *Ladies' Home Journal*. "That's a lot to juggle, so I can't have people emailing me, 'Oh, this therapist can't do it,' or 'This woman dropped out.' Fine, but just write me and tell me what your solution is as well, so I won't be surprised when the piece comes in. I don't want it to be my problem—I want you to take care of it, and tell me as quickly as possible."

One editor I spoke with told me about a very chatty writer who would email her several times a day to give her updates about how the article was going, what new information she found that day, when the article was coming, and so on. Now, think about it: If every writer did this, when would the editor actually have time to do her job?

When You SHOULD Contact the Editor

Although for many editors, the less contact you make, the happier they'll be, there will be times when you certainly should call the editor.

Clarification

If you get the assignment and don't understand something, ask the editor. For example, I received an email from an editor to accept a query of mine, but she asked me to write the article from the perspective of a newsletter editor. I was pretty sure she has just dashed off the email quickly and had really meant that I should write the article *for* newsletter editors, not necessarily writing in first-person *as* one myself, but rather than make assumptions, I wrote to check.

Likewise, one of my editors usually sends me a list of people to interview when she assigns a piece to me. Unfortunately, she tends to forget to tell me who these people are and why I'm interviewing them. Rather than playing guessing games, if I can't do a quick Google search to figure out why this person is relevant to my article, I have to ask my editor for clarification.

Ladies' Home Journal editor Chandra Czape says that a major pet peeve of hers is when a writer starts asking questions about her instructions the day before an assignment is due. When you get an assignment or a revise letter (also known as rewrite notes), the time to read it and figure out if there's anything you don't understand is within 24 hours of receipt. You will completely blow the editor's confidence if you call at the last minute to clarify what the editor wants from this article.

A Change of Direction

Call when you find something that might change the direction of your article. Let's say your assignment was to write an article about how married women are healthier than single women. But along the way, all of the research you turn up shows that married women visit doctors more, take more sick days, have more heart attacks, and so on. Now's the time to call your editor and tell her that a new angle may be in order. Of course, if you pitched the article in the first place, you are risking looking quite stupid (you should have done preliminary research before ever pitching it), but it's probably better than having the story fall apart in fact-checking right before it's scheduled to be published. If it was something that she assigned, she might have other research to show you, or she might be apt to let you take the other angle you've found.

Todd Raphael, online editor of *Workforce Management* magazine, says that his favorite freelancers are those who find new directions for assigned articles. He says that some of his best stories come from writers who have discovered things he hasn't thought of yet. "Maybe I'll say, 'Hey, I have this really great idea about Chili's restaurant,'" and they call you a week later and say, 'It was a good story, but as I was researching it, I heard this speech by the CFO that was really fascinating, and that could make an even better story for you guys.' They're not afraid to bring that up, and they were astute enough to find that hidden gem out there, yet it's still something that fits us."

Deadline Extensions

If you're going to be late for your deadline, *tell your editor*. I'm amazed by the number of editors who complain that freelance writers fail to meet deadlines. With all the competition out there, how could writers possibly not take their assignments seriously? Literally thousands of other writers are out there eager to take the place of any writer getting published, so how could anyone be so sloppy as to turn in an article late without permission?

This is an industry where days (and even hours) count, and jobs are on the line. When the editor-in-chief wants to know why there's a big gap in the layout on pages 27 and 28, the section editor who hired you is going to have some explaining to do. And there's no such thing as, "No big deal; we'll just run it next month." Issues are planned out months in advance, and usually it's not easy to swap one article for another, especially once the deadline has already passed. So if you know you need an extra day or two because of some legitimate emergency (and there are very, very few of those), you must warn your editor as far in advance as possible.

Although he remains cheerfully open to new writers, Bob Boze Bell of *True West* says that only about 10 percent of the writers he hires work out well. His most common complaint about the other 90 percent is that they miss their deadlines. Follow that with his other two complaints about writers: They're too long-winded and too whiny. "I don't have time for whiny," he says. "Doing is the best answer." But he's quick to talk about his favorite few writers, too, easily rattling off names of those who can "think on their feet," come up with great new ideas regularly, think of unusual angles, and turn in good work on schedule.

In close to seven years of freelancing, Kelly James-Enger, contributing editor at *Oxygen* and *For the Bride*, has never missed a deadline. In fact, she says, "I've only turned in an article on the day it was due twice. Every other time, I've turned it in early. Editors know that I'm anal about deadlines and that they can count on me."

When asked what their favorite freelancers do differently than other writers, every editor I interviewed mentioned meeting deadlines.

But let's say you run into a major problem: Your key interviewee is in the hospital. If you can't write the article without him, the time to call your editor is no more than five seconds after you find out this information. She may tell you to can the article, she may tell you that you must write it without him, or she may tell you that it's okay to wait it out an extra week to see if the interviewee will be able to speak with you. But don't put her in that position the day the article is due.

Some editors are more hands-on, however, and prefer to be contacted while you're working on the article. "I think I'm unusual in that regard," says Todd Raphael, online editor of *Workforce Management* magazine. "Throughout the process, I'm talking back and forth with the writer, saying, 'This is a good idea, that's not a good idea, here's who you should call, I have some ideas for you.' They run things by me and I run things by them." Todd says he loves it when writers call to discuss their work with him.

Asking your editor a few questions here or there is expected; just don't use the editor as a crutch, teacher, or mentor. That's not the editor's job. You're being paid to be the expert here. You should be able to get a feel quickly for which editors prefer to be more involved and which ones would rather not be contacted much.

I try to wait until I have at least two questions before firing off an email or call to my editor. That is, I don't want the editor to find a note from me in her inbox every day. I am respectful of her time and try to have all the important questions in a row before I contact her.

Stay on Track

If you want to become a favorite freelancer, make sure you always come through with what you've promised. While you're working on your article, go back and look at your contract or assignment sheet several times. What did the editor tell you to write? What did your query say you would write?

How closely have you delivered what the editor is expecting?

Look through your article and ask yourself this question: "Does every sentence directly relate to my article's focus?"

Did you throw in extra information? Did you fall into tangents? Steer yourself back on track. Every single sentence in your article should give the reader a better understanding of, and a new insight into, your topic.

Here is Everything I Know

Sometimes it's a real challenge to hold back from writing absolutely everything you know about a subject. Paring it down to its most interesting and relevant details takes practice. And, in my case, a day or two away from the material so I can return to it with a fresh eye.

Rather than try to impress your editor by how much research you did by cramming it all in there, think of your readers. Do they want to know absolutely everything, or would they rather have the abridged version with a little human interest and spice added?

Have you ever read a travel story (in a not-very-good-publication) where the writer began with the details of his trip to the airport, followed up by what he ate on the plane, who greeted him on the other side, what he thought of the rental car, which shops he visited . . . ? The writer was probably just trying to be thorough, but he lost track of the big picture: keeping the reader's interest. The writer has the responsibility to decide which are the most interesting parts of the article, then expand on those and leave out the boring stuff. Simple, right?

What Editors Love

When an editor compliments me on my work, in addition to the fact that my head swells a good three inches in diameter, I also pay careful attention: Exactly what is it that I've done right?

Accessibility

My former editor at *Writer's Digest*, Melanie Rigney, once wrote me a sweet note in response to an article I'd written for her. She told me that my writing was "accessible" even when I was writing heavily researched stuff.

I smiled, because I'd heard that same word to describe my writing just a few weeks prior from another editor. Accessible: Easy to read and understand. Not because my writing is "dumbed down," but rather, because it's conversational.

It takes some practice to learn how to present facts and research in a conversational manner. Rather than writing with your editor or a vast audience of readers in mind, it helps me to imagine I'm writing an email to a friend. A very well-thought out and organized email, mind you, but an email nonetheless. I imagine that my friend has asked me a question: "Jenna, I've been having so much fear about being around people and what they'll think of me. I hate being on display. It's really screwing up my life. Do you think this is normal or is there something wrong with me?"

I'll want to write back to her with compassion and hope. So, as I'm writing my article about social anxiety disorder, I'll want to tell her all about how there are many people out there who have the same problem, and that there are several ways to cure her problem through medication or therapy. I'll prove to her that these "cures" work by giving her examples of solid, recent research that backs up the claims. I'll share a story about someone else who felt just like she did and then got better. And then I'll tell her exactly what steps she can take right now to start feeling better.

In his article "Writing Effective Ad Copy" on AbsoluteWrite.com, Amrit Hallan wrote, "The reader is not interested in knowing what your product or service can do. He or she wants to know what all your product or service can do *for him or her*." Now, Amrit may have been talking about advertising, but the same principle applies to writing articles for magazines. Your words have to feel personal, not strictly informational.

Let's say you're writing an article for a magazine in Pennsylvania about new breast cancer research. It's all well and good to write, "According to researchers at the University of Delaware, this new procedure will reduce the mortality rate from breast cancer by 6 percent." But it's far better to write, "If researchers at the University of Delaware are right, 64 women in Pennsylvania who would have died from breast cancer this year will walk out of the hospital and get to watch their children and grandchildren grow up."

Make your story resonate with readers as much as possible. Make them understand how it relates to them.

Make a Dry Subject Fun

I was hired to write fishing tournament coverage for *World Billfish Series* magazine one year. I read examples of past tournament coverage on their web site, and was a bit dismayed to read how boring the articles were. The water was choppy. Weather conditions improved by mid-afternoon. So-and-so brought in a zillion-pound yellowfin tuna, which won the grand prize. Blah blah.

I decided to take a risk. I just couldn't summon the energy to write five or six articles that were this dry, so I took the chance of assuming that even die-hard fishermen just might have a sense of humor and might be interested in hearing more about personalities and stories behind the tournament rather than "just the facts, ma'am."

My first article began, "Those who remember last year's Long Island Marlin and Tuna Tournament have been offering sacrifices and shameless pleas to Mother Nature and King Neptune this week, determined not to see a rerun of last year's sloppy seas."

The next one began, "Do you suppose it's modesty or superstition? I asked most of the entrants to this weekend's Long Island Marlin and Tuna Tournament for their predictions about the outcome of the tournament, and not one replied that he expected to win. Maybe this is like the unspoken rule about not telling anyone your wish as you blow out the birthday candles if you want it to come true."

In that series, I told stories about the fisherman who showed up late to the captain's meeting because his pesky wife was in labor (in true fisherman style, he came to the meeting as soon as the kid popped out), the knot-tying instructor whose chum bucket sank because the knot came loose, and the way the winner "bled more than the shark" when he cut his hand open trying to get a look at the mako's teeth.

The editors went nuts. In a good way. They wanted to make sure I'd be back the following year, because no one had ever before made tournament coverage so entertaining. Find stories behind the stories. Surprise readers by making a fact-filled article entertaining.

Fact or Fiction?

Along these same lines, some of the best nonfiction articles read more like condensed novels. They are stuffed with sensory description and "scenes" to draw the reader into the story. We hear the "show, don't tell" rule for fiction, but many nonfiction writers overlook this. As often as possible, rather than lecturing your reader, show him. Work to let him get drawn into your story the same way you'd want him to get wrapped up in your novel or short fiction.

"Even in nonfiction/journalism we need to use conversation, anecdotes, details, examples to bring a story to life. It has to be concrete," said writing coach Jessica Page Morrell in an iVillage chat. "Even with nonfiction we write for ALL the senses."

This is especially true when writing articles about people's lives. If this is to be a profile of Fernando Lopez, don't tell us he's tall. Tell us he has to duck when he walks through the doorway. Use actions rather than adjectives whenever possible. You know the "actions speak louder than words" saying? How about "I'll believe it when I see it?" Witnessing (or reading about) a person's actions is much more powerful than hearing about the person's thoughts, ideas, and so on. So don't just tell us that Fernando is very involved with charities for children with cancer and won some fancy award; tell us about the time he volunteered to be a camp counselor and showed sick kids how to pitch tents and start campfires. Let us peek in on Fernando as he's roasting marshmallows and playing his guitar at a sing-a-long with kids who are fighting cancer.

Style

When I edited Writer Online, "You Can't Go Home Again Revisited" by Linda Moore Spencer was my absolute favorite piece. It contained this excerpt:

> **"So, it was in a small town in Utah or Ohio, in a dry spot in a conversation rife with arid patches, that I said, 'Oh by the way our family will appear with pictures in the September issue of *HOUSE BEAUTIFUL*.' There is no room for commas in a sentence of that size. 'I wrote about our house and all the men who left the women there. I think I might have even mentioned your divorce,' I tell my sister. She turns ashen."**

I think I accepted that article three years ago, and yet, that choice—the omission of the commas and the subsequent explanation of it—regularly pops into my mind as a shining example of personal writing style that works.

Depending on the piece, I may inject a running "joke" like many comedians do (coming back to the same quick punchline a few times until the audience feels like they're in on a personal joke). I may use short, staccato sentences and sentence fragments. I may use an extended metaphor, or use bullets and funny subheads.

It's important to make sure your format, structure, and tone match the magazine you're writing for, but that doesn't mean you must mimic every other writer it has published. Within the confines of the magazine's style, you can still have your own "voice," or writing style. Columnists, in particular, are encouraged to develop their own signature styles; it helps readers to remember them and become "fans." If sex writer Susie Bright's name were to be stripped off all of her columns, I'd still know it was she. Wherever she's gone—whether it's Salon.com or *Playboy* online, her blunt, colorfully humorous writing has followed.

If you have a particularly strong style, you, too, could be a columnist in the making. But know where to draw the line: When I write an article for Match.com, I have to remember that I'm writing a Match.com article, not a Jenna Glatzer article. That is, I am allowed to be creative and make style choices as long as it fits with the fashion at Match.com. Putting together a magazine is like putting together an outfit. Don't stick a pink feather boa on a business suit. Know what kind of "outfit" you're writing for, and let your article be a coordinating accessory.

Rewriting

When I asked Melissa Walker, editor at *ELLEgirl*, what kinds of writers she loves, she said, "Writers who pay attention to revise notes. Writers should always expect to do a revise (it's a happy, rare day when the first draft is approved at a big magazine), and they should do it with a good attitude. You are, after all, being paid to write and a revise is just part of the process. As a writer, I really appreciate careful and specific revise notes; as an editor, I appreciate careful attention to my specific revise notes."

Some editors at major magazines go even further than Melissa and say that first drafts are *never* approved outright. It just doesn't happen. There's always something to tweak, something an editor wants added or changed. So when you're playing with the big boys, go into it expecting to do at least one rewrite, and be willing to do more if needed. But what happens if a writer disagrees with some of the notes?

"Writers should never ignore a note because they disagree," says Melissa. "That's something to discuss with the editor, but not to ignore entirely."

And yes, indeed, you can discuss notes with your editor, but I advise you to pick your battles. Don't start a war over a comma placement or the deletion of a couple of words. But if the editor has misunderstood something or asked you to make a change that just doesn't make good sense, speak up. In a nice way. You know that cliché about attracting more flies with honey than vinegar? So it is with editors. Once an editor has given notes, there's always a certain amount of tension involved. If you haven't worked with this editor before, she doesn't know how you're going to react, especially if she's asked for big changes.

Start the conversation by relieving her fears and telling her that you are happy she spent time on this article and that you, too, want to make it the best it can possibly be. Then gently explain what it is that you disagree with and why. Sometimes it's simple enough; for example, one of my editors paraphrased an interviewee of mine in a way that was misleading. I explained to her why the paraphrase was wrong, and suggested an alternate phrasing. Problem solved. Sometimes it's a little trickier; the editor will want you to cut out a part of your article that you feel is essential, or add in something that you don't feel comfortable about adding.

Remember that it's up to you to offer solutions at this point, and that the last thing you want is to throw away all this hard work because of a disagreement. So approach the conversation with compromises and other ideas already in mind. If you can't stand the cut she made, ask her why she made it. For example, is it because she needed to trim the word count? If so, offer to cut something else instead. Is it because it wasn't clear enough? Offer to clarify it. Whatever it is, be willing to work with this editor and make her job easier.

Now let's say she wants you to add in something you can't bear to do. She wants you to add a paragraph or two into your parenting article about sending "troubled teens" to behavioral boot camps. You, on the other hand, are vehemently opposed to these boot camps and don't believe in using fear of authority and punishment as a way to teach teens right from wrong. Maybe you've even written your views about this issue before.

Your first option is to explain your position to the editor and hope she'll accept it. But if not, you must find another solution. One idea is to suggest that another writer (or editor) writes it up as a short sidebar, attributed to that person instead of you. You can't control what they do with the rest of their editorial, so as long as your byline's not on it, you don't need to feel responsible. Another is to mention those boot camps as an example of the extremes some parents go to, but ask her to allow you to present the case for why they're not a good idea.

Your final option is to walk away with a kill fee, which you might have to do if you truly feel you're being asked to write something that's unethical, false, or otherwise harmful. That's never happened to me; I've always been able to come to agreements with my editors.

You might just find that the rewrite notes you receive are actually good. You might discover that the editor has pointed out good ways to tighten up and strengthen your piece. In such cases, you can pleasantly shock the editor by expressing your gratitude. Tell her that you appreciate her notes and think she did a great job. That's what I did when an editor at *Conversely* gave me notes. He wanted a pretty big rewrite, but after I took a deep breath and read all of his suggestions, I realized how smart they were and how he was going to help me look like a better writer. The piece was much better because of it, and he helped me to grow as a writer. It was a nice treat, considering I was being paid to get this lesson.

Give genuine compliments wherever they are warranted. Did the art department do a beautiful job on your layout? Say so. Did a proofreader catch an embarrassing typo of yours? Thank her. Was the editor responsive and helpful throughout your assignment? Don't let these things go unnoticed. You might just make someone's day brighter by mentioning a job well done.

Your Friendly Fact-Checkers

Yes, fact-checkers do speak with editors. And if a fact-checker complains loudly enough that Writer X's article was full of holes, or that the source material was badly organized or unreliable, that editor might not hire Writer X again. In fact, the fact-checker doesn't even need to say a word: Your editor will see the fact-checker's copy, so if there are many cross-outs and corrections, you're probably in trouble.

And fact-checkers don't always stay where they are. Take Ted Moncrieff, for example, who started as a fact-checker for *Condé Nast Traveler* magazine and is now their senior editor. Cara Birnbaum was a fact-checker at *NJ Monthly* before becoming a senior editor at *Allure*. If you were Ted or Cara, don't you think you'd remember which writers made your job a nightmare and which ones made it a joy?

Marlinda Karo used to be a fact-checker at *Ms.* magazine, and she can tell you exactly whose work she wanted to read. "During my nine months at *Ms.*, the best freelance writer I came in contact with was Angela Bonavoglia. She was professional and had all of her materials together in an orderly fashion and working with her was a delight!"

Wouldn't you like to be Angela right now? You can make every fact-checker fall in love with you, just by using a few simple tools:

➢ **A highlighter.** It's likely you will turn in many pages of source material. Highlight the parts that you actually used in the article. Highlight the quotations you used from your interview transcripts, the studies you referenced, and so on.

➢ **A folder.** I imagine my fact-checkers smiling when they open my package to find that I've organized all of my source material into a pocketed folder. On one side is a print-out of my article, my contact information, and all of my interview transcripts; on the other side is the rest of my research material.

➤ **A pen.** Use that pen to write the numbers that correspond to your footnotes on your source material, and put your material in that pocketed folder in order. That is, if the first thing I referenced was a quotation from a book, then I'll photocopy that page from the book, write the number "1" on the upper left and circle it, and that'll be the first thing the fact-checker sees on the right side of the folder.

Give the fact-checker all the contact information you possibly can about your interviewees: address, home phone, work phone, fax, and email address if possible. You can even throw in a cell phone number if you have it.

Flexibility and Versatility

I'll never know for sure if one of my editors used me all the time because she loved my work, or because I would put up with her insane demands. She'd write to me at 4 a.m. desperately telling me she needed a piece in two days. And I'd do it. Yes, it meant all-nighters for me, and sometimes I would warn her that I wouldn't be available for these quickie assignments on a particular week when I had other pressing deadlines, but I never refused her. The pay per piece wasn't great, but considering how quickly I did them and how many assignments she gave me, I earned a lot of money from this editor and easily became her favorite.

"If someone could contribute, say, a great training article *and* a great breed profile *and* a great veterinary article, then that person would definitely be on our minds for assignments, because she (almost always 'she,' in the pet mags) had shown she could write on a variety of topics," says Moira Allen, former editor of *Dog World* and current editor of Writing-World.com. "Many, many authors are 'one-off' writers—they send in one good article or they have one subject area, but that's it."

She adds that anyone who could turn in well-written, solid, fact-packed articles that read well and weren't full of grammatical errors could very quickly and easily become one of her favorite writers.

Specializing

There's a flip side to Moira's point, too, however. Some writers become successful by showing they can handle any topic, whereas others build their reputations as the "go-to" people on specific topics.

You may choose a broad specialty, like finance, or smaller specialties within a larger category, like retirement plans, taxes, and mortgages. You may also have more than one specialty. Some editors know me as a health specialist, while others know me for specific areas of health, such as mental health or nutritional supplements. Other editors know me as a relationships specialist, and still others know me for my human interest stories.

"I have become more efficient as an article writer by using beats, just like journalists," says Meg Weaver, freelancer for magazines such as *Smithsonian*, *Popular Science*, and *The Atlantic Monthly*. One of Meg's beats is sleep. "Over the years, I've learned the basics. I no longer have to check references to understand terms such as REM sleep, sleep cycle, and even WC-1 and WC-2, the 'light-seeing' proteins. And, since it's a beat and not a narrow topic, I can write articles interesting to pretty much any audience."

A beat is any topic that has multiple article possibilities. Other examples could include diet, makeup, child discipline, contraceptives, or psychic phenomena. One writer I know has made it his beat to cover lesser-recognized behind-the-scenes aspects of the film industry. He's profiled makeup artists and set designers, for instance, and could interest a variety of trade and consumer magazines—the makeup artist could inspire a full feature article in a film trade publication, a quirky FOB piece for an entertainment magazine, a juicy tidbit for a gossip magazine, or a service piece for a women's or bridal magazine.

The key benefit of specializing is that editors will think of you when an idea is developed in-house. If an editor knows I specialize in writing about mental illnesses, and the magazine wants to run an article about schizophrenia, that editor will think, "Hey, this is a perfect article for Jenna Glatzer." And I'll get the call.

The other benefit is that it makes it easier to land the next assignment and the next, because it shows an editor that you're capable of writing well on that subject and that you have the necessary background knowledge to do the job. If I tried to pitch an article about sports to *Maxim*, I'd probably have a very hard time landing it because I have no track record writing about sports. But if I pitched them an article about obsessive-compulsive disorder, they'd take me seriously because I have built up an expertise on mental illnesses.

"If you want to establish yourself in a certain niche, pitch, write, research, study in that area," says writing instructor Jennifer Nelson, who's written for *Woman's Day*, *MORE*, and *Health*. "Start out wherever you can gain the clips on that topic and keep expanding. Before you know it, you'll have a body of work in that niche that will reflect your expertise."

You can mention your specialty or specialties in your bio (don't list more than two or three specialties at a time, and don't list specialties that are unrelated to the market you're pitching), or, sometimes an editor will ask you where you're most proficient. Sometimes, rather than running down a list, I'll tell an editor where I'm not proficient. For example, when a health magazine editor asked for my specialties, I told him I could cover anything not related to exercise. That is, I could handle general health, mental health, or nutrition, but forget me for any article about working out. The reason for this is twofold: First, I have no expertise in fitness, and second, I don't have enough interest in the topic to enjoy learning and writing about it.

Karen Asp, on the other hand, does. She advises, "Specialize in a topic you love. Then as you get the experience, you can broaden your writing. I've been a fitness fanatic since birth (and a fitness professional for the past ten years), so writing about fitness seemed a natural fit, pardon the pun. That background helped me land a spot at *Allure* as fitness columnist."

Once you have your foot in the door at a magazine, assuming you have a good experience working for them, aim to become a favorite freelancer. Do it by being reliable, accurate, nice, respectful of the editor's time, and by proposing plenty of new ideas with regularity. You can also let the editor know about any specialties you have and let him know you're available for assignments any time. You may think that's obvious to an editor, but it's not always; some writers prefer just to write articles they have proposed themselves.

When I've worked with an editor more than once, I try to keep myself fresh in her mind even when I don't have any new queries to send. I'll sometimes write notes such as, "Just checking in to see if there's anything I can do for you. I finished up my last batch of assignments today and have a relatively light schedule for the next two weeks, in case there's anything you'd like me to write." Or if I want to be less presumptuous, I might just ask, "Is there anything you need in particular? I'd love to send some new queries your way, and figured I'd ask if you're short on any topics or types of articles before I start researching."

Show the editor that you can make her job easier and that you're there for her whenever she needs you and she's likely to call on you again and again.

Chapter 14
PLAY NICE WITH YOUR EDITOR

Inside This Chapter

- **Getting personal with editors**
- **Making it to the masthead**
- **Perks of building relationships**

The Personal Touch

Earlier, I touched upon getting personal with editors. Now I'm going to give it its own full chapter, because it deserves it, and because it's one of the most important tools you have if you want to make big bucks writing for magazines.

While you must be professional and convey that you're a serious writer, it doesn't mean you have to be a robot. Perfect people are rarely interesting, and "professional" doesn't have to mean bland. You are allowed, and encouraged, to have a personality if you want editors to remember you.

Take this recent example: I pitched a story about the health benefits of yogurt to *Men's Fitness* magazine. The editor wrote back to tell me they had recently run several yogurt articles, so they weren't interested, but he loved my clips and my query and wanted to keep me in mind for assignments. How thrilled was I? A couple of weeks went by, and no assignment. So I decided to keep myself fresh in his mind.

I wrote again with a new story pitch, but it wasn't the query that was the important part of the letter. Really, it was an excuse for me to schmooze him a little. At the end of my letter, I wrote something like:

"Oh, and I'm very flattered that you'll keep me in mind for assignments. I'm up for anything, I'm great with deadlines, and you can send me the stories that other writers don't want to touch. Give me a call any time."

Well, he assured me he was still crazy about me, wanted me for assignments, and told me to keep sending him pitches in the meantime. So I did. And each time, I included a little "dig" about those assignments. In my last letter, I even started it, "Hey! Where are those assignments you promised me? I'm waiting by the phone!"

Other writers might advise never to get that bold with an editor, or never to assume a personal relationship until you've written for a magazine many times. But you have to know how to feel out an editor. If that editor had just sent me a form rejection letter, it wouldn't have been appropriate for me to engage him in this kind of informality and teasing. But from the tone of his initial response, and then from the fact that he chided me when I had a computer crash and asked him to send me back one of my query letters because I wanted to send it on elsewhere, I knew it was okay to take a little risk and keep his "obligation" to me fresh in his mind.

But, alas, he didn't respond. I realized he hadn't responded to my last couple of queries, so I called him. To my surprise, the receptionist told me he was no longer there.

Oh boy. Time to get personal with the receptionist. After all, I wasn't about to let a good contact up and die on me. "Well, that explains why he's not answering my emails!" From that sentence, she could ascertain that I had some kind of relationship with this editor, and wasn't a random wannabe writer, so she told me he had moved to another magazine. I sensed that I could have pushed her to find out which magazine, but I didn't. Instead, I asked who the new nutrition editor was.

"Well, that's tricky," the receptionist explained. "There really isn't a replacement for him yet. See, the magazine is moving its offices to New York, so we're operating on a temporary skeleton staff of only four people."

Jeepers. But I was still determined. I quickly and nonchalantly scanned my notes to find out the names of other editors at *Men's Fitness*. Never once had I spoken to the man, but I asked, "What about Dave? Is Dave still there?" Like I knew the guy. "No, he's gone, too," she said.

But by this point, I figured she thought I was tight with all of their editors, so I was able to push it a little further. "It's just that I have this great big story that I know is perfect for *Men's Fitness*, so I want to make sure I get it to the right person. Is anyone there looking at queries right now?"

No, she explained. The whole editorial department was in chaos, and nothing was being assigned until the big move. But she told me I could call the publisher—and gave me his phone number, along with the new address of the magazine, come September.

I filed this information, but figured I'd pitch the idea to a few other magazines first. I started with *Physical*. The editor wrote back to me within one day to tell me that they had just run a similar story, but he suggested three other magazines that I should contact, including *Men's Fitness*. I thought that was tremendously nice of him.

Then I wrote to my freelance writing friend, Linda Formichelli, who was the one who gave me the contact at *Men's Fitness* to begin with.

"Did you know about what's going on?" I asked, and told her that Mike and Dave were gone.

"Yes," she wrote back. "Mike's at *Physical* now."

Ah. A perfect excuse for me to build up more of a rapport with that nice editor I had just queried. I wrote back to him, thanking him for the quick and helpful response, and added a "P.S.": "I hear Mike Carlson is now with you at *Physical*. Please tell him Jenna says 'hi' and she now understands why he didn't answer her last few queries . . . ;-)."

"I would be eager to write for you anytime. I specialize in health issues (mental and physical), so if you're ever looking for a reliable and detail-oriented freelancer, I'm here!"

What? Yes, that was a winky face you saw above! No, I don't advise that you fill your emails to editors with emoticons or fancy fonts or anything, but neither do you have to be completely unfun. I have been known to trade the occasional emoticon or large font for emphasis with a friendly editor.

He wrote back, again within 24 hours, again to reject my query, but this time, he went way further. He had decided that I was someone worth working with (probably partially from my oh-so-wonderful queries and samples, but assuredly, partially because he liked my personality, too), so he told me all about their magazine and exactly why my idea didn't fit. He was far more blunt than any guidelines would have been.

Now comes the cooler part: He asked me for my address so he could send me "several copies of the magazine" so I could get a better feel for what to pitch him, and he sent me a detailed list of suggestions about where to pitch my latest query, along with suggestions for what angles I could take in my queries for different markets. And how did he end his letter to me?

"Go get 'em, Jenna!"

I immediately wrote back to tell him that he was the greatest and what a rare treat it was to find an editor like him. Two days later, I received three copies of *Physical* and three copies of their sister publication, *Let's Live*. Eyebrows raised, I read the note, which said that their sister publication's editor was also always looking for good freelancers.

Does he do that for every freelancer who comes his way? I doubt it. And what separated me from every other freelancer, is that I got personal with him. I showed that I had a bit of personality, and he showed that he had one back. And guess what? I just finished my second feature for him, and he's fantastic to work with.

I tend to err on the side of bold, rather than bland, when approaching editors. When I answer a "writer's wanted" ad, if I think I'm the perfect writer for the job,

I say so. But in a fun way. A few months ago, I read an ad from a company look-ing for people to write greeting cards and picture books. It just so happens that I adore writing greeting cards and picture books, and have experience with both. I went to their web site and found that it had a lighthearted, playful tone. So my cover letter began, "I'm your woman. No, really, I am. I've looked over your site with great delight and realized that Chameleon and I are perfect for each other."

I followed that with two paragraphs about my experience in those fields, then the line, "I'm reliable, prolific, and pretty darn cool. (And humble, too.)"

I started doing this when I realized that it worked on me. I had put out an ad looking for book reviewers who would review screenwriting books. I received letters from about 100 applicants, most of whom were ridiculously overqualified. The first person I hired got the gig because of her personality, plain and simple.

In the subject of her email, she wrote, "Look no further . . . I'm the reviewer you're looking for." Gutsy move, and could come off as just egotistical, if she hadn't written such an amusing email below that subject.

"Let me simply cut to the chase here and tell you that I am incredibly eager to write your book reviews. Now the trick is to have you reciprocate my eager-ness . . . let's see, what can I say? Well, I could sing my own praises and say that I've placed in every prestigious screenwriting contest I've entered. I could nonchalantly name drop and say that I was a semi-finalist in the renowned Chesterfield Writer's Film Project . . . " She went on to say that she could "deliciously dangle" her other credentials, "casually mention" this and that, but that she wouldn't. No, she'd rather that I hired her just because I think she's cool. She ended it with, "I'm sending you this letter in the hope that you do like the ABBA song says and 'take a chance on me.'"

And I did. Sure, there were plenty of other writers whose credentials were even better (they'd actually had screenplays produced, or lots of book review credits), but the flavor of this query let me know that (a) she'd be an enjoyable person to work with, and (b) her writing style was entertaining and attention-grabbing. And that's what my readers want.

Granted, not all editors will enjoy such "strong" approaches. One editor I spoke with thinks that pitches like this one are "obnoxious," and the editor of an English-language magazine in Germany said that she'd probably "never give this kind of person work." That's why it's a good idea to feel out an editor or company first. If it's a cold pitch, type the editor's name into a search engine and see if you can find any interviews of him, or writing that he has done. It may give you a better sense of this editor's personality and the likelihood that he would appreciate a bit of audacious fun. Also, keep in mind the company or magazine itself, and its own tone and style.

The letter the screenwriter wrote me wouldn't have been appropriate if she were applying for a writing job for, say, *Vogue*. Not because they're a bigger magazine, but because that writing style doesn't match their editorial.

I said "not because they're a bigger magazine" because I get the feeling that writers, myself included for a long time, are much more hesitant to show personality when they approach a major market. It's sort of like being at a party. If you see someone at the punch bowl, you might make some small talk, probably not think too much about it. Maybe talk a little about yourself, maybe make a joke about something in the news. But what if that "someone" is a famous movie star? Suddenly, you clam up, or you want to make sure you're saying exactly the *right* thing, so you think about your words a hundred times over before they come out of your mouth. And this famous person couldn't possibly care about your piddly little life, so you don't talk about yourself; you just bow before her and try not to say anything stupid.

We writers often have this same reverence for editors at big magazines. We don't want to say anything stupid. We don't want to overstep our boundaries. So we send off these stuffy little queries, and never have the audacity to get chatty.

That's a mistake. Editors are not deities, and for the most part, they don't expect to be treated as if they are. It's actually refreshing for most editors to see a little witty small talk in their inbox rather than dry sales pitch after sales pitch (which is what query letters are, after all. Well, not dry, we would hope, but they are certainly sales pitches). I have been most pleasantly surprised by the editors at magazines like *Ladies' Home Journal*, *House Beautiful*, *Playboy*, and *Woman's Day*—all of whom took the time to "get personal" with me, if only for a few paragraphs by email.

I still haven't written for Joel Shangle at *Fishing and Hunting News*, and I probably never will because the magazine doesn't pay well, but since my initial request for guidelines, this editor and I have traded at least a dozen fish photos from our favorite adventures. I know all about how he spent his college years writing for the Associated Press, his favorite parts of his job, and his trip to the Yukon Territory, and he knows all about my upcoming wedding, my anxiety disorder, and my catfishing vacation.

I don't have an ulterior motive here; I just hit it off with Joel and we enjoy chatting. I've recommended writers to him, but we mostly just email to small-talk and compare writing and editing experiences. However, it has crossed my mind that if Joel moves to a different (read: higher-paying) magazine, he won't easily forget me.

A great thing about building a more informal rapport with editors is that they'll be much more likely to give you tips. For example, Elaine Greene at *House Beautiful* once enjoyed an essay I sent her, but told me it was too "feel-good sweet" for their pages. She suggested other markets for it. I thanked her and kept in touch, so she mailed me clips of other essays they'd run to give me a better feel for what they were looking for. Then I praised her in an article I wrote for Absolute Write, and I pointed her to it. She wrote back to thank me for speaking well of her, and wrote, "I am dead honest, though I try to be tactful, and the thanks sometimes surprise me. I really try to help, and numerous authors *have* published in the places I suggest." She said that when there is even the tiniest bit of promise, she suggests writing workshops, and "very rarely—twice maybe in a long career—have I had to tell a persistent writer that I just didn't care for his/her style." Of course, Elaine was once a freelancer herself, so she understands our struggles.

Getting personal doesn't mean starting your correspondence with, "Hey! How's your cat? You know, I went to Rhode Island this weekend and the foliage was positively amazing . . . " No, those rumors are true about editors being busy people, and when they're at work, they actually do have to work.

In my case, the fishing magazine editor started the banter with me: He visited my web site and started asking me questions about my books. You can take clues from the editor's notes to you: The more friendly the editor is with you, the more friendly you can be in response.

The Nerve of Some People

I had been querying *Family Circle* for quite some time, and the editor often wrote me personal letters to tell me she liked my work, but that she couldn't use it for some reason or another that had nothing to do with my writing talent.

Eventually, I built up my nerve and wrote her a short letter that said something like this: "You've liked several of my queries, although I haven't quite hit the mark yet. May I be so bold as to ask if you would consider me for assignments?" I emphasized my credits again, and added a note about my strengths: that I'm easy to work with, always meet my deadlines, and turn in clean copy (meaning she won't have to fuss with my grammatical and spelling mistakes).

I wish I could neatly tie this up and tell you that it immediately paid off with an assignment, but it didn't. She wrote to tell me that all freelance assignments were based on query letters, but encouraged me to keep pitching.

Does that mean I won't use that technique again? Heck no. You can be certain I'll use it again.

If you want to be in that top 16 percent of freelancers who are earning a living wage, you must learn that opportunities rarely come to you delivered on a silver platter. You must ask for the things you want. Do you want to be a columnist? Do you want a referral to their sister publication? Ask for it.

If your queries have been met with the same sort of "we like you, but that idea's not right for us" response as I had with *Family Circle*, you might try a different tactic: Ask the editor what she *is* looking for. Drop her a note to say thanks for considering your queries, and ask if there are any topics she's looking for or any departments that are low on submissions. She just might tell you.

Get Titled: Contributing Editors

Want a coveted "contributing editor" title on the masthead? That's really just an honorary title given to the magazine's regular freelancers, you know. The title may also be conferred on writers whose names carry weight with their audience; for example, a beauty magazine may ask a famed diet guru to be a contributing editor even if she has written only a few articles for them. And the title is often given to staff editors who've left the magazine to freelance.

Sometimes it means you'll be guaranteed a certain number of assignments per issue/month/year, sometimes it means you'll get more money, and sometimes it's just an honor. If you've been freelancing regularly for a magazine for a long time, you have little to lose by asking for this "promotion."

"Little to lose" doesn't mean "nothing to lose," though—once you've been named a contributing editor, it's likely you'll be required to sign a contract that says you won't write for that magazine's competitors. This may be fine by you, or it may not. For example, I write frequently for *Writer's Digest*. Since I began writing for them, I've never approached any of their competitors, partially out of loyalty and partially because *Writer's Digest* pays better. This is a relationship I want to keep and cultivate, and possibly build up to a monthly column. So it was a no-brainer: When they asked me to be a contributing editor, I said "yes."

But what if *Men's Health* wanted me to be a contributing editor? That would probably mean I could no longer write for other men's health and fitness magazines (or possibly any other major health magazines at all). I'd have to consider the trade-off: Would they promise me a certain number of assignments per month/quarter/year? Would they give me a better pay rate? If so, it certainly might be worth it for me: I'd save time querying all those other magazines, I'd get to know this editor's style better so it would be easier for me to turn out appropriate articles, and they might even pay me more than the other magazines would. Plus, I'd have this great title to add to my bio, which I could then use when I pitched non-competing publications.

Other editors know that a contributing editor is a valued freelancer, so if I then approached a women's magazine with a query, the editor would see that a fellow editor at a major magazine thinks highly enough of me to want to work with me regularly.

I would not agree to be a contributing editor at a low-paying magazine, unless all of its competitors were also low-paying. In other words, I wouldn't accept this title from a women's magazine that pays $0.50 a word if that meant I could no longer write for the women's magazines that pay $2 a word. It just doesn't make economic sense.

So, how to get this coveted title? Most of the time, you get it by asking. Sometimes an editor will surprise you and just offer it to you after you've written for her a few times (or many, many times), but conferring titles usually isn't high on an editor's priority list, so you may have to be the one to bring it up.

Again, don't let fear stop you from taking the next step in your career. Fortune favors the brave. Take that risk. Take all the risks you can. Your career is worth it.

Pre-Queries

Now I'm going to let you in on a little secret I've never seen anyone else talk about: pre-queries.

When people are new to freelance writing, they sometimes have a hard time getting used to the idea that they don't have to write a whole article to sell it; they just have to write query letters. But for those of us who take the "time is money" cliché seriously, I advise against spending the time writing up a query letter if you're not reasonably sure it will sell.

Some ideas are so wonderful that you feel confident they'll find a home somewhere. But what about the others, the ones you *think* might sell—the ones you *want* to write but aren't sure will fit a particular magazine?

That's where the pre-query comes in. It requires a little guts, but works well for me. Instead of taking the time to research and work up a query letter, I drop the editor a quick line asking if the topic interests him.

I don't do this all the time, and I don't do it with editors with whom I have no relationship. But I define "relationship" loosely: If I've written for him before, sure, we have a relationship. However, I also consider it a relationship if he's written me personalized rejection letters, sent me samples of the magazine without my requesting them, or otherwise encouraged me to keep submitting. If we've hit the "first name basis" stage, we definitely have a relationship.

So here's a sample of a pre-query I sent a few days ago:

> **Dear Bill,**
> **Quick question before I work up a full query: Have you ever done a piece about nutritional supplements and dietary advice for people with herpes? If not, does that sound like something your magazine would cover?**

A lot of psychology is packed into those two sentences. First, I've started the note by letting him know it's just a "quick question," so he'll be inclined to answer it quickly. Then, "does it sound like something . . . " is a non-threatening way to ask this question; I'm not asking for a decision on this piece. I'm asking only if the topic might fit with their readership.

But even though I'm being laid back about it, the truth is that most people will feel some kind of responsibility if they say "yes." If this editor says that the magazine might cover something like this, when my query comes in, he'll be inclined to approve it, because he already decided and let me know that the topic is appropriate.

Even better? He might just give me the assignment then and there, without my ever writing up a full query. A few times, I've written one to two-sentence pre-queries, then gotten a call that day with the assignment. This usually works best with editors who know me well. But most editors respond with a "Yes, I'd like to hear a more detailed pitch" type of note.

If the editor says "no," that's still a positive thing to me: It means that I don't have to waste the time perfecting my irresistible query letter. And I don't have to waste the editor's time with it, either.

Reach Out and Touch Someone

Editors appreciate being thought of—not just on the day they approve your article, thus signaling accounting to send out your check, but other times, too.

Michael Sedge, freelancer and former director-at-large for the American Society of Journalists and Authors, sends editors a calendar every year in time for the holidays. This accomplishes two goals at once for him: One, it's a practical gift, and two, it is pre-printed with his name, address, and phone number. This way, if the editor uses the calendar, his contact information is on her wall every day.

If you hear your editor has been promoted, got married, had a baby, or won an award, send a card. E-cards are nice, but paper cards are nicer. Think how much it would make your day if an editor remembered your birthday or sent you a bottle of wine for the holidays. A little thoughtfulness can go a long way to show your editor she's appreciated.

ASSIGNMENT

 Editors to Remember

Editor	Magazine	Likes/Dislikes	Event/Date	Notes
SAMPLE Jenny Brill	*Nuts & Bolts* magazine	Likes Yankees, merlot	Birthday: February 12	Open to e-queries, okay to drop jokes about sports events from time to time

Chapter 15

BRING OUT THE BUCKS

Inside This Chapter

- **Considering payment rates**
- **Chasing down deadbeat editors**
- **Diversifying your clip file**
- **Networking and referrals**

No Magic Number

Whenever you're considering freelance work, do *not* judge simply by the dollar figure. On AbsoluteMarkets.com, I once listed a call for submissions for a company that makes buttons and magnets. They wanted short and funny sayings to print on their products, and they paid $40.

I got an angry letter from a writer who wanted to know why I bothered to list such lousy-paying markets. He told me that professional writers would never waste their time writing for $40.

I wrote back to tell him that I had written for this company, and I was certainly a professional writer. Then I tried to explain it in simple logic: I had a funny little idea that popped into my head one day, and when I came across the company, I realized the idea would make a good button. I sent it, and they paid me $40. That idea took all of about thirty seconds to come up with, so I got paid $40 for half a minute's work. Talk about easy money.

But this fellow wasn't finished balling me out. He wrote to tell me that although I might be a professional writer, no one who makes a *real* living bothers with such low-paying markets. I told him that I made a fine living.

Then it was time for him to truly tip the condescending scale: We obviously have different definitions of what making a real living entails, he wrote: "I'm talking about actually paying a mortgage and owning a car with the money you earn from your writing."

I told him about my waterfront property and my SUV and my investment portfolio, all financed with the money I earned from my writing, including the $40 here and there that I picked up writing button slogans. Oh, and I think I mentioned I was 25.

Isn't it great when you can render someone speechless? I never heard from that patronizing fellow again. I wonder if he ever took up button-writing.

I tell you this story to drive home the "don't be a writing snob" point. Should you spend all of your time looking for $40 markets? No way. But taking these seemingly low-paying opportunities on the side is a great way to keep money coming in.

You must consider the time versus payoff equation. If a small magazine wants an essay from you, but they want to pay you only $100, you might scoff. Or you might think to yourself, "Hey, this doesn't require any research and I can bang it out in an hour." Then you've made $100 an hour, and suddenly, the payment seems generous, not to mention the fact that adding to your résumé is always a worthy pursuit.

Points to Consider

Before deciding whether or not to accept a pay rate, consider these factors:

➤ *Time. Try to translate the fee into dollars per hour instead of dollars per word. How much time will it take you to finish the piece?*

➤ *Enjoyment. At least in my opinion, it's preferable to take a $0.50/word assignment that I'll enjoy working on instead of a $1/word assignment that doesn't truly interest me.*

➤ *Repurposing. Assuming the publication isn't taking all rights, how likely is it that you can sell reprints of this article, or rewrite it for other publications?*

➤ *Bio-boosting. Will this credit help you break in at other magazines you want to work with? Is it an impressive name to add to your bio?*

➤ *Ease of editing. You won't know this the first time you work with a magazine, but after that, you'll figure out how demanding the editor is in terms of rewrites. Are her demands time-consuming? Do you want to hurl yourself off the nearest building every time you see her emails pop into your inbox? There are one or two editors who could probably never pay me enough to make it worth it for me to work with them again, and others who I'm willing to work with for less money because they don't give me headaches.*

➤ *Probability of more work. Sometimes it may be worth it to accept less than your usual fee per article if you know a publication will provide a steady check.*

Just today, I allowed a small men's magazine to reprint an interview of mine for free. Why would I do such a thing? Two reasons: First, they were happy to give me a bio (which I used to promote my web site and my books); and second, because I wanted to break in to other men's magazines, and now I had another relevant credit to add to my list. At this point in my career, I wouldn't have spent the time writing an original article for them for free, but I'm pretty generous with my reprints.

Many writers have that "dollar-a-word" figure in their head. That's supposed to be the minimum an advanced writer will accept. But I actually accept quite a range, all depending on what's expected of me at each magazine.

I regularly write for two markets that pay me $0.50 a word. That doesn't sound very impressive until you hear that the required research is non-existent or minor, they give me long deadlines, and neither magazine's editors have ever asked me for even one small revision. I get paid on acceptance, the editors are great to me, and I no longer have to write up queries for either of them— just a sentence or two about my idea suffices.

I just contracted to write a 1,800-word feature for one of them, based on my own expertise, requiring no research or interviews. You know how long it will take me? Less than a day. So in that one day, I'll earn $900, and keep the right to reprint the article.

Compare that to some of the $2 a word markets where I've had to spend weeks researching, interviewing, transcribing interviews, writing, rewriting, re-interviewing based on revise notes, transcribing again, rewriting again, and hounding editors. Yes, it's a bigger paycheck, but the per-hour rate winds up being less than those two 50-cent-a-word markets.

Hey—Where's My Check?

> *The freelance writer is a man who is paid per piece*
> *or per word or perhaps.*
>
> —Robert Benchley

It happens often. I wish I could tell you that we are above all that, but the truth is that writers get screwed. Magazines go out of business, editors quit, they suffer long-term memory loss about the terms of your contract, or they just plain decide to be deadbeats. In my years of freelancing, I've had to chase down seriously delinquent payments about a dozen times. I was successful in about nine of those cases, and never saw the remaining three checks, which I gave up on because they were all small amounts and I decided it was a waste of my energy. If your check doesn't show up when it's supposed to, there are several steps you can take.

Your first recourse is to send a letter. Include in it a second invoice and gently remind your editor that payment is overdue, noting the original terms. If you hear nothing, it's time for a phone call to the same effect, preferably straight to the accounting department. Still nothing? If your editor has a boss, go there. Do not give up if you know you've been wronged. Don't let yourself become a doormat—you won't respect yourself, and you'll be doing a disservice to other writers by allowing the publication to get away with it.

Don't sound apologetic for reminding your editor or the magazine that you need to be paid. Think of it this way: They're making money off you. Without writers, there is no magazine. So, be polite, but increasingly firm if you don't get the response you need. Here is a sample "second notice" letter:

> **Dear Ms. Editor:**
> **According to the terms of our contract, I was scheduled to be paid on September 2, 2003, for the article I wrote for the November issue ("My Clever Title"). As of today, November 19, 2003, I have not received payment. Could you please check on this matter and let me know when I can expect payment? I have enjoyed writing for you and would like to do so again, but I need to know that your publication will honor the terms of our contract. I am enclosing a new invoice and copy of our agreement for your convenience.**
> **Regards,**
> **Jenna Glatzer**
> **cc: The National Writers Union**

(Sneaky, huh? You noticed my "cc." It's about a million times better than threatening to sue. It's just a subtle little hint that I have people on my side.) If you join the National Writers Union, their grievance department will help you fight to get the payment you've earned.

What do you need to prove your case? In a word, documentation. Technically speaking, oral agreements are binding in some states, but that's very tricky to prove. If you have a good, written contract, and your deadbeat editor/publisher has clearly broken it, then you have a solid case. Even if you didn't heed my advice and get a contract from the magazine, you should still have heeded my secondary advice and retained some kind of paper trail.

Armed with whatever paperwork you have (even phone notes are better than nothing), you can ask a grievance officer to contact the publication on your behalf. According to their statistics, they recover payment for 80 percent of authors who file claims.

However, they are not attorneys. That's the next step. Unfortunately, it's rarely worth it financially to sue a publication, unless your gripe is with a major market. Considering the time and money involved to file a claim through an attorney, you're better off trying to solve this problem on your own.

If you're not an NWU member and you've already tried writing and calling your editor about the late payment, send your invoice—by certified mail—to the accounting department at the magazine. Mark it "Overdue" and note that you will expect payment in full within 10 business days. Some writers add that they will charge interest on any balance overdue by more than 30 days.

Use Your Writing Network

Part of the power of joining a writing group is the "strength in numbers" aspect. Publishers don't want writers to find out that their terms are unfair, or that they don't pay on time. When a publisher's reputation is trashed, they realize it will be much more difficult to get top-notch writers to submit to them. Therefore, it's very important to let other writers know if you're having trouble with a particular publication.

I recently received an email from a writer, asking me if I was getting paid on time by a publisher for whom we both worked on an ongoing basis. I wasn't. She explained that she was collecting information, as her payments were quite overdue.

Word got back to the editor that her writers were talking to each other about the lagging payments. I received my check a week later.

Don't stay in the dark when a publisher rips you off. Fight for what is owed to you.

Taking Group Action

The greatest story I've ever heard about a writer fighting for payment came from one of my writing groups, the Net Wits (online humor columnists). About 100 members are in the group, and one of our purposes is to help our fellow writers when they need us.

Kim Lane, a group member, was having trouble getting paid by a certain magazine. After firing off letters of her own, with no success, she enlisted the group's help.

Every day for more than a month, everyone in the group sent a post card to the publication. The post card, in every case, contained four words: "Please pay Kim Lane."

> *Associating*
>
> ➤ *The National Writer's Union (www.nwu.org) has more than 6,000 members, and offers contract advice, grievance assistance, a media rates database, sample contracts, writer alerts, a job hotline, and events and meetings both at local levels and national levels.*
>
> ➤ *The American Society of Journalists and Authors (www.asja.org) is for experienced writers only: You must submit at least six articles published by major magazines or newspapers, or two or more nonfiction books to be accepted for membership. If you qualify, you'll get to swap information about pay rates and experiences with editors and publishers, as well as have access to workshops, private discussion areas on their web site, health insurance, a press card, a referral service for writing jobs and assignments, and online groups arranged by specialty.*
>
> ➤ *Authors Guild (www.authorsguild.org), established in 1912, is open to book authors and freelance writers, and provides contract advice, health insurance, member publications and seminars, and web sites for writers.*

Be Prepared

Knowledge is always your best defense. If you have a hunch that a particular publication isn't up to par, you're probably right. Watch for these signs:

➤ Editors who don't send you a contract.

➤ Editors who assign you several articles all at once. Before agreeing to take on more work, make sure you get paid for the first article. I've heard too many stories of writers who are owed thousands of dollars for multiple articles for one magazine; I always wonder how they let it get to that point. If you haven't been paid on time for your first piece, hold off on writing any further pieces until you've been paid. It's also a red flag because editors should want to see how you'll do on your first assignment before offering you more: An editor who wants you to write multiple pieces before having proof that you can deliver well may be desperate for writers for a bad reason—such as that none of her previous writers will write for her again.

➤ Web sites that promise to pay you per "click": Each time your article is read, you'll be paid a few cents. Most will never generate you enough revenue to see a paycheck. (Read the terms very carefully, and with a jaundiced eye.)

➤ Anyone who is not forthcoming with clear answers to your reasonable questions. If you ask, "What kind of rights do you buy?" and get a vague reply, no reply, or "I'll have to check with my superiors," don't do anything until you get a solid answer. Ditto for questions about payment, publication, etc.

➤ Publications that solicit writers all over the place. Reputable publications and editors are inundated with submissions. Most don't need to advertise at all, except for listings in the *Writer's Market*, unless they're brand new and writers don't know about them yet. If you see lots of headlines for one publication, especially including words like, "Want to see your work in print?" or "Make money off your writing today!," watch out.

➤ Editors with free Internet email addresses (like Yahoo or Hotmail). Most publications have their own web sites; even if they don't, editors should have Internet access through their office. Free email addresses are generally impossible to track, so you could be left in the dark if the user cancels her email and skips town.

➤ Any publication that is contingent upon your purchase of their product. This is known as subsidy or vanity publishing. The National Library of Poetry, for example, will guarantee to publish one of your poems, as long as you buy a copy of their anthology. Legitimate publishers pay you for your writing—not the other way around!

➤ Anyone who charges a "reading" or "editing" fee. You should never have to pay for the opportunity to have your work read and considered for publication.

➤ Those who promise that they will become a paying market in the future. This is the carrot dangled by many new publications. They begin with the (sometimes honest) notion that once they get "really big," they'll be able to afford to pay writers. Unfortunately, they usually find out two things: They can get writers to work for free (why pay?) and they never get "really big." On several occasions, I've told these start-up companies that they can hold onto my résumé and samples, and I'd be happy to write for them as soon as they begin paying. Despite several assurances, I've heard back from only one company that made good on this promise (www.Conversely.com, if you're curious).

Warnings for Writers

If you have any doubts about a publisher or editor, check in with the various "warnings for writers" web sites and bulletin boards. You can find the best ones here:

➤ *Writer Beware: www.sfwa.org/beware*

➤ *Absolute Write Bewares Board: http://pub43.ezboard.com/fabsolutewritefrm11*

➤ *ASJA Contracts Watch: www.asja.org/cw/cw.php*

Get involved with writing web sites. You'll find that many of them offer message boards where you can ask about publishers' and editors' credibility. If you ever encounter a writing scam or deadbeat publisher, be sure to let other writers know through these boards, too. The more writers share this kind of information, the less likely it is that the companies who prey off of naïve writers will succeed.

As a final rule of thumb, I refer you to the sage advice of Victoria Strauss, who maintains the Writer Beware web pages: "Money flows toward the writer, not away. The only place you should ever sign a check is on the back!"

Start-Ups: Worth Your Time?

Several experienced writers told me they won't deal with start-up magazines. On one hand, the logic is simple: New publications are a big risk. More than half of all new magazines fail within two years, according to most estimates. Some experts think that's generous; according to some reports, 80 percent of start-ups don't make it to their first anniversary.

If a magazine fails before you've been paid, good luck getting your check. That's why I have simple advice: If you're going to write for new publications, insist on being paid on acceptance.

"I have been left behind when new pubs never got off the ground," says Roberta Beach Jacobson, who's written for *Woman's Day* and *Natural Home*. "Examples are *World Travel & Cuisine* and *Surprise* magazine. But the writing life is not all rosy."

Roberta chooses to keep approaching start-ups anyway. "Most of my writer friends refuse to, so I figure there are fewer writers in line and I have a stronger chance with my queries. I find it challenging to help the editor and staff form a new publication! There are few rules until they finish a couple of issues. I've written for Wisecity.com and got $200 per reprint and they took a bunch at once."

Despite the risk, writing for a new magazine can also pay off. *Real Simple* launched in 2000, had a slightly shaky start, and as of this writing has 1.2 million readers and pays $2 a word. But even magazines with no giant publishing companies behind them can be surprising hits: *mental_floss*, started in 2001, was the brainchild of five students at Duke University who launched the magazine from an office in one of their parents' houses. Two and a half years later, the magazine can be found all over chain bookstores, Wal-Marts, and libraries. Better yet, the founders are doing monthly trivia segments on CNN, have signed a book deal with Harper Collins, have a syndicated radio show in the works, and are planning collaborations with *Reader's Digest* and Salon.com.

This magazine is definitely one to watch—they're still small (as of its 10th issue, it has 15,000 subscribers), but its sell-through rate is twice the national average: Most magazines sell about 30 percent of their newsstand copies;

mental_floss sells 60 percent. Because they're still in the "beginning stages," though, and their pay rate is not tremendous (currently $0.15–0.25/word), they're not inundated with submissions. This means that you can email their editor-in-chief, Neely Harris, and actually get a timely and personal response.

She's quick to mention that their pay rates are expected to rise: "Our pay rate will always increase based on what we can afford, and will *never* have anything to do with what we can 'get away with,' which I think is what some writers think start-ups try to do."

So, if money is your main object, this one is still a gamble, but in my opinion, a worthy gamble. Editors do remember the writers who were there from the beginning, and have a loyalty to those who got on the bandwagon before there was a bandwagon. If a start-up like *mental_floss* has a surge in popularity and pays $1.50 a word next year, flocks of writers will show up. But chances are good that editors like Neely will give the best assignments to those who showed up when she truly needed the help and have already shown her that they know the magazine and will deliver what she likes.

Don't throw yourself on every wannabe publisher with a business plan. Watch the trades and go with your gut: Is this a magazine that stands a good chance of finding a loyal audience? Are they getting media attention? Who's backing them? Are there typos all over their web site? Watch for truly promising new magazines, and if you want a chance at becoming an integral part of shaping their future, pitch early.

Diversify and Conquer

It's great to build up a relationship with one editor, or one magazine. It's super to be able to count on a regular check from someone month after month. But be careful of getting too cushy.

"*YM* was my total bread and butter—I was doing features for them, I had a column on contract, and all of a sudden they got a new editor," says freelancer Kristen Kemp. "Everyone I was working for got fired and I was out of a job. I think it's really important to have several things going on and plan on half of them falling through. If you're not doing that with several magazines, you're not covering your own butt."

David Geer, freelancer for magazines like *IEEE Computer* and *Art & Antiques*, agrees, saying the more markets you write for, the more stable your income will be. "You won't be 'putting all your eggs in one magazine,' or a small grouping. Some relationships may end or take a hiatus unexpectedly (magazines fold, editors move on), so you'll need those new relationships. New markets also help broaden your experience and expand your clip file. The more kinds of writing you've done, the more you can do."

I typically have a "front line" and a "back line" of markets; the front line includes the four or five magazines I write for regularly. The back line includes all the others I've written for just once, twice, or a handful of times. If they were good to work for, then I stay in touch with them and try to send queries every now and then, because I never know when one of my front-line magazines will disappear and I'll need a replacement for that chunk of my income.

Networking

There are two reasons to network with fellow writers.

1. Writing is a lonely profession. It's nice to connect with others who've chosen the same crazy career path.

2. Other writers have other jobs. If you're nice to them, they might just tell you how they got those other jobs, and advise you when you need a tip, some feedback, or a referral. I might not be making a real living as a freelance writer if not for the writer-friends who have advised me along the way.

There are many message boards, email lists, and organizations for writers. Many of them are specific in their intentions.

Critique groups help participants get their work into publishable shape. Other groups are meant to trade leads and business information, and still others are primarily for support and camaraderie.

As far as finding "in person" writers' groups, you have several options. First, call your local town hall, library, and YMCA. (Yeah, YMCA!) Ask if they know of any. If not, try the National Writer's Union (www.nwu.org), which organizes groups in every state. Also, the International Women's Writing Guild (www.iwwg.com) offers "zip code parties and regional clusters," where local women meet to read their works aloud and critique each other.

If you find no appropriate groups in your area, why not start one? Ask your local library if they'd mind helping you get the word out. Print up flyers and leave them at the desk. Place a classifieds ad in your neighborhood paper.

Writers' workshops can also be havens for networking. Freelancer Barbara Stahura, who writes for *Science of Mind* and *The Executive*, says, "I try to go to at least one writing workshop a year, so I've been to maybe eight all over the country so far. My experiences have ranged from nearly ecstatic to downright painful; the instructors have ranged from kind and caring to nasty, even to the point of making participants cry. Overall, however, the workshops I've attended have been helpful simply because they've allowed me to spend days at a time immersed in something I love to do and getting generally helpful feedback on my work. I don't have to worry about the daily grind for while, and I can talk for hours with lots of other writers about writing. Heaven!"

Receiving a referral from an editor is almost always a huge boon for a writer. Receiving a referral from a fellow writer can be, as well. On occasion, I have both given and received referrals to editors at major magazines.

When asked if she pays attention to referrals from writers, Chandra Czape of *Ladies' Home Journal* says, "If I respect that writer and I think she's really talented and has good instincts, then I certainly will take whomever she recommends. That happens a lot with me, actually. Of course, that only gets the person in the door; then they have to prove themselves."

Likewise, Stephanie Abarbanel of *Woman's Day* says she considers recommendations. "If you say, 'I've worked with *Family Circle* or *Good Housekeeping* or *Redbook* and I really want to work for you,' that's a leg up. If one of my favorite writers suggested you call me, that's a leg up. But the thing is, if you have style and content, that's also a leg up and you don't need either of those first two things."

Networking is not about using people. Networking is about making friends and helping each other when you can. So don't get into a "friendship" for the purpose of asking a writer for a referral. It's rude and off-putting and generally transparent. Be a friend for the sake of friendship, and if that writer later happens to offer to refer you to her editor, be grateful and consider it an extra gift. Do tell your friend that you're considering pitching an editor at a magazine she's worked for; do ask for tips; don't ask for a referral. Your friend will get the idea, and if she wants to make the offer, she will.

Writer Hangouts

➤ *For critique groups, try One Of Us (www.oneofus.co.uk) or Forward Motion (www.fmwriters.com).*

➤ *To trade leads, try the Work For Writers email list (to subscribe, send any email to WorkForWriters-subscribe@yahoogroups.com).*

➤ *MomWriters (www.momwriters.com) offers a support program, critique groups, general writers' chat, and market information.*

➤ *If you're fortunate enough to live near a city where mediabistro events are held, don't miss them! Visit www.mediabistro.com/events to find out about networking parties and panels near you, and you just might meet a real live editor and make some writer-friends.*

➤ *To find writing workshops, visit http://writing.shawguides.com, where you can search by location, date, or genre for more than 1,400 workshops worldwide.*

Understand that when a writer refers you to someone, her own reputation is at risk. She's vouching for you, and if you don't come through, or if the editor has a problem with you, that editor isn't going to be happy with your friend. The same goes for an editor who refers you to another editor, though it's less nervy to ask your editor for a referral because he has direct experience working with you and can legitimately tell a colleague whether or not you were easy to work with and a talented writer. Your friend doesn't have that same perspective.

In either case, know that a referral is a huge favor, and if someone offers one to you, look for ways to repay that favor.

Chapter 16
DELVING DEEPER

Inside This Chapter

- **What big markets love**
- **Secret magazine biases**
- **Tax basics**
- **Getting syndicated**
- **Supplemental income for experienced writers**

The Next Step

This chapter is devoted to those who are ready to get past the hobbyist or beginner stages of freelance writing. Once you have the basics down and a few credits behind you, there are new issues that you will confront. If you've been writing for small newspapers and magazines, you likely haven't discovered all of the quirky predilections of the newsstand glossies and high-profile trades. Here, you'll learn insider secrets from those who've written for advanced ($1 a word and up) markets.

You'll also learn more about a less-thrilling part of a professional freelancer's life: taxes! Yes, once you've decided to make writing your career, you'll have to learn a new set of rules about paying your taxes.

And you'll learn about other "advanced" issues for writers, such as writing columns and syndicating your work, and other options available to experienced writers.

Am I Ready?

There's no rule that says you need any particular number of credits before you start querying the Big Boys. You simply need the experience to know how to handle a professional assignment. New writers often try to jump into this lion's den too soon, and experienced writers often get so comfortable with small and mid-sized markets that they don't realize they could easily take the next "step."

When asked what she wished she had learned earlier about freelancing, writer Devorah Stone said, "Not to undervalue my time and abilities. I ended up working for so little for people who didn't respect my work." She's now written for magazines such as *Chatelaine* and *Highlights for Children*.

When you work on a major national piece, it's very likely that you'll spend weeks—or months—of your time working on an article. Sure, the pay is good, but it requires a strong attention span and the patience to get every detail right, even if that means rewriting several times. On the other hand, if you write for smaller publications, you must turn out a bigger volume of material to make a decent income. With that bigger volume comes more opportunity for variety. You can opt to write short articles for several different markets and audiences.

In general, you'll also have more editorial control and less-rigid guidelines concerning source sheets, interviewing, article focus, etc. In many small markets, my work is printed word-for-word as I've written it. This is almost never the case with large publications; many editors may have input on any single piece of writing, and by the time it appears, it may look entirely different from my original piece.

This doesn't mean that I'm discouraging you from submitting to big publications; it's quite a thrill to see your byline and your paycheck when a national magazine picks up one of your articles. Once you feel experienced enough to get in the ring with the heavy-hitters, by all means, query away!

Breaking into Big Markets

Don't expect to be assigned a cover story right off the bat. It happens, but in rare instances. A nice way to get your name known is by sending in FOB items or "fillers": a few sentences that an editor can throw in when a layout is coming up short, like a tip for removing ketchup stains or alleviating hiccups. Book and product reviews can work, too.

Many major magazines love articles about "ordinary people with extraordinary stories." Those stories typically fall into a few categories, including:

➤ People who are doing something positive to make a difference in their communities
➤ Real-life dramas
➤ People overcoming great odds or challenges
➤ Interesting entrepreneurs
➤ Couples with outstanding love stories

According to Stephanie Abarbanel at *Woman's Day*, the typical real-life drama in a women's magazine goes something like this: A couple is in distress because their son has a medical problem that doctors can't seem to diagnose. "Then suddenly you get the right doctor and he comes up with the right diagnosis and then everything's cured and hunky-dory. I hate those stories. I hate the arc. I'm always looking for a less-predictable arc," says Stephanie.

She points out that most of the real-life dramas she publishes in *Woman's Day* are medical-related, but not as simplistic. "For example, we did a piece about a woman who was forty years old, in her eighth month of pregnancy, who had a massive stroke in the middle of class. She was rushed to the hospital. The operative problem was not getting the diagnosis. The operative problem was, do we take care of the mother or do we deliver the baby? If they delivered the baby, the mother might never have been able to lift her child, she might not have ever been able to speak to her child . . . she was really losing ground fast. They opted to go increasingly invasive on the mother, but it was an ethical problem— what if the baby starts struggling? Are we duty-bound to deliver the baby?" Happily, both mom and baby did just fine, but this illustrates the type of story Stephanie prefers: "I like when there's something hanging in the balance."

It's very unlikely for you to sell a story about a woman who overcame breast cancer, or a teen who organized a food drive, because we've heard these stories

First Sale

Carolyn Chapman, a full-time freelancer in Budapest, Hungary, shares this story about her first big sale:

"The most important things for freelancers, and especially beginners, are to be persistent and to set your aims high. I live in Budapest and do most of my writing for local magazines and newspapers (which don't pay very well) and then try to re-sell them to international publications (which pay much better). I must have sent out one of my feature articles to 20 different places, mostly small publications, and then put it aside and kind of gave up on selling it. Then I happened to walk by a newsstand one day and noticed that The Wall Street Journal Europe *had been publishing a lot of articles about this topic, so I just sent in my article, not expecting to even hear back from them. A few hours later, I got a call from an editor telling me that they were going to publish my article in the next day's edition. This experience taught me how important persistence is, gave me more confidence to approach the more prestigious publications, and made me realize that I don't have to settle for the small, unheard of, bad-paying publications that I thought beginners had to start out writing for."*

a million times already. Yours would have to truly bring something new to the table. If that woman went on to do something remarkable with her life, or if that teen hand-delivered that food every day after school to people who were homebound with terminal illnesses, you might have something.

If you write about entrepreneurs, they must actually be successful. It's not likely that an editor will print a profile of a woman with a start-up company that hasn't brought in much business yet.

If you plan to write someone's love story, remember that the couples should have met in an unusual way, or overcome a severe challenge in their relationship, or done something wild to prove their love for one another. (Just as I'm writing this, I'm realizing that my parents met at a funeral!)

Make it Timely

A story that can run anytime is called an "evergreen." It's great to think of evergreen topics, because those are the kinds of stories you can sell again and again, sometimes for several years. But if you want to catch the attention of a national magazine, give the editor a reason to buy your story *now*.

Tie your topic into something that's in the news. This is called a "news peg." Keep in mind that magazines often have lead times of several months, so it can't be a fleeting news story; otherwise, by the time your story is published, it will be old news. If I wanted to pitch an article about post-traumatic stress disorder (an evergreen topic), for example, I could tie it into the war in Iraq and discuss how war veterans are at a high risk for the disorder. The war is not fleeting news; it will likely be talked about for many months to come.

If a news report came out that stated Julia Roberts is the highest-paid actor in the world, I could tie that into my article about how women are coming closer to earning as much as men do in the workplace. If I were going to write an article for women about how to get your boyfriend or husband's mom to like you, and Mother's Day was coming up, I could point out that this would be a great article for the May issue.

Tell *Your* Story

That's right: Another great way to break into major markets is by telling the story that is uniquely yours, a first-person narrative of something remarkable in your life. We all have something worth sharing: What's your story?

"Whether it's your own story or the experiences of a colorful relative," says freelancer and writing instructor Christina L. Hamlett, "Such narratives still need to address one or more of the three 'R' themes inherent in popular fiction: Reward, Revenge, and Release. Likewise, the purpose of such stories runs parallel to the three 'E's of commercial publication: to Entertain, to Educate, and to Enlighten."

In order to tell your story, you must be willing to be completely honest, even if it's embarrassing. It probably *will* be embarrassing if it's worth telling. Consumer magazines love to hear confessions, especially when they have happy endings. "How I Overcame (Blank)" is a great topic.

I've filled in the blanks with different subjects based on the market. For *College Bound*, I wrote about how I overcame leaving my high school boyfriend. For *Woman's World*, I wrote about how I overcame agoraphobia.

For your story to be salable, it has to fit two criteria: (1) It must be of interest and possible benefit to a large portion of the target audience, and (2) You must be able to add insights to the topic that have not been widely discussed before. In other words, it's unlikely that you will sell an article about how you dealt with the death of your pet, since that topic has already received a lot of attention in magazines. Unless your solution is quite unusual, this topic is too used.

However, how you dealt with the day your cancer-stricken mother asked you to pull her off life support, now that's a story. Or how you overcame fear of driving, or how you reinvented yourself when your company went bankrupt, or how you dealt with it when your teenage son got his girlfriend pregnant.

These are known as first-person service pieces. A service piece is anything that instructs the reader about how to lead a better life. When written in the first person, that service piece is rarely a cut-and-dried "how-to" piece. It's the story of how *you* handled something, with allusions to how another reader in a similar situation could use this information to help him or herself.

When you sit down to write a piece like this, imagine that a friend has come to you with a problem. It just so happens that you have gone through this problem, and have insights to share about how you did it. What would you tell your friend?

Start out by giving background into your situation: Identify the problem and its effects on your life. Then tell how you solved it, using anecdotes and quotes when possible. If you can get experts' opinions on the subject, or quote other people who've had similar experiences, all the better.

Yes, you must consider who else will be affected by your truth-telling. If your piece will prominently feature another person in your life, you must decide how to handle this. Of course, most magazines encourage (or even mandate) that you use pseudonyms when referring to a real person. But in many cases, you'll need to go further, since magazines aren't eager to be sued for libel or invasion of privacy.

To avoid getting yourself into a heap of trouble, you must be sure to do one of two things when writing about another person:

1. Fictionalize. Get rid of any easily identifiable traits and features the person may have. Don't write about his goggles collection: Turn it into a shoe collection. Don't talk about the birthmark on his knee or the twitch in his left eye: Turn it into a mole and an overbite.

2. Get a release form. When a subject signs a standard life rights release form, he or she is allowing you to write about his/her life, character, likeness, etc. in any way and for any media. These forms may be altered to specify one magazine, or limit your rights to ensure that the subject approves of the final version. Check with the magazine to find out what form they require, and if they have one that you can use.

What No One Tells You About the Biggies

Looks *DO* Matter

When I sent my first query letter to *Woman's Own*, they wrote back and hinted that they were interested in my article, which was a profile of a woman who had started her own greeting card company. But first, they wanted to see a picture of her. They wanted me to email them a photo as soon as possible before they would approve of the article.

Why in the world would a photo help them decide if she was someone worth writing about? Because—and I say this through gritted teeth—most women's magazines won't run a photo of an unattractive or obese woman. That's right: not even if the woman has done something heroic or otherwise newsworthy.

When a photographer came to shoot a photo of me for a *Woman's World* spread, he was pleased by my appearance. "You'll make *Woman's World* happy," he said. I expressed my dismay, wondering aloud if they would have been unhappy if I exceeded an imaginary weight limit.

"Oh, you have no idea. I shot pictures for [another big women's magazine], and when they saw how heavy the woman was, they killed the article." The article had been one of those overcoming-all-odds story: a woman who had adopted several kids, overcome cancer, all kinds of stuff. But because she was "too heavy," the magazine killed the article and the writer got screwed, even though there was nothing wrong with the article.

Libel means you've written something untrue or fabricated about an individual or corporation that injures the defamed person's reputation or subjects him/her to ridicule, contempt, or hatred.

Invasion of privacy means you've written something that may be true, but is private and potentially harmful to the person. According to this law, what you've disclosed must be offensive to a person of "ordinary sensibilities," and there must be no legitimate public interest in the disclosure for a person to win a lawsuit of this nature.

Is this a rare example? No way. A regular freelancer for *Cosmopolitan* instructed me to send photos with my queries, too, telling me that the editors liked to make sure their subjects were attractive.

Major magazines have age restrictions, too. If your subject is not within the target market range of the magazine, it's quite unlikely that you'll land an article about him or her. When I queried *Good Housekeeping* about an extraordinary story of a 50-something mother, they told me she was too old.

I found a younger mother, but she was in the United Kingdom. Nope. Only U.S. citizens may apply at *Good Housekeeping*, apparently.

Prevention had a more reasonable policy about age restrictions. When I pitched an article about body dysmorphic disorder to them, I told the editor that I planned to include stories from three people who had the disorder. Editor Denise Foley just asked that one of them be at least 35 years old, and she didn't care where they were from.

Exclusivity Deals

Here is another issue that came as a surprise to me: exclusivity deals.

I had a great story about a woman named Kathleen who was caring for her seven brothers and sisters, all of whom had Down syndrome. Kathleen, who was 32 years old, found out she had an inoperable brain tumor, and she was fighting to make sure her siblings would be kept together after her death. The story had been reported in only one newspaper, but based on that, Kathleen had been invited to be a guest on the Montel Williams Show.

I thought that was a great thing to mention in my query letter; after all, it showed that a major television show thought her story was worthy of air time.

Mistake. *Family Circle* wrote back quickly to tell me that once the Montel show aired, other magazines would probably pick up on the story, so they weren't interested.

Then I got back a letter from *Good Housekeeping* telling me they were very interested; however, they were also concerned about the show. An editor there asked me if Kathleen would be willing to sign an exclusivity deal that would grant them the sole rights to her story in print publications until the issue came out.

Big magazines don't want stories that have appeared elsewhere, and they don't want anyone else to be allowed to run the same stories until, at least, their issue is off newsstands.

This doesn't mean that you get to lie or cleverly omit information about where else this story has appeared or will appear. But it does mean that you shouldn't be a dummy like me and actually emphasize this as a selling point in your query.

Before you bother querying about a newsworthy, personal story to a national magazine, ask your subject how he feels about exclusivity. Tell him about the situation I just mentioned, and ask if he would agree to sign a contract that says whichever magazine runs the story would have the exclusive rights to the story for at least a month after the issue comes out.

Not every magazine will insist on this, but it's good to know up front, so you don't waste anyone's time if you find out an editor wants exclusivity. Will they pay your subject for this right? Sometimes. It probably depends on how much they want the story and whether or not they think their competitors are vying for the same exclusive.

They're Touchy About the Competition

Yes, editors read their competitors' magazines. And yes, they will be annoyed if you pitch them something that reads like it could fit into a different magazine. One way to truly impress an editor is to show him that you understand how his magazine is different.

"We're in a really competitive industry, and we have to differentiate ourselves," says Todd Raphael, online editor of the national trade magazine *Workforce Management.* "If the writer is writing an article that's just like what they wrote for someone else, then they don't quite get it." Todd is happy to explain to his writers what it is that makes his magazine unique, but he says that some writers don't listen, and he doesn't work with those writers a second time.

To gain and keep a loyal audience, each magazine must have its own voice and flavor that readers can count on. When a magazine has nothing to make itself stand apart from others, that magazine fails. Many people theorize that that's what happened to *Mademoiselle*; it had enormous competition in the women's markets and, in its last years, struggled to find its own place. Why would someone buy *Mademoiselle* instead of the dozens of other women's glossies?

That's a question you need to keep in mind when writing for a magazine—any magazine, but the high-profile ones in particular—what is it that they're known for? What sets them apart from their competitors? If one woman's magazine is known for being "traditional" and another is known for its progressive nature, recognize that distinction and don't try to "improve upon" their core concepts. A high-fashion magazine that centers around the idea that one can never have too many black stilettos isn't going to appreciate it if you quote someone as saying that women should save money by avoiding trendy things and sticking to classic clothing that can be worn season after season.

"Learn to love your body just the way it is" articles aren't going to fly in magazines that sell based on their coverlines about how to lose weight every month. Sometimes the differences are subtle: One magazine may be a bit more risqué than another, one might be geared more toward anecdotes than service pieces, one might offer daring, cutting-edge business strategies while another advocates tried-and-true methods. You can gain a big advantage by analyzing these differences and demonstrating in your pitches and articles that you understand the vision of each magazine.

And watch your queries carefully: Just about every editor I know has received a letter accidentally addressed to a competing editor.

Sex, Lies, and Magazines

In sex and relationship stories and advice columns, in particular, be aware that editors may break a cardinal rule of journalism: They'll change quotations and even entire stories just to fit with their magazine's audience. Not all magazines do this, of course, but some are more notorious for it than others. In the latter group, these articles are not sent for fact-checking, so there's no one to ensure that the quotations or stories are accurate.

One top freelancer and former staffer, who says that more than half of her credits consist of these "true" relationship and sex stories, says, "When I was at one magazine, they were making up quotes and not fact-checking them at all. You'd turn them in real, your editor would change them, and that's why they couldn't fact-check them."

If this concerns you, ask your fellow freelancers which magazines are the worst culprits, and which ones don't change or invent quotations. Fixing up the grammar in a quotation is reasonable, but be aware that some magazines completely alter a true story to make it more "juicy," more believable, or more in tune with their target audience.

"If they want to change it to make the woman sound smarter, I can call her back and say 'Is this okay with you?' But they change it so outrageously that I can't even call [the subjects]. It's embarrassing," says this writer, who is now moving her efforts away from relationship stories for just this reason. She quit writing for one weekly magazine because, as she says, "it made me so sick" that readers were being misled, but she notes that some magazines that formerly embellished these stories, such as *Glamour*, now require first and last names and phone numbers of the subjects so fact-checkers can verify their statements. Likewise, she says *Self* doesn't fabricate.

Of course, that adds on another challenge for writers: Will your subjects be willing to go on-the-record with juicy details of their sex lives, knowing that their full names will be used? Watch magazines for "names have been changed" notations, and don't accept an assignment without knowing whether or not you'll have to find subjects who are willing to be named.

Even outside of "sexy" stories, some magazines have no qualms about changing quotes. I wrote my own true story about overcoming anxiety disorder for *Woman's World*, never heard back from an editor or fact-checker about any revisions, then gasped when I saw the story in print. They had invented entire "scenes" and conversations, attributing quotations to my fiancé (who they had never spoken with) and me that made us sound so juvenile that we didn't show the article to anyone. Nor did I ever write for them again.

Writers and Taxes

First, a warning: I am not an attorney, and this is not to be construed as legal advice. What follows here is what I've learned from several tax specialists, IRS documents, and other writers. As you start to earn money from your writing, you will need to know what Uncle Sam requires of you.

Hobby vs Business

If you maintain a day job and write only a few pieces a year, earning little money and devoting small amounts of time to it, it's likely that the IRS will classify you as a hobbyist rather than a small business owner.

If you've shown a net profit from your writing in three out of the past five years, and/or if you can prove that you're making a serious attempt to sell your work (by showing copies of your query letters, taking writing courses, or even showing your rejection slips), it is likely you'll be treated as a professional.

While it's simpler to fill out tax reports as a hobbyist, and you don't have to pay Medicare and Social Security taxes, you probably won't be able to claim all of your expenses. If you want to stay qualified as a small business, do your best to show at least a small profit three out of five years.

On the Record

Keep meticulous records and receipts of all writing-related expenses, from the moment you start studying to be a writer. You must hold onto your bills, receipts, and expense records for at least three years from the day you claim deductions, but five is safer. You currently need a receipt for any deduction you claim that's more than $75.

While publishers may reimburse you for things like relevant phone calls and some travel, they're surely not going to pay for your computer, your Internet access, your bill at Barnes & Noble, etc.

However, if you keep good records and can verify that all of these expenses are necessary to your writing career, you can deduct them on Schedule C of your federal income tax return. Be sure to keep track of the dates, amounts, description, and business purpose of all of your expenses. You may use receipts, canceled checks, invoices, and so on as proof of these expenses.

According to Susan M. Jacksack's *CCH Tax Guide For Journalists*, an expense must be "ordinary" and "necessary" to your business to qualify for a deduction. "This means it must be common and accepted in your line of work, and it must be appropriate or helpful to the work you do." However, it does not have to be "absolutely indispensable."

What Are the Possible Deductions?
The following business expenses are commonly deductible if you can show they are necessary and reasonable:

➤ Airplane, bus, or train tickets
➤ Baggage and shipping charges
➤ Phone charges
➤ Car expenses (use the standard mileage rate or actual cost)
➤ Tolls and parking fees
➤ Car rental
➤ A portion of your meals and lodging on overnight trips or those requiring you to stop to rest to "properly perform your duties."
➤ Entertainment (generally 50 percent; might include taking an editor, client, or interviewee to lunch)
➤ Dry cleaning and laundry while traveling
➤ Passport fees
➤ Fax machine and computer rental charges
➤ Taxi and limo charges
➤ Tips pertaining to the above
➤ Professional conventions, writers' workshops, and seminars
➤ Overseas travel (sometimes)
➤ Computers, hardware, and software
➤ Office supplies
➤ Postage expenses
➤ Education-related expenses (books, e-books, courses)
➤ Magazines and newspapers (yes, even if you haven't written for the magazine before; if you're considering sending a query to the publication, this is a research expense)
➤ Contest entry fees
➤ Union dues and professional memberships
➤ Cameras
➤ Advertising expenses
➤ Business cards, letterhead
➤ Copyright permissions
➤ Photocopying and printing costs

➤ Legal fees

➤ Libel/liability insurance

➤ Fees for editors, consultants, proofreaders, publicists, etc.

➤ Accountant fees

➤ Bank fees for your business account

What You Can't Deduct

➤ Non-payment: If a magazine fails to pay you for your writing, you don't get to deduct that money because you never reported it in the first place (you are supposed to report income after it is received)

➤ Writing you've done for free: Let's say you donated your work to a charity—you volunteered to write their grant proposal, or articles for their newsletter; you do not get to deduct the "fair market value" of your work as of this writing, but several writers' and artists' groups are campaigning to change this rule

➤ Dues to social clubs

The Home Office

The rules for claiming a home-office deduction have been very strict, but have eased slightly over the past few years. If you use part of your home for work-related activities only, you may be able to claim a deduction for it.

The rule:

You must use a specific part of your home regularly and exclusively for work in your profession.

Translation: You can't write emails to friends in your home office. You can't visit the Dancing Hamster web site in your home office. You can't play games, balance your personal checkbook, or watch television in your home office. A good deal of this may make you shake your head in disbelief, because even employees take breaks and send a friendly email, visit silly web sites, and make personal calls from work. But the IRS is serious: If they find Tetris installed on your home office computer, or a grocery list you wrote while you were waiting for a fax to come through, you could be penalized for taking a deduction.

In addition, you must be able to prove one of the following:

➤ The business part of your home is your primary place of business

➤ You must use the space to meet clients (face-to-face)

➤ The office is not attached to the house

Your home office must be a room, or other identifiable space (a permanent partition is no longer necessary).

Okay, so you think you've got it? Then figure out the floor space of your home office divided by your home's total floor space. This is the approximate percentage of deductions you may be eligible to claim on the following:

- ➤ Mortgage interest and depreciation
- ➤ Rent
- ➤ Real estate taxes
- ➤ Insurance
- ➤ Water
- ➤ Light, heat, trash collection
- ➤ Security system
- ➤ Cleaning service
- ➤ Repairs and decorating
- ➤ Casualty losses

You can also generally deduct the entire cost of repair and maintenance on that room.

Health Insurance

Good news! Starting in 2003, self-employed people are now allowed to deduct 100 percent of the health-insurance premiums they pay for themselves, their spouses, and dependents.

Depreciation and Expensing

More good news. Although many writers don't realize this, they do have a choice about how to be taxed on some business equipment. When you buy something such as a computer, scanner, printer, or fax machine, which is expected to last you several years, most people take a depreciation deduction on its value over the course of a few tax years. But you also have the option of taking the full deduction in the year you buy certain items, which is called "expensing" and is known as the "section 179 deduction."

In 2003, 2004, and 2005, the cap has been raised: You may take a deduction of up to $100,000. When filing after 2005, ask your tax professional if the cap has changed.

Quarterly Payments

Federal income taxes must be paid all year long; employees are usually subject to withholding, meaning that the employer puts a percentage of the worker's paycheck toward income tax.

But because freelance writers are self-employed, taxes haven't been taken out of their paychecks before they receive them. Instead, writers must make estimated quarterly payments toward their taxes if they expect to owe at least $1,000 by the end of the year (as of this writing). This will help ensure that you aren't stuck with an unexpectedly big sum to cough up at tax-time. And if you were supposed to make quarterly payments and you don't, you could be in for some hefty fees.

> *Great resources for information about writers and taxes*
> ➤ *Email mediahelp@cch.com. Include your mailing address, and request a copy*
>   *of their free tax guide for journalists*
> ➤ *IRS small business resource center: www.irs.gov/businesses/small/index.html*
> ➤ *www.publishlawyer.com has great articles, including tax tips for writers*

Because tax laws for business owners can be very complicated, I recommend strongly that you consult with an accountant or attorney to help you understand what is required of you. And, yes, you should be able to deduct their fees.

Syndicate Me, Baby!

It's a freelance writer's dream: Write one column a week or month, and get paid for it dozens or hundreds of time. Why not? It worked for Erma Bombeck, Dear Abby, Dave Barry, that "Weird News" guy—why not you?

Some people may have told you that you need to have a big name (or already established column) to get syndicated. Not true! It is true that most of the big, national syndication companies won't pick you up unless you're established, but that shouldn't stop you from getting out there, pounding a little pavement, and working on syndicating your work on your own.

Humor columnist Mad Dog has been writing a weekly column for the past five years. It began as an assigned column for the *Richmond State*, which folded. Now he syndicates the column through AlterNet, a company that works with alternative weeklies throughout the country. He has also placed the column in some dailies, including the *Chicago Tribune, NY Daily News, San Francisco Examiner*, and *San Francisco Chronicle*.

"My column isn't assigned," he says, "So I do whatever the hell I want, for better or for worse. The newspapers pick up a column if they like it, so it's to my advantage to write on topics that might interest them. But I don't cater to them because the truth is that I can't second-guess what they want. There's no real rhyme or reason behind what they do like . . . each one [has] different likes and needs that change all the time."

Of course, the joy and the trouble with having your own syndicated column are intertwined. As Mad Dog said, you get to write about "whatever the hell you want," but that lack of direction can be daunting for writers. Without a guided assignment, can you write something that will interest editors and readers enough to keep coming back for more?

Finding a Topic

This is somewhat different than finding a topic for a one-time article. You have to find something you can write about every month, week, or even day, indefinitely.

That's why you shouldn't worry about narrowing down your idea too much, like you must do with single articles. Instead, find an area of interest that will provide you with plenty of material.

I syndicated three columns: A series of interviews with writers ("Words From the Wordsmiths"), a series of profiles of people with disabilities ("Faces of Ability"), and a series of tips for creative romance ("Simply Romance"). Each of these was defined enough so that an editor had a strong idea of what I was going to write about each week or month, but inclusive enough that I had a large pool of ideas and resources to come up with fresh content regularly.

Be sure the topic you choose isn't finite. For example, don't set out to write a column about "The Meanings of Religious Holidays," because the number of holidays you can write about is limited, topical (what do you do on weeks when there are no major holidays?), and you won't have anything new to say next year unless someone invents a new holiday. Similarly, don't try to work your column around a current trend. Trends are fine and dandy for articles, or even an article series, but not for a long-term column, because the sun easily sets on fads.

What You Need

First, a title. What do you want to cover in your column? Come up with a short, catchy title that encompasses what you want to write.

Next, you'll need samples. It's great if your column has already appeared in a publication, but if it hasn't, unpublished samples are okay, too. You'll need a minimum of four samples ready to show an editor.

Most columns run between 400 and 700 words, although shorter or longer may be appropriate, depending on your subject matter. For example, I had a monthly column in which I gave short tips for creative romance. This column rarely ran more than 300 words, because there was no need for more. As a general rule, keep it as tight as you can. If you can convey your message in 500 words, then there's no reason to stretch it to 600 words. Your word count needs to be consistent from one column to the next: Because the editor allocates a specific amount of space for your work, you can't write 500 words one week and 700 the following week.

Next, you need a cover letter.

The cover letter functions a lot like a query letter. You want to catch the editor's attention, convince him that your column will be interesting and relevant to the paper's readership, and that you are a capable and responsible writer who will deliver clean copy on time. No small task!

Finally, you'll need a photo. Many publications like to run a columnist's photograph. A black and white headshot is fine, or a photo that ties into your column's theme (for example, if you're writing about legal issues, you might pose with a judge's gavel). Be prepared to send it digitally or by postal mail, whichever the editor may want.

Working With a Syndicate

Yes, it's tough to break in with a syndication service. Many specialize in certain topics or types of stories, so decide carefully which syndicates might work for you. The biggest syndicates have the most clients, thus giving you a better shot of getting your column placed in many papers. However, they're also extremely competitive. Major syndicate King Features says in their guidelines that they receive 50 column submissions every week. "Of these, four to five are selected annually."

Syndicates are not keen to work with beginning writers, so it's important to show that your work has appeared in an assortment of publications. If you're going this route, send out a few articles all over the place first and sell them at whatever price you can get (even giving it away free if necessary), just to improve the variety of your credits. The syndicate doesn't have to know who paid you and who didn't, but if you can list thirty newspapers that have published your work, that will show the syndicate that your work is salable.

King Features wants to see six sample columns of no more than 650 words apiece. United Feature Syndicate wants four to six 500–600-word samples of a column that you'll write at least on a weekly basis, and says they prefer established writers or "those who already have a client list through self-syndication." Creators Syndicate "deals strictly with contract features, such as weekly or biweekly political, business or lifestyle columns," and wants to see eight to ten of your 750-word columns.

Syndication Success Story

"I know two reporters who quit their newspaper jobs and started their own one-person news services," says writer and editor Carole Ashkinaze. "The first offered coverage of all the big Atlanta stories to newspapers in other parts of the country. The second offered weekly legislative reports to tiny, rural newspapers unable to staff the state Capitol themselves. The latter was forced to admit defeat after a couple of years but had a great adventure and said she never regretted it. After a shaky start, the former regularly placed stories in the country's biggest papers and ran a small but thriving news service until he died."

> **Searching for Syndicates**
>
> ➤ *Editor and Publisher releases their Directory of Syndicated Services annually. In it, you'll find contact information (including email addresses and editors' names) for syndicates across the U.S. and Canada. Find it at www.editorand-publisher.com. Currently $20.*
>
> ➤ *Writer's Market has a section of syndicates, including their guidelines, specialties, and contact information.*
>
> ➤ *Publishers and Agents (www.publishersandagents.net) provides a submission service; they'll email your query to about 300 syndicates, or send you labels, envelopes, and letters to mail yourself. As of this writing, it costs $90 for either option.*

A syndicate will typically take half of the money you make from the column.

Self-Syndicating

To self-syndicate, your marketing campaign should differ somewhat from your single article pitches. You're going to send your proposal simultaneously to dozens, potentially hundreds, of newspapers and perhaps e-zines and small magazines. You are not expected to study every newspaper in the country and figure out where your column would fit.

Luckily, there generally aren't many fundamental differences in newspapers across the country. They have the same basic sections and formats, and, aside from the local and regional sections, cover many of the same topics.

When you propose a syndicated column, try to get the name of the appropriate section editor.

The biggest problem with self-syndicating is the snail mail/email dilemma. The problem is that most newspaper editors still prefer snail mail for column pitches, and it can get extremely expensive to send out manila envelopes filled with your proposal packets to hundreds of newspapers.

There is a way to ease the financial burden, though. First, if you're going to try self-syndicating, a web site is almost a must. Set up (or get someone to set up for you) a small web site that has all of the pertinent information: your bio, photo, synopsis of your column, and several sample columns. If you've gotten feedback from editors or readers, you may want to include that, and you may want to include the newspapers that have picked up your column.

Then send a query letter by email to every appropriate newspaper editor you can find. Don't use the blind copy option unless you have a program

---

Self-Syndication Sources

➤ *The most valuable free resource I've found is www.newspapers.com. It gives the web site addresses of hundreds of papers in the United States and even overseas. Generally, you'll find a masthead contact information on any paper's web site.*

➤ *Newslink (http://newslink.org) is another favorite. Here, you'll find links to newspapers and magazines worldwide, searchable by state, category, and frequency.*

➤ *To avoid spending all your free time searching web sites, use Bacon's media directories, Gale Directory of Publications and Broadcast Media, or Gebbie Press's The All-In-One Media Directory, all of which contain contact information (including urls and email addresses) for periodicals around the country. These should be available at your library.*

---

that can make it look like you've sent it to that person only. In the subject, type "Column Proposal" or "Syndicated Column Proposal," followed by the column's title or subject.

In the body of your email (no attachments!), give the column synopsis, your bio, and one or two sample columns. Point the editors to your web site for further samples and your photo, and give them the option of also requesting the proposal packet by postal mail. Keep track of who responds and who doesn't. Follow up in two or three weeks with anyone who hasn't responded. If they still don't respond, then you may wish to use snail mail instead, you may just keep sending them new columns as they become available, or you may choose to simply cross that newspaper off your list for now.

Ben Baker, editor of *The Wiregrass Farmer*, says the key to getting syndicated is perseverance. "Joe Klock is the most successful writer I've ever seen in this regard. Joe continues to expand his column empire by emailing his column every week to newspapers around the country, whether they asked for it or not. He's in well over 100 papers now. Sooner or later, all newspapers have a hole and having copy like Joe's to fill that space on the editorial page is like manna when you are past deadline. A few times of this and readers will let me know if they want to continue to read his stuff."

So don't give up if an editor doesn't agree to run your column regularly the first time you pitch it. You can take Joe's approach and just keep sending your column every week or month until the editor decides to run something or tells you to stop, whichever comes first.

If you do self-syndicate, you will often be asked to name your own price. The typical range for a syndicated column is $5–60, mostly depending on the circulation of the publication. You may choose to charge everyone the same amount, you may negotiate prices individually (which is what I recommend), or you may have a tiered structure based on circulation. For example, you could charge $5 per 10,000 subscribers, or set different prices for markets with fewer than 50,000 subscribers, 50,001–100,000, 100,001–200,000, and so on. Keep it reasonable, and remember that your goal is to be accessible to as many markets as possible. If you syndicate to 100 newspapers and web sites, charging only $10 a pop, that's $1,000 for every column you write. Fifty newspapers at $15 apiece earns you $750.

Other Avenues for Experienced Writers

Once you've established yourself as a magazine writer, you may find that other doors open up to you

Book writing can be an obvious extension of your work. If you're a columnist, you may simply gather your best columns into book format. If you've written quite a bit about one particular subject (the stock market, let's say), you may realize that you have enough knowledge on the topic to write a whole book about it. Or a book publisher may approach you after reading a particularly interesting article of yours.

Before accepting these opportunities, consider the time involved. A nonfiction book may take just a few months to write, or it may take years. Make sure your interest in the topic is strong enough to sustain you for all that time. Book advances and royalty rates vary widely, but most of the non-famous writers I know have gotten advances in the $2,000 to $10,000 range. I have been paid more for single articles than I have for entire books. Also, know that most books never earn out their advances, which means that it is statistically likely that you will never see a penny beyond your advance money. Of course, a select few authors make millions off of their books; research your potential market meticulously and try to determine honestly how many people would buy your book. Then assess your interest level. Then decide if it's worth it for you.

You may also be offered ghostwriting jobs—both for books and for articles. Some publishers buy the rights to people's stories, and those people may not be very good writers, or they may not have the time to write a book. In that case, someone with proven experience on the topic might be brought in to write the book. Or a person may have an idea for a book, but not the talent to write it, and would rather hire you to do it. You might get a shared credit or no credit at all. The current trend is toward a shared credit ("By Joe Schmoe with Rita Riter," where Joe is the subject of the book and Rita is the real writer).

Businesses also hire ghostwriters to write articles that they can use to help promote their businesses. For example, a florist might want to write an article for a wedding magazine so she can use the bio to plug her shop. If this florist isn't also a writer, she may look for someone who can write the article for her, and then she'll stick her name on it and submit it to the magazine.

Ghostwriting contracts are typically work-for-hire and may include clauses that stipulate that you are not allowed to use the work in your portfolio or mention that you were the writer. However, ghostwriting also can pay very well. I've known book ghostwriters who've been paid $50,000 advances (plus a 50/50 split of royalties), which isn't even the highest end of the scale. Article ghostwriters can get paid more than $1 a word even if the article will only appear in small newspapers and require minimal research.

Finally, you may get gigs as a public speaker if this avenue interests you. Writing workshops may hire you to speak about your experiences, and you may be asked to speak at events on topics you've written about. You might also be called on to appear on television or radio shows to discuss things you've written about, or to give seminars to teach people the things you've learned. Fees for speakers vary as widely as fees for writers, with some organizations paying only your transportation costs, and others paying $10,000 and up.

It may seem like "paying your dues" takes forever, but rest assured that writing careers have a habit of snowballing. Once you've begun cracking national markets, establishing yourself as an expert on particular topics, or having your bio splashed all over magazine pages, it may just be a matter of time before you're so busy that you have to turn down assignments or hire your *own* ghostwriter!

Writers who have hit this enviable level get to enjoy different perks than other writers, such as higher pay rates, editors who will actually take phone pitches, choice of assignments, and email access to markets that "won't look at email queries." If you're not at this level yet, hang in there. Put in the work, be willing to pay your dues, and be ready to reap the rewards when they come.

ASSIGNMENT

First column idea: Title_____

10 topics I can write about for this column

Second column idea: Title_____

10 topics I can write about for this column

Third column idea: Title_____

10 topics I can write about for this column

How difficult was it to think of those 10 ideas? Did you have others popping into your head as you wrote, or were you straining to come up with 10? If the ideas are coming easily, you might just have a good column in the making, my friend!

Chapter 17

THE LIFE OF A WRITER-FOR-HIRE

Inside This Chapter

- **Full-time vs part-time**
- **Maintaining self-confidence**
- **Connecting with other writers**

Going Full-Time

Most freelancers entertain the notion of ditching the 9 to 5 routine and writing full-time. Only you can determine if this is the right kind of life for you. First, remember the daunting statistics from the National Writers Union study. More than half of the writers surveyed had to keep a non-writing-related job to make ends meet. For those who worked outside of their writing career, the average work week was 52 hours. In addition, writers worked in an average of 4.6 different writing fields and genres (business writing, books, articles, poetry, etc.).

Despite the fact that writers are a very well-educated breed, they earn far less on average than equally-educated workers in other fields. Still interested?

There are no hard-and-fast rules to help you determine when it's time to quit your day job and take up writing full-time. The best I can offer you is some good, old-fashioned common sense.

Don't take your first sale as a sign that it's time to make the leap. Or your second sale. Or your 10th sale. As a general guideline, I'd advise that you don't consider making the leap until your freelance salary equals at least half of your day job salary.

Freelancing is a scary business, and there are periods of extreme financial highs and lows in most freelancers' lives.

You must have enough money saved up to be sure that you can get by for several months with little or no income in the beginning. Or, then again, you could just do what freelancer Skip Press, columnist for *Scriptwriter* magazine and author of the *Complete Idiot's Guide to Screenwriting* and several other books, did: "You'll hate me. I was on a game show and won enough money to retire for about six months," he says. Not bad! But for those of us who aren't quite so lucky, putting in some overtime at the day job may be necessary to save up enough to "invest" in your freelancing career.

You must be extremely self-motivated and disciplined if you plan to succeed as a full-time freelancer. With no boss looming over your desk, telling you to work, you must find the ambition within yourself to keep going every day. You must find a way to work without distractions from your family, or the phone, or your favorite television shows.

Even if you land assignments from top-paying magazines, there will probably never be a time when all you do is work on one article, then send a query for the next, then wait for the next assignment. The most successful writers I know have several high-paying assignments at once and continue sending out queries even while they're working on these. I'm currently working on five assignments, just sent out two new queries last night, and had one accepted this morning. I have jotted down ideas for at least a half-dozen other stories that I plan to research in the coming week or two to send out more queries. In addition, I have to recognize that an editor may call at any time to ask me to revise something I've already turned in (even if I filed it months ago), so I must be willing to be flexible.

Different writers have different "rules" for how many queries they like to have in circulation at one time. This largely depends on your success rate and will change through the years. In the beginning, you may have to send out 25 queries before you get one acceptance letter; in later stages of your career, a full half of your queries may land assignments, so you'll know to send fewer queries (or risk being swamped!).

You may choose never to go full-time, even if you feel you have the ability to do it. Keeping a day job allows many writers to keep *enjoying* writing, because it feels like a hobby. It takes the pressure off, because they're not depending on their freelancing checks. Also, they retain the social outlets of work and still have a creative outlet when they want to use it.

If you can and want to quit punching a clock, though, I wildly encourage you to go for it. Working from home can be very satisfying, and it can provide you with a brand new kind of independence. By setting your own hours, you can hang out on the beach every day, as long as you're committed to putting in long nights at the computer. Or you can take breaks to meet friends for lunch. Or you can work around the clock for three days and take the rest of the week off. Your work is portable, and it should provide you the opportunity to learn about lots of interesting topics, events, and people.

I wouldn't have it any other way.

Neither would freelancer Barbara Stahura, writer for The *Christian Science Monitor* and MSNBC.com, among others, who says, "I really enjoy knowing that I can make a good living by doing something I love this much. Writing is also rewarding for me in other ways. For one, I get to interview tremendously interesting people I would never be able to meet otherwise. I also get to do things I would normally never have the opportunity to do, like ride on a fire engine, use a $3,500 fountain pen, or get an inside look at how an artist creates. I have to research and learn about many new subjects, so I'm always educating myself and keeping my brain young. And I enjoy the challenge of trying to always make my writing more concise and elegant.

"However, my greatest reward in writing comes from those too-rare times when my heart merges with my head and I can produce a piece of writing— say, a personal essay or a poem—that truly expresses in an articulate and engaging way just what I'm trying to express. It's during those times that I'm in 'the flow,' and the only thing that has meaning at that moment is the process of writing. It's almost a sacred feeling, something to be cherished."

Do you recognize that feeling? Good for you. You might just be a writer.

But What Will They Think of Me?

You mention that you're a freelance writer at a family reunion and you can feel the snickering. You see straight into the brains of your relatives, and they're envisioning empty pockets and "will work for food" signs in your near future. Unless your articles appear in *Vanity Fair* or *Reader's Digest* every month, they're not impressed. Forget them. Be impressed with yourself.

What you do requires talent, persistence, and bravery. Every day, you're challenging your brain to come up with things no one else has thought of. You're working to find the stories that no one's paying any attention to and bring them to mass audiences. You're trying to communicate with people to help them lead better lives. And you're doing so at the risk of your own ego ("Please, editor, may I have another rejection slip?"), and, if you've gone full-time, without the safety of a weekly paycheck. You've devoted yourself to becoming a life-long learner so that you can teach other people.

Don't lose that.

The Glitz, The Glamour . . .

And . . . the other stuff.

Yeah, there's a downside to freelance writing. In fact, there are several.

It's Lonely.

There is no water cooler. There is no lunch hour with your colleagues. No one will stop by your desk with Dunkin' Donuts (unless you have a really nice spouse). What to do to combat this? I've said it before and I'll say it again: Hook up with other writers! Join writers' groups in real life and on the Internet. It'll keep you going on days you feel isolated.

It's Constant Work.

You can't be a slacker. You can't sit back and expect to make a living. You have to be your own one-man marketing team. You've got to keep putting yourself "out there," day after day, night after night, and you can never get too comfy and believe that you can turn in work that's "good enough." Good enough is never enough. Everything you turn in is a reflection of you, so every piece must be worthy of your byline.

There are Tough Deadlines.

You will get calls from editors who ask for an article overnight. You will find out that the person you absolutely need to interview is out of the country until the day after your piece is due. You will be up all night to complete an assignment. Often.

You Will Face Writer's Block.

You will have days when you feel completely uninspired, and you have no choice but to write anyway. Forced creativity is tough sometimes, but it is your job to yank out those words, and yank them out well, day after day.

However, there are also tremendous joys in this business.

Very few other careers offer the freedom, creative fulfillment, and opportunity to make a positive impact on this world that writing does. Your words can outlive you. They can outlive your children and grandchildren. They can change the course of history.

They can affect lives of strangers. They can bring hope. They can bring laughter, joy, anger, sympathy, camaraderie, understanding, insight, and faith.

You wield an enormous amount of power when you sit down to write. You are in a position to make a wonderful contribution to this world. Congratulations on choosing such a worthy profession. May you have great success in your work and in your life.

Welcome to your writing career.

APPENDIX A
QUERIES THAT LANDED ME THE JOBS

Dear Ms. Smith:

Most of the commercial crafts we're familiar with (like water taxis, mega-yachts, marine patrol, and rescue boats) are constructed with aluminum, but the pleasure craft sector is still made up almost entirely of fiberglass boats. Why?

Pound for pound, aluminum is ten times stronger than fiberglass and it weighs 20–25 percent less. This makes a big difference in power, fuel consumption, and ease of transport. Aluminum is also an extremely durable marine building material; it resists corrosion and withstands heavy wear and impact.

Aluminum boats are generally designed to have a "rough" appearance; suitable for work boats, but not as attractive in a pleasure craft. They are also generally more costly.

Today's technology may change this trend. Marine aluminum companies are working to create affordable boats with the sleek appearance fiberglass boaters are used to.

I would love to write an article for your publication comparing the pros and cons of aluminum and fiberglass boats.

I am a full-time freelance writer, and my writing has appeared in such publications as *World Billfish Series*, *Link*, *Alive*, *Adaptz*, and *College Bound*. A clip follows. Thanks for your consideration, and I look forward to your response.

Regards,

Jenna Glatzer

(All editors' and publications' names have been changed.)

Dear Mr. Smith:

When Sean Swarner was 15 years old, his doctors told him he had less than two weeks to live. The chances of him surviving were worse than winning the lottery four times over. So he did what any other reasonable person in his situation would do: He decided to climb Mt. Everest.

Sean is a one-lunged, two-time cancer survivor. When Sean was 14, he had fourth-stage Hodgkin's disease. "All my friends were out collecting baseball cards and chasing girls. Me? Well, I was sitting on the shower floor crying my eyes out because not only was I 60 lbs. overweight from the medicine, but I also had to pull chunks of hair out of the drain so the water could flow down," he says. A year later, he developed an Askin's disease tumor on his lung. The lung had to be removed.

Last May, Sean became the first cancer survivor to make it to the top of Mt. Everest, and he put a flag on the summit with the names of other people who had been affected by cancer (alive or dead). Now he's doing the same with the highest mountain on each of the continents and the North and South poles. (He's already made it to the top of Mts. Kilimanjaro and Elbrus.) He had to sell all of his possessions to raise the exorbitant fee to make the first climb.

He also started a nonprofit association, The Cancer Climber Association, to inspire other cancer survivors and patients to surpass doctors' expectations. Among other things, the association held its first "fun run" marathon this year to raise money for kids with cancer.

I think he would make a wonderful candidate for a profile in Your Mag.

I am a full-time freelance writer with hundreds of national and online credits, recently including *Woman's World, Woman's Own, Writer's Digest,* and Salon.com. I'm enclosing two clips. In addition, I am the author of nine nonfiction books.

Thank you for your consideration. I look forward to your response.

Regards,

Jenna Glatzer

Dear Ms. Smith:

Imagine living in a time and place in which a child could be turned away from necessary medical treatment and left to die because her I.Q. was too low. Imagine her parents' pleas to save her life were ignored by physicians and government officials. You wouldn't have to stretch your imagination too far; that time is now, and that place is everywhere in the world.

Katie Atkinson is a nine-year-old girl from South Yorkshire, England. She needs a heart transplant to save her life, but she has been denied a spot on the transplant waiting list because she has Down syndrome. Transplant centers routinely deny candidates with mental handicaps; in fact, there has been only one heart transplant given to a person with Down syndrome in the entire istory of the operation.

At a time when he should be preparing Katie for grade school and slumber parties, her father, Phílip Atkinson, is preparing for her funeral.

I have written about Katie and her family's plight for *Adaptz Magazine* (clip enclosed), and it met with very emotional responses from readers. I have conducted extensive research through interviews with transplant center surgeons, medical ethicists, Down syndrome activists, and pediatricians in the United States and Great Britain. I have also spoken at length with Katie's father.

I propose an original feature article, but reprint rights are available to the enclosed piece. (*Adaptz* is published only on the Internet.)

I am a full-time freelance writer with national and regional credits. My works have recently appeared in such publications as *Link Magazine*, *College Bound*, *Summer*, and *Bliss Magazine*. In addition, I run the Absolute Write web site for freelance writers (www.absolutewrite.com).

Thank you for your consideration. I look forward to your response.

Regards,

Jenna Glatzer

Dear Ms. Smith:

Think company cars, expense accounts, and a spacious office with bay windows. Who do you picture running a business this successful?

Think again. This company was the brainchild of three Boston University sophomores whose ambitions led them to thriving careers before they had diplomas to hang on the wall.

Charles Strader, Richard Skelton, and Pablo Mondal run Net One, an Internet Service Provider. The three met in the freshmen dorms, then moved into an apartment together. Opportunity knocked when Strader, who worked for the university's computer center, took a phone call from the owner of a hair salon. She sought help designing a web site; Strader volunteered, and Net One was born.

"Working closely with friends to build something we believe in" is Mondal's favorite perk. Skelton agrees. "We have great trust in each other, and feel that we're all in this together."

Considering that their only capital was a computer and a small loan from Strader's father, the guys feel very successful. "We're not millionaires, but we have goals, and we're following them," says Skelton. "I think that's true success." By any definition, Net One's roster of over 50 clients ranging from colleges to Fortune 500 companies attests to their hard work and talent.

I propose an 800-word profile for your "Students At Work" section.

I am a full-time freelance writer, and my works have been recently featured in such publications as *201 Magazine, College Bound, Bliss!, Working Women*, and Adaptz.com. Clips are enclosed.

I can provide documentation and interview notes for easy fact-checking, and could submit the completed article within two weeks.

I look forward to your response.

Regards,

Jenna Glatzer

APPENDIX B
USEFUL JARGON

Byline: The author's credit ("By Jenna Glatzer").

Callout: A snippet of your article that's repeated in larger type and/or set apart graphically on the page. Also see "pull quote."

Column inch: A term usually used only in the newspaper world, a column inch is the width of one column and one inch in height. If someone tells you he will pay you by the column inch, you will be paid according to the measurements of your published piece.

Coverline, Cutline: The description of your article that will appear on the magazine's cover. For example, *Good Housekeeping's* October 2003 coverlines include "Married for Years? 9 Ways to Revive the Passion" and "Zap! 10 Years Gone. Amazing ways to erase wrinkles."

Deck, Dek: The phrase, sentence, or paragraph below the title that tells the reader what your article is about. Usually set in italics.

Evergreen: An article that can be published anytime; it won't get "dated" quickly, unlike news-based stories.

File: Submitting a completed article. When you've turned in your article, it's been filed.

Galley: The final layout of your article, as it looks when it's going to be published. Some magazines let their writers see galleys before the issue goes to press so they can double-check for mistakes.

Graf, Graph: Short for "paragraph."

Kill fee: What you don't want to get, because it's the amount of money the magazine will pay you if they decide to "kill" (i.e., not publish) your article after you've turned it in.

Head, Hed: The article's headline (sometimes intentionally misspelled).

Lead, Lede, Led: All the same thing (sometimes intentionally misspelled). The lead of your story. The opening sentence or paragraph that "hooks" the reader.

List article: An article presented as a numbered or bulleted list ("8 Ways to Beat the Blues").

Multiple submission: Submitting more than one story idea to the same editor at one time. Some people confuse this with "simultaneous submission" (see entry).

NLT: No later than, used when referring to deadlines. Your editor may tell you he wants your article NLT September 25.

News peg: A reason why an article is timely and newsworthy.

Nut graf: The paragraph below the lead that encapsulates what the article is about "in a nutshell." Editors will sometimes ask for a lead and nut graf before accepting a query.

Primary research: Using original sources, such as interviews, personal observations, and personal documents, as opposed to using information you've read in other publications.

Pull quote: A quotation from someone you've interviewed that has been "pulled" out of the article and highlighted in bigger text, or set apart graphically in some way.

Roundup: An article that consists solely of interviews or stories from various people on one theme or topic. For example, "Five Couples Tell How They Survived an Affair."

SASE: Self-addressed, stamped envelope. (In other countries, the abbreviation SAE may be used—this stands for "stamped addressed envelope" and means the same thing.)

Service article: A "how-to" article, meant to teach the reader something to improve his or her life.

Sidebar: An auxiliary text that runs on the side or bottom of an article, usually in a box or otherwise distinguished from the rest of the layout, often giving additional resources or related tidbits.

Simultaneous submission: Submitting the same query or manuscript to more than one publication at a time.

Spec: On speculation; written without a contract or promise of publication or payment.

Subhead: Headlines within the article that break the article into sections, usually set in larger type than the rest of the article but smaller type than the main headline.

Target market: The audience the publication is trying to reach. For example, a magazine's target market might be middle-income fathers aged 30–50.

Tearsheet: An article that's been torn out of the magazine. You photocopy your tearsheets to send as clips, and/or include the actual tearsheets in a portfolio.

TK: To come, referring to a piece of information that needs to be filled in to the article at a later date.

Working title: The title of the article while you're working on it, subject to change before publication.

Zimmerman: A person who lends a human interest angle to an article, or is used as an example of the article's topic.

ABOUT THE AUTHOR

Jenna Glatzer is the editor-in-chief of AbsoluteWrite.com, the most popular online magazine for writers. She's a full-time freelancer who's written for hundreds of magazines, such as *Prevention, Physical, Woman's World, Woman's Own, Contemporary Bride, ePregnancy, Home Business,* and *Women's Health & Fitness,* and she's a contributing editor at *Writer's Digest.* She's also a columnist for Match.com and MSN.com and has written for many anthologies, such as the *Chicken Soup for the Soul* and *A Cup of Comfort* series. The best-selling author of nine books, Jenna's latest include *Outwitting Writer's Block and Other Problems of the Pen* and *Words You Thought You Knew.*